# ROCK STAR

## ROSLYN HARDY HOLCOMB

Genesis Press, Inc.

# Indigo Love Spectrum

An imprint of Genesis Press, Inc.
Publishing Company

Genesis Press, Inc.
P.O. Box 101
Columbus, MS 39703

ISBN-13: 978-1-58571-298-4
ISBN-10: 1-58571-298-1
Manufactured in the United States of America

First Edition 2006
Second Edition 2009

Visit us at www.genesis-press.com or call at 1-888-Indigo-1

# DEDICATION

*For my mama, Edith Marie Hardy (1929–2004),*
*for the gift of reading and writing.*
*I'm still missing you.*

# *ACKNOWLEDGMENTS*

Thank you, Whitney, for taking care of me so many times after I stayed up all night writing. You truly are the best husband in the entire universe. And for my sweet baby boy, Luke. How did we get so lucky? A special thank you to the Legacy crew at Mindkandy's, especially Teri. This book would never have been finished if y'all hadn't hounded me for a chapter-a-day.

For my editor, Sidney Rickman. Who knew there could be so many errors in one manuscript? Your patience, diligence and thoroughness know no bounds.

# CHAPTER 1

Callie rubbed again at the ropes that held her arms tied firmly behind her back. Her partner Tonya's enthusiasm for this type of thing was wearing a bit thin.

"Come on, Tonya," she urged looking over her shoulder. "Haven't you figured out how you want to tie this thing yet?" Tonya's only response was an exasperated grunt. "Look, we've got a bookstore to run here. Maybe you can do your research another time."

"Just a second, Callie, I think I've got it." Tonya paused, a frown clouding her pretty face. "Maybe if I tie your feet too it would be more in keeping with the character."

"All I know is the next time I get to tie you up!" Callie muttered exasperatedly.

Bryan surveyed the scene before him. Two black women of similarly slender size and above-average height seemed to be engaged in some type of bondage game. One of the women had light skin and a heart-shaped face that was accentuated by closely cropped natural hair. As for the other, Bryan did a double-take. She was without a doubt the most incredibly beautiful woman he'd ever seen. She had long, skinny dreadlocks pulled back from her face with a headband and large, chocolate brown eyes with an exotic tilt at the corners. Combined with highly sculptured cheekbones, the eyes gave her a sensual look that belied her professional dress. Even in the conservative oatmeal-colored linen pantsuit she wore with a coordinating mocha-colored shell top, her features were striking. Her companion was dressed more flamboyantly in a bright red blouse with suede appliqué and fringe and a pair of black knit boot-cut trousers. Both women were lovely, but Bryan couldn't take his eyes off the one with the dreadlocks. *God, she needs to come to L.A. She could make a fortune. I wonder if she'd consider being in a music video.*

Bryan watched for a few more seconds, then spoke up. "I thought I'd left this sort of thing behind in L.A."

Callie and Tonya both looked up, surprised to see that anyone had entered the store.

He continued, "Beautiful women into ropes. What a way to start the day. I don't suppose you do chains and handcuffs, too?" he added hopefully.

Callie blushed furiously. "This is not what it looks like." She pulled forcefully at Tonya's hands. "Come on, girl, untie me." She looked back at the smiling man over the counter. "We don't open until nine o'clock."

"It's just past nine now, and the door was open."

Her hands finally freed, Callie walked around the counter to greet the customer. She extended one newly liberated hand. "Hi, I'm Callie Lawson, and this is my partner Tonya Stevens." When the man smiled knowingly, Callie felt the heat intensify in her face. "No, not *that* kind of partner. She's my business partner…and a part-time mystery novelist." He nodded sagely. "Sometimes she has to work out the plots literally."

Bryan Spencer took the slim, delicate hand into his own, its softness in startling contrast to his own callused fingers. He stared at the beautiful woman before him, an enigmatic smile on his face as she tried to explain that she and her partner were not playing lesbian bondage games behind the counter of the bookstore. Now that they were closer, he could see that her cinnamon-colored skin was virtually flawless and almost velvety smooth. But her eyes captivated him in a way he'd never experienced before. She presented a picture of elegance, or would have, had she not been so flustered.

Callie finally fumbled to a halt in her explanations, but the sudden realization that he was still holding her hand renewed her blushing embarrassment. She pulled it away quickly, holding it behind her back as if afraid that he would take it against her will. She asked again if she could assist him.

Having decided to forego teasing her, Bryan asked for William Gibson's *Mona Lisa Overdrive*.

Callie smiled. "Hmmmm, going to read about cyber cowboys, are you?" she asked as she briskly walked past him to the rear of the store.

Bryan followed, enjoying the view of her pert bubble butt. Even encased as it was in crisp linen, it still enticed him to follow anywhere she led. *An ass like that, and she knows Gibson too.* "Have you read the book?"

Callie arrived at her destination. "Oh yes, I love science fiction, but Octavia Butler is my favorite author." She scanned the shelves. "Yep, just as I thought, we have several Gibson books. I really loved *Neuromancer.*" She turned just in time to catch Bryan checking out her backside. "Do you need anything else?" she asked, ice practically dripping off her words.

It was Bryan's turn to blush now, a reaction he hadn't experienced in quite a while. He smiled again, "No, I think I'll just browse for a while."

Callie returned to the counter, where Tonya was trying to resist a fit of the giggles. "No," she gasped, mimicking Callie, "Not *that* kind of a partner."

Callie nudged her. "Cut it out. Don't you think we've made enough of a spectacle of ourselves for one morning?"

Tonya snorted inelegantly. "What are you talking about? Dude said he's from L.A., didn't he? He probably sees this and worse on a daily basis."

Callie turned her nose up. "L.A.? For all you know he could've meant Lower Alabama! Regardless of where he's from, we don't behave this way in our store. You know it's important that we present ourselves as professionals at all times. Anyway, are you going to work this morning or this afternoon?"

Tonya turned away from the counter and started up the stairs to the second floor where they lived. "I think I'll write this morning and then spell you in the afternoon." Callie nodded and started going through the cash register procedures for opening the store. Despite her best efforts, though, she couldn't keep her mind off their early-morning customer. He was tall, at least six-two by her estimate, as he was a head taller than she, and she was five-nine in her stocking feet. His long, whipcord lean body bristled with barely contained energy. His hair was dark brown, almost black, and quite long—the ponytail he queued it into hung a third of the way down his back. But his eyes were his most striking feature. Deep-set into a long, angular face and an eerie, stormy blue, they gave him the look of a tortured poet. She wondered who he was and what he was doing in Maple Fork, Alabama. She was unnerved to have caught him checking out her backside, and hoped he hadn't noticed her giving him a similar perusal. Still, he looked vaguely familiar. For the life of her, she couldn't get over the idea that she knew him from somewhere.

"My name is Bryan Spencer, by the way."

Callie looked up, startled by the man's quiet approach. *How on earth does he move so quietly in those big clunky boots he's wearing?* "What?" She had missed most of what he'd said.

Bryan smiled. "I'm Bryan Spencer. You introduced yourself earlier, and I was too rude to return the favor."

Damn, that smile again. It really was a nice smile. She'd noticed it earlier even during their embarrassing first encounter. His teeth looked as though they'd been laid out by an obsessive-compulsive brick mason. "Oh, okay. Well, Bryan, welcome to Maple Fork. I see that you picked up two Gibson books. What else did you get?"

Bryan placed the books he held on the counter, "On your glowing recommendation, I got a couple of Octavia Butler books, too."

Callie studied the covers of the two books he had placed in front of her. "Well, you picked two good ones to start with. *Parable of the Sower* and *Parable of the Talents* are my favorites. Did you check out *Kindred,* too?"

"No, is that a good one?"

"All of her books are good, but that one is unusual in that it's primarily set in the past. So basically it's a historical set in the early nineteenth century in the South. It has time-travel in a very different way. Butler is a wonder at character development. Unlike many science fiction writers, the futuristic technology in her novels is merely a backdrop for really phenomenal characters. It's excellent and really comes to life."

Bryan turned back to the science fiction section of the store. "Then I'll get that one, too."

Callie rang up his purchases, concentrating on the task at hand to prevent her thoughts from wandering again. When she completed the transaction, Bryan smiled again and left the store. It was not until he had left her line of sight outside the store that it dawned on Callie that in recommending *Kindred* she'd suggested a book that featured an interracial relationship. Surely he wouldn't think that she was trying to make a suggestion... *Golly gee willikers, Callie. What in the world were you thinking?* She exclaimed to herself. *How big an idiot can you make of yourself in one morning?* Of course he wouldn't read anything into her recommendation. She'd suggested it to white men before, and it had been no big deal. *Yeah,* she thought with wry insight, *but those white men didn't have beautiful blue eyes and a killer smile.*

# *CHAPTER 2*

It was a busy Saturday morning at Books and So Forth. As usual, back-to-school time meant that Callie and Tonya were besieged by frantic parents trying desperately to complete school reading lists. They were always very careful to order sufficient stock to cover the schools in the area, but at least one school could be counted on to provide an outdated or incomplete list. As the only bookstore in town, they were under tremendous pressure to fulfill the requests. Otherwise the customers would go up the road to Chattanooga or over to Huntsville. Neither city was more than an hour or so away. Tonya was on the telephone now frantically trying to rush order an additional twenty copies of a book that had been inadvertently left off the high school list. Callie was trying to wait on customers and ring up purchases at the same time. They had prudently placed all the school reading list books on a table near the register. Unfortunately, that table had to be straightened up every thirty minutes or so.

"Girl, if one more person asks for *Night Weasel* I'm going to have to take hostages," Callie muttered under her breath as Tonya returned to the register. She had never been able to determine why it happened, but each year any number of people managed to mangle the title of the Pulitzer prize-winning book *Night*, by the Holocaust survivor, Elie Wiesel.

Tonya giggled. "Now remember, Callie, this is your dream…to bring literature to the unwashed masses."

Callie rolled her eyes. Then looking out at the crowd in the store, she had to snicker too. This *was* her dream. What on earth was she complaining about? She smiled as she recalled the pride and sense of accomplishment she'd felt the day the sign had gone up on the front of the store. Printed in elegant script, the sign was painted canary yellow and robin's egg blue to coordinate with the trim on the aged, red brick storefront. When the Maple Fork Restoration Committee had undertaken the task of rejuvenating downtown Maple Fork, they'd been dismissed as a bunch of crackpots. No one had believed the town could survive the loss of the steel industry. One of the first plans had been to restore the storefronts in the area to their original red brick. Each store owner had been required to coordinate trim and door colors in a way to give the entire street an enticing homey feel that made customers want to get out of their cars and walk along the cobblestone sidewalks, increasing foot traffic. Callie had chosen the bright blue and canary yellow scheme for her store. On the inside, canary yellow gave way to a soothing butter cream. With light streaming in from the four large windows in front reflecting off aged yellow pine floors, the interior literally glowed. Callie had deliberately accentuated the effect with soft, cozy chenille-covered chairs and benches all over the store to invite the readers to come in and curl up with a good book.

She and Tonya had started the store five years ago when she was right out of business school with a bright and shiny new MBA, but very little money. She'd been told repeatedly that she was foolish to start a business in small-town Alabama when she could go to the "big city" and parlay her credentials into a lucrative career. But fired up with the fever of black entrepreneurship, Callie hadn't listened to the naysayers. Enlisting the aid of her best friend Tonya, she had begged, borrowed, and leveraged herself to the hilt to open Books and So Forth.

Tonya was more or less a silent partner, allowing Callie to handle most of the day-to-day operations of the store. She'd contributed capital, sweat, equity, and her own creative flair to make the endeavor a success. Now in their fifth year with the bookstore, they were finally in the black and could contemplate finding living accommodations away from the store. And maybe even hiring some help. She and Tonya had worked extraordinarily long hours for the past five years, and Callie knew that they would have to hire someone, or the type of imaginative innovations and customer service that had made Books and So Forth a success would begin to suffer. A little rest and relaxation would give them an opportunity to brainstorm.

She made a mental note to talk to Tonya about placing an ad for a cashier.

During a late-afternoon lull, Callie and Tonya took a much-needed break to grab a bite to eat and rest for a moment. They sat down at a table in their little break area in the back of the store. The room was tiny with cinder block walls and barely enough room for a small refrigerator, a table, and two chairs. Callie did most of the paperwork for the store upstairs in their apartment, where she'd set aside an area for a home office. This room was primarily for taking a breather during a lull in floor traffic. They kept it stocked with bottled water, sodas, and snacks because they frequently had to eat at odd hours, and never knew when hunger pangs would strike.

"He came back, you know," Tonya said offhandedly as she took another sip of her iced tea.

Callie looked up distractedly from the morning receipts. "I think we're going to break a thousand dollars today. It'll be our biggest one-day total." She frowned as Tonya's statement sank in. "Who came back?"

"You know, the fine, white guy who was in here the other day. The one who was checking you out."

Callie stacked the receipts and abruptly stood up. "He was not checking me out!" She went out to place the receipts back in the register and then returned to the break area. Curious, despite her best efforts not to be, she asked with a nonchalance she didn't feel, "When did he come back?"

Not fooled for a second, Tonya replied, "He was in here in the early afternoon, when you went to make the bank drop."

"Hmmmm, did he buy anything this time?" Callie asked, the sales record still uppermost in her mind.

"Naw, he stood in the doorway, saw all those crazy folks in here and dipped," Tonya said, tossing the remains of her salad into the trash. "Of course, he could've left because he didn't see his "Nubian Goddess" behind the counter," Tonya teased. 'Nubian Goddess' was an inside joke with them, as a young man in college had followed Callie around for an entire semester calling her that. Fortunately, he had flunked out over summer break, or they would have had to resort to desperate measures to deal with him. Callie sniffed, "I don't think so. I'm sure he just came back for some more books. With his looks he doesn't have to come all the way to Alabama to get his swerve on."

"I didn't say he had to, I said he wanted to," Tonya replied.

Callie dismissed the idea, "Regardless, there won't be any swerving here, no matter how fine he might be."

"Oh, so you did notice his looks?" Tonya asked archly.

"Well, they would be kind of hard to miss," Callie replied sardonically.

"I don't know, girl, sometimes I wonder about you," Tonya replied.

"What do you mean?"

"I mean, guys are checking you out all the time, and you seem sort of, I don't know, oblivious to it. I just wonder what the deal is."

Callie wiped the table down with a sponge. "Do you really think I have had time for a man these past five years? You know the kind of hours we've had to work just trying to get this store off the ground. Besides, it's not like you're burning up in the romance department either."

"Yeah, but a fine guy like that doesn't just walk in this store every day. If it was me he'd been checking out, I would've been all over it."

A customer entered the store, triggering the buzzer designed to alert them. Callie gave a sigh of relief, happy to be extricated from the conversation, "Oh well, back to the salt mines," she drawled, turning to reenter the sales floor.

Bryan peered through the plate-glass window of the Books and So Forth storefront. In the past month he'd been back several times, but the massive crowds had been a strong deterrent to entering. Indeed, the level of activity had more closely resembled a train station back East than any bookstore he'd ever been to. The place seemed to be occupied day and night. He'd never seen anything like it. These women had to be marketing geniuses to keep their store so busy in a small town. Unfortunately, the crowds were a major problem for him. He didn't bother trying to travel incognito because he'd found that disguises usually drew more, not less attention. However, he wasn't in the mood for a bunch of screaming teenaged fans. The problem was that he had run out of books, not to mention that he wanted to see Callie again.

After some consideration, he'd decided that pursuing her might help him take his mind off the absolute shambles he'd made of his life. Since he hadn't been able to get her out of his mind for weeks, it had been an easy decision. Unaccustomed to celibacy, Bryan had concluded that his fixation on Callie could only be attributed to his lack of sexual release. He'd never been celibate before for longer than a few weeks, but at the moment he was well into his fourth month and not enjoying it at all. His breath whistled through his teeth approvingly when he saw Callie on a ladder putting some books on a high bookshelf in the otherwise empty store.

Going in, Bryan leaned against the bookcase casually, gazing up at the picture Callie made as she perched on top of the ladder. She was wearing her typical work outfit, well-tailored gray gabardine trousers and a deep rose pink sweater set and loafers. The vibrant color added to the natural luminosity of her skin. Could it possibly be as smooth and soft as it looked? Today her locks were pulled up into an elegant updo, and Bryan enjoyed the view of her gracefully curved neck and shoulders. *Is there anything about this woman that isn't sexy?* Feeling the effect she had on him and not wanting to have his arousal become evident, he finally spoke up. "Good morning."

Callie started, and bobbled a bit on the ladder before steadying herself. She looked down into a pair of familiar blue eyes. "Okay, you've really got to stop doing that!" she exclaimed.

"Doing what?" Bryan asked, pleased to have flustered her.

"Stop sneaking up on me." *And checking out my ass,* she added silently to herself. "How do you do that anyway?" she asked, climbing down the ladder. "You're wearing those big, clunky boots again, and I should be able to hear you from across the room on these wood floors."

Bryan held the ladder steady until she reached the bottom. "I've always been light on my feet. I do a lot of hiking, so I always walk with soft knees."

Callie could tell that he did get a lot of physical exercise. His thighs and legs, outlined as they were in black denim, were well-sculpted and taut. She'd always had a preference for long-legged men, and Bryan's were definitely some of the best legs she'd seen.

Bryan changed the subject. "You know, it's almost impossible to get into this store. I've been back several times, and it's always a madhouse."

Callie grinned, always happy to discuss the store's very healthy balance sheet. "Yeah, I know. It's terrific. This time of year is always very busy with back-to-school shopping. Then we wind down until the

Thanksgiving rush and Christmas. You have a problem with crowds?" she asked, looking up at him quizzically.

"Not necessarily," he replied. "I just don't want to be bothered right now. I'm here for some rest and relaxation."

Callie nodded. "That's what most folks come here for, especially all the hiking, camping, and fishing. So what can I do today to help you on your mission? Are you looking for some more Gibson books? Did you finish those Octavia Butlers?"

Bryan nodded, fairly certain that Callie didn't want to know why he needed to relax at this point.

"Yeah, and you were right. Octavia Butler is a great writer. Her vision of an apocalyptic future is almost *too* real for me, you know what I mean?" Callie nodded. "I mean, it's really possible, hell, even probable, that we'll bring about our own destruction through ignorance and greed. It just amazes me that even in a state like California they could vote to deny medical benefits and education to the children of illegal immigrants. How narrow-minded and short-sighted can you be?"

As Callie listened to this impassioned speech, she noticed not for the first time the raspy quality of his voice. He sounded as if he drank a quart of bourbon and smoked a pack of unfiltered cigarettes before getting out of bed each morning. She wondered if he smoked, but could detect no odor of cigarette smoke on him. Surprisingly, his views closely mirrored her own.

"That's the amazing thing about Butler. She projects the issues we have today to the only outcome possible in the future," she replied. "We already live in a society where access to education and healthcare is dependent on wealth. For the life of me I can't figure out why people don't understand that we are all better served when everyone has good healthcare and education."

Bryan gave her that brilliant grin again. "Will you marry me?"

Callie stepped back. "What?"

"I always told B.T. that when I met a woman who was as intelligent as she is beautiful I would marry her on the spot."

Callie smiled, "You are silly." She nudged his arm. "Who is B.T.?" she asked curiously.

Bryan leaned back against the bookcase, his arms still crossed. "B.T. is Bobby Tom Breedlove, my manager," he replied in his best corn pone accent.

Callie snorted sardonically, "Bryan, *nobody* is named Bobby Tom Breedlove."

"Well, you've got a point there. Everything else about him is fake, so I'm sure the name is, too."

"If you know the guy is fake, why on earth do you let him manage you? And exactly what does he manage for you anyway? The only folks I know who have managers are athletes and celebrities." When Bryan didn't respond, she gave him another close look, then scurried over to the magazine rack. "Oh my God. You're Bryan Spencer," she whispered almost to herself, picking up a copy of a magazine. "You're on the cover of *Rolling Stone* this month."

Bryan followed her. "Yeah, B.T. told me about that. What did they call the article? 'The Casualty Report' or something like that?"

Callie nodded, looking at the photograph of Bryan and three other young men. Bryan was in the center, dressed in black, his hair hanging loosely around his shoulders. He had another guy, a muscular redhead, in a headlock. Standing on the other side of him were the other two band members, one with closely cropped blonde hair, the other with long, artfully coifed white-blonde hair hanging in loose waves. A large hypodermic needle was superimposed over the image.

Bryan took the magazine from her hands, clearly irritated by the photograph. "It would've been nice if they'd at least talked to somebody in the band before they published this crap," he muttered to himself.

Callie looked up at him quizzically. "Why is there a big syringe across your picture? What are they trying to say? Are y'all into drugs or something?"

"I—uh," Bryan started to speak, unsure of how much information he wanted to share with a total stranger. Yet he somehow instinctively trusted Callie and was sure that he could confide his secrets to her. Then his stomach growled loudly. He recovered quickly. "Tell you what. Join me for lunch, and I'll tell you all about it."

Callie was surprised. "Lunch?"

Bryan nodded, "You know, the meal that comes between breakfast and dinner."

"Well, I don't usually go out for lunch. The store is open from nine o'clock until five-thirty, so I just grab a quick bite in the break room."

"Hell, that's got to be a violation of the Geneva Convention or something. You mean you never leave during store hours?" Bryan asked in mock astonishment.

"I don't think the Geneva Convention covers bookstores, and of course I leave the store, but I get Tonya to cover," Callie responded, getting increasingly nervous about the direction this conversation was taking.

Bryan groaned as if in excruciating pain. "Look, Callie, the lady at the supermarket down the street told me that the little restaurant next door has the best soup in the state. I was really looking forward to trying it while looking at the most beautiful woman I've ever seen…Couldn't you in the name of humanity simply sit and eat with a starving man?"

Callie giggled in spite of herself. She was nervous about the idea of having lunch with this guy, but on the other hand, it would only be next door. How dangerous could that be? Besides, she really wanted to hear his story. She couldn't believe that she, of all people, was getting all giddy over a man, and a rock star at that. But he was really nice, with a dry, self-deprecating sense of humor. She'd always been a sucker for a wry wit. While to a grown woman his being a rock star was a bit distasteful, she couldn't resist hearing more about him.

Cutting off all thoughts of felines slain by inquisitiveness she replied, "Okay, but first…" She moved within a hairsbreadth of him and looked up directly into his eyes, trying to discern any hint of glassiness or other symptoms of drug use, though she wasn't entirely sure what they were. "You need to answer one question."

Bryan inhaled her light citrus scent, enjoying the close proximity. Of course he knew exactly what she was concerned about. "No, Callie, I'm not on any illegal substance of any kind." He raised two fingers. "Scout's honor."

Callie raised a brow. "Were you ever a Scout?"

"Kicked out when I was twelve. But that time was two of the best weeks of my life." He shoved his sleeves up. "See, no track marks either. Of course, I'll be more than happy to let you give me a full-body inspection." He leered, wiggling his eyebrows suggestively.

Callie shook her head and gave him a helpless grin. "Pervert! I'll just ask Tonya to come down." She walked over and punched the intercom on the counter. "Tonya, I need to go out for lunch. Can you come down and cover for me?"

"Go out to lunch?" Tonya questioned. "But you have your lunch right up here."

Callie sighed at her friend's nosiness. "Look, I received an invitation to lunch. Can you come down?"

Tonya rushed down the stairs, almost tripping in her haste. She was brought up short when she saw Bryan standing near the counter. She inclined her head at him. "Hello, Bryan." Turning to Callie she asked, "Is he your lunch date?" Callie nodded. Tonya raised both brows. "Well, see you two later. Have fun." She waved, a sly smile on her face.

# CHAPTER 3

Granny's was crowded as usual, but Callie and Bryan managed to find a small table in a back corner. Like all the buildings in downtown Maple Fork, it had a charming exterior of aged red brick. The trim around its front windows was painted a cheerful bubble-gum pink. No one had ever bothered with signage on the door. It was unnecessary; everybody in town knew where Granny's was. The space had been expanded due to the restaurant's popularity, and now it encompassed two store spaces and had approximately thirty tables. The interior was painted bright apple green, and floral prints hung on the walls. The blue and white checkered tablecloths added to the old-fashioned ambiance. True to the name, it actually looked like a grandmother's kitchen. Callie inhaled deeply as they entered the restaurant, hoping against hope that Granny was serving her favorite beef vegetable soup and carrot raisin bread. The tempting aroma of home-baked bread and sweet, locally grown vegetables greeted her, and she smiled with pleasure. The fact that Granny only served one menu item per day was a running joke in Maple Fork, and no one ever knew what that item would be. Granny herself was a political powerhouse in the county. No one got elected to any office without her say-so, and you were likely to run into any number of politicians in the restaurant. Even the governor made a beeline for Granny's when he was in the area and had brought the vice president in during his campaign swing through the state. His aide had been rebuffed when he tried to demand that the restaurant be reserved for the special occasion. Granny didn't do those kinds of favors. The vice president had to take his chances just like the rest of Granny's loyal clientele.

Callie slid into a hardwood, straightback chair. Like everything else at Granny's, the chairs and tables were simple and plain. The food was the main event. "You know, we're very lucky that Granny opened today."

Bryan did likewise, leaning in closer to be heard over the din of the crowd. "What do you mean?" He paused. "You mean there really is a Granny?"

Callie laughed dismissively."Bryan, you're not in L.A. anymore. Of course there really is a Granny, but she doesn't exactly keep regular hours. She only opens when she feels like it."

"How the hell does she stay in business like that?" Bryan asked.

Callie nodded at his bowl. "Taste your soup." Bryan did so, and an expression of ecstasy crossed his face.

"Any questions?" Callie asked, laughing at the look on his face. "And if you think that's good, taste the carrot raisin bread." Bryan did so, groaning in appreciation of the gastronomic delight.

"Who is this woman? My God, she's a goddess of all things culinary!" he exclaimed.

"That's what everybody says." She leaned toward Bryan and whispered conspiratorially, "And every now and then, if we're really, really good, we get apple pear pie."

Bryan enjoyed this bit of silliness from Callie. Watching her full, sensuous lips purse as she spoke, he couldn't help envisioning those lips pressed against his own. Knowing the impact that train of thought would have on his body, Bryan focused on the conversation at hand. He widened his eyes and leaned in closer to Callie, raising his hand so that other diners couldn't see what they were saying. "And who do we have to kill for this privilege?" he whispered back.

Callie leaned back in her chair laughing helplessly. "According to Granny we only get pie when we *deserve* pie. Unfortunately, no one knows what it is that makes us *deserve* such an honor. Trust me, if we did, we'd do it every day." Bryan joined her in laughter as she shared additional anecdotes about the eccentric creator of the best food he'd ever tasted.

Eventually they sobered, and Callie gave him a questioning look to see if he was ready to start answering questions.

Bryan nodded. "Okay, look, I'm a musician, in a band called Storm Crow."

Callie nodded, making a motion with her hand for him to continue.

"About four months ago, my best friend, Brodie…" Bryan paused, swallowing the lump in his throat. He took a deep breath and rushed out, "Brodie died from a heroin overdose."

Callie was stunned. As far as she knew, none of her friends or acquaintances had ever used drugs, and she had never known anyone personally who'd died from substance abuse. She realized, however, that it was commonplace in the music industry. During the early to mid-1990s, rock stars had died of heroin overdoses at an astonishing rate, but it was an almost inconceivable concept to her. She placed her hand over Bryan's on the table. "Oh, Bryan, I'm so sorry." She paused as she saw a sheen of tears in those stormy eyes. "We don't have to talk about this; it's really none of my business."

Bryan was momentarily distracted by the softness of Callie's hand on his own. Although he was a very tactile person, such an innocent touch had never given him shivers down his spine. Wanting to prolong the sensation, he turned his hand upwards to grasp hers.

"No, it's okay, I want to tell you about it." He paused for a moment, startled to realize that he really did want to share this with her. Normally he had no interest in talking about his personal life with anyone. He rested his chin on his other hand while still holding hers. "Anyway, since Brodie died, I've been out of it. Acting a damned fool, as B.T. would say." He attempted a smile.

"What have you been doing?" Callie asked, concerned about possible drug use, despite his disavowal of it.

"Not what you're thinking, I'm sure. For the record, I don't do drugs at all, okay? Actually, I lead a pretty healthy lifestyle. Our bassist's girlfriend owns a holistic health store, and she has all of us on a pretty strict regimen of diet and exercise. I mean, I messed around with it when I was younger, but I learned pretty quickly that it's not for me."

He inhaled sharply as he thought about how awful the past few months had been. "Mainly I was crashing cars and getting into fights."

Callie's eyes teared. "Bryan, I'm so sorry. That must have been horrible for you."

Bryan sighed heavily. "It's getting better." He looked directly into her eyes. "Much better."

Callie suddenly became aware that Bryan still held her hand. She could feel vibrations from the contact, and the warmth tantalized her. Carefully sliding it free, she nervously picked at a piece of bread. Bryan didn't break his gaze, and finally Callie looked away. She suddenly became aware of the hubbub in the crowded restaurant. Still feeling out of her element, she stared blindly at the floral prints on the walls. Bryan leaned back in his chair and smiled cannily. He understood that he was getting to her and was pleased with the results.

"Well, anyway, B.T. got pissed with me and really reamed me out good. He told me to get out of town and gave me a plane ticket and keys to the cabin where I'm staying. I can't go back until he tells me I can."

"Good grief, was it that bad?" Callie asked, distracted from her perusal of the room.

"I pay B.T. an obscene amount of money to watch the bottom line for me, and he's convinced it's pretty bad. Plus, he thinks it would interfere with his big plans for a movie career for me."

"Movie career? Are you going to be in a movie?" Callie was surprised. She knew that a lot of musicians had ambitions in that direction, but Bryan hadn't seemed the type.

"Hell, no," he replied emphatically. "From watching some of my friends make movies and television shows, I know I would go crazy with boredom. All I want to do is play music, period. But of course, convincing B.T. of that is another story. Actually, I think the old boy was just worried about me ending up dead or in jail, and wanted to give me a chance to get myself together. Hell, we're *expected* to wreck cars and get in fights."

"Yeah, you hear about that every day almost, but it's probably for the best that you got out of town for a while."

"Yeah, I agree." He paused for emphasis, then said, "Now."

Callie looked up and got trapped in those eyes again. *I've really got to stop letting this guy get to me,* she thought. *The man is a rock star. He probably eats girls like me for...*At that thought she got a very scandalous visual and lowered her eyes, totally discomfited.

Bryan, having no idea where her thoughts had wandered, enjoyed watching her squirm in her chair. Finally he decided to put her out of her misery. "Well, I guess it's about time for you to get back to the store, huh?"

Callie looked down at her wrist. "Oh my God, I've been gone an hour and a half." She stood up brushing invisible crumbs off her clothes. "Tonya's going to kill me."

"I guess I'll take off then. Are Mondays usually less busy in the store?"

They moved rapidly towards the front of the restaurant, oblivious to the questioning looks of the other patrons as Bryan paid their check. "Usually Mondays and Tuesdays are slow days," Callie replied distractedly.

"Okay, I'll make sure I come see you on those days. Never let it be said that I interfered with the pursuit of capitalism."

Callie stopped in the middle of the sidewalk to stare at her companion, but he had already walked over to his big, black truck. With a jaunty wave, he bid her goodbye.

Callie rushed breathlessly back into the shop to face a beaming Tonya.

"How did your lunch go?" Tonya asked.

Callie stood in front of the counter, a puzzled expression on her face. "I'm not sure."

"What do you mean, you're not sure?"

"I mean, I really enjoyed lunch. Bryan seems like a decent enough guy, and he was an interesting lunch companion."

"So what part aren't you sure about?"

"It's nothing; I'm sure he wasn't serious," Callie replied, strolling over to straighten the magazine rack. Lunchtime customers always made a mess as they looked for magazines to enjoy with their meal.

Tonya followed her. Crossing her arms across her chest, she asked, "Serious about what?"

"Oh, he just said he'd come to the store to see me when we're not busy," Callie answered breezily, trying to distract herself with the task at hand. "I'm sure it doesn't mean anything."

"You're kidding, right? I told you that boy's had a case on you from the beginning," Tonya chuckled. "Of course he'll be back."

Callie picked up the *Rolling Stone* magazine from the rack. She knew she would be reading the article later anyway. "Look, Tonya, do you recognize anyone?" she asked, thrusting the magazine into her friend's face. At Tonya's gasp, she continued, "Do you really think rock stars are hanging out in north Alabama looking for a 'love connection'?" she asked, questioning herself more than her friend.

Tonya studied the cover for a moment, then flipped to the story inside. After reading for a while she exclaimed, "Damn, girl! When you go to the dark side, you really go! According to this," she gestured towards the magazine, "Storm Crow is a pretty wild band. They're huge, and their tour sold out worldwide." She paused, considering the implications of a major rock star pursuing her girlfriend, then shook her head emphatically. "But even so, he's still just a man. Just because he's a rock star doesn't mean he can't be interested in you," she pointed out logically.

"Tonya, he's a rock star. A *white* rock star."

Tonya raised her brows and gave Callie an arch look. "And this is relevant because…" Unlike Callie, Tonya had dated interracially before, had even had a long-term relationship with a white guy in college. Though nothing had come of it, she'd long since made it clear that she had no problem 'tasting the rainbow,' as she put it. "Besides, who the hell are you trying to convince here, anyway? Sounds to me like dude made it clear that he intends to see you again, and you're scared to death."

Callie leaned against the magazine rack, her head down as she tried to collect her thoughts. "Look,

Tonya, he's nice, you know, but I don't think he's interested in me that way."

Tonya snorted. "All heterosexual men are interested in all women that way."

Callie demurred. "No, I think he just sees me as a way to occupy his time while he's exiled to Alabama."

"Exiled?" Tonya raised her brows.

"Oh yeah, that's right, I haven't told you his story yet, have I?" When Tonya shook her head no, Callie slumped down on the bench in front of the magazine rack. Tonya joined her, and Callie relayed the information Bryan had shared during lunch.

"So you see now why I'm pretty sure that he's just looking for a friend, maybe somebody to hang out with while he's down here. I mean, this guy has stables of long-legged blondes at his disposal. Can you see him taking up with a skinny, nappy-headed black girl from North Alabama?" Callie asked.

It was just too scary to contemplate the idea that there could be anything more than that with Bryan. Rock stars, especially ones with more than a passing acquaintance with drugs, were way out of her realm of experience. Their lifestyle, while glamorous and exciting, had always seemed sleazy to her. Fame couldn't be all that terrific, she reasoned, or there wouldn't be so much substance abuse and other bizarre behavior. Of course, Bryan had been emphatic that he wasn't into that scene. But he had used in the past. In all honesty, she'd have to admit that she was drawn somewhat to the thrill of it all. Of course, it didn't hurt that all that excitement came in such a hot package.

Tonya stood up and began straightening the magazine rack. She was astounded that her conservative friend had not run screaming for the hills when Bryan disclosed his association with drugs and a wild L.A. lifestyle. Callie was usually not one to get involved with anything she couldn't control, and fame seemed to thrive on chaos. She wondered if Callie had any idea how much the fact that she hadn't cut him off immediately betrayed her interest in much more than a friendship. Tonya never ceased to be amazed that Callie, so savvy in anything pertaining to business, had absolutely no inkling as to how to deal with men. Even worse, she didn't even notice when one indicated in every way possible that he was smitten with her. Telling her any better now would probably only make matters worse. She'd never believe it, and it would probably only increase her resistance to Bryan. If nothing else, she would enjoy her friend's reaction when Bryan began pursuing her in earnest. In a small town, you had to take your entertainment where you could find it, and even if Callie was right, this would definitely be amusing to watch.

She casually dusted her hands together. "It's confusing all right, but I still think the boy is interested in you. I think in a month's time he could've found women all over Maple Fork to hang with if he was so inclined. After all, it's not like we don't have long-legged blondes here, you know. But then again, I guess only time will tell."

# CHAPTER 4

True to his word, Bryan continued to make his presence known at Books and So Forth. He seldom missed a day taking Callie to lunch or if it was a busy day, he'd slip in through the back door and bring both of them a meal from one of the local restaurants. He was convenient to have around, especially on days when they received large shipments of books. Stocking the shelves was backbreaking work, and Bryan had more strength and stamina than either of them. Much to Callie's surprise, he also had an admirable eye for merchandising. Apparently there were many dimensions to his artistic talent. It took some doing, but he persuaded her to rearrange the science fiction section and though she'd initially objected, a number of customers noted that it was much easier to find titles.

Callie didn't know what to make of his attentiveness, but she had to admit, if only to herself, that she liked it. Tonya, of course, read all types of implications in his behavior, but Callie convinced herself that he simply enjoyed her company and was desperate for something to occupy his time during his interminable exile. For her part, she was certainly enjoying having him around. They had so many interests in common, particularly a love for the outdoors and a fascination with history. Despite his sometimes gloomy demeanor, Bryan had a delightfully silly streak and a sense of fun that matched her own. She didn't often meet people who appreciated her sense of humor as much as he seemed to. Though flattered, Callie took care to keep herself firmly grounded in reality. Bryan just needed a distraction in his life right now, something to help him deal with some intolerable circumstances, she constantly reminded herself. It would be foolish to read anything serious into the situation. Maintaining a nonchalance she didn't feel was difficult at times, but it was certainly better than the alternative. She had a horror of making a fool of herself over a totally unobtainable man.

Given that, Callie was surprised to find herself sitting on top of Lookout Mountain in Chattanooga, Tennessee, overlooking a Civil War battlefield at eight o'clock on a Sunday morning. As a North Alabama native, she had been to Lookout Mountain many times on school field trips and such, but had never enjoyed it. It seemed that she could almost feel the spirits of the dead in this place, and no matter what time of year she went, she was always cold. She shivered now, reflecting on how this particular adventure had begun.

Bryan had dared call her at dawn on a Sunday morning. Most thinking people knew better than to

call her at that hour on the one day a week she had
an opportunity to sleep in. Of course, she thought
sardonically, Bryan frequently demonstrated lapses
in the thinking department, and she hadn't hesitated
to tell him so on more than one occasion. He had
begged and beseeched, and somehow she'd found
herself in the front seat of his truck at an ungodly
hour speeding toward Chattanooga. Bryan had been
trying for weeks to get her to go to the battlefield
with him. In previous discussions, they'd shared their
love for history; Callie enjoyed reading biographies
and social histories. Of late she'd been reading a
good deal about the Roman Empire. Much to her
dismay, she'd discovered that Bryan was absolutely
fixated on warfare and battles, the gorier, the better.
He'd spent a great deal of time researching the Civil
War battles that had occurred nearby and was particularly intrigued by the tale of a local heroine who
had done some scouting for General Nathan
Bedford Forrest. A statue in her honor was located
prominently in the middle of Broad Street downtown. The story of an Indian maiden leaping to her
death from a nearby waterfall because of unrequited
love had kept him occupied for days as he sought to
verify the story. Bryan had regaled her with tales
about his collection of war memorabilia, the center-
piece of which was a medieval mace he'd acquired in
Germany. Callie had resisted previous entreaties to
join him, but he had caught her at a weak moment
when she was barely awake.

"Bryan, are you sure I agreed to do this?" she had asked in the truck with yet another jaw-cracking yawn.

Bryan had given her a cheerful grin. "Yep, you most assuredly did. Come on, I bought you breakfast, a huge thermos of coffee, and promised you lunch. What more can a guy do?"

Callie had only snorted and poured another cup of coffee. Maybe if she drank enough, she would feel marginally human.

Now they sat side by side on the grass, the antique cannons an ominous foreshadowing of the conversation to come. They rested their elbows on their knees as they looked out over a beautiful view that had been the scene of bloodshed and horror. The mist that enshrouded the mountain gave it an air of gloom, but also one of transcendent beauty. It was that fog that had earned the famous Civil War battle the nickname, "The Battle Above the Clouds." Lookout Mountain was almost always foggy, the haze lifting only during the hottest days of summer.

"You know, I always get a funny feeling when I visit battlefields," Bryan said. "Like when I went to Gettysburg. It was really weird. The gooseflesh stood up on my arms and we whispered the whole time without even realizing it. The whole situation was eerie, and dare I say it, spooky."

Callie nodded. She had never met anyone else who had experienced the same sensation she'd felt. "It's almost like you can feel those long-dead soldiers. It's one of the reasons I've never liked to come here."

"Do you believe in spirits? I mean, like ghosts and stuff?" Bryan didn't really know where he stood on the issue, but Callie's comments piqued his curiosity. He'd come to expect the unexpected from her, and her response didn't disappoint him.

"No, not really, but I believe that maybe when there's so much violence in a place that energy could be deposited there. I don't know, I can't really say if it's their ghosts or spirits, or what, but there's definitely something. I'm always sad and depressed when I come here. And no matter how hard I try, I can never get warm."

Bryan was really surprised that Callie, who had always seemed so pragmatic and businesslike, would actually entertain so fanciful a notion.

"I definitely believe that the spirits, or 'energy' or whatever you want to call it, have remained. Sort of like a reminder of the horror of battle or something. I think about how those guys must have felt, how scared they must have been, the courage it must have taken to go forward despite their terror." Bryan shrugged and leaned forward. "Well, courage or fear of being shot by their own officers." He gave a low chuckle. "I guess under those circumstances, it would be better to face the enemy. The ultimate damned if you do, damned if you don't situation." He paused again. "After we went to Gettysburg,

Brodie and I wrote a song about it. It was on our third album."

As usual, thinking about Brodie evoked painful memories and emotions he still didn't want to confront. He had borne the guilt and self-loathing about his role in Brodie's death for months. Refusing to share or even acknowledge his grief, he had tamped it down into the dark recesses of his soul until it had manifested itself in his behavior and feelings of despair. It was as if simple acknowledgment would make the facts concrete, a reality that was more than he could bear. But somehow, perhaps it was the atmosphere of this place sanctified by the blood of long-dead soldiers, he really wanted Callie to understand the pain and abhorrence he still felt. "I gave him his first joint, you know."

Callie kept up with the topic change and knew to whom he referred. She had suspected all along that Bryan blamed himself for his friend's sad end, and now this comment confirmed it. Bryan had told her that he didn't use drugs, and she believed him, having seen no evidence of drug use since she'd known him. But he'd also told her that he'd been pretty wild in the past, and that he'd gotten drunk and crashed cars since Brodie's death. The degree of guilt and disgust had made her wonder whether Bryan had somehow played a part in the death of his friend.

She leaned back on her elbows and looked up at him inquiringly. "Bryan, did you shoot up with Brodie?"

Bryan gave her a frustrated look. "Dammit, Callie! I told you I never used that stuff! I'm clean; I've been clean for years! I've never had a drug habit, okay?"

Callie nodded. She was probably being hopelessly naïve, but for some reason, really gut instinct alone, she believed him. This was a new situation. She wasn't sure what to say, but she knew she wanted to help him. She only hoped she wouldn't make the situation worse. She took a deep breath, "So, you gave him his first joint. Did you give him his last needle, too?"

Bryan gaped at her in astonishment. He'd never expected this reaction. "What?" he asked, unsure he'd heard her properly. Her directness and honesty were traits he liked most about Callie, but in this situation, they seemed somehow inappropriate.

Callie paused. Maybe she really should just leave this alone. What did she know about helping people deal with grief? However, Bryan was still staring at her expectantly, clearly waiting for some clarification of what she'd just said. She'd already started down this path, and she could see no way to stop now. "Or maybe you have the power of life and death. What do they do, issue you a magic wand instead of a Grammy these days?"

Bryan was still speechless and could only shake his head.

"I mean, that's what you're doing, right? Blaming yourself for Brodie's death? Did you give him the needle, Bryan?" Callie asked insistently.

"No, Callie, I already told you…" Bryan growled through clenched teeth.

"Then why in God's name are you sitting here blaming yourself?" Callie yelled.

Bryan lowered his head; he really couldn't formulate a response.

Callie decided to try a gentler tack. "Look, Bryan, you've been beating yourself up for months, thinking you caused Brodie's death, right?"

Bryan raised his head, his eyes wet. "I could've stopped him, I know it."

Callie reflected on that for a moment. She didn't really know that much about substance abuse and was painfully aware that she was hideously unqualified for the role she'd been thrust into.

Callie shook her head, "Bryan, have you talked about this with anybody?"

Bryan gave a harsh laugh. "I wondered when that was coming. Ever since I got old enough to talk, one person or another has suggested that I needed to 'talk to someone.' " He mimicked the overly clinical voice of a school counselor. "Look, it's not about my potty training or being locked in closets or seeing my mom screw strangers or any of the other bullshit from my childhood, okay?" he shouted. "It's about my best friend being dead and me not doing a goddamn thing to stop it!" As if trying physically to regain control, he suddenly dropped his voice to a disconsolate whisper as he hunched his shoulders and lowered his head back down on his knees. "Callie, I don't want to talk to 'someone.' I want to talk to you."

The brief glimpse into Bryan's childhood had left Callie speechless. They'd really never talked about it before, but the picture she'd gotten wasn't pretty. He seemed hell-bent on discussing Brodie with her, here and now. She couldn't see any way out of this conversation and only hoped she wasn't doing irreparable damage. She fell back on her best tool. "Let's look at this logically, okay?"

Bryan had to smile; Callie was nothing if not always logical and efficient.

"You knew Brodie most of your life, right?"

Bryan nodded.

"You were like brothers, even closer than brothers, from what you've told me. Right?"

Bryan nodded again.

"So he knew he could come to you for anything, and you would help him no matter what."

Bryan hesitated, unsure of where this was going. "He knew he could come to me, but at the time, I was all wrapped up in this girl, and…"

Callie interrupted, not really wanting to hear about Bryan's love life. "Had you ever turned him down before?"

"Of course not, he was my brother," Bryan replied emphatically.

"Do you think he knew that he could come to you if he wanted to, and you would move heaven and hell to help him?"

Bryan paused, but then finally had to admit to himself that Brodie had to have known that he would not let him down. "Yes," he murmured reluctantly, not at all happy with the direction Callie seemed to be taking.

"So, if he knew help was available and didn't use it, what do you think that means?"

Bryan stared at her, not wanting to acknowledge Brodie's complicity in his own death.

Callie softened her tone. "He obviously didn't want help. I don't know that much about addiction, but I do know that you have to want help. You have to do that for yourself, sweetie," she murmured softly. Her voice, though barely above a whisper, resonated with tenderness and compassion. "No one can do that for you."

Bryan still didn't respond, so Callie asked another question. "Bryan, how did you find out that Brodie was using?"

Bryan leaned back until he was prone on the ground, his knees still bent, his arms stretched above his head. He seemed to reflect for a moment, then gave a heavy sigh. "You know, like I told you, we all were using stuff in the beginning." Callie nodded. "Then Brodie and I moved to B.T.'s house, and his wife Maria didn't put up with it, so we stopped." His mouth curved into a shadow of a smile as he recalled Maria's reaction when she located their stash of marijuana. She'd stormed through the house with all the force of a Valkyrie. There had been hell to pay that night, and they'd never dared try that again. Somehow, recalling the horror of watching her flush two weeks' pay had quelled any desire they might have had to attempt smoking in the house again. He hadn't seen Maria that angry before or since, but he was eternally grateful for her intervention. He continued the story. "I mean, we still drank beer and smoked weed, when we could get away with it, but it wasn't a regular thing anymore. We hooked up with Jon, and then a little later we met Twist. After that, we worked so hard we didn't have time to party anyway. I was okay with that, but now, looking back, I don't think Brodie was. Then we hit big with our second album. We moved out of B.T.'s house and lived together for a while. Brodie would go on these incredible binges. After a while I couldn't hang with the constant partying and moved out. But Brodie and I still spent most of our time together. At first Brodie was on coke. I tried it once, but I really didn't like it."

Callie interrupted, fascinated by what she was hearing. Since she'd never tried any illegal drugs, she was curious. "Why didn't you like it?"

Bryan wiped his hands over his face. "It was just too good, you know? I mean, the moment I came down, all I could think about was how badly I wanted it again. That scared the crap out of me, and I didn't want to use it again. Brodie did, though. I mean, this was the early nineties, everybody was using something. Me and the other guys pretty much left it alone five or six years ago. For me, having a life where I could write and play my music and have people actually pay money to hear it was more than enough of a high. All I ever wanted was to play music, have enough money to pay my rent and buy CDs. Storm Crow gave me all that and more than I ever thought possible. Hell, I actually own a house. Never in a million years did I ever think that would happen. I didn't need to get high anymore. I guess I grew up or something. I don't know. I knew Brodie was still using occasionally. I'd see him sometimes and he'd be really wasted, but I didn't worry too much about it. He seemed okay with just using it for partying. He was still able to function at that point. I didn't know how bad it had gotten until about a year or so ago."

"What happened?" Callie was wide-eyed as she tried take it all in.

Bryan took another tremulous breath, then continued after a long pause. "We were practicing for our tour, and Brodie kept missing rehearsals. That wasn't like him. No matter how messed up he was, he never bailed on the band. Anyway, I realized I hadn't seen him as much as usual. So I went over to his place." Bryan paused again, licking his lips and taking several shaky breaths as if steeling himself to relate the rest of the tale.

Callie could see the sweat beading on his upper lip. His color had faded as if he were feeling ill or nauseous.

"He was shooting up, Callie. I saw the needle, the works, everything. I couldn't believe my eyes." His voice shook. "And the thing is, he was so goddamned casual about it, like it was no big deal. He invited me in and tied his arm off with me sitting there. He'd already cooked the stuff. I don't think I've ever been as sick as I was when I watched him shoot that garbage into his vein. I was stunned. I mean, I knew that he liked to party, but I had no idea it had gotten like that. And it happened so fast, or at least it seemed to. Part of me just wanted to grab that poison and flush it down the toilet, but I just sat there and watched, like I was paralyzed or something. I couldn't even say anything."

Callie couldn't imagine what it felt like to see a friend, or anyone for that matter, shooting up heroin. The very thought horrified her. She reached out and touched his hand. "What did you do?"

Bryan sat up, his grim expression adding additional poignancy to the gruesome tale. She'd noted before that his eyes, already tempestuous, darkened considerably whenever he experienced emotional distress. Now they had turned almost black, taking on the appearance of a southwestern sky she'd seen once right before a tornado struck the city. She marveled at the powerful emotions that could initiate such a change. "I stayed there with him, and I tried to talk to him about getting clean. He said the usual crap, you know, about not being an addict. We fought, and he kicked me out. Then I called B.T. and the rest of the band. We tried to talk some sense into him."

"An intervention?"

"Yeah, I guess you could call it that. Brodie was like me, didn't really have any family to speak of, so it was just the band, B.T., and Maria. We didn't really get anywhere, and he never agreed to get help. But he did keep it together long enough for us to finish rehearsals and go on tour. We were about halfway done when he died." Bryan closed his eyes, obviously struggling to master his emotions. When he opened them again, the deep blue pools revealed a suffering so torturous that Callie wanted to weep. The muscles in his throat moved strongly as he choked out, "The tour, the goddamned tour! My best friend was strung out on smack, and we just patched him together enough to go on tour!"

Callie reflected on what Bryan had just shared with her. So this was the source of his self-destructive tendencies. He really hadn't caused his friend's death and was in no significant way responsible. But the guilt seemed to be eating him alive. It seemed surreal, totally alien to her, and she was clueless as to how to process it. As she struggled with her own overwhelming emotions, a ghastly thought occurred to her. "Did you find him?"

Bryan pressed the heels of his hands against his closed eyelids, as if to shut out the horrific scene. "No, Twist did. We were in London and had one more show before we were going to take a two-week break. You know, come home, regroup, then start on the American leg of the tour. Twist went to Brodie's room for some reason, and he found the body." He took another deep breath and swallowed the hotly sickening wave of nausea the memory still evoked.

"He'd been dead for hours. Apparently he'd gone to his room to shoot up as soon as we finished the show. We'd been keeping a close watch on him because it's so goddamned easy to score in London, but he said he was tired and didn't want to hang out. Hell, we all were, so we weren't suspicious. Anyway, Twist started screaming…We all ran down there…yeah, I saw him, too. He had turned blue, his mouth was all purple, the veins in his neck stood out. It looked like he had vomited. There was…" He rubbed his eyes again. "Oh God, I'd never seen a dead body before."

Callie felt like screaming herself at the picture Bryan had painted. She could not imagine what it felt like to see the dead body of a close friend. Especially a friend who had died such an appalling death. She was relieved for Bryan's sake that he hadn't actually had the initial shock of finding Brodie, but knew that seeing someone he loved in that condition had to have been incredibly traumatic.

She took a deep breath to regain her composure, "So what do you think you could've done? I mean, you tried to talk to him. You got other people who were close to him to talk to him. You were available for him. What else do you think you could've done? Do you really think he'd still be alive if you had stopped the tour? Maybe he would've died sooner. Maybe having to get it together for the tour actually helped prolong his life. Do you really know?"

"That's the real pisser, Callie. I don't know if it would've made a difference or not." Bryan sighed heavily, finally ready to acknowledge the truth. "I know you're right, Callie," he choked out, "but it doesn't make it any easier. It just seems like I put the band before Brodie's life. Did we really have to go right then? Why didn't we stop and make him go to rehab? I should've been able to do something."

"Bryan, the person has to want help. You offered help, and he didn't accept. What more was there to do?" She looked on as he put his head back down on his bent knees and brought his hands up to cup the back of his head. She could tell that he was deep in thought, but wasn't sure that her words had penetrated. After watching him for several long moments, she finally touched his shoulder. "Are you okay?"

Bryan raised his head and gave her a bittersweet smile. Then he reached out and grasped her hand in his, raised it to his lips, and gently kissed each finger. "Thank you, Callie," he said, looking intently into her eyes. "No, I'm not okay, but for the first time in a very long time, I really do think I'll be okay soon."

# CHAPTER 5

Much to Bryan's frustration, after the trip to Chattanooga, his relationship with Callie remained pretty much the same. He continued spending as much time as possible with her, but she seemingly felt, at most, a polite interest in him. Bryan couldn't help being aggravated by her behavior as he knew he had not imagined the closeness between them that day. She had given him exactly what he needed to realize the futility of blaming himself for Brodie's death. Others had given him sympathy, even pity, but Callie had been the first to make him stop kicking his own ass and look at the situation in all its sordid glory. Of course, she'd probably forced him to let up on himself only so there'd be room for her to ride his ass. He puzzled over the heretofore unknown but perversely masochistic quirk in his nature that caused him to actually enjoy and even look forward to the sarcastic little comments she was prone to make. Had he become so jaded by the way people fawned over him that he actually enjoyed being on the receiving end of her witticisms? Apparently so. He couldn't recall ever delighting in a woman's company the way he did with Callie. In all his previous encounters with women, he'd participated in the niceties of conversation only to the degree necessary to get the woman into bed, and sometimes if she was particularly star-struck, conversation wasn't necessary at all. That wasn't the case with Callie; he was astonished to find that he actually enjoyed talking to her. His celebrity status notwithstanding, she didn't pull any punches. She was a real person, with no agenda of her own. She didn't stroke his ego because she wanted an entrée into the business; she only laughed at his jokes if they were genuinely funny. And she didn't hesitate to smack him around when he needed it. He laughed to himself when he recalled an incident earlier that week.

They'd been re-merchandising the store, moving the stock around to keep it fresh and interesting. Callie didn't want customers to become too familiar with the location of their favorite items. If they had to search a little, they might find new things to buy. Better yet, they might actually have to ask, and that would give Callie an opportunity to make recommendations. Bryan shook his head; he'd never realized that there was so much strategy involved in retail. In the midst of this marketing sleight of hand, he had complained about the insipid music she had playing in the store. She'd responded with a pained look and a direct jab. "Look Bryan, I know that to you if it's not about death, mayhem, eviscerated fowl, and oozing wounds, it's not music. But the rest of us aren't looking for music to murder by." He couldn't help laughing. She wasn't the first to say that his music was a bit dark. Storm Crow was frequently compared to Alice in Chains. But no one else had ever put it in those terms or dared say it to his face.

Watching her make business transactions had become one of the highlights of his life. She'd sit perched on her little office chair, the telephone held to her ear by her shoulder as she perused the lengthy printout sheets the publishers sent. He'd sit there breathlessly waiting for that inevitable moment when she would place her pencil behind her ear. Somehow that little gesture was guaranteed to send his sexual impulses into overdrive. Damn, who would've thought he could get so turned on by a woman in business mode? He even enjoyed the little tsking sound she made whenever he did something particularly annoying. That was her most frequent reaction to his seeming inability to keep up with any of his personal belongings, especially his keys. Once when they were again delayed by the need to search for them, she'd made a wry comment that in his "other life" he probably had "people" to do that for him. He hadn't said anything, too embarrassed to admit that indeed he did. Before meeting Callie, he'd never questioned the self-indulgence of having assistants do for him what he as a grown man should be doing for himself. It wasn't as if he were to the manor born. He'd spent a considerable amount of time living on the streets. But the seductive lifestyle could grow on a person rather quickly.

He couldn't remember the last time he'd met such a genuine person. Since their trip, he felt bound even more closely to Callie, whereas she seemed to only tolerate him. He wondered cynically if she would dismiss him entirely if he didn't spend a fortune in her bookstore each week. He chuckled softly at the thought, causing Callie to raise her brow quizzically as if to inquire what he found so amusing. Bryan shook his head negatively, deciding to keep the source of his amusement to himself.

On this particular day, they'd been fortunate enough to find Granny's open and were enjoying another excellent bowl of soup.

"Okay, I've told you about me. When are you going to tell me your story?" Bryan was surprised that he was so curious about her background. Normally women revealed far more information than he was interested in. But he had learned in the couple of months that he had known Callie, that she was nothing like the women he commonly encountered.

"What do you mean? I don't have a story." Callie furrowed her brow, puzzled by his question.

"Come on, Callie, everybody has a story. I've told you all about my angst-ridden existence and my self-destructive bent. Now it's only fair that you tell me how you came to be a rising tycoon," Bryan stated emphatically.

"Actually, Bryan, there's nothing much to tell. I'm just a small business owner in a small town."

Bryan raised his brows. "Give it up, Callie, I want to hear about it."

Callie sighed, "Well don't blame me if you fall asleep in your soup."

Bryan chuckled. "Hell, I've already decided I want to be buried in it. Now come on, were you born here? Is this your hometown?"

Callie nodded. "I was born and raised here in Maple Fork. I know just about everybody."

"That must be pretty cool. I mean, I grew up in East L.A. Most of the people I knew growing up are either dead or in jail."

"It has its good and bad points," she mused.

"What do you mean?"

Callie reflected for a moment, "There have been times when I would have preferred a little more anonymity. Instead, from the time I was a little girl, people have been watching me. If I did something bad, I knew somebody would call my mama before I even got home. Actually, they still call my mama if they think I'm acting up."

Bryan gave a snort of disbelief.

"Oh, you think I'm kidding?" Callie asked insistently. "Let me give you an example. Last week I walked into Wal-Mart and didn't speak to the greeter. My mama called to ask me about it that night!"

"You're kidding."

"No, that's small-town life. It's like a cocoon, all nice and safe, but if you're not careful, a cocoon can smother you." She sighed philosophically.

Bryan nodded his understanding. "Yeah, and what is this 'speaking' thing? Everywhere I go people nod and smile. At first, I thought they'd recognized me, but then I realized they didn't know me from Adam. They were just being friendly. Is that a Southern thing?"

Callie nodded. "Definitely a Southern thing and especially a Southern black thing. If you don't speak, folks label you as siditty."

"Siditty?" He tried the word out. "I like that. Spell it," he demanded.

She gave him a speaking glance. He had to be joking. There were some words that were for speaking only. Siditty definitely fell into that category.

"But what the heck does it mean?"

"Snobbish, stuck-up." Callie took a sip of soup.

"Oh, siditty, I like that. It's sort of like Yiddish. It sounds exactly like what it means." Bryan nodded thoughtfully. "So you've never been away from Maple Fork?"

"Yeah, I left to go to college and business school."

"But since you came back here, it must not be too bad."

Callie leaned back in her chair and thought about that for a moment. "You know, when I left, I really missed it. Tuscaloosa is a much larger town than

Maple Fork and has a lot more conveniences. I also spent a lot of time in Birmingham, and it's really big. Most folks thought I'd relocate there or go to Atlanta. You know, it seems to be the law these days that all young black professionals must live in Atlanta." She smiled wryly. "Both places are full of opportunities for small business, but all I could think about was coming back home and opening my bookstore. That's all I ever really wanted to do."

"But why a bookstore, Callie?"

Callie pursed her lips, drawing Bryan's eye to that unconscious gesture as she contemplated the question. "Well, I've always loved books. I worked in a bookstore all through high school and college. I always wanted one of my own."

Bryan wondered if she had any idea how lusciously tempting her lips looked when she pursed them like that.

He raised a brow. "Just one bookstore, Callie?" he asked suspecting her imperialistic dreams.

Callie chuckled. "Okay, you sussed me out, chain of bookstores." Bryan raised his brow higher as he smirked at her response. Callie giggled helplessly at his expression. "All right, chain of bookstores, boutiques and day spas, but that will be in my new five-year plan. I'll start working on that next month."

Bryan shook his head at the oddity of sitting down and deliberately making a five-year plan, let alone actually trying to adhere to it. B.T. developed those too, and Bryan's refusal to pay it the slightest attention was an unceasing bone of contention between them.

He continued his questions. "How long have you known Tonya?"

Callie smiled. "It seems like all my life. Tonya's been my closest friend since kindergarten. She denies it, but she used to eat glue."

Bryan chuckled at the visual of the two bookstore owners as little girls doing fingerpaints and glue art together.

"We've been tight ever since. We went off to college together and when I decided to start Books and So Forth after grad school, I asked her to be my partner."

Bryan nodded. "How long have you two been living above the store? Doesn't that get annoying after a while?"

"We've been there for five years, since we opened the store. At first it was convenient, but now it's a bit impractical. We're in the black now, and I hope we'll be able to move soon."

"So where did you guys go to school?"

"The U.A." At Bryan's puzzled look, she clarified, "The University of Alabama."

"Oh yeah." Bryan nodded. "Roll Tide."

Callie chuckled. "I guess you've seen those signs up around town. The Alabama-Auburn game is this weekend."

"I guess it's a big state rivalry, huh?" Bryan wasn't much of a fan of spectator sports, except for the Raiders. He generally watched sports only when he was stuck in a hotel room while on tour.

"Oh yeah, the biggest."

"This sounds like fun. Tell me more about it."

"Let me put it this way. It's the only day aside for major holidays that we close the store."

Having spent a great deal of time in the store, Bryan was quite familiar with Callie's capitalistic tendencies, so he knew that was an incredible statement. "You close the store for a football game?" he exclaimed in disbelief.

Callie nodded. "You have to understand that this is more than a mere football game, it's absolute war. Everybody in the state chooses sides. Newcomers are given a few months to decide, and once they've chosen one, there's no going back. Folks around here take it that seriously." She smiled. "A few years ago a friend of mine married an Auburn fan. All of our friends call it a mixed marriage, and they aren't talking about the fact that they are of different races. There's nothing Alabamians love more than football, and to us the Alabama-Auburn game is the Holy Grail of the sport."

Bryan had heard about huge state rivalries in the past, but had never really paid them any attention. But this sounded like it could be a lot of fun.

"But why do you close the store? I don't think I've ever seen a time when you don't have any customers. I can't believe business falls off that badly because of a football game."

"Believe it!" Callie exclaimed emphatically. "We tried to open the store the first couple of years and got no customers. Tonya and I decided that it would be more profitable to simply close the store and enjoy the game with our families."

"Oh, you guys have a big party or something?"

"Oh yeah. My parents are the world's biggest 'Bama fans. They have a huge party with all our family and friends."

"That sounds interesting. Do you think they'd mind if I came?" Bryan asked. Somewhere deep inside he had to admit that he longed for something vastly out of his range of experience, a normal family life. If nothing else, there was bound to be barbecue involved. It seemed that Southerners took any and all opportunities to throw something dead and unhealthy on the grill. During his stay in Alabama, he had become addicted to the stuff. Grilling was a trendy thing in L.A. where everybody was into the quick and easy meal. Barbecuing, Bryan had discovered, was a totally different experience. Southerners definitely had a lock on the long, slow process. It seemed there was a barbecue restaurant on every corner. Even a tiny town like Maple Fork boasted three, and he'd sampled each one of them. His personal favorite was a little no-name dive about twenty minutes outside of town. It was a ramshackle place with a slamming screen door, plank floors, and a tin roof. He doubted it had ever seen a health inspector. A monument to the benefits of specialization, they served only barbecue ribs, no sides. Everyone knew better than to ask for such niceties as baked beans or coleslaw. Service was nonexistent; the staff was curt at best. Soft drinks were in a drink box under the counter. Yet, despite all the drawbacks, the place was always standing room only, no matter what time of day or night, and served the best barbecued pork ribs he'd ever tasted. Undoubtedly his arteries were already in a state of shock, but he enjoyed indulging his new vice. Now the idea of a gathering of family and friends, something he'd always avoided passionately, was strangely inviting.

"Bryan, you don't want to come to a party at my folks' house. I know you've been to much bigger and certainly better parties." Callie laughed.

"No, seriously, Callie, it sounds like a lot of fun. I've never been to a party like that," Bryan insisted earnestly.

Callie shook her head. "I'm sure my folks wouldn't mind another person in the madhouse they have. Sure, why don't you join us?" she asked dryly.

"Gee, thanks, I can't remember when I've had such an enthusiastic invitation," Bryan answered equally dryly. "My pride notwithstanding, I won't turn you down because I really want to come."

Callie laughed heartily. "Bryan, please come to our party. I'm sure you'll have a lot of fun," she said with mock enthusiasm. Callie was somewhat breathless. Bryan would enjoy the party; everyone always had a good time at the Lawson's annual event. But how would all this affect her? Up until this point, they'd managed to keep their relationship casual. Two people enjoying lunch and an occasional outing together—nothing more, nothing less. Meeting her family put a wholly different complexion on the matter, adding a layer of uncertainty and anxiety that could wreak havoc with an already tenuous situation.

Callie continued to stare sightlessly into her soup, puzzled as to how she had been maneuvered into inviting Bryan to her parents' home. She couldn't understand why such a huge celebrity would want to spend a Saturday afternoon watching a football game with a bunch of strangers. Somehow the man had managed to infiltrate almost every aspect of her life. He had a boundless energy level, and he seemed to fill her every spare moment. They'd gone hiking several times, and had made that road trip up to Chattanooga to see the Civil War battlefield. Sometimes she'd accompany him to the library, though she taunted him for borrowing books when he could so easily buy them at her store. He'd laughingly responded that he spent enough money in her store to equal the gross national product of a small Caribbean nation. She'd been thrilled to find that Bryan shared her passion for fishing, an interest that none of her other friends enjoyed, leaving Callie with few opportunities to indulge her mania. They had gone several times and bonded over the thrill of yet another shared activity. A consummate fly-fisherman, Bryan had never been bass fishing before and enjoyed the challenge of landing the feisty, small-mouthed bass.

He'd even tried to convince her to try canoeing or kayaking, but she had declined, citing a lifelong fear of drowning in a tiny boat with a madman. The hiking trip to Little River Canyon had been frightening enough.

They'd set out very early on a day hike along the perimeter of the canyon. Bryan had been intrigued by the prospect of hiking along the only river in the world that flowed for its entire length along the top of a mountain. On this very warm fall day, they both wore hiking shorts and boots. Bryan's long muscular legs were lightly peppered with dark brown hair, and she couldn't stop staring at them. She could almost feel that rough hair rubbing against the smooth sensitive flesh of her inner thighs. Fortunately, Bryan was leading so he wasn't aware of her fixation, but it was still terribly awkward. To make matters worse, during a brief descent they constantly brushed against one another, and her heightened awareness and nervousness had made her unusually clumsy. She'd slipped on some loose stones and Bryan had caught her just in time to prevent a nasty fall over a ledge. It wasn't the first time she'd been amazed by his stunning reflexes. The wind was knocked out of her and when she couldn't seem to catch her breath,

Bryan laid her down on the ground to check for injuries. His heavily callused fingers tenderly probed her flesh and inadvertently triggered every erogenous zone in her body. Callie brought the once-over to a halt as his touch was actually compounding her breathing difficulties. She inadvertently glanced down at the front of Bryan's shorts and realized that he was not immune to the contact either. Seeing evidence of his arousal only intensified her own response. Her body definitely longed to explore that impressive bulge. She was ashamed to admit, even to herself, that she was proud of her ability to arouse such an attractive man. But on the other hand, it was at least as frightening as the near miss off the cliff. She tried to dismiss it by telling herself that most men would be aroused by groping a woman, but somehow that argument wasn't particularly convincing.

For the most part, they only parted company when she attended church and sorority functions. Not that he hadn't tried to wrangle an invitation to join her at those events, but she didn't even want to think about the ramifications of bringing a white man to her all-black Baptist church. It was very difficult to turn him down for other things because it was so nice to have someone to explore the area with. He made even the most mundane things interesting and exciting. Tonya spent almost all her free time writing, leaving Callie alone and bored. Comfortable in her own skin, Callie enjoyed her solitude, especially as it occurred so rarely, but she always relished Bryan's company, even when he had the look that indicated a dark mood and grievous thoughts. She took immense pleasure in teasing him out of his depression. She already dreaded the day he would return to California.

Bryan leaned forward with his chin on his hand studying Callie's lowered head. He felt slightly ashamed for interjecting himself into Callie's life this way. He knew it wasn't a good idea, but he couldn't seem to help himself. He had to be with her as much as possible, and she certainly would not agree to a normal date. With a jolt he realized that he'd probably never asked anyone out on a "normal" date, and wouldn't have the foggiest notion as to how to proceed to do so. Over the years he'd had innumerable "hookups" with a multitude of women, but never a date with a nice girl. So he pretty much just followed Callie around, at least as much as she allowed. That's how he'd ended up spending the previous Sunday with her in Huntsville with her "loctician."

He'd never been inside any type of beauty establishment with a woman, but when he'd called Callie and discovered that she couldn't see him because she had a hair appointment, he'd asked to tag along. He hadn't seen her the previous Sunday as she'd gone to church and wouldn't let him come with her. He probably should be relieved that she wouldn't let him go to church. He couldn't recall the last time he was in one, and the probability that he'd be struck by lightning or descended on by a horde of locust was pretty strong. Having been deprived of his one free day per week with her increased his determination not to miss another one. It took some doing, but his persistence eventually won her over, especially when he offered to drive as an incentive. Callie hated driving, viewing the activity as a colossal waste of time. He smiled to himself as he imagined her reaction to L.A. traffic where it was commonplace to spend hours in gridlock each day. She'd been exasperated, and he suspected maybe even a bit uncomfortable with the idea of taking a white man to a black beauty establishment, but she'd agreed. During the trip over to Huntsville, she'd told him that he was probably the first white man who had ever been in this salon.

He'd had no idea that watching a woman get her hair washed could be such a sexually stimulating experience. He reflected on the double shower in his home in California and imagined giving Callie a shampoo within its steamy confines. He could almost feel Callie's coily hair against his bare flesh and became immediately aroused. He was disturbed from his reverie only when he heard the beautician ask Callie who he was. He couldn't hear Callie's response, but it sounded like a fairly noncommittal one. It seemed to satisfy the beautician anyway. After

Callie paid for her service and they turned to leave, he heard the woman mutter under her breath, "Well, what's the sense of having a white man if he can't even pay for you to get your hair fixed!"

Callie had paused and turned as if to say something to the woman, then shook her head as if thinking better of it. In his truck on the way home, Callie made a frustrated sound then said, "See, that's why I didn't want to take you with me! You hang out with a white guy, everybody assumes he's taking care of you."

Bryan couldn't believe his ears. "You mean people just assume that black women are only with white men for money?"

"Exactly! Like I'm some type of whore or something. It just pisses me off."

"Why didn't you say something to her about it then?"

"What would be the point? If somebody thinks you're a whore, what can you do to convince them otherwise?"

His confusion evident, Bryan asked, "But, why would they assume that?"

"Bryan, you mean to tell me you've read all those books about the Civil War, and you don't know anything about slavery and the relationships between black women and white men?" Callie snapped, disbelief evident in her tone. "You know, the masters in the slave cabin?" she added sarcastically.

"Of course I do. But what does that have to do with us, almost two hundred years later?"

Callie blew out a harsh breath. This was maddening. "Forget about it!"

"No, I don't want to forget about it. I mean, I've noticed the looks we get, but I didn't know that folks were thinking that you were a whore or something. I guess I'm just used to being stared at." He thought about the ramifications of the issue for a moment, and then continued, his breath whistling between his teeth. "But now I'm pissed. How dare they jump to those sorts of conclusions?"

Callie was in no mood to explain why this ancient history still had an impact today. "Bryan, why are you sweating this? It's not like we're a couple or anything, so I don't know why it concerns you at all."

"Well, it does concern me. I—I care about you, and if being with me makes people think less of you, then yes, it does concern me."

Callie, not really wanting to think about that statement, continued as if he had not spoken. "That's just the way it is, Bryan. In case you haven't noticed it, white men have always had a much higher social position than black women in this country. Black women certainly aren't the beauty standard. Most folks see us as either sex objects or baby-making welfare queens. If a white man is with us, it has to be for easy sex. Otherwise he would be with the much-preferred white woman. So they figure we're living out some jungle fever fantasy with sex as the only common denominator. I know you've heard all the stuff about black women supposedly being so incredible in bed…"

Bryan scoffed her remarks. "What do you mean about black women not being up to the beauty standard? I see gorgeous black women all the time."

Callie smirked. "Bryan, I'm not talking about models and video babes. Haven't you noticed that most of them don't have typical African features? To be black and thought beautiful in this country, you have to be as close to white as possible. You know, aquiline features, black but not too black. And you definitely have to have long, flowing hair, even if you bought it at the local wig shop and glued it in." She tossed her own freshly groomed locks to emphasize her point.

Bryan frowned with concern. "Now that you mention it, I guess you've got a point. I'd never really thought about it, but you don't usually see the darker black women in movies or anything."

Her voice tight with anger, Callie continued, "Exactly. So if we're together, and I certainly don't meet the beauty standard, then you must be using me for sex. Now do you get it?"

Bryan was taken aback by her angry tone. "Yeah, yeah, I've heard all that stuff. But women are women."

Callie pursed her lips. "Yeah, I suppose you'd be in a position to know." She paused. She'd been curious about this from the beginning. "I assume you've been with a black woman before?"

"Of course. I grew up in East L.A., there were all types of women. I've never discriminated." Bryan shifted uneasily in the driver's seat. Hopefully Callie wouldn't ask any more questions about his sexual history.

Callie sighed. That was not a subject she had any intention of pursuing. "Anyway, that's just how most folks see it. There's not much that can be done about it."

"You mean to tell me that every time I've ever been out with a black girl, people have assumed that I'm paying her?" Bryan was flabbergasted and more than mildly insulted at the notion.

"I don't know about how things are in California, but I'd say in most of the country, yes."

"That's incredible! Why haven't I heard about this before?"

"I guess none of your women bothered. Maybe they were all caught up in your rock superstardom. I've heard that fame transcends race." She added dryly, "At least as long as you don't murder your ex-wife. Or maybe y'all never had a run-in like this one. Anyway, Bryan, can we please change the subject? I really don't feel like talking about this anymore. It's not a subject I like to spend a great deal of time pondering. The situation is as it is. I don't think sweating it now will be of any benefit to anybody," she finished wearily.

Bryan, fascinated by stereotypes he'd previously had no knowledge of, wanted to continue, but he acceded to Callie's wishes. "What was that she was doing to your hair after she washed it?" he asked, referring to the technique of tightening Callie's locs.

Callie then spent the rest of the trip answering his myriad questions about black hair care, and the care of dreadlocks in particular.

All in all it had been a very illuminating trip, but Bryan had discovered yet another obstacle in his pursuit of Callie: public opinion and stereotyping. This football game sounded like a nice neutral opportunity for him to spend time with Callie, and as a bonus he would get to meet her family.

"So tell me more about your family," Bryan insisted once again. "You hardly ever mention them. Are you an only child, too?"

Callie smiled, "Not hardly, I have two younger sisters. They're sixteen."

"Two younger sisters? Twins?"

"Yeah, identical twins, they run in my family. My mama was a twin, and both her sisters have twins, too. They love your music, by the way. They'll be thrilled to have you at the house," Callie replied.

Accustomed to the racial stratification of the music industry, Bryan was surprised to find that Storm Crow had any black female fans. He'd encountered a few black guys at their concerts, but no girls. Apparently this was a demographic that B.T. had missed despite his rabid attentiveness to every aspect of Storm Crow's sales. He would enjoy ribbing him about that.

"Have they always listened to rock music?" he asked curiously.

Callie nodded, "Yeah, our schools here in Maple Fork are pretty small. Most of the classes are too small to break up into racial cliques like bigger schools. I think there's only about twenty kids in Addie and Cynthia's class. They hang together pretty closely. They seem to listen to just about anything. Mainly it's hip-hop and alternative rock. It was the same when I was in school. But you know, we grew up listening to all kinds of music. My daddy is a big Hank Williams fan, and I'd bet we have as much Patsy Cline as we do Aretha Franklin in our house. I mean, I see folks on TV and in articles talking about 'black music' and 'white music,' and I don't get it. Around here, good music is good music. Maybe it's a big-city thing. Anyway, I graduated twelve years ago, and we were seriously into grunge at the time. But I've mellowed with age, and primarily listen to soft rock and pop."

Bryan grabbed his head, feigning a mortal blow. "You mean you're not a Storm Crow fan?" He cringed as the rest of her statement sank in. "So you're the person who listens to soft rock. I wondered who they played that crap for."

" 'Fraid so, buddy. Storm Crow rocks just a little too hard for me. All that primal screaming…" She paused, looking up at him ruefully. "Oops, that's you, isn't it?"

"Uh, yeah, that's me," Bryan replied, doubly insulted. "What have you got against primal screaming?" He pursed his lips, giving her a knowing look. "In some situations it can be, shall we say…stimulating."

Callie grunted. "Maybe in the circles you travel in. It just gives me gruesome nightmares. Do you write most of your songs?" Bryan nodded. "You must have lived a helluva life. Some of that stuff is bone-chilling."

Bryan raised his brows. "I've had my share of hard knocks, but of course I do have an imagination too. Anyway, I'm willing to overlook the fact that you listen to soft rock." He winced as if saying the words wounded him grievously, "But please don't tell anybody else. I do have an image to maintain, you know."

Callie giggled.

"Now back to your sisters." He grinned wolfishly. "Nothing like impressionable young girls to inflate the old ego."

Callie smacked his arm playfully, "Bryan, I think they're way out of your league. It's all we can do to keep the boys away. Of course, being the big-time rock star you are, you might go to the head of the line."

Bryan leaned forward and stared intently into Callie's eyes. "The only girl I want is right here."

Callie tsked. This was the only difficulty in their relationship. His insistence on teasing her. "I really wish you would stop doing that."

"What?" Bryan spread his hands in an innocent gesture.

"You know exactly what I mean. You flirt with me all the time," Callie responded irritably.

"Is that some type of crime around here? A man can't flirt with a pretty girl?"

Callie was really getting annoyed now. She didn't like the idea of this guy playing with her feelings. "It is when you're just having fun at my expense."

Bryan straightened in the chair, dumbfounded by Callie's remark. Where in the hell had she gotten that idea? "Callie, I'm doing no such thing!" he exclaimed, but he could tell she wasn't listening.

"Look, Bryan, I've got to go back to work."

After giving her a frustrated look, Bryan gathered their empty plates and returned them to the counter. At least now he had an explanation for her skittish behavior. How did she get that idea in her head? A laughable concept when he had never been more serious about anything in his life. Her lips pressed together tightly, her face set into a mulish expression, she didn't look as if she were ready to hear that, though.

"Am I still invited to the party?" he asked hesitantly, certain that she would take any opportunity to retract the invitation.

Callie stood up. Though she was fairly certain that she would regret this decision, she couldn't resist the excitement of having a date with Bryan. "No, Bryan, I would never do that. My sisters would kill me. I'll see you Saturday around three o'clock." She gave him directions to her parents' home.

Bryan gave a silent sigh of relief. Thank God for her sisters. Otherwise he had a feeling he would be out in the cold. He had known from the beginning that he would have to approach Callie with care. Maybe meeting her family would give him insight into the best way to make headway with her.

❧

Callie stifled a groan as she shifted her weight from her left foot to her right. It seemed that she and her mother had been shopping for days rather than mere hours. This annual ritual of buying and cooking enough food to feed an army on retreat became more wearing each year, but somehow she still enjoyed it. As she pushed the cart down yet another aisle, she glanced over at her mother who was checking the shopping list once again. Edith Lawson was at her best scavenging for sumptuous fare for her guests. Her almost totally gray hair was done up in its usual upsweep, lending height to her petite figure. Somehow her physical presence belied her size, and Callie had seen her sweep aside much larger people, just by the force of her personality. It only took a glance to realize that Callie had inherited her arrestingly lovely features from her mother, especially the large, upturned eyes. People were constantly astounded by the close physical resemblance between them. Callie didn't see it at all. She assumed that all those people were simply seeing what they wanted to see. To her, her mother was all that was beautiful, dainty, and feminine. As a younger girl, she'd desperately longed to be petite. She'd pretty much outgrown that feeling, but she still felt like a gangly behemoth next to her mother.

Watching her mother toss another slab of ribs into the cart, Callie shook her head. "Mama, don't you think we've got enough food here already? I mean, it seems that each year we buy more and more."

Edith Lawson nodded her elegant head. "Seems like each year we have more guests."

Callie hesitated. "Well, Mama, speaking of more guests…I've invited a friend of mine to the party, too. I hope you and Daddy won't mind."

Edith paused in her perusal of pork roasts. "Mind? Honey, when have we ever had a problem with any of your friends coming to the house?"

Callie leaned down, her head almost touching the handle on the cart. "Mama, he's like, ah, he's like a celebrity, you know, really famous."

"Famous? When did you ever leave that store long enough to meet anybody famous?" *Or anyone at all*, she thought to herself. Edith was proud of her daughter's success, but concerned that since opening the store Callie had had little time for family and friends.

Unwilling to resume that long-standing dispute, Callie clung determinedly to the subject at hand. "Actually, Mama, he came to the store. That's where we met."

Edith raised her brows. "Really now. So what does the boy do?" she asked as she turned to walk toward the bread aisle.

Callie followed her mother. "Well, m'dear, I guess you would say he's a rock star."

Mrs. Lawson paused and gave her an arch look. "A rock star? What on earth is a rock star doing in Alabama?"

Callie sighed and recounted Bryan's story to her mother as she continued pushing the cart.

Mrs. Lawson brought her up short when she mentioned the drug use. "Callie, why in the world are you hanging around with some drug-using lowlife? Can you imagine what your daddy's going to say? And what about Cynthia and Addie? You know we didn't raise you like that."

"Mama, he's not like that. He wasn't the one that was strung out on drugs; it was his friend."

"Baby, you've seen those people on TV and God knows your sisters listen to enough about them and the horrible lives they lead. Jumping in and out of bed with just anybody, popping pills and whatnot like candy. We raised you to be a good Christian girl. They are not our kind of people. Those people are all about casual sex and drugs. You've seen it a thousand times."

Callie blew a long breath out between her teeth. Her mother could be incredibly exasperating at times. "Mama, it's not like that with us. There's nothing at all sexual between us. We're just friends, nothing else, okay? Look, if it's going to be a problem he doesn't have to come to the house…"

"I didn't say all that, I just don't understand why you'd want to hang out with somebody like that," her mother interrupted.

"Could you at least wait to meet him before you pass judgment, Mama? Isn't that what you've always taught us?"

Edith sighed, "Baby, you know this is for your own good." Callie didn't respond. "So exactly what is this young man's interest in you?" Edith inquired. "Surely he knows that you're not some type of, what do they call it, campie or something?" Despite her career as a librarian, Edith had a knack for mangling words,

"Mama, it's *a groupie,* and I'm sure Bryan knows that I'm not one. We're just friends, hanging out until he goes back to California," she replied flatly.

Mrs. Lawson tilted her head to the side and gave her oldest child a disbelieving look. Sometimes the girl was incredibly naïve.

"Humph. Callie, how many times do I have to tell you that men and women can never be 'just friends'? That boy's not coming to our house and meeting your folks because he wants to play patty-cake with you. As you say, I'll wait until I meet him to make a judgment, but you know your daddy isn't going to like this at all. I assume this young man is white?"

Callie wiped her damp palms on her jeans as she nodded. "I know Daddy's not going to like it, but I've brought white guys to the house before."

"Yeah, Callie, but they were just high school buddies. Y'all were just hanging out in a group. This boy is a grown man and in a very shifty business." She leaned toward Callie. "They say there's a lot of Mafia involvement," she whispered out the side of her mouth.

Callie rolled her eyes. Why on earth was her mother whispering? Did she think John Gotti was lurking around the corner in a Lucky's supermarket in downtown Maple Fork? Though she had major doubts about Bryan, Mafia involvement was not one of her concerns.

However, she could agree that she'd never dated a white man before. *Wait a minute, how did the word "date" get into this conversation?* she asked herself. *You're just friends, remember?*

"I know that, Mama, but being in a shady business doesn't necessarily mean he's shady." At least she hoped not. Edith Lawson didn't respond, so Callie added, "At least I know Cynthia and Addie will be thrilled." Callie grinned, thinking of her sisters' reactions when Bryan showed up at their door. She had decided to let his arrival be a surprise to them, and she knew they would scream in ecstasy when he arrived. She just hoped that she would have enough self-control not to scream with them. After all, behavior that was cute for a pair of teenagers would not be at all attractive for a twenty-nine-year-old.

# CHAPTER 6

Callie knelt on the kitchen floor, refilling the cooler with ice and soft drinks. People had begun arriving at the house at noon, and her parents had been up barbecuing since dawn. Fortunately, it was a nice warm day, especially for mid-November, and most of the guests were outside enjoying the unseasonable weather. They were beginning to wander back into the house as kickoff time approached, but at this moment Callie had only her own racing thoughts for company. Each time she contemplated Bryan's impending arrival, she became lightheaded and had to remind herself to breathe. She couldn't believe that she of all people was acting like an infatuated schoolgirl. It was discomfiting to say the least.

She wondered what Bryan would think of her parents' home. While the Lawsons lived comfortably on the income from Jesse Lawson's retirement from the post office and her mother's position as the local librarian, their modest split-level home undoubtedly paled in comparison to what Bryan was accustomed to. She shook her head in disgust at her own thoughts; Bryan hadn't shown any signs of snobbishness, so why was she looking for things to worry about? She looked around the spacious kitchen. Her parents had recently redone most of the house, replacing furniture and fixtures that dated from the 1970s when the house was built. They'd given it a more contemporary look by refacing the dark cabinets with a lighter wood and painting the room a bright blue. The rest of the house had received a similar face-lift, and everything reflected Edith Lawson's sophisticated taste.

As Callie finished her task, she heard the signal she had been waiting for all day: the eardrum-piercing squeal from her sisters when their mystery guest arrived. When she had told them the previous evening that there would be a surprise guest, they'd speculated wildly, but hadn't even come close to guessing their guest's identity. She could hear them in the living room literally jumping up and down with joy and excitement. Callie stood up, waiting breathlessly for her sisters to bring Bryan into the kitchen. She heard the girls gallop across the living room's hardwood floor.

The kitchen door swung open forcefully and Addie screeched, "Oh my God! Callie, you freaking rock!"

Cynthia joined in. "I can't believe it, Bryan Spencer at our house! Nobody is going to believe this! Wait until I tell the girls at school!"

Callie gave her sister a stern look. She'd warned them the previous evening that they couldn't disclose the identity of their mystery guest.

"I know, I know, we can't tell anybody about Bryan. Callie, you know we won't do that!" Cynthia gave her older sister an abashed look.

Callie shook her head at her two sisters. Unlike many twins, they actually enjoyed dressing alike and wore their micro-braided hair in identical ponytail styles. Their artfully faded jeans and matching school logo T-shirts emphasized their youth and trim bodies. They had their father's complexion, a rich chocolate brown, and their skin was silky smooth and clear. They didn't have the same sculpted features that Callie had inherited from their mother and despaired of ever growing into. Instead, their faces were more oval in shape with delicately rounded chins and upturned noses. They were, however, tall like their sister but small-boned like their mother. They were lovely in that fresh way that only teenage girls are, possessing none of the gawkishness that typically plagued their contemporaries. Both were varsity cheerleaders and boasted a self-confidence that Callie wished she had had at their age.

Bryan stood in the doorway between the girls, each arm held tightly in their grasp as they continued their joyous monologues. He smiled diffidently at Callie, happy to see her out of her usual business attire. Today she was wearing a pair of faded jeans that lovingly followed every curve in a way that his hands itched to emulate, and a loose-fitting sweat-shirt with her school logo on it. Her locs weren't pulled back today and hung well past her shoulders.

They only heightened the earthy sexiness that he had found irresistible from the very beginning. Though he had avoided just this type of scene in the past, he was willing to endure any hardship to see her as often as possible.

Callie stared at Bryan, seemingly transfixed as her sisters' chatter increased to a feverish pitch. Though he generally wore only black, today he was wearing an indigo blue long-sleeved tee-shirt that only intensified the vivid color of his eyes. His black jeans delineated every muscle in those incredible thighs, and her pulse was again sent skipping with images of those thighs locked between her own in an erotic mating dance. When she was fairly certain that she could speak without her voice cracking, she suggested that her sisters join their parents outside. Addie and Cynthia pouted, but reluctantly acquiesced.

Bryan walked slowly into the room with his usual loose-limbed grace, his eyes intently focused on her own until he was within touching distance. Callie, her own eyes widening with alarm, moved nervously away from him. Though she'd never experienced it before, she felt she was being stalked. His gaze never wavering, Bryan moved closer again, and then again. Each time he came closer, Callie backed away until finally she abruptly fetched up against the counter. Bryan brushed gently against her, sending tremors through her whole body.

"Bryan, what are you…"

"Shhhh." He gently took her face between his hands and leaned forward, pressing his lips against hers. "Open for me, baby," he murmured insistently.

When Callie felt his tongue licking delicately at her lips, she couldn't suppress a gasp, giving him the access he craved. He softly caressed her tongue with his own, trying desperately to keep the kiss tender. It was all he could do not to eat her alive, but he knew that he could easily frighten her off if he weren't careful. If he was to have any chance at all with her, he would have to temper the fierce desire raging through his body. Even as he realized this, he couldn't resist the urge to press his body into hers; he had longed to feel her against him for so long.

After a moment's hesitation, Callie moaned softly and gave Bryan even greater access to her mouth and body. She wrapped her arms around his neck, and her tongue followed his back into his mouth. She could feel electrical shocks everywhere her body touched his and couldn't resist prolonging the contact.

Her response heightened Bryan's own pleasure, and he began devouring her. His tongue caressed the roof of her mouth, and he inhaled her moan of pleasure. His hands slipped down to her hips, pressing even closer, until suddenly he realized that the kiss was exceeding the bounds of decency permissible in her parents' kitchen. He moved his hands back to her face and broke the kiss, looking down at her lovingly.

"Callie, open your eyes," he commanded, his raw voice so roughened by desire that his whisper was barely intelligible. Callie looked up at him dazedly. Her lips were swollen from his kisses, and Bryan strained under the almost superhuman effort it took to resist the urge to take up where they had left off. When he was certain he had her full attention, he continued, "Callie, I'm not playing with you." Then he released her and moved slowly away.

Callie leaned against the counter, trying feverishly to catch her breath. Every nerve ending in her body sizzled and sparked. Reaching up to touch her hair, certain that it had to be standing on end, she gaped at Bryan, unable to think clearly enough to form a single sentence.

At that moment, the back door swung open and Callie's parents entered the kitchen, bringing her abruptly back to her senses. She hastily made the introductions, forcefully keeping her voice light and casual. Her scattered mind could only focus on one thing; her parents could never discover what had just happened in their kitchen, or she'd never hear the end of it.

After placing the cooked meat on the counter, Jesse Lawson crossed the room and grasped Bryan's hand in his own. Bryan studied Callie's parents closely, realizing that while she looked a great deal like her mother, she took her height from her father. Jesse was a large, burly man, with skin that gleamed with the same tones as his younger daughters. He and

Bryan were similar in height, but Jesse outweighed Bryan considerably. Despite his age, his hair showed only touches of gray, and the laugh lines around his eyes indicated that he was a man who generally saw the humor in life. Unfortunately, he made no effort to hide the fact that he didn't find anything amusing about the current situation.

As he took Bryan's hand Jesse could feel the sexual tension coming off him in waves and turned sharply to look at his daughter. Callie moved quickly to the counter to help her mother set up trays of food, thereby avoiding her father's eye. Edith, blissfully unaware that anything untoward was occurring, chattered away about their guests. Having decided that he needed to take the measure of his daughter's friend, Jesse offered Bryan a beer and then invited him to follow him into the den to watch the pre-game show. Callie watched them depart with a sinking feeling. Why did she suddenly feel like Kate Winslet in *Titanic* watching poor Leonardo DiCaprio being submerged by the icy waves?

In the den, the real grilling began. Jesse wanted to know all the particulars about Bryan, including his background. Bryan was brutally honest, knowing instinctively that Callie's father would tolerate nothing less. He had no doubt that his family history would be problematic for this close-knit clan, but he felt he had no choice but be truthful. He acknowledged that he didn't know where his father was, and that his mother had stopped speaking to him after he kicked yet another abusive boyfriend out of the house he provided for her. Though they had no contact, he continued to pay her expenses, but had little hope for reconciliation. He recounted the tale of growing up on the wrong side of town and forming a band with his best friend Brodie, and then Brodie's death.

Jesse listened intently, interrupting only to clarify a point, or when one of the guests wandered into the room.

Finally Bryan paused, waiting for Jesse to respond to what he'd said. Instead, there was a prolonged silence. Bryan reached up and pulled lightly at his ponytail, unnerved by the deafening disapproval he sensed from Callie's father.

"Bryan, I appreciate the fact that you've been straight with me, so I'll return the favor; I don't like the idea of my daughter seeing a white man. All my life I've seen white men use and discard black women. I don't believe for one moment that you have any decent intentions towards my daughter!" he said forcefully.

Bryan bristled angrily. "Mr. Lawson, that's not…"

"Are you interrupting me, son?" Jesse asked in a dangerously soft voice.

Bryan recognized that tone. He'd heard it many times from B.T. He hastily swallowed and shook his head.

Jesse narrowed his eyes into a baleful glare as he resumed speaking. "Do you think I don't know what was going on in my own kitchen before Callie's mother and I came in?"

Bryan blushed profusely and took a sip of beer.

"I'm not so old that I don't know when a man is all twitchy around my daughter. You came into my house and didn't even have the decency to keep your hands to yourself!" Jesse finished forcefully.

Bryan could feel the cold sweat trickling down his back. Why the hell was he putting up with this? Normally he didn't take this type of crap from anybody but B.T. If he'd wanted to get his ass kicked, he could've just stayed at home and let B.T. pistol-whip him.

Jesse continued, "Now, as I was saying, I don't like the fact that Callie has chosen to see a white man. The fact that you're some drug-using rock star from California makes it even worse. But Callie is her own woman. After all, she is her mother's daughter, and strong-willed as all get out, so I have to let her kill her own rattlesnakes."

Bryan raised his brows. He was pretty sure he'd been called a reptile, but didn't dare quibble at this point.

As Jesse continued, his deep thunderous voice reverberated with positively deific tones, "I won't mistreat you, because you're somebody's child, and I wouldn't want anybody mistreating my child. But I'm telling you right here and now, boy, if my baby so much as cries while she's cutting up an onion, the only thing that'll be left of you is your haint. Do you hear me?"

"I understand completely," Bryan gritted through clenched teeth. "Now may I say something?"

Jesse looked surprised that Bryan dared to speak up, but he slowly nodded his consent.

"Sir, I just want you to understand that I care for your daughter and want a chance to prove that to you. Whether you believe it or not, I will take care of her."

Jesse rubbed his chin, glaring at Bryan from under his thick brows. He had to give the boy his reluctant admiration for having the gumption to speak up. Any number of young men in his position would have backed down. "I suppose time will tell," he conceded begrudgingly.

Jesse Lawsons's assumptions that he planned to use and exploit Callie left Bryan angry and frustrated. Obviously the man didn't know his daughter; she'd kick his ass all the way back to L.A. if he tried any funny business with her! He couldn't miss the irony of the situation; he who had never had honorable intentions towards a woman in his life had to confront skepticism the one time he actually did mean to do right by a woman. The distrust didn't surprise him, though. There were times when he doubted himself. He'd been expecting this question and had spent hours trying to formulate a response. He wanted Callie, but given his track record, he didn't know if he could sustain a relationship with a decent girl. Despite his intentions to be forthright with Callie's father, he didn't plan to tell him about his own misgivings.

Jesse leaned back and continued staring at Bryan intently, as if he were a puzzle he was trying to decipher. After what seemed like an eternity, he simply nodded his head, then turned to watch the game.

Bryan sensed that he had passed some type of test, but as he'd never been through such a ritual, he couldn't decipher its meaning. He understood that Mr. Lawson had tried to intimidate him and frighten him away from his daughter and that by not budging, he'd earned some type of merit badge. He closed his eyes momentarily, relieved to have emerged from this particular minefield relatively unscathed. He knew that he and Jesse had communicated on some primal level and that he would be tolerated as long as he didn't mess up. It was certainly more than he had expected and possibly more than he deserved. He had to suppress an inappropriate grin. Leaning back on the sofa, he relaxed and began watching the game also.

When Callie brought more food into the dining room, she cautiously glanced over at the sofa where her father and Bryan sat in companionable silence, presumably watching the game. She hadn't heard any major uproars from the kitchen, so she'd peeked in on them a couple of times and found them conversing in a reasonably civil tone. She knew from experience, however, that her father could dress someone down without speaking harshly or even raising his voice. Most of their guests had also drifted into the den and sat around the large screen television. Some of them glanced curiously over at Bryan, but as most of them were her parents' age, there was no real fear of them recognizing him. Some wondered what a white man was doing at the Lawson's house, but apparently accepted Bryan as a friend of Callie's.

Callie had to smile at the sight of her sisters sitting on the love seat perpendicular to Bryan, totally enraptured by his presence. The young men they had invited to the party sat on the arms of the seat with looks of utter disgust on their faces. They didn't recognize Bryan as a celebrity and were simply annoyed that their dates were apparently besotted with their sister's boyfriend.

Bryan looked over his shoulder as she approached and stood up. "Come on, Callie, you can have my seat."

Callie took his place on the sofa, expecting him to seek out one of the other chairs in the room. Instead he sat on the floor at her feet, leaning his head against her legs. When Jesse Lawson left the room for a moment, Bryan tilted his head back and whispered a question. "Callie, what's a haint?"

Callie lay in bed staring up at the ceiling. It had been quite late when the party ended and by the time she had helped clean up, she was too tired to go home. So she stayed at her parents' house in her old bedroom. The bookstore took up so much of her time, she didn't have many opportunities to spend time with her folks anymore, so she usually enjoyed it. On this particular occasion, however, her sisters' constant chatter and desire to share confidences until the wee hours had done nothing but wear on nerves already sensitized by Bryan's kiss. Undoubtedly most of their guests today were probably wondering about her unaccustomed distraction. She'd been totally incapable of maintaining the thread of coherent conversation, and had repeatedly had to ask "Huh?" in all but the most pithy exchanges. She supposed they would all chalk it up to that nervous breakdown her mother had been predicting ever since she opened the store. Throughout the entire day she couldn't think of anything but Bryan's comment after that brain-stealing kiss: "Callie, I'm not playing with you."

Well, if he wasn't playing, what was he doing? Callie was not a virgin, she had had what she and Tonya called an "unfortunate encounter," in college. Both she and the guy had been so nervous that it hadn't been a sterling experience for either of them. While she had a normal sex drive, and had dated some very attractive men, she hadn't met anyone who aroused her sufficiently to make her want to repeat the experience.

If she and Bryan had continued in the kitchen, they would've made love, and she wasn't altogether sure she would've cared if someone had walked in on them. She reflected on the past couple of months and the friendship they had enjoyed. Apparently what she had thought of as a casual relationship had been something entirely different to him. Of course, Bryan could simply be lying. God knows he wouldn't be the first man to say what he thought a woman wanted to hear to get into her panties. But that defied logic. After all, the man was a superstar and didn't have to lie to get laid. So simple, deductive reasoning forced her to conclude that he meant what he said.

Callie rolled over in bed, grunting in frustration. All the logic in the world didn't help if the conclusions she reached made no sense. Damn! She might as well call Psychic Hotline! She simply couldn't figure out why Bryan would choose her. Callie was a realist. She knew she was a pretty girl, some men had even told her she was beautiful, but she always took that with a grain of salt. But Bryan had access to absolutely stunning women. Women totally out of her league. Magazine articles gave detailed rundowns on his love life, and it was an impressive list of famous actresses, models, and rock stars. One even said he was once engaged to a porn star. How could she possibly compete with that? She wrinkled her nose with distaste. Did she even want to?

She glanced at the clock on her bedside table. Three o'clock. Thank God the store was closed on Sundays. It was clear that she wouldn't be sleeping tonight.

## CHAPTER 7

"I'm absolutely not believing this! The one time I decide to miss the party to stay home and write, you and that walking wet dream who's been following you around for months get your swerve on in the kitchen of your mama's house! While I'm slogging away, trying to get the murderer out of a locked room, you and old boy are bumping uglies. It's just not right!" Tonya exclaimed, almost spilling her coffee in her excitement. Tonya had decided to add a twist to the classic locked-room mystery. In this story her poor victim actually vanished from a locked room of a high-rise apartment with no visible means of escape. Callie was dying to know how she planned to resolve the story, but Tonya would never reveal her endings. She said it was bad luck, but Callie suspected that she simply didn't know yet.

Callie had left her folks' home before the rest of the family awakened. After a sleepless night, she'd decided to go home to talk to Tonya. The kitchen of their apartment had seen more than its fair share of these types of heart-to-heart discussions, and she knew that she could benefit from Tonya's greater experience and forthright honesty. Tonya had groused a bit when Callie awakened her, but she had gotten up readily enough when she realized that Callie finally wanted to discuss Bryan.

Like most of their apartment, the kitchen had a type of retro appeal with most of the furniture and accessories dating from the fifties and sixties. Though it looked very fashionable, they'd simply taken advantage of their family and friends' renovations and claimed the discards. Tonya had a flair for decorating, and the kitchen had accents of bright yellow and pink. Callie often joked that it looked like the banana and strawberry taffy from their childhood. The chrome formica table and the yellow vinyl chairs with chrome legs had been found in her Aunt Catherine's basement. The retro-50s chic had set the tone for the entire kitchen.

Callie got up to pour herself another cup of coffee. "We did not get our swerve on, Tonya!" Close, but not close enough, she thought to herself. The throbbing still had not ceased twelve hours after the encounter. Would she have survived actual lovemaking? Wrinkling her nose with distaste she continued, "And what kind of expression is 'bumping uglies'?" She began to pace in front of the counter, sloshing coffee with every other step.

Tonya just shrugged and watched Callie bemusedly, certain that she had no idea of the mess following in her wake. Neat to a fault, Callie never failed to mop up even the smallest spill. Tonya smiled gently and waited for her friend to rejoin her at the table.

Callie stopped pacing and dropped her head dejectedly. "Tonya, I'm so confused."

Tonya shook her head, astonished at what lust had done to her usually down-to-earth friend. Callie had always been the practical, sensible one. When they were in school, Tonya had gone from one relationship to another, always convinced that her new guy was "the one," only to be sadly disappointed time and time again. Callie, on the other hand, had refused to let anyone or anything distract her from her goals. She had rarely dated and had never been in love. Everyone went to her for sage advice about their own travails. Tonya had known her all her life and had never seen her this discomfited. If her friend weren't so dejected, she knew she'd be howling with laughter at this point. Maintaining her composure with great difficulty, she patted the other seat. "Okay, girl, sit down. Come on over here and tell Tonya all about it."

Callie slumped dispiritedly into her chair.

"Now, what exactly is the problem?"

"I'm not sure that he really wants me," Callie wailed. She rushed on, jumbling her words together. "And I'm not sure if I'm interested in him as a man, or if it's because he's a rock star. What if I'm some type of groupie, Tonya? I would look so ridiculous."

Tonya leaned forward with her elbows on the table, propping her chin on the pyramid she'd made of her hands. "Didn't you just tell me that this guy practically ate you alive in your mama's kitchen? What do you mean, you don't know if he wants you? Geez, Callie, does the man have to get it tattooed on his forehead? I knew you were inexperienced, but this is incredible. I can't believe you got me out of bed to ask such an obvious question!"

Callie sighed heavily. "I know he wants me sexually, but I don't think he wants a relationship. He's a rock star, Tonya. You know how they live."

Tonya shook her head at her confused friend. "Honey, all men want sex, and none of them want commitment. It's your job to make them want commitment." She reached out and took Callie's hand. "You and this guy have been hanging for a couple of months, Callie. If it was only about the coochie, he'd be long gone by now. Looking the way he does, and in the business he's in, he can get the coochie anywhere, anytime. He doesn't have to wait around for it. Hell, he could probably have it delivered!" She chuckled at her own joke. "But that's not what he's doing. He would live here if you'd let him. He's always a gentleman. He brings you lunch. Hell, he even feeds me! He takes you on outings. Works in the store like he's on the payroll, and now he's forced you to let him meet your parents. He couldn't be more old-fashioned if he were John Boy Walton. The man is courting you, honey, and you're too oblivious to know it. And as for you, you might be many things, Callie Lawson, but a groupie? Come on, no groupie on earth ever had a five-year plan. Sounds to me like you're just making excuses to get around the way you feel about the boy."

Callie's eyes opened wide in amazement. When Tonya put it in those terms, Bryan's actions made perfectly good sense. She wondered how she could have missed it. As for herself, maybe she wasn't a shameless groupie, or at least not entirely.

Tonya smiled a Cheshire cat grin. "Besides, sweetie, I've seen the way that boy looks at you. Just like he said, he ain't playing."

Callie and Tonya weren't the only ones up with the birds this Sunday morning; Bryan was up earlier than usual also. He had struggled with his desire for Callie for months, and now after the kiss in the kitchen, he felt as if he were burning alive. God, how the hell had he managed to stop? He'd never been able to before. What was it about *this* woman that made him actually want to act decently? If he'd been back in L.A., he wouldn't have cared who walked in on him and a woman. Of course, he'd never met a girl's parents before, but he doubted that fact had anything to do with it. And if he was this hot from such an innocent kiss, surely they would explode when they were skin-to-skin. *When* they were skin-to-skin? *If* they were ever skin-to-skin. He probably hadn't helped his cause any by practically inhaling the woman in her mother's kitchen. In that moment, he simply hadn't been capable of rational thought. His every instinct had screamed that he had to have her body as close to his as possible. She felt better than he'd ever imagined, and he wouldn't be able to rest until he had her. With his mind churning with those types of thoughts, sleep was impossible. So he'd gotten up for his daily run, hoping that the physical exertion would take some of the edge off.

After an unseasonably warm, even for Alabama, fall, the trees were finally beginning their autumnal display. They didn't get much of a color show in this part of the country, but the view with the river snaking below was glorious. Bryan always enjoyed running along the trails in the hills above his cabin, and as he did so on this day, he reflected on meeting Callie's family, and of course, the kiss. All in all, the previous day had gone fairly well. He was surprised that he'd been able to control himself enough to keep it decent when he and Callie were kissing in the kitchen. He didn't usually bother making out with a woman unless he was reasonably certain it would end in sexual satisfaction. But it wasn't like that with Callie. Somehow her touches both soothed and stimulated him. He looked forward to them, even though he knew there would be no sex for quite some time yet, if ever. He enjoyed touching her, even platonically. He'd never had much non-carnal contact with a woman and was pleased to find that he could enjoy it so much.

His previous girlfriends had been frustrated by his lack of casual affection. Some had even suggested that he see a therapist, but he was fairly certain he knew why he was sexually aroused so easily. For the first eighteen years of his life, his relationship with Brodie had been the only emotional connection he'd had. Nobody had comforted him when he hurt himself or given him loving caresses and kissed boo-boos away. If there were monsters in his closet, and he knew from experience that there were, it had been up to him to fight them off. His basic needs had been taken care of most of the time, but anything more than that had not been forthcoming. As far as he knew, his mother wasn't an especially affectionate woman, at least not with him. She never seemed to have any problem being affectionate with her endless string of abusive boyfriends, but apparently non-sexual contact was out of the question for her.

He craved touch and affection, but having never experienced it, he became overly excited. In the past, tenderness had been impossible for him, and usually he was very rough and aggressive in bed. Characteristically, his sexual encounters resulted in tearful and angry soon-to-be ex-girlfriends. Most of his former lovers were in the entertainment industry and didn't relish lovemaking that resulted in bruises and carpet burns. Their annoyance was aggravated by his not being particularly tender at other times and his rejection of their affectionate touches. With Callie, his usual burning desire was tempered with a surprising need to be gentle. He wasn't altogether sure of his

ability to maintain that tenderness, but he had finally
met a woman who made him want to try.

# CHAPTER 8

Callie looked out her apartment window onto the bleary streetscape below. Usually the faux Dickensian façade of downtown Maple Fork cheered her, as the renovation of the area had made the success of her bookstore possible. But today was one of those bleak fall days when the clouds seem to come down to meet the earth and bring slow chilly rain with them. Even the cheery storefronts and pseudo-gas streetlamps failed to brighten the scene. Located as it was in the commercial space above the bookstore, a more sophisticated real estate agent would probably refer to their apartment as a "loft." Here in Maple Fork it was called storage space and had been thrown in free of charge when they rented the building. Fortunately, it already had plumbing and electricity and it had taken only minimal work to make it habitable. The apartment stretched the length of the building, but she and Tonya used only the front half; the rear was dedicated to storage. It had the twelve-foot ceilings and beautifully distressed hardwood floors typical of loft apartments. Of course these floors had been distressed the old-fashioned way, by years of having boxes and crates moved across the soft pine surfaces when the owners used it for its original purpose. Tonya had been particularly enamored with the eight-foot-high fan windows and the brick walls she called "deconstructed." To Callie, they just looked like a bad plaster job.

Their friends were always telling them that their apartment looked like something you would see in New York City. Callie really loved the apartment, especially the massive eight-piece sectional. When they'd received it, the sofa had been upholstered in an unlikely shade of orange velveteen. Now re-covered in chocolate brown chenille, it resembled nothing so much as a giant Hershey bar. Callie frequently retreated to it as her favorite haven from the hectic pace she had to sustain to keep her business afloat.

Despite the dreary weather, Callie luxuriated in this lazy Sunday morning as it gave her a rare opportunity to pamper herself a bit. She looked forward to a long soak in the tub, a hot oil treatment for her hair, and treating her poor, abused feet to a pedicure. Yesterday had been a particularly grueling day in the bookstore. Publishers were sending stock in for the holidays, and she had spent most of the day on the ladder storing overstock. In her next store she would definitely remember to locate those bins at floor level. Reaching above her head with heavy books had left her shoulders tight and sore even after a hot shower, and she really appreciated an opportunity to relax. She felt a mild twinge of conscience as she and Tonya had once again missed Sunday morning church services.

Much to her mother's dismay, regular church attendance had been one of the first casualties of owning a small business. Usually she managed to at least attend on the first Sunday of each month. Receiving Communion assuaged her guilt somewhat; it proved she wasn't a total heathen. Going outside was not at all inviting on such a gloomy day. Much better to stay at home and get some much-needed personal time. Of course, she'd also have the pleasure of explaining all this to her mother, again.

As was his habit, Bryan had called earlier, looking for something to do. As it was too rainy and cold for hiking, he planned to come over later to just hang out. She twisted around on the sofa, trying to position her toes so that she could paint them more easily. Just when she was adjusted perfectly, the doorbell downstairs rang. Wondering exasperatedly who would dare disturb her idyll, Callie sighed and called out to Tonya to answer the door. After a brief interval, Tonya came back up the stairs with Bryan in tow, then returned to the kitchen, where she had been putting on the kettle for tea. Glancing over her shoulder to ascertain who their unexpected guest was, Callie immediately repositioned herself on the sofa into a more dignified posture. She was also embarrassed by the extremely casual clothes she was wearing: a pair of blue plaid flannel pajama bottoms and a coordinating baby tee-shirt. Resisting the urge to rush into her bedroom to change, she forced herself to sit still. Changing clothes would mean she was trying look nice for him, something she was determined not to do. His presence also made her self-conscious about her bra-less state and she rounded her shoulders slightly to conceal the fact, then thought better of it when she realized that given the minute size of her breasts, he probably wouldn't know the difference. Despite her anxiety, she smiled slightly as she studied Bryan's attire. Not for the first time, she speculated about his proclivity for dark clothing and wondered how many pairs of black jeans one man could possibly own. On any other celebrity, she would assume it was some type of affectation, but Bryan didn't strike her as the type to bother with something like that. He wore the same pair of disreputable boots he always wore, and had a case containing what Callie assumed to be an acoustic guitar slung across his back.

Callie capped the nail polish and hastily placed her feet on the chilly hardwood floor. "Bryan, I thought you weren't coming over until later today," she said, her mild irritation evident in her tone.

Bryan joined her on the sofa, sliding his guitar onto the floor. "I know, but I really wasn't doing anything, so I came on over. I hope you don't mind." He quickly changed the subject, knowing full well that she probably *did* mind. "Were you painting your toenails when I came in?" He looked down at her feet. Callie nodded. "You want me to finish them for you?"

An image of Bryan sucking her toes flashed through her mind, exacerbating the ache between her legs that started whenever she came within fifty feet of

this man. Her feet had always been an erogenous
zone, and she couldn't imagine anything more
dangerous than letting him get anywhere near them.
She'd probably melt into a puddle of lust-filled ooze at
his feet. "Uh, no. I'll do them later. Is that your
guitar?" She asked the obvious question just to change
the subject.

"Yeah, I've been doing some writing for the past
couple of days, and thought I might play some of it
for you and Tonya."

Tonya's cough could be heard from the kitchen.
"Sure, he wants to play his guitar for me," she
muttered under her breath. "Y'all don't mind me. I'm
just going back to my room to continue plotting grisly
murder."

Bryan took his guitar out of its case. "Is it all right
if I play a little bit?" he asked casually.

Callie nodded. She had heard some of the band's
songs, but she'd been curious to hear Bryan sing.

As he adjusted his guitar, Bryan thought back to
the conversation he'd had with B.T. the previous
evening. He'd known that a tribute concert for Brodie
was in the offing, but B.T. hadn't told him that Storm
Crow was expected to play. He had to get back to L.A.
right away so that they could begin rehearsals for the
concert. But as he'd told B.T., he wasn't sure he
wanted to do it. He'd never played without Brodie
before, and didn't know if he could. At least not right
now. He also had to consider the situation with Jon
and Twist. The other band members were undoubt-

edly pissed about the way he'd left L.A. They'd had to deal with the press and paparazzi by themselves, a position they weren't accustomed to. He'd be lucky if they only wanted to kick him out. He supposed they probably had legal grounds to sue him. Did he even still have a band? Finding out would at the very least be emotionally if not physically painful.

He thought about Twist, his short-tempered drummer. It would be a miracle if they managed to get through the rest of the tour without an out-and-out brawl. God knows they'd come close plenty of times. Almost from the very beginning, he and Twist had had a very strange and symbiotic relationship. The age difference probably contributed to the hero-worship Twist felt for him and Brodie. Twist, using his brother's ID, had lied about his age and joined the band when he was only fourteen. He had been big for his age, and it had been years before they discovered the deception. By the time they did, he was well past his eighteenth birthday, and there was no point in booting him out. The six-year age gap was most telling at times like this. Twist held him to an impossibly high standard and was the first to lose it if Bryan didn't live up to his expectations. Though this was the first time he'd fouled up, he had to acknowledge he had done so in grand style. Jon, the quiet low-key bassist, would not express his feelings as openly as Twist, but Bryan had learned long ago that his emotions ran just as deeply. If nothing else, his stay in the South had taught him the hazards of stirring up a fire ant mound, and he didn't look forward to the painful results. What would he do if they did kick him out? Where would he be without music, without his band? Would he still be that pathetic gutter rat B.T. had found years ago? Would he still be living hand to mouth, squatting wherever he could to keep a roof over his head? Would he even be alive? What would he do? No, better to put the confrontation off as long as possible. That way he could hold onto the illusion that at least part of his life was still okay.

As he had expected, when he expressed his reluctance to come home, B.T. had blown his stack and reminded him of his contractual obligation to finish the tour. Playing at the tribute concert would be an ideal way to jump-start that, as they were expected to be back on the road by January. That gave them less than two months to hire a new lead guitarist, give him time to learn their songs, and head out to begin the last half of the tour.

Of course, Bryan had known all this before B.T. reminded him. He still wanted to have a band; that had never been in question for him, though B.T. doubted his sincerity. But it just didn't feel right without Brodie. As he strummed the melody that had been going through his mind for weeks now, he realized that he also didn't want to be away from Callie. He supposed he could ask her to come with him...*Yeah, right, like she's just going to pick up and follow you back to California...Hell, she acts as if she doesn't want to go anywhere with you in Alabama.* As the thought occurred to him, he looked up and watched as Callie twisted her legs under herself in one of those fluid, boneless movements that only women seem capable of. The motion of those long, graceful legs sent a bolt of heat straight to his groin. He could feel his testicles tighten as he got an instant erection. He shifted uncomfortably on the sofa, moving the guitar to conceal his response to her sensuality. Come hell or high water, he was not leaving this woman behind when he left Alabama.

Callie watched Bryan's hands as he played his guitar. She'd never thought of the guitar as a sensuous instrument, but he stroked it like a lover. He was left-handed, and the fingers on that hand were callused and marked with tiny scars from years of playing. He'd told her that a music writer referred to him, Kurt Cobain and Jimi Hendrix as the ass-backwards club, as they were all southpaws. She remembered the feel of those long, artistic fingers on her skin. It seemed that the calluses at the ends of those fingers had found and stimulated every nerve ending in her body the day they'd kissed at her parents' house. She'd asked him about the condition of his hands and had been surprised to learn that most of the scars came from playing acoustic guitar, not the electric one as she'd assumed. Bryan had explained that since the acoustic guitar doesn't have amplifiers, a guitarist has to play harder, resulting in scars and calluses. He told her that for as long as he could remember, he had played his acoustic guitar every day, sometimes for hours.

Bryan finished one song and began another, a slow ballad. When he began to sing, the raspy quality of his voice only added to the aching that had begun with the images of toe sucking. His voice was legendary for its raw, gravely timbre, but hearing it at such close quarters was incredibly arousing.

To distract herself from those dangerous emotions, Callie waited until he finished the song and then asked, "Bryan, doesn't all that screaming and stuff you do on your songs give you throat problems? I mean, you always sound as if you've got a bad cold."

Bryan didn't look up from his guitar. "No, not really. The only time it gives me problems is when I'm stupid enough to write songs in the wrong key. My range is decent, but there are some keys that just hammer my throat."

"Why do you write in the wrong key then?" That made little sense to Callie. It would seem reasonable that a singer/songwriter would write songs he could sing easily.

He tilted his head to the side. "I have to write it the way I hear it. The music just comes to me, I don't create it." He paused to mull over the question. "I guess really I'm just a really famous and ridiculously well-paid transcriptionist."

Callie waved her hand. "I remember my pathetic attempts to write poetry in high school. I can't imagine writing a whole album, or in your case, seven whole albums. I think you're seriously selling yourself short."

Bryan began playing again.

"How do you write a song anyway? I mean, does the melody come and then the lyrics, or is it the other way around?" Callie asked curiously.

Bryan paused. He'd never been asked that question before, and it struck him as prescient that she would ask that now when he had a new song on his mind. "I guess it really depends. For me, mostly it's the lyrics first. To be really specific, the title comes first. Sometimes I'll hear something on the news or read a story and it just sounds lyrical to me." He continued, "Brodie almost always started with the melody. Sometimes I'd come up with a lyric and he'd write a really cool melody for it, but otherwise it was all about the music for him." Bryan reflected on the lengthy collaborative sessions he and Brodie had enjoyed over their career. There had been times when they would work for days without sleep, not even realizing the time had passed. As always when he thought about Brodie, painful emotions surfaced, so he resumed playing.

Callie, unsure what had caused the change of mood, decided to continue asking questions. "Have you always sounded that way?"

Bryan smiled. Such was the question of a thousand interviews. "Pretty much since puberty. B.T. says my vocal chords must have gotten stuck somewhere when my voice changed and never returned to normal. It's distinctive, though. They tell me a lot of guys in cover bands have shredded their vocal chords trying to imitate me." Bryan had never told anyone about the horror of the night his voice had broken. As if it were yesterday, he remembered screaming for hours the first time his mother locked him in the closet more than twenty years before. The next morning he'd been hoarse, and his voice had remained that way, only growing deeper and raspier when he reached puberty. Obviously he couldn't tell interviewers that little tidbit, so he'd developed a more palatable story. Bryan hadn't missed the irony of the situation. The voice that had launched his success and made him the envy of many, had been gestated in unspeakable cruelty. He wondered if he'd ever share the story with Callie. In all likelihood he probably would. For the first time in his life he wanted someone to know everything about him, dark roots and all.

He was playing a slower song she'd never heard before. Most of Storm Crow's songs were of the raw, gritty, hard-rock variety. She hadn't thought there were any ballads on any of their CDs, and she wondered if this was a new direction for the band. She looked down and saw a battered spiral notebook lying on top of his guitar case. Presumably this was his songbook.

"Bryan, are you working on new stuff for your next album?"

Bryan nodded. "None of these are Storm Crow songs, though. It's not our sound. But maybe some-body else will be interested." He had discovered early in his career that his band couldn't possibly record all of his prodigious output so he had begun writing for other musicians. His fans would be amazed were they to discover that Bryan had written in genres ranging from pop to country, and had even collaborated on a few hip-hop tunes. Those efforts were an additional outlet for his creativity, and writing for other artists seemed to enhance his writing ability. He couldn't remember a time when he didn't write songs, and was gratified that so many people clamored to record them. It was an economic bonanza also. Publishing rights were the financial backbone of the industry, and he had a considerable catalog. He reflected on the haunting melody that he had just been playing. He'd not written any words to it yet, but he already thought of it as "Callie's Song." He laughed inwardly at what the critics would make of him writing love songs, for God's sake. Some conspiracy theorists would probably point it out as proof of alien abduction.

Callie gestured toward his songbook. "Do you mind if I look at it?" He agreed, and she flipped through the tattered pages, intrigued by the raw emotions evident in most of the songs. She came across one song simply entitled "Johnny" and asked Bryan about it.

Bryan blushed furiously and reached out to take the book from her. Obviously he didn't want to discuss it, but Callie's curiosity was piqued. "Come on, Bryan, you've got to tell me about it. Who's Johnny? You had a line in there that went "Dreams of

possible connections denied by the light of day…"
What's that all about?"

Bryan tugged at his ponytail, a gesture that Callie
had come to realize indicated nervousness or discomfort. She suspected that he didn't even realize he did it
or how much of his inner turmoil the gesture
revealed. He leaned his head down until it touched
the neck of his guitar and mumbled something indecipherable.

Callie frowned, "What?"

" 'Johnny' is Johnny Cash."

"Well, what's the big deal about that? I've heard
that a lot of rockers like him."

Bryan sighed heavily. "When I was a kid, I used to
dream that Johnny Cash was my dad. You know, he
was so cool and all. I freaking worshipped him. One
day I asked my mom about it, and she laughed. Told
me that only an idiot would think that Johnny Cash
could create such a worthless child. She told me my
daddy was an even bigger piece of trash than me, but
she would never identify him." He looked out the
window to the bleak sky. "It took me a long time to
figure out that she probably doesn't know." He
exhaled forcibly, the air whistling between his teeth.
"But I still wanted it to be Johnny Cash. I started
trying to play guitar like him, dressed like him…"

"Of course! Black all the time. I wondered about
that." Callie nodded while considering what type of
woman would tell her child such a horrible thing.
Bryan didn't talk about his mother that much, but

with the information she had so far, Callie was astonished that he had made it to adulthood without going to jail or being killed. Of course, he readily admitted to more than a few hard knocks along the way.

Bryan gave a short laugh, "Now I wear it because it's just easy, I don't have to think about clothes. Besides, I've been doing it so long, people pretty much expect it. It drives Naysa, our stylist, crazy. She wants to try out all this cool stuff, and I keep reminding her to just stick to black. It makes packing easier too. She claims that I must be color blind or something. I'm not, but I just don't understand getting all uptight about clothes."

Callie shook her head. "If you weren't going to use her, why did you hire her?"

Bryan pondered that for a moment. "We hired her a few years back, primarily for videos and appearances. I loved the clothes, she has excellent taste, but I just couldn't be bothered to pay that much attention to what I looked like. But after a while, I kind of liked the convenience of having someone else do my shopping. She buys everything, including my underwear. Hell, I'd pay almost anything to have somebody take care of that! Besides, she's Twist's lady now." He snorted sardonically, "Well, at least some of the time, so we pretty much have to keep her around."

Callie pursed her lips. "Typical." Did these people have any idea just how spoiled they were? Their level of self-indulgence was just incredible.

Then after a brief pause she asked, "Did you ever meet him?"

Amazingly Bryan kept up with the transition back to the original topic. He raised his brows inquiringly, "Johnny Cash?"

Callie nodded.

"No."

"Why not? Didn't U2 do a record with him?"

Bryan again tugged on his ponytail. "I thought about it, but you know, so many of the guys I wanted to meet as a kid have turned out to be real assholes."

"Mmmm, I hadn't heard he was a jerk…"

"Oh, I haven't either. Bono said he was cool, a real righteous dude, but I just couldn't take that chance. I could have stood it from anybody else, but not Johnny. He was special. If he had turned out to be a regular sonofabitch, it would probably have pushed me right over the edge. Can you imagine what it would be like if I went even crazier?" He paused for a moment, flexing his fingers as he thought. "Johnny was the best guitarist I've ever heard. I've been listening to his music since I was a kid, and I still don't get it. He made it seem so easy. He was a natural, and unbelievably smooth." He gave a self-effacing laugh. "I'm not a natural at all. I have to work so damned hard, and still I'm not nearly as good. I couldn't have stood it if he'd laughed at me."

Callie shook her head. She was just now coming to understand why Bryan had such a low opinion of himself. *Step aside, Medea.* His mother would probably make even Euripides pause. It was horribly unfortunate that he hadn't gotten away from her until he was almost an adult. That woman had a lot to answer for. Even after all the acclaim and the attainment of "guitar god" status, he still worried that one of his heroes would laugh at him. Then again, perhaps the rejection he'd experienced at home had been the fuel to drive him to achieve that fame and fortune. She wondered how many Grammys it would take before he believed in his own success.

Bryan played another song, and as he finished, he turned to look at Callie again. "I've got to go back to L.A. next week."

Callie nodded. She had expected this for a while. He'd explained about the need to hire a new guitarist and resume their tour.

Bryan continued to pick restlessly at the guitar strings as he told her about the tribute concert for Brodie. He was trying to formulate a way to invite her to go with him, but finally decided that the direct approach was probably best. "Callie, I'm going to be out there for about a week rehearsing before the concert. I thought maybe you'd like to go with me."

Stunned, Callie could only stare at him, speechless. L.A.? Had he lost his mind?

Bryan pressed his argument. "I know it sounds crazy, Callie, but I really need you to do this. Going back is going to be really hard for me. I haven't played without Brodie before and…" He faltered, unwilling to expose his vulnerability any further.

Callie understood his misgivings about performing without Brodie, and that his ego wouldn't let him ask for her support. "Bryan, you know I've got the store here. It's coming up on the holiday season, and I can't just leave Tonya in a lurch..."

Bryan interrupted, "I know that, Callie. But you hired that new clerk a month ago. She seems to be doing pretty well. I've watched her, and she's a quick learner. Come on, Callie, it'll only be for a week. I need you to be a part of this. We'll have a great time. I'll finally get a chance to show you my house. It's right on the beach and has a view of the Santa Monica mountains. It's incredible; you'll love it." He gave her a mischievous grin. "And if you're good, I'll even show you my weapons collection."

Callie tilted her head back to rest against the high back of the sofa. This whole idea was preposterous. She couldn't just pick up and follow him to Los Angeles. Telling her folks about a trip to California would be bad enough, but going with a rock star? Having avidly watched the O.J. Simpson trial, her parents were firmly convinced that life in L.A. consisted of some type of never-ending Bacchanalian festival, and that everybody in the rest of the state was simply crazy. Her father's staunch opposition to her relationship with a white rock star would not be overcome anytime soon. And he would never agree to such a journey. Her family had agreed to be courteous to him, but that only extended so far, and certainly did not include cross-country trips. On the other hand, she felt a small thrill of excitement at the idea of actually going to L.A. with a real rock star. She'd seen the celebrity lifestyle on television, and she was more than a little bit curious as to how much of the image was true. Callie sighed. There was that brazen groupie again, longing for the excitement of bright lights, big city. This was really a bad idea, especially when nearly everything the man did made her think of taking him to bed. But even with the likelihood of impending disaster, she was teetering on the edge of agreeing to go. Then she thought about that mind-numbing kiss in the kitchen.

"Bryan, if I go with you, are you going to expect…" She took a deep breath, then braced her shoulders. "Are you going to expect sex from me? Because, well…" She shrugged uncomfortably.

Bryan put his guitar down and turned to face her. The remotest possibility of Callie accompanying him on this trip hinged on his response to her question. "Callie, you know how I feel about you, and if left up to me, we would've made love a long time ago." Callie's eyes widened. "But I know you're not ready for that, and I promise you, nothing will happen until you're ready for it, okay?"

As Callie stared into Bryan's deep-set eyes, she saw for the first time the fear that lingered there. What was he afraid of? She knew he was leery of playing without Brodie, but that couldn't explain the almost paralyzing fear she saw. In a flash of insight she understood: Bryan was afraid of losing control again and losing everything he'd worked so hard for. Could he keep it together or would he flounder again under the overwhelming grief? Suddenly she realized that she was afraid for him too. This was going to be a huge trial for him emotionally. Was he ready for it? Clearly he didn't know, and in that instant, she didn't either.

The internal debate was over; she was going to take this trip with Bryan, simply because he'd asked her to, because he needed her there with him.

"Tell you what, Bryan. If Tonya agrees to this, and my folks don't put up too much of a fuss, I'll go, but I can't stay more than a week."

That comment about her parents gave him pause. "You know, Callie, I know you and your family are very close." He paused, trying to think of a tactful way to frame what he needed to say. "But they've only met me one time…"

Callie interrupted, "Bryan, I don't think you know…"

Bryan raised his hand to halt her comment. "Please hear me out, Callie. I'm really not trying to put your folks down. I'm sure they've given you great advice over the years. You're very close to them and I respect that. Hell, to be honest I envy it. But you've had time to get to know me now. Despite what your father might say, you know I'll take care of you," he said earnestly.

Callie couldn't disagree. All logic to the contrary, she trusted this man. She nodded. "Bryan, I already said I would try to work it out. You can back off now," she admonished.

"I know, but what you said about your parents…"

Callie placed both of her hands over his and looked intently into his eyes. "Bryan, you're preaching to the choir. I'm going to try to work it out."

Bryan could barely contain his jubilation. He leaned over and grabbed her hand. "Callie, this is going to be great!"

❧

Callie rolled her eyes at the flight attendant. She and Bryan had taken a very early flight to avoid the crowds, and they were the only passengers in first class. The flight attendant had obviously recognized him and had immediately pulled out all the stops. He'd graciously signed autographs, ostensibly for her children, but she had spent most of the flight flirting with him. The only thing that prevented Callie from giving the woman a good smack was the fact that Bryan was coolly polite, nothing more. When the attendant offered him champagne, yet somehow neglected to offer any to Callie, he had called her on her omission. Of course, she had been profusely apologetic, but Callie knew a woman on the make when she saw one. Undoubtedly women threw themselves at Bryan all the time. If she were honest with herself, she would admit that the only thing preventing her from doing the same was pride. And a healthy dose of fear.

Bryan sat back in his seat, ignoring the flight attendant's machinations. He was so happy that Callie had agreed to join him that little else penetrated his consciousness. He took her hand in his and raised it to his lips. "Callie, you don't know how glad I am that you agreed to go."

"Sure, Bryan, I'm always willing to turn my life upside down and be at your beck and call," she replied sarcastically. She couldn't resist adding, "I don't know why you need me when you've got women falling all over themselves for you."

Bryan hadn't missed the flight attendant's attentiveness, and he knew that women would be an issue on this trip. "Callie, you're the only woman I want to be with. I thought we cleared that up in your parents' kitchen a few weeks ago. Yeah, there are going to be girls around on this trip. I can't avoid it; it goes with what I do, but I'm with you, okay?"

Mesmerized by those tempestuous blue eyes, Callie could only nod in agreement. Though she still didn't quite believe that Bryan was really interested in anything long-term with her, he hadn't given her any reason to think otherwise. Besides, she had resolved to just relax and enjoy herself on this ultimate groupie fantasy trip. She had all but promised her parents that she would wear a hazmat suit for the duration. She had expected them to call the pastor at any moment for a "laying on of hands" before she went, metaphorically at least, into Sodom and Gomorrah. Her father had been especially troubled, but they had finally acknowledged that she was an adult and generally made good decisions. They just hoped she wasn't going through some type of delayed adolescent phase. Callie smiled to herself. She didn't know if it was a phase, but she knew for a fact that adolescence had never felt like this.

# CHAPTER 9

Jon's guitar emitted a harsh and jarring note, and Bryan sighed heavily. This simply wasn't working. He had no doubt as to why Jon, a man famous for his rich, smooth style, was suddenly creating notes that sounded like the wailing of howler monkeys. He was angry that Bryan had abandoned them, and it showed in his playing. They'd been rehearsing for two days, and the sound just wasn't there. They weren't cohesive, and the situation only got worse the more they played. This was not just rustiness from a long hiatus; this was a band on the verge of disintegration.

They had decided to play an acoustic version of Pink Floyd's "Wish You Were Here," a very emotional tribute to their friend. But the tightness of sound that typified their performances had eluded them.

Bryan held up his hand to stop the music. "All right, guys, why don't we talk about it?" An awkward hush fell over the room. Bryan waited a long moment, then putting his guitar down on its stand, he turned to face Jon. "Look, guys, we're in trouble here. I know you're pissed off at me, and I understand why, but come on, don't you think you should at least tell me to my face what an asshole I am? I know you've said that and worse while I've been gone."

Jon looked over at Twist, who was poised like a springing cougar behind his drum kit. He ran his hands over his closely cropped blonde hair. "Dude, you just left; you didn't say anything to us. Hell, man, for months we didn't even know if we'd have a band. B.T. had to tell us what was going on. Then you think you can just walk back in here like nothing happened? What the hell was that all about?"

Bryan looked over at Callie where she sat in a corner of the rehearsal hall. She'd just returned from taking a nap in the lounge downstairs. Apparently, Jon's long-term girlfriend Cinnamon, who had been there for the first few hours, had already called it a night. Bryan thought it was terrific that Cinnamon and Callie had hit it off so well. He should've known that Callie would be fascinated by Cinnamon's owner-ship of a holistic health store. They'd connected right away, and had spent most of the time they were at rehearsals "talking shop." Bryan assumed that Twist and his on-again, off-again girlfriend Naysa were in an off-again phase. He gave a heavy sigh. Twist, who generally had the temperament of a wolverine in full-blown steroid rage, was even worse when Naysa wasn't around. Tempestuous did not even begin to describe their relationship; she was one of the few people who would stand up to him and give as good as she got. Usually he'd be so angry with her, he wouldn't have any irascibility left to direct towards anyone else.

Bryan shook his head. Given the vibe in the room, he'd need an archangel complete with a flaming sword to get out alive. He gave a self-deprecating snort. He'd spent most of his life doing things that were unlikely to earn him any tender mercies from God; divine intervention in this situation would not be forth-coming.

Callie had been with him for all the endless hours of rehearsal. He couldn't have done it without her, and he was grateful for the support. But he sensed that dealing with Jon and Twist was going to be tougher than any performance. He had expected a confronta-tion from Twist, but was surprised that Jon had been the first to fire off at him. Generally Jon, with his Beach Boy good looks and soft voice, was so low-key and mellow that people were tempted to check his pulse. The fact that Jon had spoken up was an indi-cator of just how tenuous the situation was.

Bryan turned back to him. "Man, you're right, I messed up. When Brodie died…"

Twist threw his drumsticks across the room, so angry that his numerous freckles stood out like little sparks on his normally pale face. "Goddamnit, Bryan, I'm tired of you acting like you're the only one who loved Brodie. We lost our friend, too! Jesus, man, you're not the one who walked into that…," he faltered and took a deep breath to calm himself, "that hotel room. I was!"

Bryan inhaled sharply as he tugged on his pony-tail. Twist was the youngest and had always been the most volatile member of his band. He was quick to feel slighted and tended to get angry very quickly. As his nickname indicated, he would change personality without warning. Bryan had learned to handle him after years of experience, but they had never had a crisis of this magnitude before. He struggled to find the right words to mend the rift he'd caused, but he was frustrated, too. These guys were his family; they should understand him better than this.

"Look, man, did you want me to die, too?" he asked exasperatedly. "You know what it was like before I left. Eventually I was going to kill myself or somebody else. That's why B.T. wanted me out of here. But I never ran out on you guys. You know I wouldn't do that!"

There was a long pause while everyone digested what had been said. But he could still feel the anger simmering in the room. When he looked at Callie again, she leaned forward in her chair, her face rapt with interest, giving him a slight nod to let him know that he needed to continue.

Bryan stood up and began to pace. "This is the first time I've ever let you down. Do you really think I wanted to do it? Goddamnit, I didn't have a choice. I had to leave. Can't you understand that?"

Still there was no response. Bryan could suddenly feel the anger coming over him in waves. Fear tightened his chest, constricting his lungs so he couldn't breathe. What would he do without his band? The pounding in his head intensified, and fear rose up in a wave of clammy sickness. Suddenly he was there, back there in the bottom of the closet where his mother used to leave him when she went out. She'd started locking him in after social workers came by in response to complaints from neighbors that he played in the streets at all hours of the night. The overwhelming fear that she'd forget he was there had left him paralyzed and helpless, and those feelings returned now with a vengeance. *Breathe, man, breathe.* He struggled to swallow his fear. No, no, he wouldn't go there ever again.

Abruptly he turned and started yelling as loudly as he could. "All right, what is it, Twist? What the hell am I, your daddy? What's wrong? You needed your daddy here to hold your hand?" he shouted belligerently, straining past the tightness in his throat. "You want to kick my ass because I wasn't here to hold your hand?"

"Bryan," Callie said urgently, moving towards the stage, "please don't do this." What on earth had gotten into him? Callie experienced a brief moment of fear as she saw a side of Bryan he had never shown her before, a dark, raging facet of his personality that he generally hid with sarcasm and genial good-naturedness.

Bryan couldn't hear her through the roaring in his ears and the pounding in his chest. He wiped his sweaty palms on his jeans. What would he do without his band? He struck out again. "Come on, Twist, you're the big badass. Everybody has to walk on eggshells around you! So now what's it going to be? You've always wanted to do it, so come on then. Come on, what's keeping you? Come on, bring your punk ass on over here and kick your daddy's ass!" After years of handling Twist and his hair-trigger temper, Bryan knew exactly how to elicit the desired response.

"Punk ass? Who the hell are you calling a punk ass? At least I didn't run!" Twist jumped up from his drum kit and charged.

Jon knocked his chair over as he leapt and grabbed Twist before he made it to Bryan. "Ah, come on, dudes, cut it out," he said, breathless from trying to hold a squirming Twist.

Callie had sprung from her chair when Twist charged and now she put a calming hand on Bryan's shoulder. After a long moment he began to feel the tension ease from his body and he relaxed his pugilistic stance. Callie pulled him over to the chairs where she'd been sitting to give him a chance to calm down. She couldn't believe the anger she felt coming off him. He was actually trembling with rage.

Jon struggled with Twist for quite a while longer before he calmed down enough for Jon to release him. They both sat down on the floor, astonished by what had happened. Talented, strong-willed people were bound to clash from time to time and they'd had many fiery battles in the past. But they'd never come this close to actual blows before.

Both Bryan and Twist looked on in amazement when Jon suddenly stood up. His face flushed, his voice trembling with emotion, he began to rock back and forth. "Look guys, this just isn't right, okay. I have no intention of going out on tour with you two acting like spoiled brats. Do you think this is what Brodie would've wanted?" Jon raised his voice to a normal level, which was the equivalent of anyone else shouting. "We've spent most of our lives building this band. Are you two going to flush it just because of your huge egos? I'm sick of the whole thing, and I'm not going to put up with it. Either we're a band or we're not. Just let me know what you decide." He turned to walk out the door. His movement finally jarred Bryan and Twist out of their stunned paralysis.

Twist jumped up and grabbed his friend's shoulder. "No, nobody's going anywhere, we've got to talk this thing out. If you leave, who the hell's going to talk? Me and him?" He jerked a thumb towards Bryan. "I don't think so. I'd rather cut the bastard's heart out," he finished lightly. True to form, Twist's hair-trigger temper had spent itself. His temper was like a lightning strike while Bryan's resembled a hurricane.

Jon didn't resist as Twist pushed him back down on the floor and sat beside him.

Bryan pulled the elastic band off his hair, letting it hang free while he rubbed his temples between his thumb and forefinger. Then he leaned back, staring at the ceiling while he tried to find the composure to say what needed to be said. What the hell had that been about? He hadn't felt this out of control since he was a kid. The desperation and utter hopelessness that had dominated his life before music, before B.T., had suddenly returned with a vengeance. Music had saved his life. He couldn't afford to lose it. His foundation had always been insubstantial, and now it was collapsing beneath his feet. God, even Jon was pissed with him, and he'd never seen him pushed beyond even keel.

He swallowed the huge lump in his throat. He had no idea what to say, but he had to say something. "Look, guys, do you want me out? Do you want me out of the band? I mean, I would understand. I left you two here to face all the craziness by yourselves, and I understand that you're pissed. But I really didn't mean to do it, and I'm sorry. But haven't I always been straight with you guys? Don't I at least deserve something for that?"

Jon and Twist considered his words. He was right; he'd always been straight with them. Even though he and Brodie had written most of the songs, their money cut, even from the publishing, had been divided equally. He and Brodie had dismissed their protests about the inequity. If it was for Storm Crow, they all shared equally. Too many bands had fallen apart over royalties, and money simply wasn't worth it. He had always been very careful to make sure all of them were included in publicity or articles about the band. Everyone knew that Storm Crow was Bryan's band. He was the unchallenged star of the group. The media couldn't get enough of that tortured poet visage and sometimes surly attitude. But he had never hogged the limelight, nor did he dominate the band as many others in his position had done.

Twist got up from the floor and began to pace. "Dude, it's not about the money or publicity! Yeah, you and Brodie were always fair about that." Twist paused. "It's like, well, I know you and Brodie were together since you were kids, but it just seemed like sometimes, man, you guys shut us out. Like you were one band, and we were another. It didn't feel like Storm Crow was about the four of us. Then when Brodie died…" He took a deep breath, his eyes closed as if to shut out the horrific reality of Brodie's death. When he opened them again, they were moist with unshed tears. "When Brodie died, you didn't turn to us, you ran away, like we didn't matter. Like we weren't a part of this too. We were supposed to be in this together, but we weren't."

Bryan latched onto the first part of Twist's statement. "Man, we've talked about this before. The lead singer almost always gets the attention…"

Twist interrupted, "That's not what I'm talking about! Weren't you listening? Hell, I'm glad I'm not the one reporters are following around. I sure as hell haven't enjoyed having them all over me while you've been gone. I just want us to be like brothers again, you know, like when we started out. Remember how close we got when B.T. would make us practice like twenty hours a day? And we would go to Maria and beg for mercy?" Bryan nodded. "Man, that was so hella cool. Now it's like we've split up, but we're still together. It's been driving me crazy, man. I just want to be included. We should've been able to talk about this. We should have been the first people you turned to, but you left us, like we weren't family. That's all I'm saying."

Bryan nodded and glanced over at Jon who seemed to be in full agreement with Twist. He'd had no idea that his bandmates felt this way. He'd always thought of them as his brothers. Really they were the only family he had. It surprised him that they didn't know that. Then again, he'd never told them.

"Look, guys, I can't tell you how sorry I am. But I'm with Storm Crow until the day I do die, okay? I'm not going anywhere, and you'll always be my brothers." He choked up and had to stop talking for a long moment, then resumed. "When Brodie died…" He took a deep breath. "All kinds of crazy stuff went through my mind, but I didn't for one moment think about breaking up the band. I might not have acted like it the past few months, but I love you guys. You're all the family I've got. I'm not out unless you kick me out."

Twist hung his head. "I guess we just freaked out a little. You know with both you and Brodie gone, we kind of didn't know what to do."

Bryan nodded. He certainly knew how that felt. "I know, I didn't know either. That's why B.T. sent me away before I did something that even he couldn't fix.

Losing Brodie really messed up my head, but I can't lose you guys too."

Jon seemed contemplative for a moment. Then he walked over and picked up his guitar and nodded to his bandmates, "Let's do this."

Bryan shrugged his aching shoulders. He couldn't believe it had taken until after two o'clock in the morning for them to get it together. They had been playing for eighteen hours straight, and he was exhausted. Though he was still worried about the tension in his band, he had been reassured when Twist walked over to him as rehearsal broke up and asked, "Hey, dude, what's up with Callie?" He'd introduced her earlier, and he'd known that they were curious about her but were too proud to ask. Twist had been absolutely flabbergasted when he'd simply replied, "She's my mate, man." He smiled to himself; they'd always treated Twist like a kid brother because he was so much younger than the rest of the band members. From the beginning Twist had looked up to them, and his hurt over Bryan's defection was genuine. But Bryan was pretty sure that they would be able to work out any remaining tension once they got back on the road together. For him, being on tour was a real bitch. The constant time zone changes were absolutely exhausting, and he was always tired because it was impossible to sleep. Even the most stringent contract riders didn't ensure good food, so more often than not he had an upset stomach. They usually weren't in a city long enough to really enjoy it, and he spent most of his time in a boring hotel room looking at daytime television. Little wonder that some rock stars trashed luxury hotels rooms as a hobby. Many record companies even built escrows into contracts to cover such damage. Being on the road was a trial by fire; it either brought a band together or destroyed it. Storm Crow had always gelled on tour, and Bryan was confident that this time would not be any different.

He glanced over at Callie in the passenger seat of his pickup truck. She was sound asleep with her head pressed against the glass of the side window. She looked so youthful and pretty when she was asleep. Her dreadlocks were pulled back, and her face looked soft and vulnerable. She wasn't accustomed to their late hours and had taken to napping whenever the opportunity presented itself. Bryan smiled. She was a game one, all right. This lifestyle was difficult to say the least, but she had hung in there with them through fights, temper tantrums, and hours only the local winos kept. But now they were headed home. Something about that seemed so right. Home with Callie. His grin grew wider; he wondered if she knew she snored.

Callie awoke with a start, disoriented. It took a moment to recall that she was at Bryan's house in Venice Beach. When they first arrived, she had been surprised at the grittiness of the neighborhood in which Bryan had chosen to live. She'd assumed that he would live in Malibu or even Carmel, but she should've known that an alternative rock superstar wouldn't live in such sanitized surroundings. The edginess and eclectic nature of Venice Beach suited him far better than any ritzy upscale neighborhood. In Venice Beach multimillionaires rubbed shoulders with street performers, seemingly in comfortable accord. She'd never seen anything like it, though of course, she'd actually seen very little of it.

They had arrived late the previous Saturday, and since then she had not gotten to bed before three o'clock in the morning. She couldn't believe how hard the band worked. So much for the glamour of drugs, sex, and rock and roll. She and Tonya had worked to the point of and beyond physical exhaustion many times when they first opened their store, but at least they weren't required to sound good while they did it. She'd always dismissed rockers as a bunch of overpaid, spoiled brats, and that element certainly had a presence. But the brats weren't successful for long. Maintaining a career in this industry took nothing less than selfless dedication. As a small business owner, she could respect hard work, and these people made promoters of the Protestant work ethic look like slackers. Today, if she was right and it was Wednesday, they'd be auditioning a new guitarist, and she was sure that would result in more endless sessions.

The tribute concert was on Saturday, and while the band seemed ready for that performance, she could tell that Bryan was anxious about hiring a replacement for Brodie. They apparently had a number of candidates. The band seemed to be more concerned about chemistry than with actual talent. Bryan was adamant that guitar licks could be learned, but he didn't want some jerk to come in and ruin their already fragile vibe. They'd even briefly toyed with the idea of going with just Bryan on lead guitar, but most of their music had been written with two leads, many with difficult contrapuntal harmonies. Those would be impossible to duplicate without another guitarist.

She glanced over at the clock. It was almost ten o'clock. Despite the late hours, she knew Bryan had already been up for quite a while. Apparently he needed very little sleep. She hadn't kept such hours since she first opened the bookstore, and even then she hadn't sustained the brutal pace for long. Bryan had probably already gone for a run by now, and was almost certainly in the kitchen preparing what she had come to think of as a typical L.A. breakfast: fruit smoothies, fresh fruit, and whole-grain muffins. She just couldn't understand how celebrities could be so obsessed with healthy foods and at the same time use enough illegal substances to undo any benefit. She shook her head as she stretched and got out of bed. Oh, the life of a rock star.

After her shower, Callie padded barefoot into Bryan's kitchen. She really liked his house, just as he'd told her she would. Small compared to some of the celebrity homes she'd seen on television and in magazines, it had only three bedrooms and two baths. Given Bryan's penchant for the color black, she'd been surprised to see that the house had been done in very soothing neutral shades, with subtle touches of sage green. The guest bedroom where she was staying soothed the senses with lush green tones, and reminded Callie of the fern forest at a botanical garden she'd once visited. Like most of the houses in this area, it was designed to take advantage of the ocean view, and the den had French doors that opened directly onto the beach. The ocean view with the Santa Monica mountains further up the coast was breathtaking. The only hint that a rock star lived there was the four Grammys in the den, an absurd amount of electronic equipment, and, of course, the guitar picks that were scattered throughout the house.

Callie couldn't understand it. Bryan littered every room of the house with guitar picks, yet he seemed to be on a perpetual quest to find them. She'd even found one in the refrigerator, and suspected there was one in the coffee canister, but he'd snatched the container away before she had a chance to check it out. Bryan did some production work at home, using his Macintosh computer. In the interest of self-protection he hadn't put in a studio for fear he'd never leave home, instead spending all his time mixing and remixing music, probably never finishing a recording. Having lived in the house with him for a week, Callie could certainly understand the problem. Bryan would be better off doing his recording in a studio, where there would be "people" to help him keep up with his equipment.

Though she had teased him about it, Callie couldn't believe that he really did have a full-time staff person that he paid to do all those pesky little things he didn't want to be bothered with. She'd met his personal assistant, Kelly, earlier that week. To para-phrase the perky redhead, her job responsibilities included everything from aspirin to Zeppelin. As in Led Zeppelin, she'd clarified for Callie's benefit. After all, given the level of self-indulgence in this town, it would not have been at all surprising if Bryan had an airship stashed somewhere. Cataloguing his massive CD collection was another one of her tasks. Fortunately, she seemed to be up to the job. Her tiny frame bristled with energy, from her bright red hair in its short, spiky cut to her curvy, little toes that were resplendent in multicolored nail polish. On the day they met, she wore a bright pink denim jacket with matching capri pants. Callie would have thought such a bright color would clash with Kelly's vivid coloring, but somehow it didn't. Everything about Kelly from her incandescent smile to her bouncy walk and infec-tious enthusiasm for her work just screamed ex-cheer-leader. For some reason, perhaps her bubbly effervescence, or the nail polish, she made Callie think of a Rainbow Brite doll she'd had years ago. She was the first female acquaintance of Bryan's Callie had met who didn't have any romantic interest in him. Their camaraderie, built over years of working together, was that of brother and sister. It was fun to watch her take care of him. Callie was fascinated when Kelly told her that, along with her many other tasks such as picking up dry cleaning, arranging his schedule, and maintaining his truck, she was also responsible for keeping up with Bryan's keys. Callie stored that little nugget of information for later use. When she'd teased him about it before, he'd never let on that he really did have someone to do that for him.

Casually dressed in loose cotton knit shorts and a T-shirt, Callie halted abruptly when she noted B.T. sitting at the kitchen table. She had met Bryan's colorful manager the previous Saturday when they arrived, but had not seen him since. Given his good-old-boy guise she'd expected some type of reaction from him about her being black. But if he had any concerns in that area he had not expressed them during their long ride from the airport to Bryan's house. Of course, he had been so busy berating Bryan for all manner of shortcomings, some going back ten years, that he might simply have run out of breath before he got to the race issue.

Bryan was standing at the counter, as she'd suspected, making a breakfast smoothie. B.T. was scolding him for the lack of "real food" in the house.

Bryan turned when Callie came in. "Good morning, Callie. Want a smoothie and a muffin?"

Callie walked past him to the coffee maker. "If you had any humanity at all, Bryan, you wouldn't keep a girl out all night and then expect her to start her day drinking something that looks like algae."

B.T. laughed in approval. "Just like I told you, Bryan, get some bacon and eggs in this house. Nobody wants to drink that green crap but you." He paused. "Now don't forget that Maria is expecting you two at the house tonight for dinner."

"For crying out loud, B.T., you know we've got the auditions," Bryan responded irritably

"Look, son, this is my wife we're talking about here. You know how she is. I made the mistake of telling her that you brought a decent girl back with you from Alabama and now nothing will do but you bring Callie to meet her. She's expecting y'all at six."

Bryan shook his head, knowing that telling Maria "no" was fruitless. "Well, we won't be able to stay for long."

Callie gave them both an exasperated look. She was definitely not up for meeting the woman that Bryan considered to be his mother. "Uh, guys…"

B.T. stood up and started moving towards the back door. "I guess I'll be on my way."

"Are you stopping by the auditions?" Bryan began sipping his smoothie.

"Yeah, I'll be there for awhile, but I've got lots of appointments today," B.T. replied as he walked out the door.

Callie raised her voice. "Bryan, did it occur to you that I might not want to have dinner with B.T. and Maria tonight?"

Bryan shook his head. "Do you think I do? But I don't think we really have a choice in the matter, Callie. Maria's been like a mother to me. I can't hurt her feelings." *Or piss her off*, he added to himself. He'd been on the receiving end of Maria's tongue lashings before. Though generally sweet and loving, Maria clearly wore the pants in the Breedlove home. B.T. always responded good-naturedly when he was teased for being henpecked and would usually reply with a big grin, "Y'all just remember that a hen only pecks one rooster, and I'm the cock of the walk."

Callie took one of the muffins Bryan offered and sat at the table with her coffee. "What time do auditions start?"

"Not until about two, so we've got a little time to look around the neighborhood. This is really an interesting place. I think you'll like it a lot."

After breakfast Callie and Bryan wandered around Venice Beach. Callie had wanted to look particularly cute for Bryan and wore denim shorts and a knitted top that showed occasional glimpses of her midriff when she moved. She could see the appreciation in his eyes as he stared, seemingly fixated on her bare legs. As they descended the steps to the street, he realized that her midriff was exposed when she moved and immediately took her hand in his. He held onto it the entire time they were sightseeing, not releasing her unless it was absolutely necessary. Callie didn't really mind, though she felt obligated to make a principled objection. She was amused that he was being so possessive when there were so many women clad in considerably less.

Of course, Callie didn't relish the sight of the scantily clad women who wandered the street. She wondered at the bravery of women willing to roller blade in thong bikinis. She'd regularly glance at Bryan to see if he was checking out the view, but he seemed to be quite blasé about the whole thing.

Venice Beach was like nothing Callie had seen in her life. Often she was left staring in wide-eyed amazement at the many street performers. Terrified that he would lose a limb, Callie couldn't tear her eyes away from the man juggling chainsaws, and another one balancing women on his chin. She just couldn't take it all in. They posed to have their portrait done in pastels by a street artist who was amazingly quick. He sketched them in fewer than ten minutes, somehow managing to capture the essence of their personalities in just a few brief strokes. Much to her surprise, no one harassed Bryan, though any number of people recognized him. He explained that as a resident, people respected his privacy and kept their distance. It was another thing he loved about the neighborhood. Besides, Callie thought, with some of the antics going on in the streets, having a rock star walking around seemed almost mundane.

Bryan enjoyed seeing everything through Callie's eyes. Her excitement and wonder brought new life to what had become all too commonplace to him. He had noticed her attempts to catch him checking out the other women and couldn't help feeling slightly smug at her uncharacteristic display of jealousy. Finally, with her hand still held firmly in his own, they reluctantly returned to his home.

# CHAPTER 10

The Breedlove home epitomized what Callie had expected of the Hollywood lifestyle. A large, Spanish colonial-style bungalow, it had a traditional terra-cotta tile roof. The lush, tropical landscaping lent the home an inviting and restful facade that in no way minimized the glamour of the setting. Set back from the street with a wrought-iron gate and a long approach ending in a circular driveway, it was the type of place that might be seen on *Entertainment Tonight*. On the other hand, Maria Breedlove was nothing like Callie expected. Given that the woman had to handle a character like B.T., not to mention Bryan with his sometimes difficult personality, Callie expected her to be large and imposing. Instead, Maria was a tiny woman who barely reached Callie's shoulder. She flitted around the room, reminding Callie of the small brown wrens that made themselves at home outside her apartment window. She and B.T. made an incongruous couple, she small and delicate, he large and brusque in his standard seersucker suit and a giant cigar clenched firmly in his teeth. Maria was admonishing Bryan now for not coming to see her more often.

"You finally meet a respectable girl, and you really thought you would get away with not bringing her home to me." Maria shook her head.

Bryan gave her a hug. "Maria, I'm sorry. We've just been so busy."

"I know, darling, always, always, that's your excuse. But still, how could you possibly be too busy to see me?" She wagged a finger at him. Then, as if resigned to never resolving that dispute, she turned her attention to Callie. "Okay, let me get a look at you." She reached out and grabbed both of Callie's hands, pulling her forward from where she'd been hiding, partially behind, and partially beside Bryan. "Oh Bryan, she is a lovely girl, but much too skinny. Come, come, Callie, you must come into the kitchen and let me fatten you up. Running around with Bryan you'll never get any decent food," she said, tugging Callie towards the kitchen.

Callie looked back over her shoulder and gave Bryan a bewildered look, frantically signaling for him to join them. In what was clearly a coordinated stratagem, B.T. grasped Bryan's shoulders firmly and directed him towards the den. Bryan simply shrugged and gave Callie a sheepish grin. Callie took a deep breath and resigned herself to being alone with Maria in the kitchen. Though she couldn't be sure, she suspected that she was well on her way to an interrogation the likes of which hadn't been seen since the Spanish Inquisition.

Callie looked around the spacious kitchen, which was obviously the domain of a gourmet cook. The six-burner Viking stove looked straight out of a five-star restaurant and had all the markings of daily use. In keeping with the Spanish colonial style of the house, the floor was covered in terra-cotta tiles, with a coordinating backsplash and borders in bright Mexican tiles. The well-seasoned pots hanging from the pot rack overhead and the glass-front Sub-Zero refrigerator added to the impression that this was actually a cooking kitchen, not a designer's idea of what a kitchen should look like. Watching Maria bustling about, it was clear that despite their obvious wealth, she did most of the cooking without assistance from a cook or other "help."

Without inquiring as to whether Callie could cook, Maria handed her a bunch of vegetables and asked her to prepare a salad as she made Bryan's favorite shrimp chimichangas.

"So, do you cook for my boy when you're back home?"

"No, not really, Mrs. Breedlove. Back home I own a bookstore, and I spend most of my time working there," Callie replied, tearing the romaine lettuce into bite-size pieces.

"Ah, a career woman," Maria muttered to herself as she folded the shrimp mixture into the crust.

Callie didn't know what to make of that comment, so she chose to remain silent.

"How long have you two been in love?"

Callie bobbled the lettuce as she gasped out, "Mrs. Breedlove…"

Maria interrupted, "Please, call me Maria. Breedlove is such a ridiculous name, if I hadn't loved Robert so much, nothing in the world would have made me take it."

Callie puzzled over that for a moment, then realized that Robert was B.T. "Okay. Anyway, Maria, Bryan and I aren't in love," she said, firmly shaking her head for emphasis.

Maria turned away from the stove. "Oh really? Are you saying that my boy would bring a girl home to me that he didn't love?"

"Uh, Mrs. Breed…" Maria raised a brow imperiously. "Sorry, Maria. I thought you pretty much insisted that we come to dinner."

"My boy didn't have to come, did he? You've known Bryan long enough now to know that he doesn't do anything unless he wants to. Besides, he met your folks, didn't he? Why wouldn't he bring you home to meet his family?"

Callie wondered irritably if there was anything that Bryan hadn't told B.T. If he'd told him about the kiss in the kitchen, she would kill him!

"Robert told me that your father really put him through the wringer. Bryan doesn't have to put up with that just to be with a girl. Yep, my boy is definitely in love."

Callie had no intention of responding to that statement and worked in silence.

Then, "Robert said you really helped Bryan deal with Brodie's death."

"I don't know if I helped or not…," Callie responded tentatively.

"Of course you did. My Robert wouldn't have said it if it wasn't so."

Callie rolled her eyes, fairly certain that Bobby Tom would say pretty much anything, but thought it would probably be better to allow Maria to maintain her illusions.

Maria continued contemplatively, "They were both my boys. I remember when Robert brought them home. My poor babies were like abandoned puppies…"

Callie interrupted, "I thought they were already teenagers when they met B.T.?"

Maria corrected her. "Initials are what you embroider on your underwear when you go to camp."

"But isn't that the name he goes by?"

"Yes," Maria replied snappishly, "but I don't have to call him that, do I?"

Callie raised her brows and wondered if Maria had ever told B.T. that his name belonged on his drawers.

Maria continued, "Anyway, yes, they were seventeen or eighteen years old. But they'd never had anybody to care for them. They were desperate for love, but it scared them too. It took months before they'd even return a hug. What kind of people are fortunate enough to have such fine sons and then just throw them away as if they're garbage?" she asked forcefully. Maria had obviously gone off on this tangent before, and didn't seem to really expect a response, which was a relief to Callie as she didn't have any idea of what she should say. "All I can say is, it's fortunate I never met either of their so-called parents." Then as if suddenly recalling Callie's presence, she ended her diatribe. "Anyway, it was a tough time." She turned back to the stove. When she spoke again her voice was hollow with grief. "Robert and I never had children of our own. Now I know the pain of losing one of my babies, without having the pleasure of holding that child to my breast." Then she smiled. "But now my other boy has brought home a nice girl, and there'll be babies for me and my Robert."

"Maria…," Callie tried again to interject. Where had she gotten these ideas from? Did she act like this every time Bryan brought a woman to the house? Then she remembered that Bryan had told her he'd never brought anyone home before. Well, she could certainly understand why!

"You'll take good care of my boy. You two are crazy in love with each other, there's no doubt about that. You can see it all over your faces. I've prayed that he'd meet a good girl, and you know the Lord answers prayers. Come on, let's get this food on the table. As usual, my boy is in a hurry."

Callie gave up disagreeing with Maria. After all, who was she to argue with a deity, and she didn't mean the Lord. She had quickly realized that like her own mother, Maria suffered from what Callie jokingly referred to as "little woman syndrome." Having lived with a mother with the disorder for years, she recognized it in Maria immediately. Both were tiny women who could steamroll an opponent without mussing their hairdo. Neither woman would back down from her own viewpoint, and both would walk right over you if you allowed them. And even worse, they had the ability to make you adore them despite their assertive tendencies. She meekly finished the salad and followed Maria into the dining room, though she made a mental note to find a mirror as soon as possible to see exactly what, if anything, was showing on her face.

Dinner was a festive affair with Maria playing queen bee over everyone. She forced food onto them, insisting that both Bryan and Callie were much too skinny, and remonstrated B.T. for eating too much fatty food. She continued to probe into every aspect of Callie's life. Bryan took it all in good humor and kept giving Callie amused looks and smug grins. She in turn pantomimed the injuries she intended to inflict on him for putting her through this. Fortunately, they had a built-in excuse to leave shortly after they finished dinner.

As they walked to the door Maria harangued them to give her plenty of advance notice to prepare the wedding. She'd never been the mother-of-the-groom before and really looked forward to it. And of course, they were not to wait too long to present her with lots of lovely grandchildren; twins might not be a bad idea. After all, they weren't getting any younger. Callie had no idea which couple she referred to, and didn't dare ask.

Once they escaped to the truck and their hosts had returned to their home, Callie began punching Bryan in his arm repeatedly for not warning her about his surrogate mother.

Bryan doubled over with laughter, holding up his hands in defense. "Would you have come had I told you about her? Besides, I put up with worse from your dad!"

Aside from his inquiry into the etymology of the word "haint," they'd pretty much avoided discussing Bryan's conversation with her dad. Bryan hadn't needed to understand that a "haint" is a ghost to recognize an implied death threat when he heard it.

Callie squeezed the back of her neck and exhaled, the breath hissing through her teeth, "God, from the way folks are acting, you'd think we were a couple of horny teenagers. My folks trying to scare you away, your folks rushing us to the altar. What's wrong with people that they don't understand that we're simply…well, you know." Callie fumbled to a halt, flustered by the effort to define their relationship. Even she had to acknowledge that she and Bryan had gone past the "friendship" stage quite a while back, but she had no idea what to call their relationship now.

Bryan chuckled at her confusion, "Did you tell Maria that we're just, 'you know'?"

Callie sucked her teeth. "I don't think anyone has told that woman anything since 1965. No, to hear her tell it, we've got one foot on the altar and the other on a banana peel."

Bryan laid his arm across her shoulders and leaned forward, resting his forehead against hers. "How do you know we don't?" he asked quietly.

Mesmerized by the loving regard she saw in his eyes, Callie didn't reply as Bryan leaned forward to place a velvety soft kiss on her lips.

Callie had almost grown accustomed to her response to Bryan's touch, but the newness of the kiss seemed to suck all the oxygen from the truck. She felt as if a large hand was squeezing her heart, leaving her breathless and lightheaded with the wonder of it all. Instinctively she parted her lips, inviting his tongue inside for further exploration. Bryan stroked her tongue and the inside of her mouth as if it were a soft-serve ice cream cone. The very delicacy of the gesture seemed to heighten her arousal, and when Bryan removed his tongue in an attempt to break the connection, she followed it back into his mouth, setting off another chain reaction of desire. Bryan finally grasped her chin and firmly moved away to end the kiss, all the while mentally damning the responsibility that necessitated doing so.

He knew without a doubt that he was falling in love. He wanted this woman as he'd wanted only one thing before in his life: music. She awakened a hunger in him that even music couldn't assuage. God only knew what Callie was feeling with all this "you know" stuff. Surely she knew that he wasn't toying with her, but she seemed unwilling to acknowledge the power of what was happening between them. Of course, he understood her hesitancy. Given his background, very few normal women were willing to throw themselves into the breach. His celebrity status only exacerbated the problem, and as if that wasn't bad enough, she had family opposed to interracial relationships. But if nothing else, his childhood had given him a formidable drive and determination, and he'd never wanted anything as much as he wanted Callie. He knew that she was attracted to him. He just needed to convince her that his feelings for her were genuine, not an insurmountable task in his estimation. He cleared his throat. "Are you sure we have only one foot on that banana peel, Callie?" He started the truck and backed out of the Breedloves' driveway.

The auditions were far less grueling than Callie had anticipated. It was a deceptively simple process; each guitarist would play a song of his choice on the acoustic guitar. Those who played well acoustically were asked to play another song on the electric guitar. Finally, they were invited to jam with the band. Very few of the musicians made it to this point, making Callie wonder if they would ever find a new guitarist.

Fortunately, the very first candidate after the dinner break stood head and shoulders above the rest. His name was Thaddeus, and he was the strangest looking person there. In a crowd of tattooed, longhaired rockers, he was dressed neatly in a pair of pressed chinos, a button-down shirt with a sweater vest and looked to be about seventeen years old. Seeming painfully shy, he didn't look up once during his entire set. Callie initially wondered if he had come to the wrong place, but she could tell from Bryan's reaction to the first chord the young man struck that he was the one. As one body, Bryan and the other band members walked over to their instruments and joined him. Despite his traditional manner of dressing and diffident manner, he fit in seamlessly with the rest of the band, and Callie could see the relief on Bryan's face. Thaddeus quickly ran through a medley of Storm Crow songs, displaying an admirable knowledge of the band's catalogue. His aptitude meant that the transition to a new guitarist would be much smoother than anticipated. After they finished the set, they dismissed the other applicants and offered him the job on the spot, after confirming that he was of legal age.

Naysa, the band's stylist, looked Thaddeus over carefully. "You know, I think I could work with this." She gestured towards his outfit. "A kind of nouveau geek look would be perfect." She tapped one sleekly manicured nail against her perfect white teeth as she circled around the youngster. A petite Japanese girl with dainty doll-like features, Naysa wore her straight dark hair in a short pageboy hair cut with bangs. The style, commonly called the China doll, emphasized the dramatic slant of her eyes. Her cowboy hat, leather vest and vintage jeans created a unique look that had contributed to her success as a stylist for celebrities. On her tiny frame and with her strongly Asian features, the dichotomy of the look was arresting.

Thaddeus gave her a bewildered look. He obviously had no clue as to what she was talking about, but was so mesmerized by her striking beauty that he really didn't care.

Unaccountably disturbed by Thaddeus' openly besotted gaze, Twist spoke up, pointing out the guitarist's obvious youth. "Hey, kid. What was your name again?"

"Thaddeus."

Twist rolled his eyes. "Mind if we call you Thad?"

Thad nodded his consent. "That's what everybody calls me, except for my mother. She always calls me Thaddeus," he said, nervously looking down at his watch. "Uh, guys, it's getting late. I've got to go home now and tell my mom I got a job."

As the rest of the band looked on in amazement Thad packed up his gear and left. They couldn't restrain their laughter as they anticipated the fun they would have on the road with this naïve young innocent. Twist was particularly happy to have someone in the band who was younger than he was. Some of the ribbing he'd received could now be directed towards the neophyte. He smiled to himself. Young Thad would definitely be a welcome new addition. Of course, there was the issue of his mother. He hoped she didn't have to come along on tour. It would definitely put a damper on their less wholesome activities. He'd also have to keep an eye on him around Naysa. Not that he was jealous or anything, he told himself smugly. Maybe he'd be able to introduce him to a nice girl who was more his type. If the poor lad got tangled up with a hellcat like Naysa, there wouldn't be anything left to go on tour with.

# CHAPTER 11

Callie looked out over the crowd, shaking her head in bemusement. The event looked more like a madhouse than anything she'd ever witnessed. She and Bryan were attending the pre-tribute publicity party, and it seemed that every reporter and photographer in the world was in attendance. Callie had tried frantically to convince Bryan that she shouldn't go, but he had been adamant that he needed her there. When she'd packed back home, she'd had no intention of attending the gala, so she hadn't brought any dressy attire. With the whirlwind schedule of rehearsals and auditions there had been no opportunity to shop, and she was concerned that her clothes weren't suitable. Naysa allayed those fears by advising her that dressing casually for all occasions was one of the fringe benefits of being a rock star. Bryan was dressed in his standard all-black attire, right down to his seedy-looking boots. Callie breathed a sigh of relief when she realized that her over-dyed boot-cut jeans and simple white cotton wrap top were not at all out of place. There were plenty of people there who wore dressier clothes, but according to Bryan, they were mainly wannabes, hangers-on, and groupies. The people who were regulars at such events had a look of studied insouciance. Others attempted that same practiced indifference, but somehow on them it came across as an almost sad desperation. This was especially true of the celebrities who had not had a hit in a while. Their eyes overly bright, collagened lips pried apart into smiles that were more like grimaces, they worked the room with a near fiendish intensity.

Though she'd seen a lot of celebrities on television and in magazines, somehow they looked much more synthetic in the flesh. Most of the women, and a sizable percentage of the men, seemed to have had "work" done. Of course, the scant amount of clothing the women wore made going under the knife an absolute necessity. Callie and Bryan spent a brief moment on that chicken and egg discussion. Did they get surgery to accommodate the nearly nude fashions? Or were the women dressed so skimpily to flaunt their new bodies? Either way, they wore so little clothing that Callie wondered why they even bothered. Never in her entire life had she seen so many immobile bosoms. She couldn't believe that people actually did that to themselves on purpose. Bryan had to nudge her several times when she was riveted by a particularly preposterous endowment.

Members of the press and music industry insiders inundated Bryan. Callie was relieved when he gave the brush-off to two unctuous-looking men who tried to talk him into a new management deal. Though B.T.'s practices were unorthodox, Callie knew he had

Bryan's best interests at heart. These other men didn't look to even have hearts, at least none without stakes driven through them. Others approached him about becoming a solo artist. Jon and Twist were particularly attentive during those conversations because rumors were circulating rapidly about a solo project for Bryan. Despite his constant denials, people assumed the stories were true, and everyone wanted a piece of the deal. The interactions had all the complexity of a minuet. As one group drifted away, another swooped in. In their attempts to isolate Bryan, the various toadies simply ignored Callie or tried to brush her aside. It amused her that no one bothered to ask her name. Most of the people acted as if they didn't see her. They had a way of quickly assessing her status and then dismissing her. Callie didn't mind, because being a nobody in this town definitely had its benefits. Bryan held onto her like a lifeline and only relinquished her to B.T. or Jon when he absolutely had to for a publicity photo. She didn't want to appear in the type of stories she usually read about celebrities. Bryan soothed her anxiety by assuring her that the focus would be on him, and though she'd be included in the photo, she'd just be dismissed as another "unidentified girlfriend." Hearing this, Callie breathed a sigh of relief.

Callie struggled to maintain a casual demeanor while being introduced to the dizzying array of celebrities, some of whom were legends in the music or film industry. She didn't want to embarrass Bryan

by acting like a star-struck country yokel. Anthony
Kiedis lingered to talk to Bryan. From their hushed
tones and solemn expressions she assumed that they
were discussing Brodie. Anthony had tried desperately
to intervene with Brodie, who had been one of his
closest friends. He'd also tried to stop Bryan's self-
destructive downward spiral after Brodie's death. The
enthusiasm of his embrace with Bryan demonstrated
his joy in finding his friend in a better state of mind
and back in the fold. Callie could tell that some of the
celebrities were true friends of Bryan's, and shared his
grief about Brodie. They generally maintained a low-
key manner, and tried to approach when the paparazzi
were not present to avoid creating a scene. Others,
however, were patently seeking publicity and a boost
for their own careers. Bryan's graciousness with the
latter surprised Callie. She thought it was rather
ghoulish to attend such an event just for publicity, but
upon reflection she realized it was not much different
from people back home who attended funerals for an
opportunity to gossip and wear nice clothes. Bryan
apparently accepted such behavior as being an innate
part of the entertainment industry and wasn't taken
aback by it.

Not to her surprise, an amazing number of the
half-clothed women approached Bryan, and just in
case he hadn't seen their best assets, struck artful poses
that displayed their charms in a favorable light. Bryan
coolly introduced her to each of the women, keeping
his eyes firmly fixed on their faces. Callie picked up

on the subtle body language differences that indicated which women Bryan had slept with. It quickly became obvious that he hadn't lied when he said he didn't discriminate. If there was a racial group not represented in the bevy of beauties, Callie didn't know what it was. After watching the little impromptu rainbow coalition for a while, she couldn't resist taking another dig at Bryan. "So you've been basically having yourself a little rainbow orgy, haven't you?"

"Not on purpose," he replied with a brow deeply furrowed with concern. "And calling it an orgy is a bit much. They were mostly threesomes."

Callie gave a disbelieving snort.

"Okay, foursomes, at the very most," he conceded.

Callie left the topic alone for the moment, but she had every intention of revisiting it. She didn't intend to miss this marvelous opportunity to put Bryan on the hot seat.

With so many groupies trolling for new celebrities present, the whole room vibrated with sexual energy. Bryan had made snide references to the type of activity common at such events, but Callie was somewhat skeptical. Why would people risk behaving so scandalously with all these reporters and cameras around? Time and time again, she'd seen celebrities rant against the paparazzi and their invasive tactics. Bryan explained that their protests were a ploy, that most of those people would kill their own mothers to be on the cover of *People*. Later, when she briefly left Bryan's side to go to the ladies' room, she accidentally opened a closet and found one of the lovelies Bryan had introduced her to earlier performing a lewd sex act on a well-known movie producer. She rushed back to Bryan's side and breathlessly shared the news. Bryan merely grinned at her and advised that the young lady in question was legendary for her technique and carried the nickname "Miss Goodhead" proudly. He likened her to the infamous groupie Cynthia Plaster Caster, except that she lacked the talent to make plaster casts of her partners' penises. Instead she confiscated their underwear as a trophy of her conquests. When Callie inquired as to his level of acquaintance with the young lady in question, Bryan gave her a mock salute and responded, "Ma'am, all my underwear is present and accounted for." Afraid of what else she might encounter, Callie didn't leave Bryan's side again.

Despite their attire, most of the women were cordial, though some couldn't resist making remarks about her outfit or obvious lack of surgical augmentation. One even slipped her a business card and encouraged Callie to hurry on over to North Roxbury to see the "plastic" who did "her work." It didn't take long for Callie to determine that 435 North Roxbury housed some of the most legendary plastic surgeons in town. Callie pursed her lips. She really had to wonder about people who carried a surgeon's business cards with them. However, Bryan didn't seem to think it was odd at all.

Watching the women brought to mind the comments her mother had often made about the importance of maintaining a healthy diet and eating heartily with family and friends. According to Edith, people who didn't eat properly ended up cannibalizing each other. Watching the bared claws tonight, Callie was convinced that there was more than a grain of truth in her mother's comment. The women weren't trying to be mean, or at least most weren't, but in this impossibly competitive society, they used every tool available to gain even the slightest edge. And cattiness seemed to be the weapon of choice. Towards the end of the evening, Bryan introduced her to "a friend" with the unlikely name of Chasdity, with a "d," no less, a tall, leggy redhead who Callie suspected was his most recent girlfriend. Callie had never met anyone who spelt their name when introduced and wondered idly if the "d" stood for dingbat.

After the introduction, Chasdity exclaimed, "Oh, I just love your accent! I've never met a Southerner. Say something else!"

Callie pointedly ignored her order, pretending to be engrossed in another conversation. She had no intention of taking commands and performing like a trained seal. When Chasdity didn't take the hint and repeated the request and Callie again didn't respond, she asked Bryan where they'd met. When Bryan explained that they had met in Alabama, Chasdity expressed disbelief and then waved her hand towards Callie. "Alabama! Well, that explains your outfit. Oh, you poor thing, it's so like Bryan to rush a girl away from home without giving her a chance to pack or even do any shopping. I can't tell you how many times he's done that to me!" She then lapsed into her best attempt at urban black speech. "Give me a call, girl-friend, and I'll give you the hook-up. Can't have you running around looking all 'Bama, now can we?"

Callie sucked her teeth. Nothing irritated her more than white people who felt they needed to "talk black" to her. She pointedly gave a once-over to Chasdity's obscenely short, low-cut dress and dryly commented, "No, I don't think so. My taste is a little bit different from yours. I only dress like a stripper for costume parties, but if I ever decide to do it again, I'll be sure to give you a call."

Chasdity gasped indignantly, and Bryan shook with laughter as he choked out an excuse to move them to another group before she could respond.

"I can't believe you ever dated that woman!" Callie hissed at him.

Bryan shook his head, sure that Callie didn't really want to know how little "dating" had actually tran-spired. "I wouldn't exactly call it dating. We only went out for a couple of weeks, but I don't know how I put up with her either."

Callie sat in the audience, transfixed by the band's performance. Bryan, Jon, and Twist sat on a stage illu-minated only by a lone spotlight. They were the last performers in an evening that had been taut with emotion. Bryan's voice was even huskier and rawer than usual, and Callie couldn't stop the tears as he wailed out an exquisitely painful rendition of "Wish You Were Here." On her right, Maria had her head on B.T.'s shoulder, and he comforted her as tears ran unabashedly down his face. Callie couldn't get over B.T.'s open grief. Given his usual gruff manner and fixation on the bottom line, she'd had no idea that Bryan and Brodie were anything more than just a column on his balance sheet. This was yet another dimension of their extraordinarily complex relationship.

She had heard Bryan's CDs, and he had even performed for her in her home, but nothing compared to seeing him in his element. Bryan made each person in that audience feel as though he were performing for them individually. Callie was moved beyond words that he would be this open and honest, especially as she knew what that openness cost him in terms of his own vulnerability.

When the band finished, it felt as though everyone was collectively holding their breath, the tension as taut as a bowstring. Then, as if someone had thrown a secret switch, a clamor arose as the audience jumped to its feet en masse and applauded thunderously. The earsplitting applause continued until the band consented to an encore, and then resumed again. If there had been any doubt as to the stability of this band, they were allayed in that instant. Storm Crow was back and better than ever.

Though there were no invitations, and no previous plans, somehow it was simply understood that everyone would return to the Breedlove home after Storm Crow's performance. No hangers-on were present for this private time. Callie looked around the crowded den in wonder.

Bryan stood back, somewhat aloof from the group, looking on as his friends dealt with their emotions in various ways. Maria had deliberately made the Breedlove home a sanctuary for them all, and he had never appreciated it more than tonight. Jon frequently suffered headaches after performances, and Cinnamon was massaging his current one away. It seemed as though she and Jon had been together forever. He could hardly remember her as the ragtag little urchin she had been when she first began to follow the band from venue to venue, utterly besotted with the bassist. Poor Jon hadn't stood a chance. As an adult, she closely resembled her name with her long golden brown hair and lightly tanned skin. She preferred vintage clothing, and tonight her dress consisted of layers of various shades of amethyst silk which swirled around her sylph-like frame.

He glanced over to the corner where Twist and his girlfriend Naysa were talking quietly with Maria. Apparently they were on-again for the moment, but that had been known to change with the Gulf Stream. Naysa's delicate loveliness was set off by the cream silk poet's shirt she wore with a long denim skirt and concha belt. Each time he looked at her, he was newly amazed that someone who looked so exquisite could spew such an astonishing array of multi-syllabic profanity when she and Twist were brawling. Curiously, Naysa had no difficulty getting along with the other band members. Indeed she was one of the sweetest, most easygoing people he'd ever met. She'd been with them for five years, far longer than any of their previous stylists, who usually ditched them as soon as they discovered the band's disdain for fashion and determination to dress as they pleased. Naysa and Cinnamon were quite close, but somehow that compatibility didn't translate to Naysa's relationship with Twist. He'd heard some of their friends refer to them as "Twist and Twistette" because her personality changed so drastically when they were together. Bryan didn't understand them at all, but somehow she had hung in there longer than any other girl Twist had dated. For that, she certainly deserved combat pay.

When they'd first returned from the concert everyone had been quiet and subdued, but as the group relaxed with wine and good food, the gloom lifted somewhat and they began sharing Brodie stories. Twist related a particularly raucous incident which had occurred back when the band first started out. They were playing the college circuit and had a gig in a small Southern town. After some discussion as to the location, they eventually agreed that they were in Tallahassee, Florida, home of Florida State University. They were too wired and keyed up to sleep after the show, so everyone had congregated around the hotel pool to let off some steam. Several six-packs and at least one bottle of Jack Daniels later, they were feeling no pain.

When under the influence of alcohol, Brodie had a habit of kissing any and everybody, male or female, full on the lips while making declarations of undying love. Unfortunately for the group, two teenaged boys walked by and witnessed him kissing Bryan, and made a crude comment. Brodie taunted the boys, eventually encouraging them to show their tits. The comedy of errors began when a pre-teenage girl, who, unbeknownst to the group, was in the pool with her father, assumed that the comments were directed towards her. Upon being informed of this, the father came over to defend his daughter. Fortunately, an alert security guard, who was an off-duty police officer, noted the impending slaughter, and came over in time to prevent the melee. When he inquired as to the source of the enmity, the father explained what he thought had happened. Bryan, who was at least as wasted as Brodie, had defended his friend with the exaggerated indignation of the truly drunk. He had manfully declared that Brodie would never make such a comment to a young girl, that it was the young boys he was talking to, and that the boys had started it by making nasty remarks about their kiss. The police officer looked on in increasing disgust as he continued this tirade. Jon, realizing that Bryan wasn't helping matters, tried to quiet his friend before they were all locked up. Fortunately, the police officer was accustomed to drunken disturbances and merely sent them all to their rooms. He did warn them however, that he didn't ever want to see their perverted asses in his town again.

By the time Twist finished the story, they were all doubled over, gasping for air. That was how most of the rest of the evening went, with the ones who loved Brodie best remembering him fondly. The gathering became a celebration of the life of their friend, and Bryan rejoiced, surprised that it felt so good to look upon Brodie's life joyfully instead of dwelling on its tragic end. Brodie had always been down for a party, and Bryan knew he would have had a great time at this gathering, especially as they were totally focused on him. When the evening finally wound down, everyone exchanged joyous and tearful embraces. They had a ways to go yet in the grief process, but they had navigated a difficult and important step tonight.

Bryan stood in front of the French doors, staring sightlessly out at the ocean. The party at the Breedloves' hadn't ended until very late, and despite the eventual joy of the gathering, he was still too keyed up to sleep. The arousal he always experienced after a performance had not abated, and he had no outlet for that energy. When he was younger he'd availed himself of one of the many groupies waiting after the show. With age had come wisdom and realization of the perilous nature of his behavior. In more recent years he was usually in some type of a relationship, but even then he didn't usually have sex after a show. Under the best of circumstances he wasn't particularly civilized in bed, and in the heightened state of arousal he experienced post-performance, any number of women had told him he was downright scary.

Of course, the only woman he wanted these days was standing behind him, frantically pretending that there was nothing between them. He knew that she was not yet ready for a sexual relationship. He'd invited her along on this trip hoping for an opportunity for them to get closer, and he believed that they had. She'd been a bulwark during the madness of the past week. He had kept her close to his side the entire time because he wanted to make it clear to others that she was important to him. If he had not literally held onto her, they would've simply brushed her aside as a nonentity. Callie had been accorded the respect she deserved. Unfortunately, the endless contact had done nothing to soothe the constant state of arousal he'd experienced since they'd first met. He was close to the edge now. He sighed and leaned his head against the glass. Going for a run would probably calm him down, but somehow the prospect of the solitary exercise didn't appeal to him.

Callie fidgeted nervously at the bar, watching Bryan as he stood by the French doors, apparently brooding. Tonight his hair was unbound from the usual ponytail, and he was dressed in a black linen shirt and black jeans. He didn't wear his hair loose often, and it gave him a savage look that only heightened her awareness of him and his potent masculinity. She hadn't been able to keep her eyes off him all night, and the need to touch him was almost uncontainable. When he had been performing, the sight of his hands strumming the guitar had left her squirming in her seat, picturing those long fingers caressing her body. She had to get herself under control. His sojourn in Alabama was over now, and any type of sexual involvement was out of the question. Knowing this, however, had no effect on her arousal level. The throbbing between her thighs had not eased up in the slightest.

Earlier, she'd prepared a gin and tonic just to have something to do with her hands and it sat now on the coffee table, the ice completely melted. She couldn't understand what was going on with Bryan. The whole time they'd been in L.A., he had been openly affectionate and friendly towards her. He'd held onto her throughout the pre-tribute concert events, introducing her to everyone as his "good friend, Callie," whatever the hell that meant. He had been somewhat distant and strangely quiet at the Breedloves, and now he seemed cold and brusque. She didn't know why. She'd initially thought that perhaps the evening had evoked the grief and despair he had been struggling with for months, but the pleasure he'd shown during the party was genuine. Besides, he'd been grieving the whole time they'd known each other, and it hadn't caused him to behave this way. Maybe he was just tired. God knows she was.

"Well, Bryan, I guess I'll head off to bed now. It's late; are you going to bed soon?" When she received no response, Callie approached Bryan and placed a hand on his shoulder. She could feel tension and energy emanating from every pore, but didn't understand the source. His shoulder muscles were bunched beneath his shirt. Callie tsked. "You're all tied up in knots." She began massaging his shoulders, using some of the techniques she'd learned from watching Cinnamon.

A low growl came from deep within Bryan's chest, and he moved abruptly away. "Don't touch me, Callie," he said in a harsh rasping tone.

Deeply hurt by his rejection, Callie stood looking at his back. "Good night, Bryan." She turned towards her bedroom, knowing only that she had to get away from him before the tears began falling.

Bryan heard the emotion in her voice and knew that he had hurt her. He couldn't let her leave this way. He grabbed her arm, pulling her body to his. "I'm sorry, Callie, but I can't keep doing this," he muttered almost to himself.

"Can't keep doing what?" Callie looked up.

Bryan looked down into beautiful, chocolate-brown eyes swimming with tears and knew that he was lost. His eyes fell on her luscious lips and he couldn't restrain himself any longer. He leaned over and forcefully captured her mouth. Before Callie even had a chance to gasp, his tongue was mating with hers. He pulled her closer, shivering with delight from the feel of her body so close to his. He'd wanted to do this for so long that he was almost mindless from the pleasure.

Callie felt as if she was caught up in a firestorm, unable to think or even breathe. All she could do was feel the feverish desire this man started in her, and she wrapped her arms around his neck, desperate to get closer.

Bryan slid his hands down to Callie's hips, pulling her into his hardness. The rounded curves of her bottom felt tantalizingly ripe and full in his hands. He pulled her even closer, trying to absorb her into every cell of his being. It seemed that he'd been waiting forever to feel those lush globes under his hands, and though he wanted to linger, his hunger was riding him hard tonight. His hands reluctantly left her hips and moved to the front of her wrap top. He'd suspected that she wasn't wearing a bra, and his sensitive fingers quickly confirmed it. Her breasts sprang free. He'd been longing to see them and wasn't disappointed. Their sweet, little conical shape was a bold invitation to his seeking mouth. He was intrigued by the puffiness of her areolas and the faint contrast between them and the rest of her skin, and he couldn't resist the need to feel their velvety softness. The tightness of her tiny, chocolate nipples showed her level of arousal and as he took one, then the other, into his mouth, he was astounded that the reality could be so much better than his fantasies.

The soft wetness of his mouth pulling on her nipple in a way that she had only imagined was almost too much for Callie. She pressed herself even closer to Bryan and began to move her hips against him, desperate to ease the throbbing in her womanhood.

Bryan gasped. The sensation of her moving against his erection was simply too much. Suddenly his grip became bruising as he moved his mouth back to hers, devouring her, not leaving her any opportunity to breathe. He sucked on her tongue like a starving man, and when he moved down to her neck, she suddenly felt the sharp nip of his teeth as he bit and sucked forcefully.

Bryan inhaled deeply, trying to slow his headlong rush into passion. But the aroma of their co-mingled scents permeated his senses and did little to abate his arousal; indeed, it only increased its fierceness. He didn't want to frighten her, but he couldn't contain the powerful hunger to consume her.

"God, Callie, I've got to have you," he groaned, capturing her lips again. As his tongue tangled furiously with hers, he moved his hands back to her breasts, grasping the tips and teasing them into even greater arousal.

"Please baby, please baby, please," he whispered, his tone so guttural that Callie could barely understand him. He slid her shirt off her shoulders and moved to caress her neck, ears, and shoulders with his lips and tongue. His hands moved urgently to her jeans and he slipped his hands inside to feel her wetness. Finding the evidence of her arousal took him to the brink. He was so far gone at this point that he barely knew what he was saying or doing. His entire being was focused on one thing, the complete possession of her body. He had to do it now. There was no way in hell he'd be able to stop.

Callie could feel the tremors going through Bryan's body and his level of excitement raised hers to a fever pitch. As she felt him kneel before her, sliding her jeans and panties down as he went, her legs became so weak she could barely stand.

Bryan spread her legs and used his fingers to stroke her nether lips apart. A low growl escaped from deep in his throat as he inhaled her womanly scent. He brought his head forward to capture her sensitive bud gently between his lips. Callie let out a groan of utter surrender. He stroked the nubbin with his tongue, then began to lick her in long forceful strokes. Callie's legs collapsed, and she leaned on him to prop herself up. As he brought her to completion, Callie grasped his hair in her hands and held him as close as possible to the source of her pleasure.

When he knew she'd reached her plateau, Bryan slid down until he was prone on the floor, pulling Callie down with him. His hands went to the fastening of his jeans, and he opened them, frantically freeing himself. He searched desperately through his pockets for the small foil packet, then sheathed himself. He pulled Callie astride him, and grasping her hips, lowered her onto his erect manhood. Feeling her tight wetness around him, Bryan clenched his teeth, and his head strained back, the cords in his neck standing out as he struggled for control. He continued to raise and lower her on his shaft, the pleasure intensifying to dizzying heights. He could tell from the tightness of her body that it had been a long time since Callie had been with a man.

"So tight, so wet, oh God," he growled, his body straining with the effort to limit the force of his thrusts. He didn't want to hurt her but he'd never felt anything like this and controlling the need to plunge deeply into her succulent body was almost impossible.

Callie tensed as she felt her body spread inexorably by the pressure of Bryan's engorged manhood. For a moment she didn't think he would fit, and she strained a bit to adjust to the size of his thick head. When he slipped inside, she gasped. All her inner nerve endings tingled as she was completely filled with his broad length. Her one "unfortunate incident" had not prepared her for the reality of making love with Bryan Spencer. It was as though he'd branded her as totally his. No other man would ever suffice. She unbuttoned his shirt, sliding it off his shoulders. Sweat was gleaming on his golden chest and she stroked it, loving the feel of his slick, hot skin under her hands. She lowered her head and slipped her tongue around one of his nipples. His silky fine chest hair feathered around his nipples, trailing down his torso in a thin line to his groin where it thickened into a full pubic bush. Driven by something primal deep within, she wanted only to give him the same pleasure she'd enjoyed earlier. She moved her hips forcefully up and down on his shaft, squeezing him with her inner muscles.

Bryan tensed even further, the shudders rippling through his body more powerful than ever.

"Oh God, oh God, oh God," he moaned, rolling his head from side to side. His control slipped another notch. "God baby, you feel so good. You're making me crazy!" he strained out as his hands flexed forcefully on her hips.

Catching sight of Bryan's extremity pitched Callie into a second orgasm. When Bryan felt her muscles begin to clench spasmodically around him, he knew he couldn't hold back any longer. His back arched almost impossibly as he reached his own release.

After maintaining that posture for what seemed like an eternity, Bryan sank back onto the floor, taking a limp Callie with him. She pressed her fevered face into the curve of his neck as the tremors continued to arc their way through her body. It seemed that the exquisite sensations would never cease. They were almost frightening in their ferocity. Their bodies gradually calmed as they lay in a boneless heap on the floor.

# CHAPTER 12

Bryan stirred briefly from his position under Callie, smoothing his hands over her back to rouse her. He wanted to stay intertwined with her forever, but was concerned that he might have hurt or frightened her.

"Callie." When there was no response he shook her slightly. "Callie, baby, are you okay?" he rasped.

Callie murmured something unintelligible into his neck, and he shook her more insistently. "Baby, are you okay? Did I hurt you?"

Finally Callie raised her head and peered down at him as if in a daze. "Whaaaa...?"

"Are you okay? I didn't hurt you, did I?" he asked anxiously.

Callie continued to stare at him blankly as she gradually collected herself.

"Oh my God," she murmured as she moved completely off him, her movements jerky and disjointed. She wiped a hand over her face. "What did I do?"

Bryan sat up immediately and reached out to touch her shoulder. "Sweetheart..."

Callie began to collect her clothing. Still feeling disoriented, she held her shirt up to cover her nakedness. She knew only one thing for sure: She had to get away from Bryan as quickly as possible.

Bryan grabbed her shoulders firmly. "No, Callie, you're not leaving me."

"But, Bryan…"

"Listen to me, Callie. You knew this was going to happen sooner or later." He looked down ruefully at the faint marks on her hips and breasts. "I'm sorry I hurt you and no, I didn't intend for it to happen tonight, but we were going to be together eventually, and you know it."

Callie still reached for her clothing, trying frantically to move away from his hands. "Bryan, just let me put my clothes on…"

Bryan brushed her locs away from her face. "No, Callie, you've got to go home tomorrow. Just stay with me tonight, please." He leaned forward, his mouth mere centimeters from her own as he whispered, "Baby, I'll be leaving soon, and we won't be able to be together for a long time. I just want to hold you. Please stay." Bryan was almost desperate to continue their embrace. The need to have more of her was urgent. Now that he'd had her, he had no intention of ever letting her go.

When Callie moved hesitantly under his hands, he moved them to her shoulders, stilling her as he captured her lips in a tender kiss. He moved away slowly, until his lips were a mere hairsbreadth from his own. Staring down into her liquid brown eyes, he implored, "Callie, stay with me."

Callie breathed in deeply, closing her eyes as she reflected on what had just happened. To do so would only make bad matters worse as far as she was concerned, but the invitation to spend the night in his arms was impossible to resist. She leaned forward, placing her head on his shoulder.

Bryan moved his hands up, cupping her head to his body as he inhaled deeply. She would stay. All was not lost.

As the fingers of dawn painted a pastel palette across the sky above the Santa Monica Mountains, Bryan woke to a dream fulfilled. Each time he'd awakened during the night, he'd looked down on the vision Callie made lying against him and simply couldn't believe that his fantasies had come true. Though they had made love only one additional time, the sensation of her flesh against his was as intimate as the most carnal act. One of her arms was flung across his chest, and her thigh lay across his hips. Her hair was strewn over his chest from where her head rested on his shoulder. He rubbed it in circular motions against his skin. As he had suspected, the soft coily texture was extraordinarily sensual. He lay back in the bed, luxuriating in the feel of her silky flesh against his own. But she had an early flight and he had to talk to her before she left. There was no way he was letting her leave until they came to some type of understanding. He gently shook Callie awake. "Come on, sweetheart," he murmured. "We need to talk."

Callie and Bryan sat facing each other on a beach that was abandoned at this early hour. Clad only in his pajama bottoms, Bryan's legs were splayed to the outside of hers. He held both her hands firmly ensconced in his own as he tried to formulate the best way to tell her what was in his heart. He knew he was unlikely to get another opportunity to talk to her like this, and was terrified that he would botch it. He'd never wanted to express such feelings to a woman before, and didn't know where to begin. He waited until she raised her eyes inquiringly.

Taking a deep breath he began. "Callie, last night was the most incredible night of my life. For the first time in my life, I felt…" He fumbled, unable to put such wondrous emotions into words. "I can't even tell you what I felt, but it was unbelievable. I wish things were different, and I could take as much time as I want to be with you, but I've got to finish up this tour. There's no way out of it." He rushed on when she didn't respond. "Do you understand what I'm saying?" He took another deep breath and held it, afraid of what Callie's answer would be.

Callie had lowered her eyes the instant Bryan mentioned the previous evening. "Bryan, I don't think any of this is a good idea. There are just way too many things separating us."

Bryan placed a finger under her chin, raising her head until her eyes met his own. "Callie, the only thing separating us right now is you. We are two people who care about each other. Are you going to throw that away because other people don't approve, or because of the business I happen to be in?"

Callie broke eye contact and lowered her head again, but couldn't think of anything to say.

Bryan continued, "Callie, like I told you last night, you knew damned well that this was going to happen sooner or later. Okay, the physical part happened sooner than I had planned, but baby, we've got something here, something I've never had before…" He broke off, unable to think of anything else he could say that might convince her.

Callie knew she was being unfair to Bryan. He was right. Deep down inside she had known that their relationship would eventually come to this, and if she hadn't wanted it, she should have stopped it long before they slept together. Breaking it off now would make things even more difficult. She lowered her head to her knees. "Bryan, I do want to be with you," she admitted, "but…"

Bryan pulled her closer, relief making his body go limp. "Let's not think about the 'buts' right now."

Callie turned her head to look at the seagulls diving for their morning meal. "It just seems to me that it would be simpler for us both to just let it go."

Bryan cuddled her against his chest. "Callie, I don't think either of us has ever taken the easy way out, no real reason to start now."

From that position, nestled in the warm safety of his arms, Callie couldn't think of any real reason to start either.

Callie and Bryan stayed on the beach for as long as they could, but eventually they had to get ready to go to the airport for Callie's flight back to Alabama. Bryan would be staying in L.A., rehearsing for the resumption of Storm Crow's tour. Callie had packed the previous day, so it was really just a matter of checking the house to ensure that she had not left any of her belongings behind. As they sat in the kitchen enjoying one last cup of coffee before they departed for the airport, Bryan slid the tiniest cell phone she'd ever seen across the table to Callie. Smaller even than a pager, it gleamed with an odd metallic sheen.

She picked it up and examined it curiously.

"I've always refused to have a cell phone before. There are times when I don't want to be in contact with anyone, but that doesn't apply to you. With this cell phone, I'll be reachable twenty-four hours a day." He took it from her hand, and flipped it open. "I've got one like it. Yours has my number programmed in it. You'll be the only person to have that number, so you can reach me any time you want, okay?" He handed the telephone back to Callie. "I've got a manual and an extra battery for it around here some-where, but it seems pretty easy to operate. This way we'll be able to stay in touch, no matter where I am."

Callie continued to examine the cell phone. "It's really tiny," she mused. "Do you think you'll be able to keep up with yours?" she asked, an impish glint in her eye.

Bryan smiled at her. "I always hold onto what's important to me." He gave her a pointed look. "It's a trait commonly found amongst gutter rats like myself."

Callie had to laugh at his self-deprecating humor. "Bryan, I'm really going to miss you," she murmured, quietly reaching for his hand.

Bryan gave her big grin. "You could always come with us. It would be a blast," he continued enthusias-tically. "We've got some great cities left, especially Miami. I love Cuban food. Have you ever tried it?"

Callie shook her head. "No, Bryan, I've never had Cuban food. But I'd have to be crazy to go on tour with you and your band. One week with you guys has aged me at least ten years! I don't know when you people sleep, and my God, the amount of beer y'all drink would keep a brewery in business for centuries. No, that's okay, I'll return to my nice, quiet, sane bookstore."

Bryan smirked at that comment. He'd spent enough time at Books and So Forth to know that the largest collection of kooks he'd seen outside L.A. patronized it.

They reminisced a bit longer about the insanity of the previous week, postponing their departure as long as possible. When it was impossible to delay the inevitable any longer, they began loading Callie's belongings into Bryan's truck for the trip to the airport.

Try as she might, Callie could not resist the need to hold onto Bryan as long as possible. She feared that she was making a spectacle of herself, but at this point, she was beyond caring. Bryan felt much the same way, and they spent most of the time they waited in the VIP lounge quietly embracing each other. They remained entwined until final boarding call, then reluctantly separated, knowing it would be a long time before they had this pleasure again.

Callie snuggled down deeper into the warm confines of the fluffy pink quilt on her bed, still using the cell phone. It was after midnight, and she had had a very long day. Bryan's schedule was still insane. The band's rehearsals were often overly long because they were really feeling the vibe. With the time difference, his promised calls usually came very late in the evening. As she yawned her way through each work day, Callie would remonstrate with herself to cut the conversations short, but she never did. She took so much comfort in talking to him while lying in bed, she couldn't bring herself to limit the time. So what if she sleepwalked through most of her days?

"Okay, Bryan, you've really got to stop doing this."

"What, a guy can't even send his lady a teddy bear these days?"

"Bryan! He's four feet tall, for crying out loud," she exclaimed, looking exasperatedly at the gorgeous Steiff teddy bear that sat in the corner of her bedroom. His biscuit-colored fur had a sheen and luster present in only the most high-end stuffed toys. The fluffy white fur on his belly and snout was especially luxurious, and Callie had been compulsively stroking it since it arrived that afternoon.

"Nonsense," Bryan replied. "Three and a half at the most!"

Callie tried the reasonable approach. "Bryan, he's bigger than my mother."

"Callie, I've seen garden gnomes bigger than your mother," Bryan retorted.

Callie giggled into the telephone, enjoying this frivolous exchange with Bryan as she had all the others they'd had since she returned to Alabama. They'd developed a pattern: The UPS man delivered her daily gift, and she and Bryan would argue over that gift during their nightly bedtime telephone call. Over the past couple of weeks the gifts had varied from the sweet and simple—three-dozen pink tulips, her favorites ascertained from a very cooperative Tonya—to the ridiculously extravagant—a ten-carat, though Tonya claimed it was at least twelve, pink sapphire line bracelet. She'd never seen pink sapphires before, but Tonya, a font of information on just about every subject, told her that sapphires come in many colors. Along with the more familiar blue they could also be yellow, pink, green, or red, the red being known as rubies.

Though it was breathtakingly lovely, she had every intention of returning the bracelet to Bryan, despite his protests, as soon as possible. Unfortunately, she'd just been too busy in the past few days to do so. At least, that's what she told herself. Deep down, she had to admit that the gift was enchanting and she was loathe to part with it. However, her dignity and self-respect demanded that she object to his generosity. She'd seen too much of that type of thing in L.A. The bear was absolutely beautiful, but Callie had no doubt that he'd cost a small fortune.

"Bryan, I thought we'd agreed, no more extravagant gifts," she persisted.

"Extravagant? Look, it was either the bear or a pink Jaguar."

"A pink Jaguar?" Callie gasped. Had the boy totally lost his mind? A frown marred her smooth brow as she pondered the next question. "And who buys a pink Jaguar?" She paused for a moment, stunned by the prospect of driving around Maple Fork looking like a Mary Kay lady going through a midlife crisis. "For that matter, where on earth do you buy a pink Jaguar?"

"This is L.A., baby," Bryan replied breezily. "For enough money, you can get whatever you want. But anyway, Jon said you struck him as more of a Volvo kind of girl. I could see his point. You know, with you being an emerging robber baron and all. Unfortunately, there's a six-week waiting list to get them in pink."

"Bryan, don't you dare buy me a pink Volvo!" Callie shrieked into the telephone.

"Why not?" Bryan asked, puzzled. "Tonya said pink was your favorite color. But that's okay. I'm sure they wouldn't mind if I ordered another color. What would you like? Or would you prefer the Jaguar after all?" he asked hopefully.

"Bryan!" Callie shouted. "I don't want you to buy me a car at all. Actually, I don't want you to buy me anything else, period, okay?" When Bryan didn't respond, Callie asked, "Why do you keep buying me stuff anyway? Aren't you supposed to be rehearsing? You must spend all your time shopping."

"I don't know, it just seems like when I'm buying presents for you, we're closer or something. I got so excited when I found the bracelet because I could just imagine the look on your face when you opened the box. The guy at Harry Winston's showed me all kinds of stuff, but when I saw the bracelet, it just reminded me of you, so pretty and elegant. The stones kind of flashed and sparked, the way your eyes do when you're annoyed with me. I just knew you would love it. I think that's the cool part of it, imagining your reaction. I've never felt like this before. Sure, I've given women stuff before, but usually it was, you know, a part of the deal, and I usually sent Kelly to pick something out. With you, it's different, you're different. I like looking for things that'll make you smile, that you'll think are nice. It's been lots of fun. I think in a way it helps me deal with being away from you."

Callie smiled. She knew she would keep the bracelet now. How could she resist when there was such sweet sentiment behind the purchase? He was like a young boy with a crush, making daisy chains for the little girl down the street. Probably the world's most outrageously expensive daisy chains, but daisy chains nonetheless. It was absolutely delightful, and a far cry from what she'd originally thought.

Bryan went on, "I guess if I can't be with you, I can send something to be with you. Like the bear. If I can't sleep with you, at least he can."

"But he's four feet tall, Bryan. Why did you get him so big?"

"Well, you're a pretty fitful sleeper. I figured you'd lose a smaller bear," he chuckled.

"I am not a fitful sleeper," Callie protested indignantly, even though she knew that both Tonya and her sisters had made the same claim and refused to sleep with her under any circumstances. "Anyway, Bryan, I'm not the type of girl who sleeps with a stuffed animal. I think it's sweet that you want to buy me things, but could you try not to be so excessive? There's no way I can explain such expensive gifts to my family. I don't want them to think that I'm…well, you know."

"You don't want them to think I'm keeping you?" Bryan asked softly, irritation evident in his tone.

"Well, yeah."

"Callie, it's not like that."

"I know that, Bryan, but I don't think I could possibly explain it to them. So no pink Volvo, okay?"

Bryan's breath whistled as he blew it out between his teeth, not trying to hide his annoyance as he reluctantly capitulated. "Okay, baby, no cars." He paused for a moment. "What about Christmas?"

"No cars for Christmas, either, Bryan."

He laughed irreverently. "You know that's not what I meant! What are you doing Christmas? The guys and I have decided that things are going so well that we're going to take a couple of days for the holiday." His voice dropped to a seductive whisper. "I miss you so much. baby. Would it be okay if I came back down there for a visit?"

"Oh, that would be great! I'd hoped y'all would break for the holidays, but I wasn't sure you'd be able to. It would give my folks a chance to get to know you better, and you could help out in the store. This time of year we need all the help we can get." Callie chuckled at the last comment. Clearing overstock bins was not her sweetheart's idea of fun.

"Okay, I should've known you'd find a way to get more free labor out of me. I assume I'll be staying with you?" Bryan asked, making love again foremost on his mind."

"Actually Bryan…" Callie hesitated, she knew this was not going to go over well. "I don't think that would be a good idea. I don't want Cynthia and Addie to think that I'm sleeping around. My folks said if you came they'd like it if you spent the holiday at their house." Bryan yelped into the telephone just as she'd known he would, but at least he hadn't started swearing. Yet. "Don't worry, I'll be there too."

"Yeah, but who's going to call in the S.W.A.T. team?" Bryan retorted irritably. "Callie, I don't think staying with my girlfriend's parents is ever a good idea. Especially when her daddy's already made it clear that *he don't like my kind around there*," he said in such an excellent imitation of her father's big booming voice that Callie couldn't help laughing.

"Bryan, we'll have a great time." Then at his snort of disbelief, "Okay, we probably won't have a great time, but I really need to do it this way. Please? I want to see you, but I can't just pretend my family doesn't exist."

Bryan groaned inwardly. Clearly there would be little or no opportunity for him to have her sweet body again, but he couldn't resist doing anything Callie asked of him. "Okay, I'll come to Alabama and let your dad kick my ass, *again*, but you're going to owe me big time." He perked up. "What about after Christmas? We're doing a gig up in Canada for New Year's. It's just a warm-up really, to give Thad a chance to adjust to playing in front of a crowd. He's really going to lose it. That boy just doesn't like playing in public, but anyway, it's at this really cool ski resort. You'll love it. There's a great spa, so you can even say you're doing research for your five-year plan to dominate the American economy."

"You've already had poor Kelly buy my ticket, haven't you?" Callie asked suspiciously, knowing how Bryan operated.

Bryan hooted with laughter, but didn't deny it. "You do know me so well. So, will you come?"

"Yes, Bryan, I'll be there," Callie agreed, relieved that he'd capitulated so easily and agreed to stay with her parents. Another cross-country trip paled in comparison.

The conversation continued as Callie asked about the band and Bryan told her how well Thad was working out. He explained that the situation was still strained at times, but they were playing great. Adversity sometimes produced the best music, or so Bryan sincerely hoped. Like all the other nights they strung the conversation out for as long as they could, but eventually they had to say goodnight.

After she hung up the phone, Callie lay in bed staring at the bear she'd decided to call Bartholomew. Somehow he looked right at home in her bedroom. Her taste was very tailored and the soft pink tones of her bedroom were absent of any lace or flourishes. Tonya referred to it as the "ruffle-free zone." Of course any bedroom would be plain compared to Tonya's, which in Callie's opinion resembled an upscale bordello. Decorated in bright jewel tones, everything in Tonya's room was festooned with ruffles, lace or bows, and sometimes all three. Tonya called it her "girlie" room. Callie preferred much softer, relaxing hues, and of course, a clutter-free environment. Her large brass bed was a hand-me-down from another relative, and the cozy pink quilt had been made by Big Mama, her father's mother. Callie studied Bartholomew a little longer, then feeling lonelier than she had in her life, she pulled the bear into bed with her. Wrapping her arms around the furry creature, she fell into the first peaceful slumber she'd had since leaving L.A.

# CHAPTER 13

Tonya moved another stack of books, paused to wipe the sweat off her brow, then glanced back over her shoulder at Callie. "So when were you planning to tell me that you and Bryan did the 'do' while you were in L.A.?"

Her question was greeted by a resounding crash as Callie knocked over the pile of books she was moving out of the overstock bins. "Tonya," Callie hissed in a high-pitched whisper, "did you forget that Cynthia and Addie are here?"

Tonya merely shook her head. "Callie, they're in the break room getting something to drink, and you didn't answer my question," she pointed out.

Callie flopped down on the floor next to the stack of books she'd knocked over. It was well past midnight, and she was exhausted. Christmas Eve was only two days away, and they would open early with all kinds of door busters and special discounts for their early-bird customers. This was an ideal opportunity to eliminate their overstock and remaindered books, but keeping the shelves stocked was back-breaking work. With extended hours the store was open until nine o'clock the week before Christmas and customers were taking advantage of the specials. Cynthia and Addie had come down to help them restock the shelves, tidy the store and help maintain attractive merchandising.

Callie looked up at Tonya balefully. "How did you know?"

Tonya sank down beside her friend on the floor. "Let's see, you come back glowing like an alien invasion, and old boy starts inundating you with diamonds and pearls and you didn't think I'd guess what happened? Hell, I started to ask how it was, but I think it's obvious because dude's been spending money like Tiffany's is having a fire sale."

Callie buried her face in her hands, mortified by the accuracy of what Tonya was saying. "Tonya! He's only sent one piece of jewelry, and I had every intention of sending it back."

Sharp as ever Tonya caught her slip of the tongue. "Had every intention? Hmmmm, what happened to 'most definitely' sending it back? Told you those twelve carats would grow on you!" she added smugly.

"Hush, I don't want Cynthia and Addie to hear about it! You know what my folks will think!" Callie paused, reflecting on what Bryan had said the last time they'd discussed this topic. "You know, Tonya, when he first sent the bracelet, I thought he was trying to buy me or treating me like a kept woman. I told you that." Tonya nodded. "But the other night, we talked about it again, and I could see that he just really wanted to give me something pretty. It wasn't about trying to own me or anything. I think I was being unfair to him."

Tonya pursed her lips, "What do you mean by unfair?"

Callie rubbed her hands over her thighs as she tried to frame her words. "I think I was holding him to a different standard than I would a black man. I mean, would I have questioned a black man's motives in giving me a bracelet? I think I let other folks' stereotypes mess with my head. I know Bryan better than that. He's not that way, and I shouldn't have thought it for a moment." She paused to mull over that thought. "Did you have these problems when you went out with Nate?" Callie referred to the white guy Tonya had dated when they were in college. She hadn't asked too many questions about the relationship at the time, assuming that he was just another one of Tonya's flights of fancy. The relationship had lasted more than a year, though, which was much better than her usual track record.

Tonya laughed self-deprecatingly. "I don't think Nate and I ever got that deep. We were too busy doing other things." She stared off into space as if lost in thought. "I never looked at it that closely, but you know me, I never really gave a damn what other people say. Folks have been calling me a whore since high school, big deal," she said dismissively.

Callie saw through the bravado. She remembered those rumors and knew how much they had hurt Tonya as they both had been virgins until they were in college. Nate had been Tonya's first, and the relationship had lasted until he went off to join the Peace Corps their junior year.

"So what's the deal between you two?" Tonya asked.

"I guess you could say we're dating. He said he wants to be with me as much as he can, and I want that too."

"Cool, so when are you seeing him again? Didn't you say they're about to go out on tour soon?"

Callie began straightening the books. "Yeah," she said glumly. "They're going back on the road in January. He'll be here day after tomorrow. He's spending Christmas here at my folks' house, and then we're going to Canada a few days before New Year's. After that, who knows?"

"Callie, why are you leading that boy into the lion's den? You know how your daddy feels about white men, especially white men who are trying to get," she paused with a wink, "have gotten into his daughter's drawers." Then the second half of Callie's statement sank in. "You're going to Canada with him for New Year's? Wow! Have you told your folks about that yet?"

"No, I haven't told anyone besides you." Callie tried to change the subject by asking, "Do you think you'll be okay with the store? The literacy group and the financial planning workshops don't start back up until after New Year's. It's only for a few days, and

Cynthia and Addie are out of school and they can help. Plus Roshonda…"

Tonya interrupted, "Of course I'll be okay. That's why we hired Roshonda in the first place, remember? So that we could have a personal life. Of course," she continued sarcastically, "some of us have way more life than others." Much to Callie's chagrin, she wouldn't be distracted from the previous topic. "But you still didn't answer my question. What about your folks?"

"Tonya," Callie said earnestly, "I really like Bryan, and I want to spend as much time with him as possible. I know Daddy will be difficult, but I don't think they'll do anything to hurt his feelings. I just want them to get a chance to know him as a person, you know? Not as the 'long-haired, drug-using rocker from California,' but as Bryan, the man I lo…" She stopped. Where on earth had the "l" word come from? "Anyway, Tonya, I miss him. You know how the poems and stuff talk about missing somebody so much you ache?" Tonya nodded. "I always thought that was a bunch of nonsense. Now I know better. A thousand times a day I think of something I want to tell Bryan about, then by the time he calls I've forgotten, and we end up just sitting there breathing into the telephone because we don't want to hang up. I didn't think it was possible to miss somebody so much."

Tonya hadn't missed her friend's slip of the tongue, but deciding that Callie had been tortured enough for one long day, she reached over and gave her a brief hug. "Girl, you know I understand, but…"

"I know, but I'm an adult now. I've never given my folks any reason to question my judgment or choices. I know they don't like it, but they'll have to live with it. Being with Bryan is worth it."

Their little chat was disturbed by a shout from the stockroom. "Callie," Cynthia called, "your cell phone is ringing." She rushed into the room giggling. "I think it's your boyfriend."

Callie snatched the telephone from her hand and answered it, then walked to the back of the room for privacy to talk to Bryan.

"Did you see that cell phone he got her?" Cynthia asked Tonya. "It's the latest Motorola, and it's titanium plated! I can't wait until I can finally tell the girls at school about all this. They're not going to believe it! It's the most awesome cell phone in the world, and he gave her a direct line! That's sooo romantic!" she gushed.

Tonya grunted in disbelief at Cynthia's enthusiasm. "Oh yeah, nothing says 'I love you' like titanium plating."

"No, baby, please, I can't take anymore. We've got to stop now," Bryan gasped, moving away from Callie on the sofa. It was Christmas Eve, and Callie and Bryan were supposed to be watching a movie in the den of her parents' house. The rest of the family had retired for the evening, leaving them alone. Bryan couldn't believe Callie's behavior. He'd come to Alabama firm in his resolve to keep his hands to himself while in the Lawson home because he had no intention of getting dressed down again by her father. Unfortunately he hadn't taken Callie into consideration when making that resolution. He hadn't a clue as to why, but his usually reserved Callie had suddenly turned playful. From the moment he arrived, he'd known he was in trouble. She'd jumped into his arms and planted a huge wet kiss on him right in front of her family. Bryan wasn't sure but he thought he'd seen Jesse Lawson grow fangs right before his very eyes. During the embrace he'd been careful to keep his arms splayed to avoid even the appearance of having initiated it.

Fortunately her family hadn't noticed when his eyes crossed from the bolt of desire that shot through him when he felt Callie's bare foot stroking his calf during dinner. Despite that close call, she had resumed her antics while they cleaned up after dinner, playfully popping him on the backside with the dish towel.

The soft, wet kisses they'd shared since her family had left the den had quickly evolved into deep, passionate exchanges. And somehow they'd wound up prone on the sofa, feverishly straining to fit their bodies together in a way that was not possible through their clothing. The fierce grinding had stressed his perilous control to the point that he either had to end the embrace or make love to her right there on the sofa.

"But I missed you," Callie pouted petulantly, as if that excused the way she had jeopardized his life. She leaned against him and reached up to stroke his hair. "I really, really missed you."

Bryan disengaged again. "Callie, you know how your father feels about me. He made it clear that he didn't appreciate me disrespecting his home the last time I was here. What if he'd walked in and caught me between your legs like that?"

Callie crossed her arms across her chest. She knew Bryan was right, and she really did appreciate the way he was working so hard to make a good impression on her family. He wasn't accustomed to having to behave in any prescribed manner; indeed, people generally went out their way to accommodate him.

"I'm sorry, sweetie, I know I've been a bad girl, but I can't seem to help it. I guess I've gotten used to having you around, and now that you're not here…" She shrugged. "I realize what a big part of my life you really are."

Bryan smiled. "I feel the same way, Callie. That's why I don't want to mess things up with your folks. I know they're very important to you, and I want them to at least trust me to take care of you and respect their home, even if they can't come to like me, okay?"

Callie nodded, seeing the logic in this. "I think dinner really went well, don't you? You and Daddy talked about football and stuff."

"Yeah, he's a big Titans and Falcons fan, and I really like the Raiders, but all in all, it was pretty cool. That's why I don't want to blow it by having him catch us making out on the sofa like a couple of kids." He leaned over and brushed her hair out of her face. "But I can't wait until we get to Whistler. I'll show you how much I've missed you." Then he goosed her. "You'll definitely pay for your misbehavior at the dinner table, young lady," he growled.

Callie giggled. "I couldn't help it, you were being just too well-behaved. 'Thank you so very much, Mrs. Lawson,' 'I've never had such an incredible meal, Mrs. Lawson,' 'May I assist you in clearing, Mrs. Lawson?'" She mimicked his deep, rasping voice.

" 'Could I blow your nose for you, Mrs. Lawson?' I just couldn't take any more!"

Bryan continued to tickle Callie, delighted by this change in her manner towards him. It was yet another intriguing dimension of this complex woman he adored. Now if he could only survive it for two more days.

He moved over to the end of the sofa, pulling Callie with him to rest her head on his shoulder. They sat contemplating the fire he'd built earlier. He suspected he'd impressed Callie's father with his ability to build a fire and chop and gather wood. He had B.T. and his endless attempts to "make him into a man" to thank for that. While B.T. was no outdoors man, unless you counted his fanatical golf game, he had insisted that Bryan and Brodie learn manly skills.

Callie's mother seemed to be warming up to him. She'd just beamed when he insisted on clearing up after supper. He'd even heard her tell Jesse, "That boy might not be so bad." Jesse had only grunted in response, but it had to be a step in the right direction. He pulled Callie closer. Two more days of sexual frustration wasn't too great a price to pay for the type of progress he'd made. He stroked her shoulder. Soon, very soon, he'd have her all to himself in the snow-capped peaks of the Canadian Rockies.

The next morning Bryan awakened to the sound of Cynthia and Addie knocking on everyone's door to awaken them for the highlight of the day, at least as far as they were concerned: the opening of the Christmas presents. Though it was barely seven o'clock, he was already awake. Callie had given him advance notice of her sisters' Christmas morning wake-up call. He lay in bed until he heard the family members move downstairs, then got up and hastily dressed in black jeans and a charcoal gray fisherman's sweater. He didn't bother to put on his boots and instead padded downstairs in his stocking feet.

The smell of sausage frying and coffee brewing greeted Bryan. Cynthia and Addie had begun breakfast as early as possible in an effort to speed everyone along to the main event. He followed his nose into the kitchen. He found Callie, as he'd known he would, at the coffeepot getting fueled up for the day. She looked deliciously rumpled in a pair of snug-fitting jeans and an oversized red crew-neck sweater. She gave him a somnolent glance and it was all he could do to resist the urge to take her back upstairs to her bed, or his bed, or for that matter, any flat surface. When he found himself contemplating the mechanics of making love without a flat surface, he moved to pour his own cup of coffee to distract himself from his prurient thoughts.

Fortunately Addie announced that breakfast was ready, and they moved to join Mr. and Mrs. Lawson in the dining room. Though most meals in the Lawson home were eaten in the kitchen, Christmas was a special occasion. Edith Lawson had set the table with her Christmas china and they drank their orange juice from her wedding crystal.

Addie and Cynthia had prepared homemade biscuits and scrambled eggs with cream cheese and sausage. Fresh fruit rounded out the meal. Much to the girls' dismay, everyone ate their breakfast in a leisurely fashion, making polite conversation about the issues of the day. Jesse Lawson especially enjoyed teasing them about their presents.

"I don't know why y'all are in such a rush. I've told you girls already, you're not getting anything but coal and switches," he drawled laconically.

Both girls happily joined into what was clearly a family ritual that was enjoyed by all. They pouted and made doe eyes at their father and Addie even managed to produce a tear or two until Jesse finally relented.

"All right, y'all might have a gift or two under that tree," he conceded.

They both rushed over to shower him with hugs and kisses. "Thank you, Daddy!"

Finally the family moved from the table to the den, where the eight-foot Christmas tree was surrounded by mounds of presents. Callie and Bryan shared the love seat, while Edith and Jesse sat on the sofa. Addie and Cynthia rushed over to sit on the floor next to the tree.

As the girls took turns calling out each person's name and handing them their presents, Bryan was surprised to find that each family member had bought him a gift. He hadn't expected it, though he had brought presents for each of them. He had spent a great deal of time thinking about Edith Lawson's present before finally deciding on a simple gold circle pin. It was perfect for so classy a lady, but not so expensive that it would be daunting. He had originally planned to give Jesse Lawson season tickets for the Tennessee Titans, but abandoned the idea when he realized that Jesse might think he was trying to use his money to exert undue influence on him. Not that Bryan was above trying that tactic, but he had enough savvy to know it probably wouldn't work. Besides, he needed to keep something in abeyance in case he really screwed up. He had learned strategy at the knee of a master. B.T. would be extremely proud. Instead, he gave him two tickets that were good for the home game of his choice. Cynthia and Addie were thrilled with their Apple iPods. Fortunately the portable MP3 players closely resembled ordinary personal stereos so the Lawsons didn't know how expensive the little gadgets were. He'd also given them Steiff Teddy Bears, though theirs were considerably smaller than the one he'd given Callie.

Edith Lawson presented him with a lovely pale blue cable-knit sweater and told him, "You can't wear black all the time, son. It's just not natural. And the color will look pretty with your eyes."

Callie doubled over laughing at the expression on Bryan's face. "My goodness, Bryan, what are you going to do about your image? You can't be seen in real live colors," she gasped as she struggled to get the words out around her the bubbles of laughter.

Bryan gave her a surreptitious pinch and assured her mother that he'd be more than happy to wear anything such a beautiful woman recommended. Callie rolled her eyes at his flowery language. Jesse Lawson gave him a Leatherman pocketknife, and Cynthia and Addie gave him a set of guitar picks and elastic bands for his hair.

Addie smiled up at him shyly. "Callie told us you're always losing your picks and hair bands, so we gave you super-sized boxes."

Much to their delight, he gave each girl a peck on the cheek. "It's so nice to have my own personal elves. Now if you could only find a way to help me keep up with my keys."

Callie sighed dramatically. "Hey, there's only so much us curly-toed creatures can do. Helping you keep up with everything you lose would be a full-time job."

"Yeah," he whispered back, "but I give great benefits."

Addie and Cynthia's second gift to Bryan was a double picture frame. On one side was a snapshot of Callie as a baby, on the other a more current portrait taken when the family did a session with a local photographer the previous summer. Callie was wearing a simple rose-colored wrap dress, her hair was pinned up and she had the same shy smile he remembered from the first day they'd met. In the baby picture she looked to be about a year old and was clad only in a diaper. Her hair formed a huge curly afro around her head and she was grinning, showing all four of her teeth. As he gazed intently at the baby picture, he felt a warmth and tightening in his chest as he suddenly realized that he wanted a replica of that tiny, chubby-cheeked creature of his own. He wondered how Callie would feel about having his babies. Callie had moved over closer to look at the pictures, and when she glanced up, their eyes locked. She knew he'd been thinking about babies. She lowered her eyes immediately, surprised by how much she wanted them too.

She moved back over to her end of the love seat and watched closely as he opened her present to him. It had taken hours to purchase the autographed

Johnny Cash boxed CD set on eBay. She was convinced she had paid far too much for it, but when she saw the way his lips trembled as he traced the signature with his finger, she knew that it was worth any price. When he turned to look at her, the emotion in those tempestuous blue eyes was more telling than even the most passionate kiss.

Knowing his penchant for giving her extravagant presents, she opened her gift very cautiously. All the goodwill he had engendered from her family during this trip could be undone in that very moment. The box was small, just the right size for another shockingly expensive piece of jewelry, but instead it contained a small card indicating that she was the recipient of the complete six-volume set of Edward Gibbon's *History of the Decline and Fall of the Roman Empire.* The gift was pricey, but it was not the type of thing a man would give his kept woman.

The gift pleased Edith Lawson as well. As a librarian she realized its expense, but more importantly, it showed that this young man understood her daughter and was clearly on a mission to win her heart. If he'd taken the time to appreciate what such a gift would mean to Callie, she could no longer doubt his intentions. Especially in light of the fact that he was willing to go out of his way to impress her family. She would still watch Bryan closely, but she was more than half convinced that he was sincere in his feelings for her daughter.

Callie looked up at Bryan, one eyebrow raised inquiringly.

Bryan knew exactly what that silent query meant. His Callie was mercenary to the end. "Yes, Callie, I bought the set through Books and So Forth. Tonya helped me. And yes, I paid retail."

Callie grinned at Bryan, happy that such a lucrative sale had been channeled through her store. Then maintaining a sedate demeanor in front of her family, she reached over to give him a brief peck on the lips.

Bryan grinned back, "Now don't forget, you'll have to share. I've always wanted that set for myself."

# CHAPTER 14

Vancouver, British Columbia, was one of the most breathtakingly lovely cities Callie had ever seen. As they drove up the mountain towards the ski resort Callie thought that the copywriter who had coined the slogan "From Sea to Sky" in describing the city, had earned every penny of what was undoubtedly a huge bonus check. Deep, crystal-clear alpine lakes were surrounded by spiraling snowcapped peaks. Having grown up in a region of tall, skinny, loblolly pines, Callie was astounded by the height and size the pines here attained. Expecting the type of arctic weather for which Canada was famous, she had been surprised to find that it wasn't much colder than it had been in Alabama when they left. Bryan explained that this part of Canada was actually rain forest and experienced moderate temperatures because of the warm, Pacific currents. Callie was surprised to learn that there were rain forests at this latitude, but was grateful for the pleasant weather.

The resort was designed like a lodge. The main building, the hub, housed the public spaces, restaurants, and meeting rooms. It was connected to the various chalets through a courtyard. The owner of the resort was a friend of B.T.'s and, as Storm Crow would be playing there on New Year's Eve, Callie and Bryan were rushed through check-in procedures with a minimum of fuss. Their chalet was dominated by a massive slate fireplace that was complemented by natural stone flooring and oversized furniture. The living room opened into a small kitchenette and there were also two bedrooms. However, it was understood that they would be using only one. After arriving in their room, Callie and Bryan moved into each other's arms for a long embrace. The lack of close contact during their stay at Callie's parents' house had been brutal for both of them. Callie almost purred with pleasure from being in Bryan's arms, and Bryan closed his eyes, savoring every moment. In all too short a time, he would be separated from her again.

The other band members had already arrived and had left a message for Bryan and Callie to join them for dinner at seven o'clock. Bryan groaned when he got the message. He'd planned to order room service, have a leisurely dinner with Callie, then spend the rest of the evening making up for their long separation. He looked at Callie, noting her drooping shoulders and the shadows around her eyes. The cross-country trip had been hard on her. Though they'd only had to change planes twice, it had still been a grueling trip. Maybe dinner with the guys and an early bedtime would be better. After all, there was always the morning...

"Baby, you look really tired. You want to lay down and take a nap? We've still got a couple of hours until dinner."

Callie snuggled her face closer into Bryan's neck. "Are you going to join me?"

Bryan grinned widely. "I don't think I've ever had a better invitation."

∽⚬∾

Dinner was a riotous affair. The main restaurant, with its stone walls and timber-framed ceiling, was filled with après-ski revelers, and Callie and Bryan's table was one of the rowdiest. Soothed by one another's presence after their extended separation, they had overslept and joined the others much later than scheduled. This, of course, caused rife speculation as to why they were late. Callie blushed furiously. Though she and Bryan hadn't made love, she was terribly disconcerted that everyone assumed they had. Bryan, who was not embarrassed in the least, finally took pity on his shamefaced girlfriend and shushed the rest of the band members.

Callie was disappointed to discover that she would be the only woman on the trip. Apparently Twist and Naysa had had yet another disagreement and she had decided not to come. Cinnamon was spending the holidays with her family and hadn't joined them either. Callie liked both women and had looked forward to spending some time with them on this trip, especially when the band was rehearsing.

As the evening wore on the teasing got progressively worse. Undoubtedly the copious amounts of wine and beer added to the merriment, but soon the conversation turned to various exploits of Storm Crow on the road in previous years. Twist was clearly trying to impress Thad and elevated the raunchiness level with each subsequent beer. Groupies were a favorite topic and Callie was fascinated when Twist mentioned a unique interlude that had involved Bryan, crunchy peanut butter, and an especially enthusiastic young lady.

"Bryan, what on earth did you do to that poor girl, and why did it involve crunchy peanut butter?" Callie asked, wide-eyed at the possibilities. Everything she could think of seemed preposterously uncomfortable and maybe even dangerous.

Bryan scratched his head. "Well, I do prefer crunchy, but everybody knows it only works with the creamy kind," he responded obliquely.

This was greeted with hoots of laughter from the band, and Bryan joined in when Callie hissed her irritation. "What only works? What did y'all do?"

Gasping for breath, Bryan rasped out, "Believe me, baby, you really don't want to know. Besides, I was much younger then. I haven't touched the stuff in years."

Jon and Twist booed their disbelief at Bryan's comment. "Okay, I swear, I haven't done peanut butter in months." He glared at his friends, daring them to say otherwise. "And you guys really need to give it a rest."

They calmed down somewhat, and the rest of dinner was more subdued. They made arrangements for an early morning ski run on one of Brodie's favorite trails. In keeping with Brodie's impetuous nature, it was a double black diamond, one of the toughest courses at the resort. It would be challenging to everyone but Twist, who was the daredevil of the group. They looked at the run as a tribute to Brodie and a welcoming ritual to Thad, who had fit in with the band as if he'd always been there. Callie intended to sleep in, then join Bryan later on one of the green trails, maybe a blue one if she hadn't lost all her skiing ability. She'd learned to ski on a school trip to Vermont and was happy to hear that skiing on powder was significantly easier than on the wet snow back east.

The exercise would be good for Bryan, but she worried about the emotional catharsis that might occur. Although Bryan seemed to have put Brodie's death in perspective as a tragedy, one he didn't have the power to prevent, would making this ski run evoke memories and emotions better left undisturbed? Additionally, she had studied the map of the route they planned to take, and was concerned about their skiing such a dangerous trail. While they all seemed to be experienced on this particular course, they'd never skied it under stressful circumstances. Bryan probably wouldn't have a breakdown or anything that dramatic, but his feelings could distract him from what he was doing, and on a course like that, inattention could be dangerous.

As the sun rose over the jagged spires of Blackcomb Mountain, Callie awakened to Bryan's soft, loving kisses on her neck and face. His hair unbound, his eyes heavy-lidded with desire, Bryan was stroking and caressing her body to arousal. Callie smoothed her hands over the golden flesh exposed by his lack of a pajama top. Bryan's long torso and arms were defined by sleek, ropy muscles, and his lanky form radiated heat, a warmth that her own body longed for.

Bryan slid his hands along the curves of her thighs underneath the short cotton knit nightgown she'd donned the previous evening after he rejected her flannel "granny" gown as something old ladies wore to bed. As he again kissed the side of her neck, Callie asked about the ban on sex for athletes. Bryan replied that obviously none of those guys had awakened with her in his bed.

Callie demanded that Bryan do a striptease, slowly, planning to enjoy every moment of having a hot rock star in her bed. Bryan got out of bed and languidly doffed his pajama bottoms, clearly savoring Callie's delight in his body. He insisted that Callie reciprocate, and she did so awkwardly, but with a certain amount of pride because his eyes caressed her every curve.

They continued the teasing foreplay for as long as they could until suddenly the need to join their bodies overwhelmed them. Bryan moved his hand from her thigh to the center of her womanhood, caressing her to even greater readiness. Then he moved between her parted legs, and Callie gasped as he finally brought their bodies together. The pleasure was excruciating as Bryan took his time dragging out each stroke for maximum sensation. Finally toward the end, he could no longer control himself, and his movements became fierce, almost harsh as his body crashed into hers. Callie felt the incredible release of her completion just as Bryan, with a final thrust, was catapulted into his own orgasm. He growled his fulfillment as his body shuddered uncontrollably.

When he could catch his breath, he grinned down at her wolfishly. "See, those jocks don't have a clue what they're missing."

❧

After his morning ski run with the rest of his band, Bryan and Callie enjoyed a leisurely lunch before hitting the slopes together. He didn't say anything about the morning's activities, other than that they had all made it down the mountain without incident. Since he seemed to be in a good mood, Callie assumed that all her worries were for naught, and her own spirits lifted. It took her a while to get her form back, but before very long, she was skiing quite proficiently on the green trails.

They stopped for a while to watch Twist and Thad snowboard in the half-pipe. His bandmates tried to convince Bryan to join them, but he demurred, reminding them that the resort belonged to one of B.T.'s numerous friends, who no doubt was also part of the legendary grapevine he cultivated. Given his reaction to Bryan's previous episodes of recklessness, B.T. would probably have a seizure if he ever heard about the treacherous ski run they'd taken that morning. God forbid word should get back to him that his band was anywhere near a half-pipe.

They spent most of the rest of the afternoon skiing together and then Bryan convinced her to join him at the top of the mountain for the last run of the day down a blue trail. Callie initially declined, but she really did want to see the view from the summit and knew she would enjoy the challenge of skiing a more difficult course. As they rode the ski lift to the top, Callie looked out on the breathtaking view of the valley below. Even in Vermont, she'd not seen mountains this imposing; they seemed unreal, magical. Unlike the lifts back east, these lifts were enclosed to protect the rider against the biting cold, and their sliding doors made them resemble tiny subway cars.

It was so cold at the top of the mountain that Callie was thankful that she had worn her heavy duty gloves and hat. Callie skied the blue trail with very few mishaps; though there was one bad moment when she planted her pole and her hand sank wrist-deep into the snow. She regained her composure very quickly and aside for some balance checks and skidding, her performance was not nearly as bad as she feared. Through it all, however, she looked forward to a long soak in the hot tub that evening.

# CHAPTER 15

Callie paused in the doorway of the penthouse suite and nervously smoothed the sleek bottle-green silk jersey dress down over her hips. It was New Year's Eve and she was looking forward to a romantic evening with Bryan at the resort's party. Storm Crow was playing during the early part of the evening, so she had to enter the party alone.

Though she was nervous about attending yet another party with still more strangers, she thrilled with the anticipation of seeing the look on Bryan's face when he saw her in this dress. She had purchased it several months previously on a rare shopping excursion with Tonya to Birmingham. The dress had hung like a rag on the hanger, and initially she hadn't understood Tonya's enchantment with it. But once she tried it on and realized that it caressed the curves of her body like a lover, she appreciated her friend's enthusiasm. With no inkling as to where she would wear such a garment, she'd purchased it. It couldn't have been more perfect for this occasion. She hoped to leave an indelible imprint in Bryan's memory for the long months of separation that lay ahead.

According to Bryan, most of those in attendance would be the movers and shakers behind the music industry, producers and studio executives. B.T. apparently wanted them to know that Storm Crow was in good shape despite their recent troubles. Before Brodie's death, B.T. had been poised to negotiate a new deal for Storm Crow and thought they'd had a good chance of getting the money and other perks they demanded. Of course, the other executives had begun circling around the moment they thought there was a possibility of snagging the band for their own stable. B.T. knew their record company would hear about the interest the other executives were showing and would quickly come to the bargaining table. He was certain that with a good showing here, they'd be back on track to making a good deal.

Bryan had teased her that given her background and financial acumen, she would probably feel more comfortable with this crowd than he did. An avid reader of business magazines and journals, she recognized a few of the men as giants in the entertainment industry. As she looked around the room, she quickly realized that there were also movie and television executives present. She wondered what B.T. was up to. Bryan had told her that B.T. wanted him to do commercials and movies, but he'd declined. Clearly, that old boy wasn't taking no for an answer.

As she continued to study the guests, Callie realized that this was indeed a party for the industry's power brokers. Most were older, overweight, and balding, but had the requisite nubile young things on their arms. Regardless of whether they were music executives or talent, it seemed everyone in this business went for the stationary synthetic breasts and bleached hair. It quickly became apparent that she would be the only black woman present. There were a few black men in attendance, but they too had queued up for the Barbie parade. It would be enough to give a black woman with her own unaltered breasts an inferiority complex if she hadn't seen the way Bryan's eyes lit up each time he saw her.

She let her thoughts drift back to the previous evening when, almost numb with exhaustion and truly aching in places she didn't know she had, she'd joined Bryan in their private outdoor hot tub. Each chalet had a small patio with an eating area and a Jacuzzi. The patio was open on one side only, and the top was open to the sky. The layout granted a limited amount of privacy without detracting from the view. She couldn't wait to tell Tonya about the indescribable decadence of sitting outside in a Jacuzzi in the snow. Warm to her bones, she had leaned her head back against the rim of the tub and let the snowflakes fall down onto her face like icy little kisses. By the time she'd indulged in a sinfully delicious hot apple pie cocktail, she was almost purring in contentment.

Gradually as some of their soreness eased, they'd moved their swimsuit-clad bodies closer to one another. Eventually Callie had positioned herself between Bryan's legs and leaned her head back against his shoulder. He put his arms around her waist and as usual when they were in close proximity their hands started to wander and they began kissing. Soon they were far steamier than the hot tub. Though they desperately wanted to make love, they'd had to acknowledge that physically they simply were not up to the task. This was her last night in Whistler, however, and Callie had no doubt as to how the evening would end.

Tonight was the first time she'd seen the band in formal attire. She wondered what type of elfin magic Naysa had worked to get the band to wear tuxedoes. The stylist often lamented that she had no idea what they paid her for since they never took her advice. Callie gave Bryan a lingering look. In jeans the man was, as Tonya would say, a walking wet dream in a Prada tuxedo, he was simply devastating. The jacket hung off his broad shoulders and tapered to showcase his slim hips, and the tailored fit of the trousers left no doubt to his vibrant masculinity. He had left his hair loose, and had already unfastened his bow tie and the first few buttons on his shirt. The combination gave him a rakish look that was almost criminally sexy. Now as she stood waiting for him to notice her, she shivered with excitement at the thought of being in his arms again.

Bryan locked eyes with Callie from across the room. He'd been watching for her all evening, and could scarcely believe the vision she made standing there in the doorway. Her hair was pulled up into an elaborate upsweep, and the dress hugged every luscious inch of her body from her neck to her feet. He nodded his head toward her, appreciating the conservative lines of the dress, until she began to walk towards him, and he noted that it was slit almost to her hip on one side, emphasizing the long, sexy length of her legs.

Bryan had a momentary lapse and forgot he was performing as he watched her approach. He'd always known that Callie was a sensuous creature, but usually she muted that effect with low-key, modest attire. But tonight she seemed to be reveling in her femininity. Even her beautifully manicured feet looked erotic in strappy little silver high-heeled sandals. He could feel all the blood drain from his head and he stared in wonder as she moved sensuously toward him. Without breaking eye contact with him, she paused near the stage and with a languid gesture, reached over to pick up a champagne flute from a passing waiter and took a long sip from it. When she lowered the flute, Bryan watched, mesmerized, as she licked away the residue on her lips with a slow flick of her tongue.

Realizing that he had no idea what he was playing anyway, Bryan brought the set to a close. He never noticed that his bandmates were watching the suggestive little byplay between him and Callie with amusement. It was clear to them that Bryan was beyond sprung and didn't care who knew it. Twist was appalled by Bryan's behavior. Though he'd never admit it to anyone, Bryan was his hero, and he'd never thought he'd see the day when Bryan would totally lose it over a woman. Usually Bryan didn't allow anyone to touch his guitar or his microphone, but he walked past both, leaving them for the roadies to remove. Twist shook his head, vowing that he would never fall for one woman. There were simply too many available to attach himself to just one.

Blissfully unaware that his friends had placed him firmly in the "whupped" category, Bryan moved quickly to Callie's side. Now he could see that the dress was literally backless from her neck to the curve of her magnificent bottom. Bryan whistled to himself. No wonder every man present had gone on point when she entered the room. Despite the presence of all the silicone-enhanced bottle blondes, most of the men were craning their necks to check Callie out. Bryan moved in closer, making eye contact with several of the onlookers, sending the message that Callie was with him. They quickly looked away, tacitly understanding the unspoken hands-off signal.

"Has anyone ever told you that you're a goddess in green?" he whispered into Callie's ear.

"Goddess, Bryan? Don't you think that's laying it on a bit thick?"

He brushed his hips against her backside, ensuring that she felt his arousal. "No, that's laying it on a bit thick."

Callie rolled her eyes at the crude double entendre.

"I know a vision when I see one."

As Bryan moved in closer, his hands automatically moved to her waist. "May I have this dance, sweet baby?"

With that, Callie moved into Bryan's arms and they began to dance, their bodies swaying in accord to the jazz band that had replaced Storm Crow on the stage. They had never danced together before, and as always when she was in his arms, the room and everything in it ceased to exist for Callie. Bryan danced with the same elegant grace he lent to all his movements, and it seemed as though they were floating on air. She snuggled in closer, resting her chin in the curve of his neck.

Bryan stroked his hands up and down Callie's bare back, thinking he'd never get enough of the feel of her skin under his hands. As she nuzzled closer, he enjoyed the sensation of her coily hair against his neck. Her light, womanly scent set his mind to wandering lasciviously. Smoothing his hands from her waist to her hips and back again, he luxuriated in the silky feel of the fabric against her even silkier skin. He made another pass over her hips, then paused with sudden realization. "Callie, what are you wearing under this thing?"

Callie gave a nervous little laugh, then whispered, "Chanel N° 5." At Bryan's stunned expression, she continued, "I couldn't wear anything else. The dress is too clingy, the lines would show."

Bryan caught his breath as his body tautened with immediate arousal. He instantly grabbed her hand

and began moving towards the door, but Callie dug in her heels and wouldn't move.

Callie pouted, "It's not midnight yet, Bryan. I want to be here for the balloon drop." She pointed toward the vaulted ceiling of the penthouse, where nylon mesh held thousands of gold and silver balloons.

Bryan paused, eyeing her sexy pout with wry amusement. "You did this on purpose, you little tease. You knew the minute I saw you in that dress I wouldn't be able to wait to get you out of it."

"Come on Bryan, it's only a few minutes until midnight. We've never danced together before," Callie reasoned, batting her eyes at him flirtatiously.

With that, Bryan capitulated and they began dancing again. Callie's dress was so thin that she could feel the movement of each muscle in his long torso and her body responded with with even greater excitement, a fact that was made evident by the bold display of her nipples through the thin silk. They moved closer to the glass wall of the penthouse, enjoying the view of the city lights below. When the clock finally struck midnight, Bryan pulled Callie to him for another mind-numbing kiss, leaving her so bemused that she didn't even see the balloons dropping around her. This time when Bryan reached for her hand, she followed him eagerly.

When Callie and Bryan entered their chalet, she was surprised to find it lit by candlelight. Presumably the steward had returned to their rooms after she left, tidied up a bit, and left champagne, truffles and at least three dozen pink roses. Callie turned to look at Bryan, who only gave her a mischievous grin.

"Champagne?" he asked, moving towards the low console.

They slowly sipped the champagne, eyeing each other over the rims of the glasses. Bryan looked as if he wanted to devour her. Despite her longing to be consumed, the predatory look in his eye made her nervous.

Bryan seemed to sense her trepidation and moved behind her, wrapping one arm around her waist while he removed her champagne flute from her hand with the other. After setting down the glasses, he began to slowly kiss and then stroke her neck with his tongue. Gradually he smoothed his hands from her waist to her stomach and then up to caress her breasts. Her nipples puckered in his hands as he swirled them gently with his fingers.

Callie's response was immediate and fierce. She pressed back harder into him until she felt his masculinity twitch against her buttocks. As she began to grind her luscious bottom into his hardness, she heard him gasp against her neck. The moisture pooling between her legs signaled her intense arousal, and she began moaning as her body greedily sought what it craved. Suddenly, it became too much, and

Bryan took her hand to lead her into the bedroom. When he steered her over to the bed, Callie automatically moved to remove her shoes. Bryan halted her with a roguish shake of his head.

He slowly moved his hands across her shoulders, slipping the dress down to her waist. He fondled her bare breasts with their tiny, dark nipples. Then with a shimmy of her hips, Callie shed the dress and it lay at her feet in a pool of green silk. She stood proudly before him, wearing nothing but a pair of stiletto heels. Bryan slid his hand down from her breasts to her womanhood cloaked in a nest of curly black hair and slipped his fingers between her swollen lips, stroking her to a fever pitch. A low groan escaped his throat as he felt the wetness that streamed from her body. Her womanly scent, already nearly unbearable in its power to stimulate him, intensified with her arousal, and his nostrils flared as he sought to inhale as much of it as possible. He couldn't wait; he had to taste her now. He laid her down on the bed and lifted one slim leg and ran his callused palm down to her foot. He began placing slow, drugging kisses along the arch of her foot, up to her calf and finally to the apex of her thighs.

Callie writhed on the bed, arching her hips to bring herself ever closer to the source of her satisfaction. Bryan took her love button between his lips and sucked on it gently while he swirled it with his tongue. Periodically, he gave long, broad licks along her moist petals. Callie was beyond comprehending anything but intense pleasure. Under his sensual ministrations Callie pitched into an orgasm so intense she almost lost consciousness. When he felt the final tremors of her orgasm leave her body, Bryan hastily disrobed and joined her on the bed, immediately mounting her and thrusting his erection to the hilt into her tight wetness. Callie gasped at the sensation of being filled and instinctively wrapped her legs around his waist.

The feel of her silky thighs and stiletto-clad feet around his hips was almost too much. It was all Bryan could do not to come that very instant. He clenched his teeth and partially withdrew to dull the sensation. Then he began a slow steady grind, pressing his body urgently against hers. He slid his fingers down between their sweaty bodies and stroked her pleasure center. Her thighs clenched even tighter around his hips as her body convulsed in yet another orgasm.

Bryan was so close to the edge he could feel the feathery sensations along his spine. He wanted to prolong their lovemaking for as long as possible, to store up this pleasure for the long drought ahead. Deep in his primitive center, he wanted to leave his mark on Callie so that she could never imagine being with anyone but him. When Callie's second orgasm coursed through her body, he felt her fingernails bite into his flanks, sending his over-sensitized nerve endings into overdrive and pitching him uncontrollably into his own release. He rasped her name as his hips slammed inexorably into hers and the unbearable pleasure coursed through his body.

Callie moved sensuously under Bryan, basking in the feel of his weight pressing her into the bed. His hair hung down on either side of her head, enclosing them in silken intimacy. She stroked her hands over his sweat-slicked back. With sudden clarity she understood the meaning behind the lyrics to Stephanie Mills' "I Feel Good." Her entire body had been loved and she felt totally complete, possibly for the first time in her life.

With a groan Brian finally moved his body off hers. She reached over and stroked his hair away from his face. "You know, we never got around to eating any of those truffles, and I could use some more champagne."

Bryan wrapped his arms around her, pulling her up to rest on top of him. He gave her a lascivious grin. "Actually," he murmured as he stroked his hands over her backside, "I was thinking about calling room service to order some crunchy peanut butter."

Morning came all too soon for Callie and Bryan. They had been insatiable, reaching for each other again and again in the night, making love beyond the point of exhaustion, beyond even knowing whether their bodies were capable of further pleasure. It seemed that if they could just maintain the physical connection, they would never have to be parted. Folly it was, since they both had grueling flights before them the next day, but they couldn't seem to stop.

Despite his rather checkered romantic history Bryan had never felt so powerfully sexual in his life. He had had Callie so many times the previous evening that he had lost count, yet his first thought upon waking was that he wanted her again. It was insane to continue to make love to a woman to the point that coming was actually painful. He winced as he moved gingerly on the bed, his body sore and tender. Poor Callie was probably in even worse shape. But as she had been a willing participant, and oftentimes instigator of their epic lovemaking session, he had to assume their craving was mutual.

Falling in love scared the hell out of him, but there was no way he could deny feelings this intense. Callie was his mate for all time. It was as simple as that. She had to know it by now, but he suspected that unless he said something, she would continue to refute the overriding emotion that lay between them.

Bryan pulled Callie closer, nuzzling her neck. "I can't get enough of you. I think I'm going to start calling you 'Cocaine Callie.' You're worse than any drug. The more I have, the more I want." He took a deep breath. It was now or never. "I think you know this already, but it's time I tell you anyway. Callie, I love you, and when this tour is over it's going to be all about us, okay?"

Callie shifted in Bryan's arms, the slight movement engendering a groan as she felt the impact of previous evening's activities. Despite her physical discomfort she didn't regret one moment. She looked into his turbulent blue eyes. The love she saw there was evident, and she had lost the will to deny her own feelings some time ago. "Bryan, I love you too, and it's already all about us," she whispered.

Bryan grinned, and then with a whoop of joy, he began to tickle Callie until she laughed helplessly. The upcoming months without her would be unbearable, but then she would be with him for the rest of their lives.

# CHAPTER 16

Callie stretched and yawned, rubbing wearily at her bleary eyes. It was an early Thursday morning, and she was waiting for the truck that delivered their periodicals. Thursday mornings were always particularly wearing because the truck delivered at seven o'clock, and they had to have the magazines merchandised by the time the store opened at nine o'clock. The big chain stores got the prime delivery times. As an independent retailer, she had to take the delivery schedule that was left. Today she was barely awake. Over the months Bryan had been on tour they'd gotten in the habit of talking on the telephone until the wee hours of the morning. The band had played in Miami the previous evening, and Bryan had called her shortly afterward. He was always wired after a performance but for the first time their conversation had slipped into the realm of phone sex. They had been particularly long-winded and hadn't said their good-byes until dawn began lightening the eastern sky. Consequently, Callie had gotten only a couple of hours of sleep. The lengthy separation was agony, and though they only had about six weeks to go, it seemed a lifetime. Callie couldn't shake her gloom and depression. Since Books and So Forth had had its best fourth quarter ever, she should've been overjoyed. Instead, she'd merely recorded the data on the spreadsheet. Even the development of a new five-year plan failed to cheer her. Nothing seemed worthwhile if Bryan wasn't there to share it with her.

They'd only had two opportunities to see each other in the past few months, Bryan had sent for her and her sisters to join the band in Atlanta when Storm Crow played there. Cynthia and Addie were included as a special treat, even though their presence meant that he and Callie wouldn't be able to make love. She'd also joined him in Jacksonville, Florida, over a long weekend made possible when an extra show was added to the bill. That weekend had been wonderful, punctuated with long walks along the St. Johns River, and midnight suppers in his suite. Other than that, they'd had to make do with lengthy telephone conversations. Callie was thoroughly frustrated, both emotionally and physically.

She peered out the back window as she heard the truck pull up. The driver greeted her perfunctorily and then began unloading boxes of periodicals. Callie checked each crate before signing the bill of lading, and the young man was on his way, the whole transaction having taken less than thirty minutes. She groaned; ten boxes of magazines to put out this morning, God, she hated the first of the month! Callie looked up as Tonya joined her, carrying a mug of coffee in each hand. They sipped the steaming beverages for a few moments before beginning to place the stock. Each set of publications was bundled together with plastic wire tape that usually just zipped apart, but today had to be cut with a box cutter, adding long minutes to an already annoying task. They worked through the magazines in companionable silence until they got to the tabloids. Callie had always hated them, seeing them as disseminators of lies and human misery. Of course, they were quite popular, and the one time she'd tried to discontinue selling them, she'd seen a noticeable drop in revenue. She picked up the last bundle, sighing with relief at the prospect of finally finishing this chore.

Tonya was idly contemplating a plot twist for her book when suddenly she heard a piercing screech. She turned to see Callie dropping the bundle of magazines as if it were a live snake. Tonya rushed to her side, looking at her uncomprehendingly as Callie continued to scream and point at the magazines. Tonya looked more closely and saw a picture of Callie and Bryan together on the cover of *The Naked Truth*, a particularly repulsive tabloid. The heading over the picture screamed "Best Lay I've Ever Had" in bright fuchsia 48-point type. Callie finally stopped screaming, but she still stared at the magazine cover in a state of shock. Realizing that this crisis was going to take a while to resolve, Tonya hastily scribbled a sign to indicate the store was closed for inventory and taped it to the door. She returned to Callie's side and gently eased her onto the bench. Then she brought her a bottle of water from the break room. Callie just held the bottle, her eyes still transfixed on the appalling headline.

"Okay, Callie, this is probably not as bad as it looks," Tonya soothed, disturbed by the chaotic emotion she saw in her friend's eyes. "I mean, those tabloids have titles like that all the time, just to get folks to buy them. Usually there's nothing to the story."

Callie reeled in greater shock; she'd been so flummoxed by the photograph that she hadn't considered the possibility that the story could be even worse. She pulled the top copy of the magazine out of its bundle and hastily turned to the center spread, her eyes widening in ever-greater horror as she read the story. Apparently it was an "exclusive" given to the magazine by an "insider," identified only as "an intimate friend of Bryan's." According to the "insider," Callie was a call girl who used the bookstore as a cover for her nocturnal trade. As per the "insider," Bryan had been forced to resort to prostitutes because, "He likes rough sex, and no decent woman would have him." The "insider" went on to say, "He probably took up with a black girl because everyone knows they're really wild like animals and will do anything in bed."

Tonya, who was reading the magazine over her friend's shoulder, shook her head in dismay. "Damn, girl, you told me about you and Bryan in the Jacuzzi, but you didn't mention y'all were bare-assed naked." She gestured towards a photograph of Callie and Bryan in an outdoor hot tub. The grainy texture of the image was a dead giveaway that it had been taken with a telephoto lens.

Callie turned on Tonya with a shriek. "That's not us in that picture! I mean, yes, that's us, but we had our swimsuits on the whole time. Look at that picture! It's obviously been Photoshopped!" She pounded the magazine. "Those aren't my breasts, those are L.A. breasts! My breasts move!" She shook her shoulders to illustrate her point, then screamed in anguish as she crumpled the magazine. "I can't believe these people. I knew they were evil, but this is incredible!"

In addition to the damning hot tub photograph, there were three others, including one that Callie found particularly poignant. The picture had been taken at the pre-tribute party, and showed Bryan standing behind her, his arms encircling her waist while he placed a kiss on the side of her neck. The party had been winding down, and they'd thought all the paparazzi had left, but obviously they had been mistaken. Apparently they were so absorbed in one another, they hadn't even heard the shutter go off. Her face glowed as if illuminated from within, and he looked so achingly tender in that moment that she wanted to weep. Their feelings were evident for all to see. Under normal circumstances, Callie would have treasured it as evidence of Bryan's regard for her. But accompanying the garbage in the article as it did, it only sickened her. It cheapened their love, turning something sweet and pure into something tawdry.

When her cell phone began to ring, Callie grabbed it from where she wore it clipped to her belt and stared at it as if she had no idea what it was. She couldn't possibly talk to Bryan right now. What on earth had she been thinking? A relationship with a rock star was out of the question. People would constantly be lying about who and what she was. What would her folks think? And what about Cynthia and Addie? She was their big sister and had always tried to set a good example for them. Now the whole world thought she was a prostitute. Her poor sisters would be made fun of at school. Her family had always been so proud of her; now they would all be so ashamed.

All the hopes and dreams she'd so carefully laid out in her five-year plan would come to naught. Who would finance any of her plans now? Nobody would be willing to invest in any of her projects. For the first time in her life Callie knew overwhelming despair. Suddenly she burst into tears and threw the telephone. It hit the wall with a muted thud, and skittered across the floor. As Tonya looked on in astonishment, Callie ran up the stairs.

Tonya moved slowly over to the cell phone where it lay on the floor, still ringing. Thank God for titanium plating, she mused to herself as she picked it up, hearing, as she expected, a distraught Bryan on the other end. When he realized that Tonya had answered the telephone, he inquired as to Callie's whereabouts. Tonya paused, looking reflectively up at the ceiling until she heard the unmistakable sound of the shower running in Callie's bathroom. Callie tended to take long showers when she was upset; it seemed to soothe her.

"I think she's taking a little water therapy at the moment," Tonya replied. She didn't quite know what to make of the situation yet, but she suspected that it was going to be much worse than she had initially thought.

Bryan sighed. He had noted Callie's water habit also. "So I guess she knows about the story, huh?" He had been hoping against hope that she had somehow missed it, and the whole thing could just blow over without causing too many problems.

Tonya didn't respond, unwilling to share any more information than she had to. Bryan knew the bookstore schedule as well as she did, and he had to know that Callie would have seen the tabloid first thing that morning.

"Is she very upset?" he asked worriedly.

"I'd hazard a guess that she's pretty much devastated. I don't think she wants to talk to you right now. Actually, I don't think she wants to talk to anybody right now," Tonya replied coolly.

He had expected no less from Callie's best friend, and he certainly didn't deserve anything more. It was barely nine o'clock in Miami. After playing the night before, he and Callie had talked all night and he hadn't gone to bed until almost five o'clock in the morning. Though he usually slept no more than four hours, performing seemed to increase his requirements. Sleep deprivation certainly wasn't helping matters any.

It had never occurred to him that he wouldn't be able to talk to Callie, but that seemed to be exactly what Tonya was telling him.

"Tonya, I know she's upset, but I didn't do anything! I don't know what the hell happened. I can't believe they attacked her like this!" Bryan explained frantically.

"Look, Bryan, I don't know if she plans to talk to you. She's really freaked out. Give her a chance to calm down, okay?"

Bryan sighed heavily. He wanted to talk to Callie, now. "Just tell her, I love her, okay? Will you at least tell her that for me?" he pleaded.

Tonya relented, just a little bit. "I'll tell her Bryan, but I've never seen her like this. I don't think she'll be listening. I closed the store," she added just before she hung up. Tonya knew that Bryan would understand that they would close the store only under the direst circumstances. She wanted him to know how much of an impact this was having on Callie. She felt a certain amount of guilt. After all, she had encouraged Callie to be with Bryan, and this was the catastrophic result. It was vindictive, but she wanted Bryan to experience some of the remorse and despondency she was feeling.

Bryan flopped back on his bed, wanting to scream with frustration. He couldn't recall ever having been this infuriated before. He had to get to Callie right away. Everything they had together, the trust he'd worked so hard to build, was being destroyed by that stupid article. But he couldn't leave now. Storm Crow had to play another show in Miami before moving on to Houston. He was bone-weary of the tour and being without Callie, and now this filth had bubbled up from the very sewers of hell. He wanted to go see about Callie immediately, but leaving now would mean the end of his band. Jon and Twist had forgiven him for his previous transgression, but there was no chance in hell of them being so understanding if he ditched them again.

He pulled his hair into a quick, shaggy ponytail. Getting some help for Callie was crucial. He couldn't go to Alabama, but maybe B.T. would be able to help out. She would need someone to give her some directions on how to navigate the paparazzi minefield that was sure to be set off by this article. No one was better at that than his manager. B.T. had called him first thing that morning and faxed him a copy of the article. He'd immediately realized the implications and quickly called Callie. From the very beginning he'd tried to be careful to shelter Callie from this type of publicity. But he'd never dreamed she would be attacked with slander so terrible. He was a public figure and fair game in their eyes. Hell, there were even times when they'd courted negative publicity because it was so good for sales. But this…Callie was a private citizen; she should've been off limits. At worst, he'd expected a photograph where they referred to her as the "unnamed woman" accompanying him. They'd done it just that way countless times in the past. It was an unspoken rule that in general the tabloids left people alone unless they were in the business. It was inconceivable to him that they would violate her privacy and distort the truth to this degree. This was not the way the game was played. He just didn't understand it.

He mused on the problem for long moments, and then the answer hit him with all the subtlety of a cruise missile, Chasdity! Of course, she was the "insider" with the information. That evil bitch had gone to the tabloids and used them to attack Callie. Damn! He'd had no idea she was that vindictive. He shook his head. This made no sense; she'd walked out on him! Why did she feel the need to seek revenge? But what about B.T.? They wouldn't have dared do such a thing without running it past him first.

Bryan propped himself up against the padded headboard and called B.T. back, puzzled by the fact that his usually crafty manager had apparently been caught flat-footed by the story. B.T. had low friends in high places, and very little caught him unawares. When his manager came on the line, Bryan demanded some answers.

"Hell, boy, even the best grapevine breaks down some of the time!"

Something about the statement rang false with Bryan. B.T. bragged all the time that he had a better network than any government agency. He even went so far as to boast that the president called him for intelligence. Though that was probably an exaggeration, it wasn't much of one. If there had been an actual communication breakdown, B.T. would've been the last person in the world to acknowledge it.

He pushed the issue, "Come on, B.T., that's bullshit, and you know it. You've got your finger in every game in town. Hell, you started most of them, so don't try to play me like that."

B.T. gave a heavy sigh. "You always were a smartass." This sharp line of questioning was surprising coming from Bryan. Usually he didn't inquire too closely about this area of the business, finding it distasteful and annoying but a necessary evil. If he told Bryan the truth he would come unglued. He tried to prevaricate and appeal to sentimentality.

"Look, I've been with you for fifteen years. Don't you think I try to take care of you?"

Bryan was on a low simmer. This day was getting worse by the second. He wasn't where he wanted to be. The walls of the hotel were closing in on him, and his mood was deteriorating rapidly. B.T. was up to no good, adding to his frustration with this attempt to make an end run around the topic by playing on their personal relationship.

Bryan clenched his teeth, holding onto his temper by the barest strand of a thread. "B.T., I just called the woman I love. A woman who just had her world knocked off its foundation by a story. A story that my manager, a man who has a network the CIA would envy, to whom I pay an obscene amount to prevent such things, somehow managed to let slip through the cracks. Cut the crap, B.T., it doesn't work with me," he snarled, biting off each sentence with a sharp click of his teeth.

For the first time in many years, B.T.'s thick corn-pone accent slipped as he gave an answer that he knew could destroy their very lucrative relationship. "Bryan, I thought it would be easier to let it go this way," he murmured softly.

Bryan pulled his hair in frustration. "B.T., what the hell are you talking about? Easier than what? Death by a thousand cuts?"

"I just thought it would better for your career if you didn't get so serious about a black girl," he mumbled.

Bryan was astounded. He couldn't believe his manager would say such a thing. "B.T., what in the hell are you talking about?" he asked, enunciating each syllable as if suddenly he doubted who he was talking to. "I don't believe this is coming out of your mouth. You and Maria had her in your home. What in the hell kind of racist bullshit is this? Don't you think you're taking the redneck charade just a bit too far?"

B.T. tried a soothing tone. "Bryan, you just haven't thought about the impact that dating her might have on your career..."

Bryan snorted, "B.T., try another one. I've dated girls of other races before, and you never even noticed. And all you've thought about for the past fifteen years is my career; you know damned well you've never missed a trick. Try another one!"

B.T. had heard Richard Nixon lament once that unlike Ronald Reagan, he had not been able to plead stupidity. No one would believe for one moment that he had not had total and complete control of everyone in his administration. Nixon was simply too savvy. Apparently he was about to be hoisted on the same petard. There were times when being intelligent and crafty was an outright pain in the ass. People just didn't understand.

"Okay, okay. I just never thought you were serious about her. Even when you brought her to the house, I thought you were just making nice with Maria. Good God, Bryan, you've slept with some of the most beautiful women on the planet! How was I to know that you would lose your mind over a skinny little bookworm from Alabama? She's a nobody. I thought at the very least you'd go for an actress, even a porn star, but a bookstore owner?" B.T. seemed sincerely perplexed by Bryan's choices. "So no, honest to God, I didn't think there was anything to it. Why do you think nobody bothered y'all in L.A.? I got the word out that she was just another flash in the pan, hardly worth noticing."

Bryan could scarcely believe his ears. He couldn't believe he'd known this man for fifteen years and didn't really know him at all.

"B.T., I can't believe you're saying this. You have to know me better than this. Callie is not a nobody, she's the woman I love, and I'll take her over any porn star or actress," he growled into the phone. He paused for a moment, contemplating the rest of B.T.'s comments. He'd always known that his manager worked hand in hand with the paparazzi, but he'd had no inkling of just how Byzantine the relationship was. "Okay, okay, as usual you were in bed with them, so what the hell happened?"

B.T. squirmed uneasily in his chair; he hated when Bryan asked these types of questions. Despite his rough reputation, Bryan was really too sensitive for this business. "You and her in Whistler is what happened," he said defensively. "I send you up there to impress the suits, and you spend your time making goo-goo eyes at each other! Everybody said y'all could've set the damned place ablaze on New Year's Eve. After seeing you together nobody believed that there wasn't anything going on between you two. It was clear that you were beyond whipped. I couldn't have stopped the story if I wanted to!" he blustered.

"Did you want to, B.T.?" Bryan asked sadly, seeing his manager's true character for the first time. He wasn't naïve. B.T. had always had reptilian tendencies. It was almost impossible to survive in the music industry without them. But he'd always been his snake. When had he turned?

"No," B.T. admitted begrudgingly, "I didn't want to stop it. You know how this business is. Every little thing counts against you. Especially right now when I'm trying to re-negotiate your contract, and then there's the movie deal…"

"Movie deal?" Bryan interjected wearily. They had discussed this so many times. He couldn't believe the man was still trying to pull this one off. "B.T., I told you a long time ago that I have no intentions of making any movies. What in the hell are you talking about?"

"Yeah, I know you don't want to make any movies right now, but you never know. You're a good-looking kid, definitely leading man material. They've been sending some really good scripts. It could put you over the top. I get offers for commercials and licensing all the time. I've told you again and again that you have to keep all your irons in the fire, and getting serious about a black girl could only screw that up!"

"Screw what up, B.T.? Even if I gave a good goddamn and you know I don't, plenty of rockers have dated or married black women! Look at David Bowie. He married a black woman, and the man's a frigging legend. Jagger has a biracial daughter and nobody's bigger. This is bull, B.T., and you know it! You let your own prejudices derail my relationship."

"Yeah, he married a black woman, a goddamned supermodel! Did you have enough sense to do that? God knows plenty of them have thrown themselves at you. No, you had to go find some little nobody in Alabama. Sure, you can marry a black supermodel and it might be okay, but then again, you might have to be around for thirty years like Jagger and Bowie. Those guys can do whatever the hell they want. I know it's hard to believe, but you can't. No, I couldn't take that chance, you've got a big future ahead of you, and I wasn't going to watch you wreck it over a woman."

Bryan's voice softened. "How quickly you forget, B.T. Do you remember how you felt when Maria's folks did this to you? They didn't want any gringos in the family. Remember how that felt?" Maria came from a family of wealthy vintners with an aristocratic lineage going back for generations. They'd done everything in their power to prevent a nobody like B.T. from marrying into the family. All his success had meant nothing to them, as he had no pedigree to speak of. "Remember what you told me, B.T.? Never let anybody or anything come between you and your woman. Do you remember that?"

"Of course I remember that! But this isn't about me. I'm not a rock star. I don't have an image to maintain, you do!" B.T. blustered.

Choking with rage, Bryan managed to yell into the phone, "Was that your call to make, B.T.? Was it?"

"I know you, boy. Once you decide you want something, there's no way to shake it loose out of your head. You wanted this girl, and I didn't have a chance in hell of talking you out of it. Especially if I started talking about what it would do to your career. The way you've been behaving, you act like you don't give a damn about it anyway. I figured a story like this would do the trick without hurting you or your career too much," B.T. replied, still trying frantically to explain his behavior. This conversation was going downhill fast, and he saw little opportunity to salvage their relationship.

Bryan ignored the reference to his previous bad behavior. "What about her career, B.T.? She's a business owner in a small Southern town. What did you think would happen to her? Do you care that people all over the country think she's a whore?" he snapped.

Then the unthinkable occurred to him. "Did you plant the story?" Planted stories were fairly commonplace, and B.T. did it anytime the band hit a publicity lull. He'd always cleared it with them before, and the stories had always involved other celebrities. While the idea that he would do such a thing without his consent would've been inconceivable before, now it seemed almost plausible.

B.T. gasped indignantly, "No, I didn't plant the story! You know I always ask first. You're like my own kid. Do you think I'd do that to you?"

"But what about what you've done to Callie?" Bryan yelled. "If you really loved me like a son, you couldn't hurt somebody I love…" He broke off as raw emotion choked his throat. "You're right, this won't hurt Storm Crow too badly. Hell, it'll probably be good for the band." Tears welled up in his eyes as his voice dropped to a rasping whisper. "But you've destroyed the woman I love. You've wrecked us, killed our relationship, man. Just like always, I trusted you with her, to help me take care of her, and you betrayed both of us." He took a deep breath, trying to ease the excrutiating pain in his chest. "And you know what's funny?" He paused, pained laughter welling up from his throat. "You know what's really funny, B.T.? I called you to go help her, to help me protect her. How stupid could I be, huh? Yeah, I was going to send you to Alabama so I wouldn't have to leave your precious band. I took your advice, B.T., and thought about somebody other than myself. Too bad, you were only talking bullshit as usual. I'm such an idiot! It never occurred to me that you'd had anything to do with this." Bryan took deep gasping breaths, trying to calm down before he became totally overwhelmed. "I suggest you find yourself another boy. As of right now, you don't work for me anymore."

With slow deliberation, Bryan replaced the receiver in the cradle. The dark chasm that had been with him since childhood yawned before him again, its pull almost tangible. He'd always seen B.T. as a father, the man who had rescued him from a fate worse than death. Now it was apparent that he'd never been more than a commodity to the man he'd loved for almost half his life. The betrayal on top of the realization that he'd probably lost Callie seemed more than he could bear. It was worse than losing Brodie because B.T.'s treachery had been a deliberate act. When the telephone began to ring, Bryan stared at it were as if it were an alien object. Then with a fierce movement, he pulled the cord out of the wall, flinging the telephone across the room. He sat there on the edge of the bed for a long moment, then slid down until he was sitting on the floor. He stayed in that position for what seemed an eternity, his body limp with anguish. Time came to a standstill as the agony reverberated through his very core. He sat there, motionless, almost as if the slightest movement would loosen the fragile link to his psyche, leaving him once again adrift in the void. Then, when he could contain it no longer, a sound heretofore heard only on concert stages around the world erupted from his throat. The primal scream that had sold millions of CDs now marked a raw pain Bryan could express no other way.

# CHAPTER 17

Edith Lawson looked up from the book she was reading. It was after eleven o'clock, and Cynthia and Addie had gone to bed an hour ago. Jesse was on an overnight turkey-hunting trip with friends, and she was in bed, taking advantage of his absence to indulge in some late-night reading. Jesse had taken these trips every spring for as long as she could remember, and had yet to bring home a single bird. His lack of success indicated that these excursions were probably more of an escape with his friends than any desire to actually acquire any turkeys. It was probably for the best that he didn't know that she enjoyed these little breathers as much as he did.

She frowned. There it was again, the unmistakable sound of someone on the stairs. She hadn't heard the girls' door open, and no one else was supposed to be in the house. Just as she was about to get up to investigate, Callie appeared in the doorway of the bedroom. Only this was a Callie she'd never seen before. Her face was swollen to the point that she was almost unrecognizable. But even worse were her eyes, the eyes so like her own. Usually so alive with intelligence and simple joy of life, they were black pits of despair. Her shoulders slumping with dejection, Callie shuffled over to the bed and threw herself sobbing into her mother's arms.

"Callie, what on earth…" Edith gathered her oldest child to her. "What's going on, baby? You can tell Mama."

Callie gasped and continued to sob as if her heart were breaking.

Edith patted her back. "Baby, what's wrong, what's happened? Are you okay? Did somebody hurt you?"

Callie only shook her head and mumbled something incoherent while her weeping escalated.

Edith continued to rock her daughter back and forth, knowing that she would eventually share whatever was causing her to cry so inconsolably. Finally, after several long moments, she decided to try again.

"Come on, Callie. You're starting to scare me now. You've got to tell me what's going on," she said insistently. She handed Callie tissue from her bedside table.

"Darling, is it Bryan? Did y'all have a fight or something?" Edith knew that Callie had been unhappy because of their long separation, but she'd seemed content with the direction the relationship was taking. She couldn't imagine what could've happened.

Callie paused in blowing her nose, and shook her head again. "No, Mama, it's worse than that." She settled herself on the side of the bed and told her mother about the tabloid story.

Edith listened in horror as Callie recounted the tale. "How can they say such things? Who told them this filth? How dare they call you a whore?"

"Mama, they make things up. That's why I've always hated the tabloids." At that moment she vowed that she'd never have them in her store again. She shuddered, if she still had a store. She looked hesitantly into her mother's eyes. "You don't believe any of it, do you?"

Edith Lawson tsked. "Callie, I know what I raised, and I didn't raise no trash." By all appearances, Callie was on the verge of collapse; the swelling of her eyes indicated a very long crying spell. "When did you find out about this?"

"First thing this morning."

"Honey, why didn't you call me?"

"Mama, I think I was in shock, I couldn't do anything. We didn't even open the store today, I just lay there on the bed staring at the ceiling and crying."

Edith nodded her understanding. "Does Bryan know? What did he say? Surely he knows what to do."

"I haven't...I haven't talked to Bryan. He called this morning, but I...I couldn't talk to him." Callie began quietly weeping again. "Mama, I'm going to lose everything...everything I've worked for all these years. People are going to think I've done terrible things," she whispered, her throat aching with despair.

Edith pulled Callie to her. "Callie, that's nonsense. You're not going to lose anything because of these filthy lies. Folks in this town know you. They've watched you grow up. They're not so ignorant as to believe any of this mess," she said fiercely. "There's nothing to be done tonight, but they're going to regret messing with my child," she swore. She peered at her daughter's swollen, tearstained face. "But you need to lie down before you fall down." She pushed the bedcovers down to allow Callie to recline next to her. "Lay down here next to Mama and rest, baby. It'll all look better once you've had some sleep."

Callie smiled at her mother as she curled up beside her on the queen-sized bed. She had had less than five hours sleep in the past twenty-four hours. Mama was right. She did need to get some sleep. Mama still had her back; maybe they could figure a way out of this mess.

❧

"Bryan, I didn't ask Robert, I asked you. Now tell me what happened!" Maria snapped.

Bryan groaned. These early-morning telephone calls were killing him. He had spent all of the previous day trying unsuccessfully to contact Callie. Today the band had a morning flight to Houston. At least it was direct; Bryan was in no mood to deal with airport personnel any more than he had to. Now

Maria was picking at the ugly wound left by B.T.'s betrayal. For the love of God, couldn't she at least let it scab over first? How did he tell a woman that the man she'd been married to for thirty years slithered around on his belly?

"Maria, I really don't think it's my place to tell you…" He tried to sidestep the issue.

"Bryan Andrew Spencer, start talking! Do you want me to come down there?" Maria had known from the moment she saw the tabloid story that something had gone seriously awry. Though she maintained a careful façade of blind wifely devotion, she was not oblivious to her husband's machinations. When she'd mentioned the article to him, he'd mumbled something indecipherable. He'd done like-wise when she asked about Bryan and the band. In their many years together, he'd never directly lied to her, but he was a past master at misdirection. If she wanted a direct, honest answer, Bryan was her only recourse.

Bryan pressed the heels of his palms against his eyes; a sleep deprivation headache throbbed there with sickening intensity. He tried to hedge again, "Oh geez, look Maria, we just had some artistic differences…"

"Okay, so now you think I'm stupid?" Maria snapped in disgust. "Artistic differences? I know my husband. Robert wouldn't care if you played 'Chopsticks' every night as long as you could make money doing it! This is your last chance, Bryan. I want to know what happened, and I want to know now!"

Bryan sighed. Clearly she was not going to leave him alone until he told her the truth. "Maria, B.T. let a story run…"

"That story that was in *The Naked Truth*? I wondered about that. You're angry because that story got out? I assumed it was something you guys cooked up for publicity."

"Maria, do you really think I'd let them call Callie a whore for *any* reason?" Bryan asked indignantly. Didn't anybody understand how important Callie was to him?

"Well," Maria reasoned, "you've done some pretty ugly stuff in the past. I remember when you got engaged to that porn star…"

Bryan didn't want to talk about past publicity stunts. "Maria, that was not an engagement. Hell, I never even dated her. She was just in the video and B.T. thought it would help sales if the story 'leaked' to the press that we were engaged. I didn't have anything to do with this crap. He did it on purpose, Maria. He back-doored me so he could break me and Callie up."

Maria paused, stunned by this revelation. She knew her husband was capable of all manner of skull-duggery, but this defied reason. "Why on earth would he want to do that? You were happy with Callie, happier than I've seen you in years."

Bryan choked off a laugh. "He said…he said that getting serious about a black girl would be bad for my career."

"Bad for your career? Who cares about that? She was terrific for you. Why, that hypocrite! Is being married to a Latina bad for his career?" Maria broke off mid-tirade; this wasn't helping Bryan. She would take this up with Robert himself. She continued in a more soothing tone, "Hold on, precious, I'll deal with Robert."

"There's nothing to deal with, Maria, I fired him," Bryan said emphatically.

"Now, Bryan, don't make any hasty decisions. I'll take care of this. How's Callie holding up?"

"She won't talk to me, but Tonya says she's in pretty bad shape. They closed the store the first day, but now they've reopened and the paparazzi are there all day." He gave a harsh laugh. "Tonya thinks it might actually have helped sales. People are so interested to see what all the fuss is about that they are stopping by the store. But apparently even the prospect of making more money hasn't cheered Callie up in the least. She doesn't know how to handle this, Maria. I can't go to her. If I walk out on the guys again…" Bryan broke off. The prospect of losing both Callie and his band was too horrific to contemplate.

Maria tried for a positive outlook, "Bryan, it's only been two days. You know how these things go.

I'm sure a bigger story will come along soon and knock this right off everybody's mind," she consoled.

"They called her a prostitute, Maria! Do you understand what that means to someone like Callie? She lives in a small town; everybody knows everybody. She's always been a good girl; she's not one of these party girls I usually hang out with. She's a real person with a real life! This is going to destroy every dream she ever had." He took a deep breath. "Maria, I love her, I've got to do something!"

Maria heard the desperation in the voice of her last remaining child. Unlike her husband, she understood the depth of emotion he felt for Callie. "Bryan, do you trust me to help?"

"Maria, you know I love you, I'd trust you with my life. But B.T..."

"Don't you worry about B.T. I'll take care of that," Maria vowed, using his nickname for the very first time in Bryan's memory. Apparently B.T. had lost his "my Robert" status.

Bryan was resigned. He was going to have to rely on Maria to help Callie, as he wouldn't be able to do so himself. "Okay, Maria, please help her. If she'll talk to you, just tell her I love her, and I'm so sorry I broke my promise."

The hand on his shoulder was rough, the voice horribly familiar. "Come on, boy, wake up, we've got a lot of work to do and not a whole hell of a lot of time to do it."

Bryan opened one stormy blue eye, convinced that he had to be having a particularly ghastly nightmare. Perhaps it was alien abduction, or maybe he was having an episode of sleep paralysis like he'd seen on the Discovery Channel last night. That was the only conceivable explanation for the fact that Bobby Tom Breedlove was in his room at the Four Seasons-Houston, rudely shaking him awake.

Though he was fairly certain that he didn't want to know, Bryan felt compelled to ask his former manager the obvious question. "B.T., what in the hell are you doing in my room? Who gave you a key?" He rubbed his hand over his face, making a mental note to have whoever was responsible fired. "For that matter, what in the hell are you doing in Houston?"

B.T. waved some legal documents in his face. "This is why I'm in Houston. We've got a lot of work to do…"

Bryan sat up on the bed. "B.T., I don't give two good goddamns about you or your contracts. You don't work for me anymore."

B.T. blustered, "Boy, who gives a damn about a contract? We'll deal with that later." His sharp glance indicated that there would indeed be a reckoning later. "These are divorce papers. Maria said she'd file them in two weeks if I don't get you and Callie back together." B.T. began to pace. "What the hell did you tell her, anyway?" he asked accusingly.

Bryan looked at B.T. in astonishment. He'd never thought Maria would go this far. It had never occurred to him that she would play the ultimate trump card. "I told her the truth, B.T. Why would I lie to her? You're a scum-sucking maggot. I thought it was time she knew that."

B.T. had no doubt that Maria, who knew him better than any human being on earth, was already more than aware of his character flaws. But he was shell-shocked by her draconian reaction to this situation. Frankly, as he'd pointed out to her, he'd done far worse. But of course, he'd never interfered with Bryan's love life before. Apparently that was the Rubicon he was never permitted to cross as far as Maria was concerned. It would've been nice if she had told him that in advance. It seemed only fair that if she were going to draw a line in the sand, the least she could do was tell him about it! They had had many disagreements over the long years they'd been together, but she'd never made this type of threat before. She had told him, without equivocation, that the fate of their entire marriage hinged on his ability to repair the damage he'd caused.

Why the hell had he brought those boys home in the first place? Damn, they'd been nothing but trouble! But extraordinarily profitable, he had to admit. B.T. had a brief moment of panic. For the first time in his life he doubted his own abilities to manipulate events. He'd felt he was taking his life into his own hands in boarding that flight to Houston to confront Bryan, but frankly he'd had no other choice. Bryan was one of the most mule-headed people he knew, and he wouldn't talk to him unless he was forced to. No other means of communication would work. He had to resort to a face-to-face confrontation. He truly expected at least a broken nose for his trouble, but thus far Bryan hadn't resorted to violence. B.T. wasn't sure that even he could deal with Bryan in his current mood, but the time for self-doubt and reflection had long passed. He simply didn't have time for such indulgences now.

"Well, that's neither here nor there. I've got to get your woman back or I'm going to lose my wife. So we've got to get to work."

Bryan didn't respond. He had no intention of trusting B.T. again.

B.T. wanted to strike him in exasperation but knew that would definitely not get him what he wanted. Bryan was perfectly capable of hitting back, and right now he looked as if he'd like nothing better than an excuse to kick his ass. With great trepidation, he decided that he'd have to go with the one trick he almost never used: the direct, honest truth.

B.T. waved the divorce petition in Bryan's face again. "I know you don't believe a thing I say, but if nothing else, you've got to know that I'll do anything to keep from losing Maria." His voice cracked and he paused briefly. "Hell, maybe I haven't played fair with you, I probably haven't played fair with anybody, but you know I love Maria. There's no way in hell I can live without that woman and you goddamn well know it. Will you please help me get her back? I know you don't owe me a damn thing, Bryan. But could you find it in your heart to help me?"

Suspicious of B.T.'s motives, but somewhat mollified by the humility he had shown, and the fact that B.T. had at least as much to lose as he did, Bryan moved to the edge of the bed to hear what B.T. had to say. He had always suspected that B.T.'s seemingly indomitable drive for financial success was based in Maria's family's rejection of him. He was determined to keep her in an even grander style than she was accustomed to in order to prove them wrong, no matter who he had to walk over to accomplish his goal. Bryan could empathize with B.T.'s feelings, but he'd be damned if he was ever going to trust him again.

"Okay, look, this weekend Storm Crow's going to be on *Saturday Night Live*." Bryan raised his brows. "Yeah, I know Audioslave was supposed to play, but the producers booted them for y'all," B.T. replied briskly. "Y'all are a bigger story right now." His quick grin froze in response to Bryan's snarl.

Bryan marveled at his former manager. B.T. had pulled yet another behind-the-scenes maneuver. "Yeah sure, just what we needed, another reason for Chris to be pissed at me," he snapped sarcastically. He and Chris Cornell, the lead singer for Audioslave, had a long-standing feud harkening back to Chris' Soundgarden days. At this point, Bryan couldn't recall what had initiated the bad blood, but he was pretty sure this wouldn't help.

"Oh, and guess what? Harley Joseph will be the guest host." B.T. grinned again, knowing Bryan would be impressed with his awesome feat. Booking a band on such a high-profile show at this late date was an almost unheard of accomplishment, and with Harley hosting, the ratings would in all likelihood go through the roof. This would give Bryan an opportunity to solicit some positive publicity about his relationship with Callie.

Damn! This was a coup even by B.T.'s standards. Harley Joseph was the star of one of the season's biggest new shows, *The Shelter*, about the director of a group home for runaway teenagers. Though the show had the potential to become downright treacly and clichéd, Harley's edgy and flawed character kept it fresh and cutting-edged. Harley was the brightest star of the television season and a lead contender to be *People Magazine*'s next 'Sexiest Man Alive.' But even better for their purposes, Harley and Bryan were good friends who hung out regularly whenever they happened to be in the same city. They'd met when Harley approached him to do the theme song for *The Shelter*. The song had been a big hit for the band, and Harley and Bryan's friendship had taken off. Bryan wondered whose bed B.T. had gotten into to secure this gig.

B.T. continued enthusiastically, "Anyway, I've already booked you guys to go to New York

Wednesday for the show." He lowered his head, then looked up at Bryan through half-closed lids. "By the way, do the guys know what happened?"

Bryan gave B.T. a disbelieving look. "Of course they do. What the hell did you expect me to tell them?"

"All right, all right." Bryan was astonished to see that B.T. actually looked embarrassed. "Anyway, I've booked you on a couple of shows while you're in New York. You'll do Letterman and Conan. I'm still working on Leno."

Bryan stood up; his intimidating stance was not at all diminished by the fact that a pair of Calvin Klein briefs was his only attire. He moved as close to B.T. as possible. "I just want you to understand one thing, B.T. I'll do this dog and pony show because it'll help get those maggots off Callie. But I want the dogs called off today. I don't want another reporter anywhere near Maple Fork. You understand me?"

B.T. nodded eagerly. "No problem, I'm already working on that."

Bryan paused for a moment, looking down as he collected his thoughts. When he looked up again B.T. stepped back, unnerved by the fierce rage he saw in his protégé's eyes. For a brief moment Bryan reminded him a snarling wolf, and he thanked whatever gods that might still have an interest in him that his rage was directed at someone else. "And B.T., I don't care if it takes every dime I've got, I want *The Naked Truth*'s ass on a platter. I don't care what we have to do, but I want them to pay. When I'm through with them, they'll never mess with Callie again!" Bryan growled grimly.

B.T. rubbed his hands together sinisterly, happy to see that at least for the moment, Bryan was actually angrier at the tabloid than he was at him. He'd hoped he would want to take this tack. He loved it when a plan came together. "It's all part of the plan, my boy, it's all part of the plan."

## CHAPTER 18

Callie smiled and thanked the customer as she handed over her purchases. There were still at least three customers waiting to check out, and she had never needed a cup of coffee so desperately in her life. Surely one more cup was all it would take to ease the throbbing tension headache that had her in its unrelenting grip. At the very least it would clear her mouth of the sawdust taste that left her feeling as though she'd licked the floor of a barn. The noise level in the store strained nerves already made sensitive by lack of sleep. Over the past couple of days she had grown accustomed to the constant buzz of reporters and photographers milling around the door of Books and So Forth. Yesterday several had come into the store harassing her and the customers. Initially, she'd simply tried to ignore them, but when they started asking customers how they felt about shopping in a store with a bordello upstairs, she'd called the sheriff's department to have them removed. The deputies had made it clear that they could not come into the store unless Callie gave permission. Thus far, the reporters seemed to be complying with the orders. Though she was appreciative of the deputies' assistance, their intervention had presented another set of issues.

Shortly after the deputies left, Callie was flat on her stomach on the floor trying to rescue several magazines that had fallen behind the magazine rack when she looked up into the corpulent belly of Graham Pettway, the local sheriff. Scooter, as he was called, at least behind his back, had attended high school with her and Tonya. Though he wasn't stupid, everything about him gave the impression that he was not particularly bright. He was tall and balding and had somehow managed to combine a mullet with a really bad comb-over. With the greasy strands of hair falling to just above his collar, he looked like Billy Ray Cyrus' "Where Are They Now" picture. Though sheriff was an elected position in Etowah County, Scooter had pretty much inherited the job from his deceased father and had run unopposed in the previous election. Having basically won a job no one else wanted, he took a great deal of pride in his alleged law enforcement abilities, and vowed to stamp out crime in Maple Fork, whether any existed or not. Having retrieved the wayward magazines, she got up with a cheerful greeting. Scooter was rarely seen anywhere near any type of reading material, and he quickly made it clear that this wasn't about books.

The sheriff rocked back on his heels, a mean feat considering the proportion of belly he had to cantilever in that position. "Callie, you know everybody in town is talking about that story."

Callie rolled her eyes. "Scoo…I mean, Sheriff Pettway, I know you're not coming to talk to me about that."

"You know I'm all about enforcing the law, and if you've got…" he glanced around at the other customers and lowered his voice. "Working girls operating out of this establishment, I'm going to have to bring you up on charges." Scooter prided himself on being up to date on police lingo. Apparently no one had bothered to tell him that police shows on television are not the best source of information.

"Who in their right mind would try to run a business like that in Maple Fork? We're an hour or more away from any major city!" Callie exclaimed, her irritation evident. She knew Scooter would sell his own mama for political advancement, but this was a new low, even for him. "Sheriff, the story was in a tabloid, for crying out loud, not in a respectable newspaper."

Scooter nodded knowingly, rubbing his chin in a way that would probably look intellectual on anyone else, but somehow made Scooter look dumber. "I know all about those drug-using Hollywood types. I saw you flitting around with that rocker and I knew something was up then. I told my deputy that anytime you see a white man with a black woman, there's some shenanigans going on."

Callie had to bite her lip to contain the impulse to ask Scooter if he knew that from experience. Of course, he'd have to pay a woman to sleep with him, that is, assuming that he could even find his manhood under that massive belly.

Scooter continued spewing his senseless invective. "What else could it be besides prostitution? You're trying to be like that Heidi Fleiss, and I'm not going to have any of that going on around here, so you just know that I've got my eye on you!"

Callie was amazed at her restraint. Had she not had a store full of customers, she would've given Scooter an earful for his blatant disrespect. The foul racism was astonishing for an elected official who was supposed to work for all the citizens of Maple Fork. There had been some talk about him being unnecessarily rough with black suspects, and now she could see the source of that behavior. She knew he was only looking for an excuse to arrest her, so instead of giving him the tongue lashing he deserved, she gave him her sweetest smile. "Tell you what, Sheriff, why don't you watch me real closely right now. I'm about to go to work."

Scooter perked up. "Really?" he asked eagerly. "What are you about to do?"

Callie walked briskly towards the break room. "I'm taking out the garbage. Last night I saw a huge rat out by the dumpsters. I'm sure you'll want to visit your kin."

It took him a moment to digest and interpret the insult. Then he stopped in mid-stride and looked around the room. Clearly the presence of customers prevented his responding as he would have liked.

Instead, with a grunt of frustration, he turned and left the store with an ominous, "I'll be back."

Callie crossed her arms across her chest, primarily to restrain the urge to shove him out the door. "I'll be waiting, jackass," she muttered under her breath.

Even with the paparazzi being kept outside, she still had to deal with the people inside the store. There had been a sudden influx of customers generated by the media's presence. There hadn't been this much excitement in town since Emmitt Whitehead's emus got loose and ran right down Broad Street. It had taken days to round up all the contrary birds. Of course, there hadn't been any television cameras or reporters around when that happened. A regrettable fact actually. Nothing like a rampaging herd of emus to drive even the most determined paparazzi out of town.

Even during the holidays, they never had crowds like this. The participants behaved as if in a poorly choreographed square dance; the people came to rubberneck at the reporters, and the cameras recorded the people. Under better circumstances, Callie would've been amused. Of course, the situation would have been funny only if the cameras were *not* pointed at her. Fortunately for her balance sheet, some of the people actually chose to buy books and magazines while they were there, so at least the fiasco had a profitable silver lining. She, Tonya, and Roshonda had worked constantly for the past two days, both on selling and restocking the shelves. Though the store was usually crowded on Saturdays, today it was almost standing room only. *There couldn't possibly be this many people in Maple Fork,* Callie thought. Maybe folks were coming in from some of the surrounding communities to participate in the spectacle.

Callie was ringing up sales while Tonya and Roshonda helped customers on the floor. She was gratified that at least the townspeople did not seem to believe the tabloid story. Some of the customers had gotten quite ugly with the reporters and others had reminded Callie that they knew the stories were all lies. They'd known her since she was a child, they'd said, and certainly knew her better than a bunch of California crazies. She didn't have the heart to tell them that *The Naked Truth* was headquartered in Florida. As far as her neighbors were concerned, everything that was evil or insane had to come from California or New York. Besides, Florida wasn't really a Southern state anymore. With all the snowbirds, it had pretty much become a suburb of New York City. Their support had lifted her spirits somewhat, and she was able to work during the day with some semblance of normalcy. But she still couldn't bring herself to talk to Bryan. She didn't really blame him for what had happened. In truth she faulted herself. After all, she'd entered a relationship with the man knowing full well how treacherous fame could be. Her daddy had always warned her that her good name was all she had.

Well, she had jeopardized hers for…for what? Callie squelched the tiny voice that told her she'd risked it all for love. Sometimes love simply wasn't enough, she whispered to herself fiercely.

She thought it best to simply make a clean break with Bryan and leave it at that. The tour would be over in a week or so now, and she could make arrangements to return his gifts to him. Surely he would understand what that meant. If not, she would probably have to talk to him briefly, but by then she would be feeling stronger and better able to handle it.

Ever since the story had broken the telephone had rung constantly with other tabloids wanting to get "her side of the story." She wondered if tabloid reporters had moonlighting jobs as telemarketers. The similarity in their technique could not be mere coincidence. No matter how many times she declined their absurd offers, they continued to call. Every time she left the building there was a photographer there to snap her picture. How many shots of her taking out the garbage or making the daily bank drop could they possibly need?

There was a brief lull in the clamor from the reporters, and then the door buzzer rang. Resigned to having to deal with yet another customer, Callie looked up, pleasantly surprised to see Granny, owner of the restaurant next door, striding purposefully towards her. Granny was a very large woman, standing well over six feet. She had a massive bosom and in her youth she had been called a handsome woman. Now she was simply stately. Her mahogany-colored skin was still smooth and soft as a girl's though she had to be well into her seventies. She'd told Callie once that she never went to bed without smoothing Vaseline on her face. That ritual had apparently left her skin virtually wrinkle free. Callie was overjoyed when she saw that Granny carried what had to be one of her legendary apple-pear pies. It had been months since Granny had made one. Though she'd had no appetite for days, the sight of that succulent pastry set her mouth to watering. Granny placed the pie on the counter, then pulled Callie aside. There was a disgruntled murmur from the waiting customers when Granny pulled Callie away, but Granny quelled any discord with a sharp glance and a raised eyebrow.

"I wanted to tell you that I know that what they said about you and that boy isn't true. I saw the two of you coming in and out my restaurant for months, and I've been around long enough to know true love when I see it. I had that for nearly forty years with my husband." She took a deep breath, plainly still mourning a man who had been dead for nearly ten years. "You don't see it too often these days. Most of these young folks don't know their ass from a hole in the ground!" She put her hands on her hips. "But you two have it and better not nobody come in my place and say otherwise." She nodded towards the front of the store, where the reporters could be seen through the window. "One of those flea-bitten dogs had the nerve to come in my restaurant today. I told him we don't serve animals, to get out of my place."

Despite her misery, Callie's mouth curved in amusement. Earlier that day, one of the reporters had decided to go to the bakery down the street for doughnuts and coffee. Mrs. Reynolds, who owned the bakery, had chased the poor man out of her store. Brandishing a baguette like a billy club, she'd pursued him all the way back down the street. Callie blinked rapidly as the tears suddenly welled up in her eyes; she hadn't expected this outpouring of support. Damn! She cried so easily these days! She gave Granny a quick hug. "Thank you so much, Granny, I really appreciate it."

Granny returned the embrace and gave Callie a brief kiss on the top of her head. "Don't let all this get you down, baby. It'll be over soon, and these numbskulls will go and harass somebody else. You stay strong now, you hear?"

Callie smiled and gave Granny a quick nod. "Yes, ma'am, Granny, I hear."

❧⚶☙

From her position near the greeting cards fixture, Tonya watched the interaction between Callie and Granny. She was grateful that so many people had shown their support for her friend. Callie had always maintained a low profile, never wanting any attention at all. She'd spent her life cultivating a good image and was well-known as a decent girl. For her to suddenly be inundated with this type of publicity was incredibly unfair. After Callie's breakdown on Thursday, she'd returned from her parents' home on Friday morning at seven o'clock ready to go to work. Though she'd looked tired and worn, she'd worked through the past two days with an energy that was only belied by the emptiness in her eyes. Callie was hurting. Those who cared about her knew she was keeping it together by sheer force of will. She had often joked that her mother was a "steel magnolia," but it was evident that she too possessed a will of iron. Tonya admired her friend, but was worried for her too. She heard the sobs through Callie's bedroom door each night, and could tell that she was getting little sleep and that the coffee she drank constantly was all that was keeping her going. When they were in their apartment, Callie carried Bartholomew with her everywhere and slept with him each night. This could not continue. The girl was wasting away right before her very eyes.

With Callie's full knowledge, Tonya had talked to Bryan several times per day since the story broke. She would not go behind her friend's back, even though she felt that the situation would only be resolved by Callie talking to Bryan. But her stubborn friend wouldn't relent. Bryan and Callie were in equally bad shape, though Callie seemed to be handling it better. She couldn't believe that Bryan managed to go on stage and perform each night, when as best she could tell, the man could barely maintain a coherent thought. He began every conversation inquiring about Callie's well being, and then he would just repeatedly ask her to tell Callie he loved her. Tonya had agreed to pass on the message, and had done so, but Callie had responded with only a blank stare. Tonya could tell that neither was sleeping much, and both were exhausted and numb with hurt and despair. Callie insisted on the separation, even though they both desperately needed to be together.

Tonya had a sneaking suspicion that Callie intended to continue ignoring Bryan until he simply gave up and stopped calling. She shook her head. Evidently the girl didn't have a clue as to the type of man she was dealing with. It hadn't taken her very long to realize that Bryan intended to hold onto Callie regardless of what her intentions were. To a man like Bryan, her refusal was immaterial. He would go away only if he knew for sure that Callie didn't want him, and no one who had ever seen them together would ever believe that. Though normally she would stand behind whatever decision Callie made, given their pitiful state, Tonya appreciated Bryan's obstinacy. He had called her earlier in the day and told her that they had a plan in the works to resolve this mess, and that the reporters would be gone by the end of the day. He'd also told her that the band would be performing on *Saturday Night Live* that weekend. Tonya was going to make sure that Callie watched it. Maybe seeing Bryan again would force her to come to her senses. She was relieved to hear that their media siege would soon end, but she just hoped that whatever they had planned for Saturday night wouldn't spark it again. Callie's nerves were pretty much stretched to the limit. If she had to endure much more of this insanity, those reporters would really have something to talk about.

Callie lowered her head as her father said grace. This command performance for Sunday dinner at her parents' home was not what she had planned for this evening. After the hellish week she had been more inclined to crash and burn in the privacy of her own apartment. However, her mother had warned her that as soon as her father returned from his hunting trip he'd want to see her. Given his misgivings about her having a relationship of any type with Bryan, she knew this meal would be anything but pleasant. She just hoped that he would wait until after dinner to upbraid her.

Hoping for the best, Callie asked her father about his hunting trip, and they exchanged general pleasantries. The roast chicken, mashed potatoes with gravy and green beans were delicious, and though Callie had little appetite, she enjoyed the comfort food. Addie and Cynthia did their best to help and talked animatedly about everything they could think of. They related anecdotes about school and cheerleading, and relayed gossip about various classmates and even a few teachers. Callie was grateful for their ability to fill the awkward silences with incessant chatter. Her brain whirring with confusion, she contributed little to the conversation. Then just when she thought they'd get through the meal without any fireworks, Jesse looked at her pointedly and asked about the tabloid story.

Resigned to her fate, Callie responded with a cheerful optimism she didn't feel, "Daddy, I don't think it's going to be a big deal. The reporters seem to have left yesterday, and I haven't seen anything else about it on the news," Callie answered, hoping against hope that he'd be satisfied with her answer and leave the matter alone. But of course this was only the first salvo of what was bound to be a long drawn-out disputation.

"Yeah, Daddy," Cynthia piped up, "the reporters probably left to cover Lainie Ellison's disappearance. You know that girl on the TV show *High School Blues*. They say she was probably kidnapped for ransom. Her daddy's the richest producer in Hollywood. He developed the show just for her. It's been on the news since yesterday evening. Everybody's talking about it." Despite their youth, Callie's sisters understood the pressure she was under and made an effort to help with diversionary tactics.

Jesse ignored Cynthia's comment and stared down the table at Callie. "Do you really think people are going to forget that horrible story, not to mention seeing naked pictures…?" he asked incredulously.

"That wasn't me!" Callie interrupted, "Daddy, you know I'd never allow those kinds of pictures!" Callie felt the heat rise in her face. Though she knew the photos were fake, everyone else would assume they were seeing her nude body.

Jesse took a deep breath. "I know it wasn't you, but everybody else thinks it was," he replied in a calmer tone.

"No, everybody doesn't, Daddy. The people who know me, they know better. Folks all over town are telling me…"

"That's the point," he bellowed. "Everybody doesn't know you! I can't believe you're trying to play this whole thing off like it's some type of joke. Seems to me that you're just making excuses so you can go on seeing that boy. Just like always, another white man had his fun, and the black woman is branded a whore while he moves on and finds himself one of his own kind to marry! Didn't I tell you better?"

Callie's lowered her head as the tears ran silently down her cheeks. "I'm not seeing him anymore," she murmured softly.

"What?"

Calllie raised her voice, though still barely above a whisper. "I said, I'm not seeing him anymore. The relationship is over." Through her veil of tears Callie could see the hurt and pain masked with anger in her father's eyes. She couldn't help recalling other times in her life when she'd seen similar emotions reflected in their obsidian depths. When she was five, he'd been teaching her to ride a bicycle and she'd somehow gotten away from him. An oncoming car had caused her to brake suddenly and she'd fallen off the bicycle and broken her arm. When her father caught up with her, he'd blustered in anger and yelled at her for riding away, even though she could see tears shimmering in his eyes as he inspected the damage she'd done to her arm. When she was in high school, he'd remonstrated against her accepting a date with Timothy Little, the object of her eleventh-grade crush. Of course, she'd impulsively agreed to go out with him and had been devastated when he stood her up. Her father had raged for days and reminded her that he'd told her that Timothy's folks were no account, and that Timothy was no good. Then as now, she could see her own pain mirrored in his eyes, but he'd never admit it. Covering his concern with anger was simply the way her father coped, and over the years they'd all learned to understand and accept it, at least most of the time.

"Well, hell, the damage is done now, isn't it?" he snapped. "Everybody thinks my daughter is a whore. Did you think about how your mother and I feel? How about your sisters. Don't you think they're going to be teased at school?" Jesse exclaimed belligerently.

Cynthia and Addie gasped and whirled in unison to challenge Jesse's statement, but they were quelled by a sharp glance from their mother.

Edith Lawson had had enough. "Jesse, can't you see the girl is upset? Do you really think you're helping the situation any?"

Jesse wasn't ready to back down. "Edith, I can't believe you're questioning me on this. Didn't you tell me that Sheriff Graham Cracker himself came by to question Callie about running a prostitution ring?" Jesse blustered, using yet another one of the sheriff's derogatory monikers. "God only knows what's going on with that boy, and they've dragged your daughter's name through the mud and you're yelling at me?" His jaw tightening in consternation, Jesse stared at his wife as if she'd suddenly become deranged.

"Jesse, I didn't raise my voice once. You know nobody takes that so-called sheriff seriously. He only came by for political purposes. Anybody with any sense knows nobody would run a prostitution ring out of this town. Now, I understand you're upset, but Callie is a grown woman and perfectly capable of making her own decisions. I agree that this is a terrible thing, but neither of them is at fault here," she responded in a reasoning, conciliatory tone. "Callie is going through a tough time, and she needs all our support."

"It most certainly is his fault," Jessie replied insistently. "He promised he'd take care of our child, and this is what happened. But you're on his side anyway. All he had to do was play nice during Christmas dinner and buy her some books and you suddenly think he's the best thing since sliced bread," he continued, annoyed that anyone would question his support for his oldest child. "And did I ever say I didn't support her? Did I? I just didn't want the girl branded a white man's whore in front of the whole country. Is that too much to ask?"

"Jesse, she said she's not seeing him anymore. Isn't that enough?"

Callie tilted her head back against the chair and rubbed her hands over her eyes, trying to stop the flood of tears. It seemed that she'd spent the past few days doing nothing but crying. Things had always come so easily for her. She'd never really had any serious upsets to cry about before now, but apparently now she was going to get a lifetime's worth of misery in one fell swoop. Nobody seemed to understand that she loved Bryan and her heart was breaking in two. Or maybe they just didn't care. Her father seemed to be so fixated on getting his "I told you so" in that apparently her feelings didn't matter. The throbbing in her head still hadn't eased up, and her misery increased with each word her father spoke. Finally, she had to speak up or drown under the weight of her despondency.

"Daddy, I made a mistake. I should've listened to you. You're right. Are you happy now? I messed up, and I dragged the whole family through the mud. All right? You have your pound of flesh," she whispered hoarsely. It took everything she had to keep from screaming out her anguish. "Can we leave it alone now? I'm really tired, and I simply can't take this." Shaking so hard she could barely stand, Callie moved away from the table. She nodded toward her mother. "I'm sorry, I'm sorry I embarrassed you, I didn't mean to," she whispered. She coughed as her throat tightened. This was too much. "Mama, I'm sorry, I know

I'm being rude, but may I be excused? I'm going home." With that she moved slowly towards the front door, without waiting for her mother's response. The rest of the family sat in stunned silence until they heard the door close quietly behind her.

Jesse sighed as Edith, Addie, and Cynthia gave him disapproving looks. Being the sole male in a house full of women could be heaven or it could be hell. He'd screwed up on an unprecedented scale and wondered how long hell would last this time. His women could turn this house into a fortress and shut him out for weeks, barely speaking to him. All the little niceties he had grown accustomed to, like the girls bringing him his slippers or keeping dinner warm for him, would disappear in a flash, leaving him to fend for himself. After so many years of pampering, it was an impossible adjustment to make. They had him on tenterhooks, and they knew it.

Even Addie, who'd always been a "daddy's girl" was looking at him as if he'd just kicked a kitten. Well, he had to admit, in a way he had. He'd never seen Callie look so wretched, and he should've left the situation alone. But it still angered him that she'd allowed herself to be used that way, even after he'd warned her of the probable consequences. Feeling impotent to do anything about his child's pain, he'd done the boneheaded thing and struck out in anger. He sighed to himself. Easy enough to figure that out now, but why hadn't he realized that before he attacked her that way?

He stood up, moving towards the closet to get his jacket. "I'm going to apologize to Callie. I really put my foot in it."

Addie gave him a wide-eyed stare, her luminous brown eyes deep pools of concern. "You want me to go with you, Daddy?" she asked, afraid that he would lose his temper again. She couldn't believe that her precious daddy had been so mean to Callie. Since the story came out, their telephone had rung incessantly with friends calling to get the scoop. There was bound to be vicious gossip in school, but she and Cynthia knew that Bryan and Callie were in love, and they stood firmly behind their big sister.

Jesse tugged gently at one of her braids. "Nope, that's quite all right, little doll. I've eaten crow before. I know just how to season it."

# CHAPTER 19

"Damn, dude, you look like something Dr. Frankenstein wouldn't dig up. What the hell happened to you?" Harley Joseph stood in the doorway of his dressing room. He narrowed his piercing green eyes and peered into Bryan's reddened pupils. Then he looked hurriedly past Bryan to Jon. "Jesus Christ, man! Is he using?"

Bryan punched him in the shoulder. "Damn, man, I'm not dead yet! You don't have to act like I'm not here." His body shuddered as he was assaulted by another racking cough. "And no, I'm not using. What the hell made you ask such a thing?"

Harley gave him a speaking glance. "Obviously you haven't looked in a mirror lately. Here, man, sit down before you fall down. These cheap bastards would probably make me clean up the mess if you dropped dead in my dressing room." He pulled out a chair from the table. Accustomed to the lavish spending typical for a hit television show, Harley had not yet adapted to the shoestring budget of a long-standing production like *Saturday Night Live*.

Bryan sat down gratefully as he was seized by yet another coughing attack.

Harley looked up at Jon again. "Aren't you guys supposed to be performing this weekend? This guy sounds like he needs to be in the hospital. I don't want him to upstage me by dying in the middle of the show," Harley added facetiously, only half in jest.

Finding no other chairs available in the tiny space, Jon sat down on the table. "I think he's just got a cold. He'll be all right if he gets some rest. He hasn't been sleeping since that crazy story came out."

Harley nodded. "Yeah man, that's a mess there. What the hell happened? I know you haven't had much long-term success with the ladies, but when did you start resorting to call girls? Last time I saw you, you and Chasdity had hooked up. Surely you didn't blow that relationship up too?"

Bryan gave him a disgusted look, "Callie is not a call girl! Your good friend Chasdity made all that crap up and gave it to the tabloid," Bryan rasped, reminding Harley that he'd introduced him to the starlet.

Harley winced, idly scratching his blonde head. "Well, you know what they say about a woman scorned. She didn't seem particularly upset when I left L.A. What the hell did you do to her?"

"I didn't do anything to her and she sure as hell wasn't scorned," Bryan replied, contempt dripping from every syllable. "Hell, she dumped me!"

Harley pursed his lips in confusion, a particularly arresting gesture in such a saturnine face. "Interesting. Chasdity's been around a while. She knows the score;

she has no problem with the pay-to-play routine. That's why I passed her on to you. I figured that was one even you couldn't mess up. So what brought out her vicious streak?"

"I don't know. The only thing I can figure is she got pissed off about a confrontation she had with Callie at the pre-tribute party. As usual, she blew it way out of proportion. It wasn't that big a deal. God, I hate melodramatic people."

Harley sobered, giving Bryan and Jon an encompassing glance. "Sorry I couldn't get back to the Left Coast for that. The shooting schedule for the show is a real bitch."

"No problem, we knew the deal." Bryan started coughing again, his shoulders shaking with the effort.

Harley waited until the coughing fit eased up. "So who is this Callie? If she's not a call girl, where is she? Even you couldn't have destroyed it this quickly. I saw the pictures." He gave Bryan a knowing look. "Nice tits, but I always took you for an ass man."

"Those aren't her breasts!" Bryan hissed through his teeth. "She's not some groupie, she's my girl, so don't talk about her that way."

Harley raised both hands defensively, leaning back away from Bryan's vehemence, "Oh. Sorry, man. Hell, I didn't know." He looked over at Jon. "Whupped, huh?"

Jon nodded. "Totally."

All three laughed as Bryan made no attempt to deny it.

Bryan made an encompassing gesture towards the dressing room. "What the hell are you doing here anyway? Why aren't you back in L.A. helping Myron deal with Lainie's kidnapping?" Myron Ellison and Harley were long-time friends. In addition to Lainie's show *High School Blues*, Myron also produced *The Shelter*.

Harley made a moué of distaste, "Kidnapping, my ass! Don't talk to me about that spoiled little bitch. Myron should've beaten her ass a long time ago! She probably had herself kidnapped or ran off with some drug dealer or something. Besides, I've bailed on this show one time too many. I had to do it this time; I ran out of lies."

Bryan shook his head. Harley had told him about Lainie's repeated attempts to get him into bed. Even if Harley had been stupid enough to ignore the age difference and possible statutory rape charge just for a young piece, he certainly wasn't prepared to give up his long-time friendship with Myron for it. Lainie had always been a brat. He hoped for her sake that this was just another one of her ridiculous stunts.

Harley returned to the subject of greatest interest, Bryan's love life. "Where is the lovely Callie? If she's got you in this kind of shape, I know you didn't leave her behind in L.A. for all the other coyotes to get their hands on her."

Bryan rested his chin on his hand. "She doesn't live in L.A., so at least I don't have to worry about that, but she won't talk to me. All this stuff was too much for her. I think she's dumped me."

Harley was puzzled by Bryan's response. "You think she's dumped you? Well, that's nothing new. They all dump you eventually. I don't get it. Women go nuts for you. They say you've got a face like a fallen angel, but your bedside manner couldn't be more Neanderthal if you shaved your back. So, I'm not surprised you got dumped again, but don't they usually do it to your face? Why don't you know whether she's dumped you or not?"

"I told you, she won't talk to me." Bryan didn't bother to dispute Harley's comments about his romantic track record. Harley had been his friend for a while, and pretty much everything he'd said was true.

Harley snorted. "Like that's ever stopped you before!"

"In case you haven't noticed, man, we're trying to wrap up a tour here." He nodded significantly at Jon. "I can't just take off to see what's going on with Callie. We've got a few more dates after we leave here, and then I'm going back to Alabama to see her. I'm going to get her to talk to me." He gave Harley a wry glance. "Besides, why are you so fixated on my love life? Hell, at least I'm not sneaking around to see my lady!"

Harley's complexion blanched under his light tan. "What the hell…" he began, then seeing Bryan's smug smile, decided he wouldn't give him the satisfaction of asking how he'd acquired his information. Bryan couldn't know too much. For once in his life he'd actually been reasonably discreet, and he'd thought he and the lady in question were the only parties privy to their relationship. He grinned back at his pal, indicating that there would definitely be a reckoning at a later date. The poor guy wasn't up to it right now. It would hardly be sporting. But when he got on his feet again…

Harley nodded knowingly. Bryan's presence in New York City was an interesting plot twist in Storm Crow's ongoing drama. He leaned against the edge of his dressing table, contemplating his friend. An unusual choice for a leading man, Harley was tall, slim and blonde, but he was not the California beach blonde so prevalent in films and television. He was a Nordic blonde, with the wide sensuous mouth and the sculpted cheekbones commonly seen amongst the Russian Tartars. His deep-set, heavy-lidded peridot green eyes punctuated an almost unreal male beauty. Fortunately for the sake of his masculine pride, his love of extreme sports had left him with a nose that had been broken frequently enough to make him aristocratically handsome, rather than beautiful. Indeed, the bumps in it were so arresting there was a running joke that he'd had them put there, possibly by surgery. Regardless of how he'd acquired his distinctive nose, it added an air of danger and interest to his cover boy good looks. His puckish personality was the complete antithesis of the brooding roles he usually played. People were always astonished to learn that Harley liked nothing better than a practical joke, and he would put in endless hours of effort to ensure that his victims were caught in his web. His vivid green eyes gleamed devilishly as an idea occurred to him. "You know what? I think Ms. Chasdity needs to be put in her place."

Bryan glanced up at him, recognizing the unholy glow in Harley's eyes. He really didn't care what happened to Chasdity, but he didn't have time right now for another one of Harley's elaborate schemes. Frankly, he'd had enough plots to last a lifetime. "What are you talking about, Harley? Chasdity is the least of my concerns right now."

Harley began laughing out loud. "Oh man, this is killer. Yeah, man, I know you only want to get your woman back, and I doubt if this will help, but God it's going to be so funny." When he realized that Bryan was not joining in the fun, he gave him a disheartened look. "There you go again, 'Monster of the Minor Chord.' Lighten up, dude, why don't you?" He'd given Bryan the nickname when a music writer called him the "Master of the Minor Chord." Harley had hooted hysterically and claimed that his friend was more "monster" than "master." It had stuck, like all too many of the names Harley generously bestowed on his friends. He used it as much as possible, especially when he wanted to get Bryan's goat, which was most of the time. When Bryan still didn't respond, he threw his hands up in disgust. "It won't involve you anyway." He moved towards the door, muttering to himself. "Now if I can convince these cheap-ass producers to add a sketch this late…"

Bryan stared at the door Harley had just exited through, then up at Jon. "I wonder what the hell he's up to?" His comment about undercover romance must have hit closer to home than he'd initially thought. He hadn't known Harley for very long when he discovered his friend's tendency to use humor and sarcasm to cover his own pain. Anytime anyone dug too deeply, he would start pulling pranks and practical jokes like crazy, feverishly trying to distract them. Bryan had been in on a number of them. It was said that even Mel Gibson could not top him in utter deviousness. Fortunately for all concerned, his masterpieces were generally played out behind the scenes.

"I don't know, dude." Jon wasn't particularly concerned about Harley's plan. Frankly, as far as he was concerned, Chasdity deserved whatever she got. He had witnessed the tête-à-tête between Callie and Chasdity, and Chasdity had gone way over the top in response to what was really a very mild putdown.

At the moment, though, he was quite worried about Bryan. His friend hadn't slept much before the story broke, but it hadn't seemed to affect him too much. Now, in just a few short days, he'd lost weight he couldn't afford to lose, his skin was drawn and pale, and he had dark circles under his eyes. Bryan was almost always wired, alive with barely contained energy. Now his usual lively demeanor had taken on an almost feverish intensity that none of them had seen before. When they weren't playing or rehearsing, he was on the telephone, either trying to reach Callie or talking to Callie's roommate. The cold had started two days ago, and Bryan still hadn't taken the time to rest. The coughing fits were clearly draining him, but he'd insisted on seeing Harley before they rested back at the hotel. He'd become more unreasonable as he got sicker. The others had gone to their rooms, but Jon had accompanied him, fearing that he might lose consciousness in transit. Bryan had dismissed his concerns, but he hadn't protested too hard. Jon suspected that he also knew he was in bad shape.

Jon touched Bryan lightly on the shoulder. "Hey, dude, we've got a while before rehearsals, so why don't we go back to our rooms and get some rest? Kelly got you some cough medicine and some aspirin, and I think you should take it and then get some sleep."

Bryan rose slowly from the chair. "Since our host has apparently abandoned us, that's probably the best offer I'll get all day."

❧

The body against his was wonderfully familiar; he knew every soft sensuous curve. Callie was kissing the back of his neck while her hands stroked over his arms and chest. She moved down, taking each nipple in her mouth in turn. Bryan's body convulsed at the first exquisite contact. Then he sighed, bereft as her lips moved downward. Callie followed the line of hair from his chest to his abdomen. Her lips pursed, and she sucked gently at his flesh as she continued. Her tongue flicked out periodically, as if she'd tasted a particularly tasty morsel.

Bryan was in a daze; Callie had never made love to him like this before. His every nerve ending humming, he waited for Callie to reach the center of his arousal. His muscles tautened with each caress. It was almost beyond bearing. When he felt her soft lips slide over the head of his arousal, Bryan almost erupted in rapture. Trying desperately to prolong the pleasure, he moved his hips away from Callie's questing lips and tongue. But she would not be denied and followed him eagerly. Bryan gave in to the bliss as her tongue stroked along his hardened length. She took him into her mouth, her tongue again circling the head of his manhood and moaned as if pleasuring him was also a turn-on for her. The little kitteny growls were viciously arousing. It was all he could do to contain the scream of ecstasy when her soft hand moved up to gently caress his testicles. They tightened even more in response to her touch. Then she moved to engulf his entire penis, her soft wet mouth suckling gently on the length. Bryan couldn't hold it another moment: His back arched until only his shoulders and heels were touching the bed as his body shuddered convulsively in release.

Bryan sat up suddenly, his body drenched in sweat. Damn! He'd been having that recurring dream again, a replay of their last morning in Jacksonville. God, he had to see her. He couldn't sleep, and when he did, she haunted his dreams. He'd been sure the cold medicine he'd taken earlier would guarantee a restful sleep, but he should've known better. He didn't know how much more of this he could take. Four months of celibacy broken by only occasional sex had been difficult enough, but now not knowing when or if he'd be with Callie again was driving him insane. Twist had suggested that maybe he should start dating someone else. The very thought of touching another woman sickened him. No other woman would do, he had to have Callie. His body taut with longing, he moved over to the window. The view from The Mark Hotel had always been one of his favorite things about New York City. Now he didn't even see sparkling vista of 77th Street below. With a sigh, he moved over to his guitar, knowing from experience that he wasn't going to get any more sleep tonight. Might as well do something productive with the insomnia.

From the wings, Bryan looked on as Harley and one of the actresses from the show did a sketch that was a brutal full-frontal assault against Chasdity. Though very much an inside joke, those for whom it was intended would recognize the vengeful strike for what it was. In the sketch, Harley was a Wall Street type out on a date with an actress, who, with heavy make-up and assorted padding, was a dead-ringer for

Chasdity. If there was any uncertainty as to who was the brunt of the joke, they removed any doubt by calling the character Puriti with an "i." Over dinner Harley's character earnestly told Puriti that he loved her deeply and wanted to see the real authentic person she was underneath. It took a great deal of persuasion, but eventually the young lady agreed to allow her swain to view her au naturel.

The next scene showed them back at her apartment. Harley waited anxiously while Puriti undressed on the other side of a screen. As she removed each article of artificial enhancement, she tossed it over the screen, as Harley cheered her on. Harley grew increasingly leery as the expected wigs, falsies, nail-tips, and even fake buttocks flew over the screen. His eyes widened in escalating horror as prosthetic arms and legs followed those items. Then the young lady whispered breathlessly that she was ready for him to join her behind the screen. He moved very woodenly towards her. His face was a study of concern as he was clearly worried as to what he would find when he turned that corner. The camera focused on his face as the air was rent by his horrified screams. Then the camera panned down to the bed to show a large drawing of a stick figure on the white sheet.

Bryan tried to suppress his laughter, knowing that it would likely trigger another bout of coughing, but each time he thought about that stick figure drawing and how aptly it described Chasdity, he was overcome again. Chasdity had gotten what she deserved, but now he had to get through this show. Storm Crow had performed earlier in the broadcast, and they were setting up to do their second song. Earlier in the week the band had been playing the piece he thought of as Callie's song. He hadn't given it a title yet, but he'd been kicking it around for months and finally had some good lyrics. Since their separation, he'd taken the portrait from Venice Beach and the photographs her sisters had given him at Christmas around with him. One night when he was once again staring at the Venice sketch, the words to accompany the music which reflected all the longing and desperation he felt just fell into place. Though songs sometimes came that easily, usually writing was grueling work. Bryan had little doubt that this song was going to be incredibly important to his relationship with Callie, if she was willing to listen.

Due to the cold his voice was very fragile so they had been using the song as a warmup. One of the producers had heard them and insisted that they play it tonight. Bryan had initially protested. But most of the furor over the tabloid article had died down and the media focus had been redirected to Lainie Ellison's disappearance. For a moment he'd wondered if B.T. had actually engineered the kidnapping as a diversionary tactic, but his manager had assured him that he didn't generally make a habit of breaking laws that would land him in a federal penitentiary for the rest of his life. He'd seemed genuinely hurt that Bryan would even consider such a thing.

Regardless of how the reprieve had come about, Bryan didn't want to initiate more speculation by singing a song that was so out of character for the band. But on further reflection he realized that he really had nothing to lose, and that this might actually help his cause. He wanted the world to know how he truly felt about Callie, that she wasn't some passing fling, but the lady in his life. More importantly, he wanted her to know that. Apparently she'd forgotten that last morning in Whistler, and he wanted to remind her of the commitment they'd made. This performance would spark such a firestorm that most people would forget about the tabloid article or dismiss it as the trash that it was. Of course, everyone on the planet would know about his love life, but they thought they knew that now. At least this way everyone would know the truth, not a bunch of lies dreamed up by a vindictive woman.

Bryan tried to warm up his voice again, but stopped when he began coughing. No point in trying anyway; he had very little voice left. Fortunately, they'd practiced with Thad harmonizing on the chorus; otherwise they wouldn't have had a show. His falsetto, which was erratic at best, would not be putting in an appearance tonight. He'd literally blown his vocal chords on the first performance and would have to struggle to get through Callie's song.

Thad's singing ability was a bonus they'd discovered by accident when his mother happened by one of their rehearsals and asked why Thad wasn't singing. It was all they could do to restrain their laughter when she added that he sang almost every Sunday in the church choir. How had they managed to hire a bona fide choirboy? They'd all had a grand time teasing Thad about it and had tried in vain to get him to sing for them. Bryan didn't understand it; the kid was an absolute guitar virtuoso, and unbelievably talented, but he could perform only if he totally blocked the audience out. Otherwise he freaked out. They'd finally given up trying to goad him into a performance. He'd only agreed to sing tonight because Bryan simply wasn't up to the task.

Bryan was actually grateful that his voice was so weak; it never would've occurred to him to have another voice on the song, and it sounded immeasurably better with Thad. Twist kept teasing them that they had a Simon and Garfunkel type harmony which only made Thad more uncomfortable. Jon had finally put a stop to it, by reminding Twist that they might have to call on him to sing next.

Bryan smiled genuinely for the first time in a week as he and the band moved onstage. Sometimes the best plans required no planning at all; they simply happened serendipitously. Too bad B.T. had never figured that out.

Callie and Tonya sat on the living room sofa, waiting for Storm Crow's next number. Callie had already told Tonya about the incident with Chasdity, and Bryan had shared his suspicions about the source of the story with Tonya. They'd both laughed raucously at the Puriti with an "i" sketch. They laughed even harder when Callie recalled her mother's warning about the mean-spiritedness of hungry people. Callie assumed that Bryan had also told Harley about what had happened and the sketch was the result. By the time it was over, she actually found herself feeling sorry for the poor girl.

Appalled, Callie commented on Bryan's physical condition. Tonya dryly replied that they both looked as if they'd been "rode hard and put away wet." Callie could hardly argue the point. During this past week she'd had occasional glimpses of herself in the mirror. If she'd ever looked worse, she was grateful that she couldn't recall it. Despite the judicious use of Visine, her eyes had not regained their normal hue, and her skin had lost its wondrous sheen. Even her hair, normally so vibrant and healthy, hung in lackluster strands around her face.

Bryan's voice was even hoarser and raspier than usual. Tonya had told her that he had a cold. But despite his condition, Bryan's fierce masculinity reached out to her just as powerfully as ever. His physical and emotional vulnerability provoked her to the point that she wanted nothing more than to rush to the airport and get to New York as soon as possible.

She no longer doubted that he needed her as much as she needed him. Watching him perform, she realized the futility and cruelty of ending their relationship the way she'd planned. She would have to talk to him and tell him her decision and the reasons behind it. However, she wasn't sure she could actually survive the pain of doing that in person. Certainly she was not up to the task right now.

Callie leaned against Bartholomew, rubbing his soft fur as she anxiously watched the television. The band had acoustic guitars and sat in the same formation they had used for the tribute concert. She wondered briefly if they were going to do an encore of that performance. Then they began to play, and Callie immediately recognized the melody. It was the song Bryan had played that day he'd asked her to come with him to L.A. She had a brief flashback to the sweet memory of that rainy fall day, and the joy in his eyes when she agreed to go. The tenderness of the music evoked so many painful memories that it literally took her breath away. She began to shake uncontrollably when she realized that the song Bryan was singing was about her and the way their relationship had been destroyed by outside forces and events they couldn't control. Everything else fell away; there was no one in the room but her and Bryan. It was just as it had been at the tribute concert. Bryan had the power to make a person feel as if he were singing directly to them. That he was making that person privy to emotions that he would not share with anyone else. But in this instance, Callie knew that this song was truly for her ears only. The fact that there were millions of other listeners was irrelevant; this was her song and he was singing it to her. Like the troubadours of old, he'd put his feelings to verse and was serenading his lady. The intimacy of that moment was almost tangible, and she began rocking back and forth as she realized the depth of this man's love for her. Then Thad joined in, harmonizing on the chorus, his high sweet tenor in stark contrast to the low timbre of Bryan's voice. The combination of the two voices sent chills down Callie's spine. She was surprised that Thad was willing to sing on stage because he had seemed so painfully shy and self-conscious. Even now, he didn't look into the camera once, but kept his eyes lowered to his guitar. Somehow the additional voice elevated the song's emotional power, and Callie began to sob.

Tonya looked on in wonder as Bryan told the world how much he loved Callie. Almost paralyzed with astonishment, it was all she could do to move closer to Callie in an attempt to console her. Much to her surprise, tears formed in her own eyes. She'd never expected him to make such a bold declaration. They both stared at the television, transfixed as Bryan finished the song and then looked directly into the camera. His tempestuous blue eyes ablaze, he huskily whispered a proclamation for the entire world. "I love you, Callie."

Callie gasped suddenly as the room grayed around the edges. For a moment she was sure she was losing consciousness. His voice sparked memories of those mornings when she'd awakened spooned in his arms, to his whispered declarations of love. His declarations had possessed the same raw emotion and gravely tone. She could almost feel his breath on the back of her neck as he murmured it to her. But he had said it on live television!

Tonya rocked her friend's slack body against her own. Damn! Dude really did know how to throw down the gauntlet. If anyone had any doubts about his intentions, he'd disabused them of those notions as patently as possible. Not to mention placing the ball firmly back in Callie's court.

Callie raised her head from Tonya's shoulder. "He really loves me, Tonya. He just told the world that he really loves me."

Tonya looked at her friend speculatively. "Yep, I'd say he did. Now the question is, what do you plan to do about it?"

# CHAPTER 20

Callie stared at Marjorie Peters' retreating back as she exited the store. So this was what it felt like to have the whole world all up in your business. Marjorie was the Sunday School teacher at Callie's church and the biggest gossip in Maple Fork. Actually, some said she was the most prolific scandalmonger in the tri-county area. She truly lived by Alice Roosevelt's old maxim, "If you don't have anything good to say, come sit next to me." Callie shook her head in utter disgust; Marjorie was the umpteenth person to ask her what she intended to do about the situation with Bryan. Was there anybody in the whole damned state who hadn't watched *Saturday Night Live*? And didn't any of these people have lives of their own? If she knew what she was going to do about "the situation with Bryan" would she be standing here in the middle of her store feeling like a hieroglyphic?

Meanwhile, Bryan seemed to have embarked on the official "Tell the World Their Business Tour," with appearances on all three late-night talk shows. Somehow he made it seem as though she'd rescued him from the brink of despair and self-destructive grief. Incredulously, she listened to him reveal the whole story with stark honesty.

To his credit, no one was talking about the story in *The Naked Truth* anymore. Instead, they were talking about Callie in terms usually reserved for the likes of Mother Teresa. And public opinion, in its usual fickle fashion, had turned against the tabloid. Under attack from what seemed like every celebrity in Hollywood and even some television news pundits, they had issued a formal apology and retraction and had even offered to make a substantial donation to Callie's favorite charity. Callie chewed her lip; in some ways she actually regretted the tabloid's quick capitulation. She had enjoyed the assaults on them and regularly watched the tape of Bill O'Reilly's comments. His voice shaking with righteous indignation, the commentator had upbraided the tabloid for its slanderous attack on a non-celebrity, a regular "working stiff," and demanded an apology.

She knew she had achieved true "fallen woman" status when she received a telephone call from celebrity attorney Gloria Allred's office offering to file suit for a substantial sum against the magazine. The representatives had pointed out to her that in addition to being slanderous, the story was also quite sexist and demeaning to women everywhere. Callie sucked her teeth, tempted to add that it was racist as well. As she had told Bryan, regardless of what went on in California, most people still didn't like seeing a black woman with a white man. Especially a white man who was as famous as Bryan. The law firm's offer would give her a chance to get back against a publication that had maliciously tried to ruin her life. Though sorely tempted, years of litigation did not appeal to her. More than anything, she simply wanted to get on with her life, not become entangled in endless legal retribution. Though she'd declined the offer, somehow the story had leaked to the press. She was fairly certain that it was Allred's potential involvement that had caused *The Naked Truth* to offer the quick recantation, apology and monetary award. Though she shuddered at the thought of actually taking what she considered to be blood money, she knew that there were several black entrepreneurial organizations that could use the capital. They had been immeasurably helpful to her, and she looked forward to being able to reciprocate.

For the first time in a long time, Callie was in the store alone. Roshonda had asked for a well-deserved day off, and Tonya was giving her manuscript some desperately needed attention. Tonya's editor was the only person calling them more often than the tabloids. In all likelihood Tonya would make her deadline, but it would be a near thing. She'd almost stopped writing altogether as she pitched in to help Callie deal with the crisis. Customers were still coming in at a steady clip, mainly to be nosey, but fortunately the reporters hadn't returned en masse. Generally there were one or two a day, content to snap a quick photograph and then go on their way.

Presumably the number of reporters dwindled because they were still covering the disappearance of that poor girl, and while Callie felt terrible for Lainie's family, she welcomed the reprieve. B.T. had given her a brief primer on how to handle the media last week. He had cautioned her that it was better to simply let them take the picture than to resist and to do her best to ignore them. She'd followed his advice, and for the most part, even the most notorious ones had been only minimally obnoxious.

Well, except for the one she'd found in the bottom of her closet that morning. She'd originally thought he was a burglar or worse and screamed the house down. Tonya had run in carrying her trusty Louisville Slugger. The guy had cowered there, begging them not to kill him, and presented his press credentials. They quickly determined that, having gained entrance with a credit card, he had been there for only a brief period, and not all night as they'd initially feared. Scared witless, he'd immediately confessed that he only wanted to get pictures of the rooms where the working girls supposedly did their business. Callie had a brief moment of gratitude that he hadn't gone into Tonya's room; one glimpse of that Mae West fantasy and nothing would've convinced the guy that there weren't any call girls there. He hadn't had a chance to take any incriminating photos, but they confiscated his memory card anyway and agreed to let him go. They'd called the locksmith right away to put on a dead-bolt lock on both their doors. Though the situation was bizarre to the extreme, it wasn't nearly as bad as some of the stories B.T. had related during their conversation the previous week. She couldn't imagine what it felt like to have paparazzi popping up in the bathroom, or hanging out of helicopters to get photographs. Sometimes they even yelled racial epithets or insults at celebrities to spark a reaction and "juice up" the picture. God, there had to be an easier way to make a living.

The *Saturday Night Live* performance had created quite a stir, and the first call after the show had come from Addie and Cynthia. They'd been so excited that they were nearly incoherent. Finally they'd calmed down enough to ask Callie when she was going to New York. They'd been bewildered when she'd assured them that she had no plans to do so.

"What more can he do?" Cynthia had screeched. "Callie, he told the whole world that he loved you. Isn't that enough? Even Daddy had to shut up after that! Did you hear him, Callie? Oh, it was so romantic. It gave me goose bumps the way he sang with his voice all bugged out. It was so cool."

Callie hadn't responded to the statement about her father. She was still smarting from his biting criticism two weeks ago. Though he'd come to her home shortly thereafter to apologize, and in his own gruff way had tried very hard to be loving and supportive, she was still hurt by his outbursts. She doubted he'd had a sincere change of heart, but accepted his apology because she didn't want to be the one to continue the hostilities.

Callie didn't know how to answer her sister's inquiries. She wondered what all these busybodies would say if they knew that Bryan had not called her or Tonya since appearing on the show. The only time either of them had heard him he was either on the radio or television. "Portrait," better known as "Callie's Song," had become an instant hit and was in heavy rotation on the radio stations. It seemed that MTV was broadcasting the *SNL* performance in a continuous loop. Every channel surfer on the planet had probably seen it at least once. She'd fielded requests from every talk show in existence, including some she'd never heard of. The only one she found even marginally tempting was Oprah. She adored the self-made woman, and would've been more than happy to talk with her about any other topic except her love life. With minimal participation from her, the situation was already outlandish. If she actually joined in the media circus it was bound to spin out of control. Besides, she didn't want to come across like the instant celebrities from all those so-called reality shows. They were famous for being famous, and had never really done anything to justify all the attention. No one would be interested in her if Bryan had been just a regular guy from down the street; she didn't want to exploit his fame that way.

*Cosmopolitan* had called to interview her for a story called, "How to Catch Your Own Rock Star."

Despite her refusal to cooperate, they were apparently rushing the issue to press to take advantage of all the media hype. She couldn't wait to see how they were going to write a story about her love life without interviewing her. Of course, *The Naked Truth* had apparently had little difficulty doing so. Why would *Cosmo* be any different? The telephone calls had tapered off somewhat after Callie made it clear that she wasn't giving interviews to anyone at any price. So much for her mercenary streak. If she'd taken even half the offers, she could have been a reasonably wealthy woman.

Just when she thought the situation couldn't get any worse, Sheriff Pettway had returned with a warrant to search her garbage. What was it going to take to get rid of this guy, a silver bullet? Perplexed, she'd simply stared at the document for a long moment, and though she really didn't want to know the answer, she had to ask why he wanted to search her garbage.

"Callie, I know you madams have gone high-tech these days. They tell me y'all even take credit cards. I figure I'll find the evidence in your trash. Besides, I know you people are big on practicing safe sex. If I find condoms out there, I can use our high-tech techniques to collect DNA evidence," he blustered self-importantly.

Callie wondered if Scooter even knew what DNA was. She knew for sure that he couldn't spell it. How high-tech could his collection methods be? After all, this man had bragged continuously for three weeks when he got a new bug zapper. He'd ceased his crowing only when the mayor threatened to put him in the contraption. Callie shook her head and led Scooter to the back of the store where they disposed of their garbage. Trash was picked up only once per week, so the dumpsters were quite full. She stood there and watched for a while as he and his deputy began pulling out the large trash bags. He had been so smug and superior she refused to tell him that she shredded all her documents, especially credit card receipts. With all the identity theft going on, she couldn't be too careful.

She was occasionally surprised however, at comments from people she would previously never have thought to be racist. Made self-conscious by the South's dismal racial history, the white people tried diligently to couch their opposition to her relationship with Bryan in inoffensive terms. The blacks were much more direct in their approach. The warning shot had come from the extremely Afro-centric leader of the African tribal dance class they had bi-weekly at the store. Their confrontation had been very heated, and the instructor threatened to cease teaching at the store. Deeply wounded, Callie had calmly told her to do what she felt was right. Thus far, the classes had continued on schedule, but the atmosphere was noticeably frigid between them. On more than one occasion she had been heard to ask how such a conscious-appearing  sister had turned into such a monumental sell-out. Quite a few black people had protested losing another one of their best and brightest to "the white man." As one of the church sisters put it, "It's bad enough that the first thing black men do when they get a little money is get a white woman. Now black women are doing the same thing. What's going to happen to the community?" Callie didn't know what to make of that. Would folks have been less concerned if she had been unattractive and less successful?

Attending church or any church activities had become almost impossible. Though the pastor of her church remained above the fray, his parishioners had not and some had even spouted the same vitriolic rhetoric she'd heard in other places. They could not be dissuaded, even when Callie protested that she would not be leaving the community for any reason. Dating a white man did not obviate the fact that she'd been black for twenty-nine years and was unlikely to change anytime soon. Most wounding was her eventual realization that all her activism on behalf of the black community apparently meant nothing if she dared violate the most crucial taboo for a black woman: dating a white man. Some of the women she sang with in the choir had been especially hateful. It had been unbearably painful when they whispered "white man's whore" under their breath as she entered the choir stand. Much to their dismay, Granny heard them and called them on it.

"Hmmmph, I can't believe all these supposed-to-be-sanctified folks are up in this church picking on Callie for loving somebody. If the church isn't about love, what is it about? And y'all know the only reason you got something to say is because you ain't got no man at all!"

Callie smiled as she recalled Granny's strong support. The women had slunk away; nobody dared talk back to Granny.

Much to her surprise, many of the comments were positive and the town was absolutely abuzz with interest in her love life. Of course, it didn't take long to realize that a great deal of that support came from people who had an eye towards capitalizing on the situation for their own benefit. Thus far, she had fielded dozens of requests for an entrée into the music industry. That had provided a great deal of comic relief, as people had taken to coming into the store to demonstrate their various talents. At any moment a seemingly normal customer would break into song or dance and sometimes most impressively, both. Their repertoire included everything from spirituals to operatic arias to hip-hop.

The butcher had entertained them all with a soliloquy from *Hamlet*. Callie wasn't sure exactly what his intentions were because she doubted that Bryan could get him into television or film, and the fact that he was pushing fifty made him an unlikely Hamlet, anyway. She was careful not to mention that to him, though. After all, the man had unlimited access to some very large knives. Not to mention his pride and joy, a brand-spanking-new meat grinder with which to dispose of any grisly remains.

Through all the insanity, though, Bryan still had not called. It was almost surreal. He'd been calling continually for days but now that she actually wanted to talk to him, nothing. She could only conclude that it was just as Tonya had said. He'd put the ball in her court, and the next move was hers. Of course, she didn't even begin to know what she wanted. Actually, that wasn't completely true. She knew without a doubt that she wanted Bryan, but was she willing to risk having something like this happen again? There was no way she was going to become like those sad creatures she'd seen in California, mere appendages of whatever celebrity they managed to pull cover with. Callie had every intention of continuing her own life, and to the degree that it was possible, putting every aspect of her five-year plan into place. Could she do that while married to a superstar rocker? And who had mentioned marriage anyway? Bryan had said that he wanted to be with her, but there had been no proposal in the offing. After all, what did 'it's going to be all about us' really mean? At the time she'd thought it meant marriage and long-term commitment. Now she wasn't so sure. For all she knew, he didn't even believe in marriage. They'd never really discussed it, and given his background, it wouldn't be surprising if he didn't.

Callie was saved from her confused musings when Granny came bustling into the store. She stood and glowered down at Callie from her impressive height for a long spell, then asked the question that seemed to be in the forefront of everybody's mind.

"Granny, I don't know what I'm going to do," Callie responded resignedly.

"You do know that boy isn't going to wait for you forever? Many a woman's missed out on a good man on account of listening to other folks," Granny lectured her insistently.

"I know that, Granny."

Granny pursed her lips, shaking her head decisively. "No, I don't think you do. I think you're letting all this foolishness folks are talking keep you from doing what's right for you. I've always thought you were a right smart young'un, Callie, but in this you're acting like a dumb missy."

Having Granny's respect was very important to Callie, and she tried to explain. "But Granny…"

Granny held up her massive hand to cut off any comment from Callie. "You listen to me. I don't want to hear nothing you've got to say because frankly right now you're not operating in your right mind, and it's bound to be stupid."

Callie's eyes widened in disbelief, but she didn't dare open her mouth.

"You young folks think you know everything, and you haven't lived long enough to know nothing. But I tell you what I'm going to do. I'm not opening the restaurant until you do the right thing. I'm not feeding people who don't deserve feeding." With that, she turned with all the grace and dignity of the Queen Mary under a full head of steam and stalked out the store.

Callie choked back the urge to scream. Oh hell, this was all she needed. If Granny went on strike, people would probably picket her store. She'd just gotten rid of the reporters and now she'd have a whole new gang of crazy folks at her door. The whole damned town would be at her throat if they were cut off from their soup! Not for the first time Callie wondered if she wouldn't be better off just seeking another zip code. She'd heard that Fiji was wondrous this time of year.

After Granny departed, Callie moved slowly over to the bench in front of the magazine rack and gingerly lowered her body to the seat, both hands tenderly holding her head as if afraid that it might fall off otherwise. Her mind whirled as she came to what had previously been an untenable conclusion. The butcher, the baker, and now the official soup maker. How had she lived in this town her entire life and never noticed that it was inhabited by full-fledged lunatics?

# CHAPTER 21

The knock on the door was loud and insistent. Callie bolted straight up in bed, startled from a restless slumber. Her abrupt movement almost knocked Bartholomew to the floor, and she righted him from his precarious perch on the edge of the bed. Disoriented for a moment, she looked around trying identify the source of the disturbance. "What in the world…" But all she heard was the insistent rain, unusual for late spring, that had lingered all day. Just as she glanced over at her bedside clock, the knock sounded again. "Who on earth is knocking at one o'clock in the morning?" She jumped out of bed, hastily donning her bathrobe to cover her short cotton nightgown.

She met Tonya on the landing. After contemplating for a moment who the caller could be, they moved cautiously down the stairs, Tonya at Callie's back, carrying her upraised baseball bat. Callie hoped it wasn't Sheriff Scooter. At this point she'd have no qualms about introducing him to the business end of that bat. The knocking continued as they very hesitantly approached the door. It was unlikely that anything good was showing up at this hour. When they reached the bottom of the stairs, Callie called out from the safe distance. The reply gave her a start and she turned to give Tonya a disbelieving glance, then rushed to unlock the dead bolts.

"Bryan, what are you doing here…" Bryan cut off that question by immediately pulling Callie to him in an all-encompassing hug. She relaxed against him for a moment, just absorbing the wonder of his presence, but abruptly backed away when she realized he was soaking wet.

Bryan pulled her back up against him, closing his eyes as an intense wave of pleasure washed over him. "God, baby," he murmured against her neck. "God, just give me a minute."

Tonya put her bat down, then leaned casually against the stair rail. Crossing her arms over her emerald green velvet robe, she drolly commented, "Damn boy, what took you so long? I was seriously starting to wonder about you."

Callie and Bryan were too absorbed in each other to respond. Finally giving a sardonic snort, Tonya turned and made her way back up the stairs.

Callie finally broke their embrace. "Bryan, you're soaking wet. Did you bring a change of clothes? I know you've had a bad cold; you're going to catch pneumonia." She took his chilled hand, leading him up the stairs to her apartment. Bryan nodded his affirmation to her question, and hoisted a disreputable-looking duffel bag onto his shoulder. Once they reached her apartment, Callie directed him into her bedroom to change clothes while she went into the kitchen to start a pot of coffee. Apparently Tonya had already beat her to the task and stood leaning against the counter looking at Callie expectantly. Callie shrugged. She didn't have any idea what she was going to say or do.

Tonya gave her another significant look. "Callie, I haven't said anything all this time while I watched both of you wallow in your own misery." She paused, then gave Callie a sheepish grin. "Besides, I have to admit I felt a little bit guilty because I pushed you to hook up with him, and all this stuff happened. But he's come to you now. Don't mess this up."

"Tonya, nothing's changed. He's still famous. I can't live with that. I just can't," she whispered disconsolately.

Tonya threw up her arms in disgust and then left the kitchen to return to her bed. Callie moved to pour coffee for herself and Bryan, then took the mugs into the living room. As she sat down, Bryan came out of bedroom, toweling his hair dry. His black jeans and dark gray vintage Led Zeppelin T-shirt hung on his spare frame, telling the story of his recent weight loss. Bryan, like many other rock stars, had a fondness for vintage rock-and-roll T-shirts. Naysa had told Callie that she found them at Lo-Fi, a vintage clothing store in L.A., and for all its casual appearance, that T-shirt had probably cost a fortune. According to Naysa, the shirts were one of the few sources of sartorial excitement within the band, and the only truly fashionable thing she had little difficulty getting them to wear. Little wonder then that she had standing orders for them as they came in, even though the prices sometimes topped out at better than five hundred dollars as competing stylists drove the prices up.

Of course, none of this was on Bryan's mind at the present. Feet bare except for a pair of athletic socks, he padded over to Callie and took the mug she offered before sitting down on the sofa next to her.

Bryan took a few appreciative sips. The rain had left him more chilled than he'd realized. Then he said, "I know you know why I'm here. Since you won't talk to me on the phone, could you please be so kind as to tell me what the hell's been going on?"

Callie shifted restlessly under the intensity of his dark-blue gaze and moved over into the corner of the sofa, resting her head against the sofa's high back. She had never thought that Bryan would just show up like this, and was totally unprepared to deal with him. She had gone to great pains to avoid just this confrontation and his tone made it clear that this was going to be as tough as she'd expected.

"I don't know, Bryan. All of this has been so confusing. I just didn't know what to say to you."

"Did you have to just cut me off like that? I had no idea what the hell was going on with you!"

"I didn't mean to hurt you, but I just don't think I can be with you…"

"What the hell are you talking about?" Bryan shouted. "I knew this would be tough on you, Callie, but I thought you had more backbone than this." He ran his fingers through his damp hair in frustration, his efforts adding to its disheveled look. "Yeah, the reporters suck, but it's not the end of the freaking world. They will eventually go away and suck some other poor bastard's blood."

Callie couldn't believe he had the audacity to say such a thing. "Backbone? How dare you? Do you have any idea what I've been through these last few weeks? Do you?" she shrieked.

"Yes, Callie, I know exactly how bad it's been. Remember, while you were giving me the brush off, I was talking to your roommate. At least she had the decency to talk to me," he snapped back irritably, his entire body practically crackling with his anger.

"No, I don't think you do. You couldn't possibly know what it's like to have hundreds of people in your store all day long…"

Bryan interrupted, "Callie, I live with it every freaking day! I've been dealing with it for at least ten years, ever since the band hit big, and pretty much even before then."

Callie continued as if he hadn't said anything. "Reporters beating on the windows, hiding in my closet…and a redneck sheriff going through my garbage. I'm not a rock star, and I shouldn't have to put up with this!" she shouted.

Bryan was caught off guard. "Reporter in your closet? Sheriff in your garbage? Nobody told me about that. Are you okay?"

"Do you care, Bryan? Do you really give a damn?"

"Callie, I don't even believe you could ask a question like that. What the hell else do I have to do, woman, to convince you how I feel? Frankly, I'm getting tired of the whole damned routine," he retorted wearily.

Callie closed her eyes. He had every right to be angry. She was being incredibly unfair to him. "You're right, Bryan, I don't have any doubts about how you feel."

Bryan threw his hands into the air in mock wonder. "Well damn! Stop the presses. Callie finally admits that she knows I love her. I guess I should be grateful for that anyway," he returned snidely. "So what is it, what's the problem, Callie? Why are you doing this to us? Don't you think I deserve some type of explanation?"

"Bryan," Callie sighed, moving closer to him, "it's a lot of things. You know I had doubts from the very beginning…"

Bryan gritted his teeth. "Doubts I thought we overcame a long time ago." He didn't know how much more of this he could take.

Callie, sensing that he was at the end of his patience, decided to compromise. "Bryan, I really don't know what I want, okay? Maybe to you this is all normal, but for me, it's been really freaky. Can I please have some time to work it all out?"

Bryan was in no mood for anything short of unconditional surrender. "Jesus, Callie! You've had weeks, while I've just been hanging on wondering what the hell was going on. What more do you need to work out? Look, Callie, do you have any idea what I've gone through to get here? I landed in Atlanta barely an hour ago, caught absolutely the last flight after our show!

Thank God for the time difference or I never would've gotten out. At the airport, I hired a taxi to get me here. I've got to be back in New York by this time tomorrow night. I'm tired as all get out, but I had to talk to you." Bryan paused and took a deep breath as he realized he wasn't being totally fair to Callie either. After all, she didn't even know the whole story. He flopped back on the sofa. "The worst thing is, I haven't even told you what all is going on. You've got to hear everything before you make any decisions."

Callie looked at him apprehensively. What more could there possibly be? She didn't know if she could stand it if this situation got any worse.

Bryan didn't really want to tell Callie about B.T.'s involvement in this whole fiasco; she was already skittish enough and ready to bail on him. But if he kept this from her, it was bound to flare up someday and then she'd accuse him of lying to her. As he tried to collect his thoughts, his eyes drifted over her legs left bare by the short terrycloth robe she was wearing. She was sitting lotus-fashion with her legs up on the sofa facing him. He ran one finger up and down her firm calf. The feel of her skin beneath his hands was still a powerful lure, and he was momentarily sidetracked as he began to recall how that warm golden brown skin felt under his lips. He'd always thought Callie's skin looked like cinnamon dipped in honey, and after the long drought he could think of nothing that would taste better.

"Baby, do you have any idea how much I want to make love with you?" he whispered, his voice raspy with desire.

Callie gave him a longing look. She was more than willing. Being with Bryan had awakened all her carnal desires, and her body craved the physical satiation he offered.

"No." He shook his head firmly, needing to convince himself more than anything. "Much as I wish it was otherwise, there's no way we can get through this without talking first. I just hope you don't get pissed off and stop speaking to me again when I tell you what happened."

"Bryan, I wasn't angry with you, I just…"

Bryan placed a gentle finger against her lips to silence her. "I know. Well, actually, I don't know, but you haven't heard the whole sorry mess yet, either." He sighed heavily. "Just relax and let me tell you a story." She might not have been angry before, but Bryan had no doubt that by the time he related B.T.'s perfidy, he'd be lucky if the fireworks didn't set the building ablaze. He then relayed the tale of B.T.'s complicity in their story being published in the tabloids.

"Why that…" For the first time that she could recall, Callie was at a total loss for words. She hadn't felt this confused since that day in first grade when her father accidentally dropped her off at the wrong school. "I can't believe this. You mean he put us through all this just to break us up?"

Bryan felt compelled to defend his former manager. After all, fair play was fair play. "Actually, he didn't start it, he just didn't try to stop it."

Callie's eyes widened in amazement. "Don't you think you're splitting hairs here? What possible reason could that man have for trying to break us up?" Her teeth snapped together as the obvious motive occurred to her. "It's because I'm black, isn't it?"

Bryan really didn't want to get into this area, recognizing its relationship-wrecking potential. He thought back to the conversation they'd had that day they'd gone to get Callie's hair done. God, he'd been so naïve! "Callie, I know you tried to tell me all this…but I didn't listen. It never occurred to me that anybody would give a damn who I fell in love with. I really did think all that was ancient history and didn't have anything to do with us. I was such a frigging idiot. Baby, I'm sorry…"

Callie shook her head as she interrupted him. "You don't have anything to be sorry about. How would you know? You didn't have any experience with it. I, on the other hand, knew better." She continued regretfully, "I don't know why this caught me by surprise. I should've been expecting it all along."

Bryan shook his head mournfully, his self-disgust evident. "Well, you did tell me, but I was just…I don't know, I was just so happy that I couldn't believe that anything like this would happen. And I never thought they'd go after you. Baby, I'm so sorry I didn't take better care of you. My only excuse is, I thought B.T. had my back. I won't make that mistake again."

"Hmmmph, I just can't believe this guy. If he had problems with our being together, why didn't he say something earlier?" She sat up as a thought occurred to her. "Did he say anything to you about us?" Surely Bryan wouldn't have kept something like that from her.

"No, he never said anything to me about us being together hurting my career or really anything at all. He seemed indifferent, but that's how he's always been about my relationships, unless it was with somebody he could use for publicity. Not that I would've given a damn if he had said anything. But I know he didn't mention it to me because he knew it wouldn't have done any good," Bryan replied, his rising anger evident in his tone.

"Well," Callie said resignedly, "I should have been expecting this. I know how people are." She paused for a moment. "Did you tell Tonya about this?" she asked sharply. She'd be deeply hurt if her friend had kept such earth-shattering news from her.

"Good God, no! What do you think I am, nuts?" He couldn't miss the irony of that comment. "Okay, so I am nuts, but I do actually function quite well despite my assorted personality disorders. Besides, even Charlie Manson would be sane enough not to tell Tonya something like this. It was all I could do to get her to talk to me in the first place. If I'd told her about B.T.'s involvement…" He shuddered. "It's too awful to contemplate."

Still confused, Callie frowned as she struggled with the niggling little inconsistencies in the story. "But,

Bryan, he called me, he told me how to deal with the reporters and everything. What was that all about?"

Bryan was mesmerized by the hint of cleavage visible above the rose-colored fabric of her robe.

"Bryan? Are you going to answer me?" she asked insistently.

Bryan wiped a hand across his face. "Sorry, baby." He grinned sheepishly. "I just got distracted for a moment." He frowned as he recalled her last question. "Yeah, B.T. had to come back around. Dude didn't really have any choice in the matter. Maria had him by the short hairs."

"Maria?"

"Yeah, believe it or not she threatened to divorce him if he didn't make things right."

"Wow." Callie couldn't think of anything else to say. During their encounter in L.A., Maria had given her the impression that she was blindly devoted to her husband. So much for first impressions.

"I know, I couldn't believe it, either." Bryan continued ruefully, "Old boy hunted me down in Houston and asked me to help him. Then he got us on *Saturday Night Live* and all the gigs on the talk shows. He also called off the reporters." He held up his hand to silence her when she opened her mouth to speak. "And no, he didn't have Lainie Ellison kidnapped to take the heat off us."

# CHAPTER 22

Callie screeched in amazement, "Good grief, Bryan! I never thought he had!" Had things really gotten that bad? Did Bryan truly believe his manager was capable of such a monstrous act? Or was he just seeing his manager through his anger and pain?

The television mogul's daughter had been returned that morning, unharmed. The situation was very mysterious, and rumor had it that her father had paid a monstrously large ransom to get her back. The family had made no comment, other than that they were happy to have their daughter back. It was shaping up to be much more than a seven-day wonder, with speculation running rampant that she'd been sent to drug rehab, or had run away to escape her father's overbearing management of her life. There was even some talk of a secret boyfriend, or maybe even a pregnancy, but those rumors were summarily dismissed because Myron Ellison kept very close restrictions on his daughter. Whatever the circumstances, Callie could truly empathize with the girl and her family. She hoped they'd be able to rid themselves of the paparazzi quickly. Surely Myron Ellison's money would help in that area.

Callie studied Bryan's wan features. Though he tried not to let on, the pain he felt from B.T.'s betrayal was obvious. Bryan was wearing his hair down tonight, and it hung like dark silk halfway down his back. It was mussed from the rough towel drying and his repeatedly pulling at it as they worked through the complex emotional issues that were keeping them apart. Bryan's feelings and loyalties ran deep. He and B.T. had always had a strong relationship, and he'd tolerated behavior from his manager that no one else could have gotten away with. She had no doubt that Bryan had a great deal of respect for his manager, but she also knew that Bryan loved B.T. deeply. This had to have been a hellish situation for him.

"Bryan, how are you feeling about all this?" she asked quietly.

Bryan took a deep breath, raising his shoulders, then lowering them, as if forcing himself to relax. He moved to get up as he tried to change the subject. "You got any food around here? I didn't get a chance to eat and I'm starving."

Callie grabbed his arm, pulling him back down onto the sofa. She gave him a disapproving look. "Bryan, you know better. I know you've got to be hurting. B.T. is like a father to you. Has been for years. You can't just tell me that he's betrayed you this way and you're perfectly okay with it." When he still didn't respond, she gave in begrudgingly, muttering under her breath about his obstinacy as she got up from the sofa. "Okay, I'll make you a sandwich, but you know we've got to talk about this."

By the time Callie returned from the kitchen with a ham and cheese sandwich, piled high with lettuce and tomato just as she knew he liked it, Bryan had moved over to the window. He pushed the light muslin curtains aside to stare out at the streetscape below. Maple Fork was, of course, bedded down for the night. The rain had finally ceased, and the town gleamed wetly under the illumination of the artificial gas streetlights. When he realized she'd returned with the sandwich, he moved to the sofa and sat down. He took several bites and chewed for long minutes. Then he took a couple of sips from the fresh mug of coffee she'd brought with the sandwich. He had used the food as a distraction, but he really was hungry. The meal served on the airplane had been inedible and he hadn't wanted to take the time to eat once he arrived in Atlanta. Consequently, his last meal had been early the previous day. Finally, when he was about halfway finished he glanced over at her expectant face. He had no choice but to resume the conversation.

"Damn it, Callie, there's just some things that are better left alone," he replied irritably. Why did Callie have to continually probe at his feelings? The last thing he wanted at this moment was to expose himself any further. Besides, she was using this as a distraction, just as he'd done with the sandwich, to keep from having to address their own issues.

"Between us, Bryan? Are you saying that there are things that shouldn't be discussed between us?" Her hurt feelings were evident in her soft tone.

Bryan gave her a speaking glance. "What *us*, Callie? Is there an *us*?"

Callie lowered her head but didn't answer.

Bryan reached over and put a finger under her chin and raised her head until her eyes met his. "Is there an *us*, Callie?" he asked forcefully.

Callie's eyes pooled with tears. "I don't know, Bryan, I just don't know."

Bryan gave a snort of disgust, then resumed eating his sandwich, taking sips of coffee between bites. Apparently she still wasn't ready to talk about what was going on with her. He'd be patient just a little longer. "I don't know how I feel about B.T. I think the man saved my life, Callie. Matter of fact, I know he did. If I'd stayed out there on the streets like that, God only knows what would've happened to me. Everything I am, everything I've ever wanted to be is because of him. I don't know if I can do this without him and Brodie too."

He shifted on the sofa, his voice tremulous with anger. "I thought he cared about me, Callie. I thought he really gave a damn about me as a person. Now I know that I'm just another product to him. He was willing to ruin our lives to protect his interests."

Callie moved over closer, wrapping her arm around his waist and laying her head on his shoulder. She searched desperately for words to console him, but none were forthcoming. The situation was so over-whelming, everything she could think of sounded trite and meaningless. "Sweetie, I'm so sorry. I don't know what to say."

Bryan pulled her against his chest. "There's nothing much to say. I fired him, but I know I've got a hell of a legal battle ahead. And then there's Maria, the one person who actually does give a damn. This is going to be awful for her. She's going to be so hurt, I don't know if she can take it. God, what a mess!"

Callie nuzzled into her favorite position beneath his chin. She knew what she had to say, but it was a major struggle to utter the soothing words. "You know, maybe it wasn't just his interests he was protecting. Maybe he really did think he was taking care of you too. I mean, you've told me that over the years you've pretty much let B.T. run the show. He's never inter-fered with your love life before, but maybe he really was just desperate and did what he thought was right." Much to her surprise, she found that she could over-look her own issues with B.T. if it would give Bryan some measure of relief from the emotional burden he was laboring under. Reflexively, she wanted to agree with Bryan's decision to cut B.T. out of his life. It would certainly be a more comfortable existence for her, but it would undermine the closest thing he had to a family. Could she let him do that, especially when he'd already lost the man he considered a brother? Unfortunately with family, sometimes a person had to take the bitter with the better, as her mother would say.

She reflected on B.T.'s very real grief the night of the tribute party. The man had not been mourning his balance sheet. He cared about Bryan, and more importantly, Bryan loved him. B.T. was not the ideal manager, but he had been considerably better to Bryan than many of the other managers out there would have been. She shivered as she recalled the shifty men she'd met at the tribute party. B.T. stood head and shoulders above most of the managers in the music business. Bryan could most assuredly do a whole lot worse. Another of her mother's sayings ran through her mind: better the devil you know than the devil you don't. All in all, Bryan would be better off holding pat with the hand he'd been dealt.

Bryan perked up as her statement sank in. "Do you really believe he thought he was looking out for me?" Despite his anger, he couldn't keep the hopefulness out of his tone.

Callie nodded. "Bryan, I really don't think B.T. intended to hurt you. I don't think he's evil." She snorted with laughter. "Twisted as all get out, and definitely amoral, but I really do believe he thought he was looking out for you."

Bryan shook his head, awed by her defense of a man who had caused her so much pain. He'd never known anyone with such a capacity for forgiveness. "I can't believe you're willing to forgive this guy. You're incredible."

Callie could only smile in return. She hadn't exactly forgiven B.T. for his involvement in this whole mess, but she did believe that he'd had Bryan's best interests at heart. Besides, a break with him would probably hurt Bryan much worse than it would B.T., and Maria would be wounded more deeply than either of them. Callie had no doubt about Maria's love for Bryan. She had put her marriage on the line for his sake. She could understand Bryan's reluctance to hurt her. They would tangle with this issue for a while, but as long as they handled B.T. carefully, there was no real reason to dissolve the relationship. Despite his anger and pain, Bryan would eventually see the wisdom of this course of action.

They sat comforting each other for a long time, simply absorbing one another's presence after their long dry spell.

After a while, Bryan stirred. "So, Callie, now that we've dealt with everything else, what about us?"

Callie frowned. She'd put this off for as long as she could, but apparently her hour of reckoning was at hand. Bryan would not be put off any longer.

She pursed her lips as she formulated what she needed to say. "Bryan, do you remember those women we saw in L.A.? You know, the ones who are always looking for the next celebrity to attach themselves to?"

"Yeah, Callie, I'm passably acquainted with the breed," Bryan responded dryly, wondering what the hell this had to do with them. Surely Callie didn't think he was still involved with those women.

Callie spoke rapidly, her words rushed, as if afraid that if she didn't say it now, she never would, "See,

Bryan, I'm not like them. I've got my own life. I'm a businesswoman. I can't be like those women in L.A., just following you around from place to place, like some type of accessory. I don't want to live off you and be rewarded with extravagant shopping trips and expensive jewelry. I've got my younger sisters and the rest of my family to think of. I just can't act like that." She paused, looking up at him tremulously, not sure of his reaction. She didn't want to hurt him, but she couldn't live that way. But then again, giving Bryan up would be devastating. She wanted both and hoped he would understand.

Bryan frowned in puzzlement. "Callie, what on earth are you talking about? When did I say I wanted you to do that? I think it's a good thing that one of us knows how to make money. For God's sake, haven't you seen all those broke-ass ex-rock stars on *Behind the Music*? In case you haven't noticed, I've got one crafty sonofabitch for a manager. Hell, by now he's probably got more of my money than I do and in a few years I'll be lucky if I can get a gig playing 'Freebird' at a Holiday Inn in Eastaboga!" he roared, infuriated that Callie was still hung up on the notion of being his kept woman.

Callie doubled over, unable to contain her laughter. Bryan was truly incensed. She could all but see the sparks flying from those deep blue eyes.

He continued at full rant, "I may not be too terribly bright, but I do know the difference between a good woman and a pay-to-play girl. Please give me some kind of credit, okay?"

Callie was still gasping with laughter and couldn't respond.

Bryan calmed down, unable to maintain his anger in light of her silly response. When she finally stopped laughing, he captured her face in both his hands. "Callie, you are the woman I fell in love with all those months ago. That's who you are, and that's who I want you to be. My own personal budding tycoon. You know I love it when you're all in your business mode negotiating deals; it's so goddamned sexy. You don't know how many times I've wanted to slide you right out of your tastefully tailored pants and take you right on top of your desk, especially when you have a pencil behind your ear. It's probably given me a fetish."

Callie gaped at Bryan in amazement. She'd never had any inkling that he'd been thinking that way. A pencil behind her ear was sexy? Who knew? She thought back to all those late nights Bryan had been in the store with her while she ordered books. Perusing long printouts from the various publishers, she'd frequently had a pencil behind her ear. When things were really frantic she'd sometimes have pencils behind both ears. She shivered delightfully as she thought about her response if he'd followed through on his inclinations.

"You've got your own gig, baby, and that's great. Go take over the world, give Bill Gates a run for his money. I never thought for one moment that I'd just be able to attach you to my life. God, Callie, I could've had that years ago with dozens of women. That's not what I want; I want us to make a life together, as partners, as equals." He looked into her luminous brown eyes. "Is that what all this was about? Were you going to dump me because you thought you were going to have to give up everything to be with me?"

Callie nodded, her eyes now sparkling with tears, moved by the wonderfully beautiful things he'd said. He was offering her everything she'd ever wanted. He was giving her the world. But did she dare take it? "I thought it would be better if I just let it go. I'm not sure I can handle all the reporters and stuff and I don't want to give up everything I've worked so hard for. I know it was wrong of me not to talk to you about it, but I—I didn't know what to say. I knew I couldn't look you in the eye and tell you how I felt, so I thought if I refused to talk to you you'd eventually stop calling." Callie shook her head, shamed by her cowardice.

Bryan leaned his forehead against hers. "God, baby." His voice choked with emotion. "Please, please promise me one thing. Always at least talk to me first. I've been going out of my mind worried about you. I know I probably drove Tonya crazy calling all the time, but I had to know you were okay. I can't promise you that the paparazzi won't bother us. Sometimes little things you do get a lot of attention, especially on a slow news day. They're unpredictable, but I promise I'll do a better job of taking care of you."

"I'm sorry, Bryan. I'd already realized that I'd have to talk this out with you, but I didn't think I could do it. It was so unfair, I really am sorry." She moved away from him to look into his face. "So is it okay if I take some time? I mean, I won't stop talking to you again, but I just need to think things through." She lowered her eyes, then looked up with a tremulous smile. "Besides, you still haven't told me exactly what type of relationship you want with me."

Bryan grinned down at her, then shifted to remove something from his pocket. He took her left hand in his, and slid a ring on her finger. "I thought that was obvious. I'm asking you to marry me."

Callie gave her ring finger an astonished glance, dazzled by the beautiful heart-shaped pink sapphire ring that now adorned it. She looked back up at Bryan, speechless with wonder.

Bryan continued determinedly, "I bought that when I bought the bracelet. I've always known you were meant to be my mate. To be with me forever. Have my children and kick my ass for the next fifty years. It's a pretty big order. I need a woman, Callie, not a little girl. Which one are you going to be?" He paused to give her a chance to respond. When no answer was forthcoming, he continued through clenched teeth, "You take all the time you need. You make goddamned sure of what you want, because once you're mine, I'm never letting you get away from me again."

# CHAPTER 23

Callie lowered her head to the kitchen table. "Oh, no, Mama, not you, too. Just for the record, I haven't the foggiest notion what I'm going to do about Bryan. I swear as soon as I do, I'll put it on a billboard, okay?" Relocating to the South Pacific and living in a thatched hut in the middle of nowhere was becoming more desirable by the second. She probably wouldn't even look too bad in a grass skirt. Snap back to reality. Knowing her luck, some intrepid Fijian would trek endless miles into the jungle just to inquire about her love life. Callie had known she was in trouble when her mother showed up on her doorstep a few minutes ago with the ominous statement, "We need to talk." But then again, what else was new?

Edith took a deep breath. Unlike her husband, she tried not to interfere unless Callie came to her first. She'd waited for several weeks, and other than the first night after the story came out, Callie hadn't mentioned anything about Bryan. She had just continued on as always, working harder than ever. Edith had even made a point of going to the store regularly to offer moral support, something she hadn't done since their first year, but Callie had not confided anything to her. She could see that her child was in pain, but evidently if she wanted to know how Callie felt, she'd have to ask her directly. "Callie, do you love Bryan?"

Callie raised her head from the table, leaned forward with her elbows on the table and her chin resting on her clasped hands. "Mama, I..."

"Callie, it only requires a yes or no answer. Do you love the boy or not?" Edith interjected sharply.

There was no way around it. She couldn't lie to her mother. She closed her eyes, unable to look at her mother directly. "Yeah, Mama, I do, but..."

"But what? Good Lord, Callie. I know this situation has been awful, but are you really going to throw your relationship away because of it?" Edith asked, incredulous about the huge mess her usually level-headed daughter had made of what really was a fairly straightforward matter. Callie had never before doubted what she wanted or how she would go about getting it. Edith shook her head. Bless her heart, clearly the child had been so focused on her career that she didn't even begin to know how to deal with men and relationships. She had no idea how the child had gotten along unaided for this long. This madness had gone on long enough. If she didn't give the poor girl some direction, she'd never get out of this on her own.

"Mama, he's a big rock star. I don't know if I can be with a rock star," Callie sighed miserably.

"Callie, didn't you know what the man did for a living from the beginning?" Edith asked exasperatedly.

Callie nodded, "Yeah, Mama, you know I did."

"And if you didn't think you could handle it, why did you jump in bed with him?"

"Mama!" Callie gasped. Her mother never commented on her sex life. Of course, up to now she hadn't had much of one to engender any discussion.

"Please!" Edith sniffed indignantly. "Your father and I were young once, you know. I know what it feels like to be all hot and bothered over a man." She grinned knowingly. "Besides, you young folks act like y'all invented sex. How do you think you got here?"

Callie covered her ears, wrinkling her nose with distaste. She really didn't want to think about her parents having sex. "Mama, I don't want to give up my life. I have my future all planned out, and I don't know if I can have that with Bryan."

Edith gave her daughter a look of patent disbelief. What was this child doing? Callie had never been one to run and hide. What was going on? Her voice sharp with exasperation, Edith replied, "Callie, don't you think that maybe, just maybe, you need to discuss this with Bryan? Why are you putting up all these road-blocks?" She frowned, leaning forward on the table as she recognized the real source of her daughter's anxiety. She hesitated, knowing Callie wasn't ready to hear this, but nothing would be resolved until she did. "Now baby, I know this is going to hurt your feelings, but you know I wouldn't tell you this if it wasn't true.

I don't think any of this has anything to do with Bryan. I think you'd be acting crazy with whatever man you happened to fall in love with."

"Mama, what…"

Edith held up her hand to silence Callie's interruption. "Hold on there, baby. If you think about it, you'll know I'm telling the truth. All your life you've had to be in control of everything. That's why you hardly ever dated. Being in love is too messy, too uncertain for you. I remember even as a skinny little girl, you refused to participate in any games that you didn't have complete control over. Everything had to be in exact, precise order. You're the only child I know who didn't like surprises. You wanted to know everything well in advance, and hated last minute changes or anything impulsive."

Callie couldn't catch her breath to formulate a response; she'd had no idea that she came across that way. Over the years people had teased her about her controlling personality. Tonya could keep up a running monologue on the topic, but it had never occurred to her that it might be the cause of her romantic ambivalence.

Edith continued, "I guess maybe at least some of this is our fault. We probably didn't let you have enough say in your life as you were coming up. We've tried to do better with your sisters. That's the good thing about parenting more than one child; you get to learn from your mistakes and improve your technique. But that's neither here or there now. I know you were happy with Bryan, Callie, and I know you have been absolutely pitiful these past few weeks. And it hasn't just been those nosy reporters and assorted other crazy people you've had to deal with. You've been handling crazy folks for years. Every nut in Maple Fork hangs out in this store. Most of your so-called customers either are or need to be medicated. You encourage it with all those classes and groups you have here, so you've got to be used to them by now. No, you're unhappy because that boy is not here, and you might as well admit it. Now, you're a grown woman, and I can't tell you what to do, but, baby, you've got to know how foolish this is. Either you want the man or you don't. If you want him, none of this other stuff matters. You'll take him regardless of what he does for a living."

She paused for a moment, evidently searching for a way to illustrate her point. "Callie, what would you do if instead of being a rock star, Bryan was blind or handicapped in some way? Would you break up with him then?"

Callie was indignant. What kind of woman did her mother think she was? "Of course not, I would stay with him and help him."

"So why can't you look at his career as something of a handicap that you have to help him with? Inconvenient for sure, but it doesn't change who he is." Edith Lawson knew from Callie's stunned expression that she had scored a direct hit. It was time to leave her to reflect on what they'd discussed. She was confident that this daughter who was so much like herself in temperament would make the right decision. She got up from the table. "I'll leave you to think about that. There's really nothing more for me to say." As she walked past her daughter, she wrapped her arms around her shoulders and gave her a kiss on the top of her down-turned head. "I love you, baby. I hope you'll make a decision you can live with."

Callie closed her eyes as she inhaled the Youth Dew fragrance her mother always wore. The scent of lilies and cinnamon evoked sweet memories of other times she'd been consoled. This time, however, was different. Mama wouldn't be able to fix this. She was on her own this time. With eyes that reflected her mental anguish and discord, she watched as her mother departed the kitchen.

Callie waited until she heard the front door of the apartment close behind her mother, then leaned back in her chair. Was what her mother said true? Was she some type of commitment-phobic control freak? She had to concede that she liked to be in charge of things because she knew she could do them right. She paused, that thought reverberating through her head. Oh God! That had to be the first article of faith of every control freak on the planet! Okay, she admitted with sudden self-knowledge, she was somewhat controlling, but did that explain her confusion and conflict about her relationship with Bryan? Her mother's statement whirred through her mind: "Either you want the man or you don't." That was the core of the matter right there. Bryan's career was tiresome, and would be a pain in the ass from time to time, but it didn't change who he was, or how she felt about him. Oh God! What if she'd ruined everything by being silly and stupid? She took several deep breaths. Her next move was clear, as it had been for weeks. But she'd been trying desperately to run from the truth. She prayed with that same intensity for the strength to follow through on the only decision she could live with.

Bryan looked out over the sold-out crowd in Madison Square Garden. This was their third sold-out show there and the last show of the truncated Storm Crow tour. Nineteen thousand eager fans had paid upward of fifty dollars each to see this show, and the band was determined to do their best. They were famous for giving very long performances, and this was one of their longest, clocking in at over three hours. The adrenaline surge of playing before a packed house had carried them through countless songs, each one played more intensely than the previous one. They had their fans in the palms of their hands and they knew it; it was now only a matter of bringing the show to a close with a bang, and they had just the song to do it. The arena was a sea of pinpoint lights as thousands of cigarette lighters flickered in response to the opening chords of "Portrait," the only ballad the band had ever played. Bryan was pretty much over his cold, and was capable of singing the song unaided, but Thad still joined him on the chorus, and their harmony had lost none of its emotional impact. His body slack with physical and emotional exhaustion, Bryan held the microphone tightly as he crooned the ode to his unrequited love. His despair over his loss fueled the song's poignancy and many in the audience were openly weeping. Bryan felt like crying himself; he had been so sure that Callie would call in the week since he returned from Alabama. He simply didn't know what else he could do to apologize for the mockery his fame had made of her life.

He blinked rapidly, his eyes moistening with sudden tears as another wave of hopelessness washed over him. And that's when he felt it, the vibration of the cell phone he had kept in his pocket for months. Much to his own surprise, he hadn't lost the thing once. Kelly claimed that it had to be some sort of record. He paused for a moment. Perhaps he was mistaken. Then it buzzed again. It could only be Callie; no one else had the number. Unwilling to risk losing this opportunity, only God knew if she would call again, he immediately raised his arm to stop his bandmates' playing, then reached into his pocket for the telephone. Thad and Jon who were standing on either side of him both moved over closer to see what was going on. They quickly realized that he was answering the telephone, and Thad relayed that information to Twist who sat behind his drum kit shaking his head in disgust. The crowd could see a close-up of Bryan on the huge wide-screen monitors on either side of the stage so they knew what was happening. Most of the crowd had followed Bryan and Callie's tale and had little doubt as to who the caller was. The murmur that had begun when Bryan stopped playing rose to a thunderous crescendo when their guess was confirmed by Bryan's ecstatic expression as Callie told him, "No, Bryan, this time, I'm coming to you."

From the wings of the stage B.T. watched Bryan's activities avidly. Fortunately Bryan was not able to see his face, because he could not hide his gleeful expression as he watched Bryan answer the telephone. Despite his recent setbacks, he knew a marketing bonanza when one was handed to him. He turned to Kelly. "What brand of cell phone is Bryan using?" he asked sharply.

Kelly, totally enraptured by the romance of the scene, looked up at B.T. quizzically. "What?"

B.T. waved his hand dismissively as he walked away reaching for his own cell phone. It really didn't matter. With today's technology, he could have a bidding war to put any number of brands in his star's hand. Bryan couldn't even complain about the boredom of shooting a commercial. He'd already done the hard part. Even better, he had done it without any manipulation, so he couldn't blame it on his manager. B.T. grinned widely as one of his favorite marketing executives came on the line. "Paul," he began in his best "Let's Make a Deal" tone, "you're not going to believe what just happened here." His Southern drawl deepened as he switched the cigar to the other side of his mouth and continued his pitch. "It's a gold mine you'd be a fool to pass up…"

Kelly turned to stare at B.T.'s retreating back. It hadn't taken long for the old boy to return to the art of the deal, she thought ruefully. She'd missed him. She had to admit, begrudgingly, that old shyster kept things hopping.

After she finished speaking with Bryan, Callie wandered into her bedroom and sat on the edge of her bed contemplating what she'd just done. She felt a warm tingly glow all over, just as she always did after talking to him. More than anything, that feeling convinced her that she'd done the right thing. She looked down at the fiery glow of the heart-shaped ring he'd given her. She hadn't been able to bring herself to take it off, even though it had spawned even more gossip about their relationship. He'd known all along they were fated to be together, that she was, as he called it, his mate. What had taken her so long to come to the same conclusion? Impatient now with all the time she'd wasted, she jumped off the bed and rushed over to her closet, pulling her suitcase down from an upper shelf. Realizing that she would need assistance to get packed quickly, she called out to Tonya, who immediately rushed into the room.

"What's going on?" she asked, frowning with concern at the urgent nature of Callie's call. Seeing her friend with a suitcase, she hurried over to her side. "Where on earth are you going, girl?" For a brief moment she wondered if Callie had decided to follow through on her threat to relocate to Fiji.

When Callie turned to face her, the beatific glow on her face gave mute testimony to what had transpired, and Tonya grinned in return. "You called him?"

Callie grabbed her friend in an enthusiastic hug, almost screaming in her excitement. "Yes! Yes! I did!" Then she giggled. "You're not going to believe this, but he was on stage at Madison Square Garden!"

"You're kidding!"

"No! And he answered the telephone in front of thousands of people." Callie couldn't stop laughing, her effervescent mirth indicative of her relief from the burden she'd been laboring under for weeks. It felt so good to be happy again. The release of it all made her giddy and lightheaded.

"Girl, will you stop laughing and tell me what he said?" The joy was contagious and Tonya began bubbling with merriment also.

Callie sobered, hesitating as she pulled open her lingerie drawer. "He wants me to come to New York, Tonya. Actually he was coming here, but I think after all the changes I've put him through, I should go there."

Tonya nodded approvingly. "Yeah, I think you're right. When are you leaving? Have you gotten a ticket or anything?"

Callie paused. She'd grown so accustomed to traveling with Bryan and the way his 'people' handled everything, she hadn't thought about making travel arrangements. She glanced down at her watch; she really needed to get packed as soon as possible. She continued pulling clothes out of her chest of drawers.

"Tonya, can you go online for me…" Callie faltered as her cell phone began to ring. It was Kelly, Bryan's personal assistant, calling to confirm flight arrangements for the next day. Callie collapsed on the bed in another fit of giggles, Oh God, she loved that man!

# CHAPTER 24

"Dammit, Kelly, can't you drive any faster?" Bryan yelled, frustrated that a simple trip to the airport was taking so long. He knew he should've gone to Callie; he hated waiting around like this. After Callie's call last night he'd rushed to his dressing room as soon as possible to make travel arrangements for her. Fortunately Madison Square Garden had excellent security, and the band got to their dressing room without having to navigate the usual gauntlet of zealous fans and assorted hangers-on. Jon in particular preferred solitude after a show, and usually wanted only Cinnamon there to help him with his headaches. Bryan had been thrilled to discover that Kelly, with her usual efficiency, had already arranged Callie's transportation to New York City. In his delight Bryan had picked his petite assistant up in a bear hug and offered her a twenty percent pay increase. Of course his bandmates had followed him into his dressing room and had a great time teasing him about his behavior on stage. They were pretty sure that no one had ever answered the telephone during a concert before. Of course, Bono had made those legendary calls to President Bush during a U2 tour, but answering a call was an entirely different matter.

Through the fog of his euphoria, Bryan barely heard anything that any of them had to say. He had gone back to his hotel room and spent the last twelve hours counting the minutes until he would see Callie again. Of course, he hadn't factored in the ridiculous amount of time it took to actually get to the airport. He knew he should have driven, but Kelly had absolutely insisted that after weeks of little sleep, compounded by a nasty cold and a grueling concert schedule, he was in no shape to take on New York traffic. He was sure she was right, but God, he hated waiting.

Kelly gave her boss a malevolent glance. Despite her staunch objections, he had insisted on accompanying her to the airport. He'd been determined to go even when she reminded him that some airport employees act as spotters for the paparazzi, and his antics the previous evening were bound to set off a firestorm of new publicity just as the story was dying down at last. Bryan had made it clear that he didn't give a damn. He wasn't giving Callie an opportunity to change her mind, even if he had to do the hated talk-show circuit again.

At the airport Bryan shifted restlessly in his seat as they queued up to the Delta terminal. Finally, almost sizzling with impatience, he left Kelly to park the car and jumped out to sprint up to the gate. Kelly shook her head. Obviously Bryan had lost his mind. She just hoped he didn't get tackled. Running anywhere in the vicinity of an airport was liable to get him shot in these times of heightened security against terrorism.

Bryan arrived at the gate, only to realize that Callie's flight wasn't due for at least an hour. He checked the board; at least the flight was still on time. He began to pace impatiently. What if she'd changed her mind? This was it; he couldn't put his feelings on the line like this again. What more could he do? He had been willing to do anything to get her back, but damn, a man had to draw a line somewhere. In an effort to maintain a low profile he'd tucked his ponytail, distinctive for its length and color, into the back of his black denim work shirt. He tugged on it now in irritation, not really caring if he drew unwanted attention to himself.

Knowing that he would go insane if he didn't have something to do, he recalled the Starbucks he had passed on his way to the concourse and decided to go back and get a cup of coffee. Perhaps that would help take some of the edge off his frayed nervous system. As he strolled back down the hallway, he recognized at least one, possibly two, paparazzo. He paused. Maybe if he asked them to lay off…Nope, that almost never worked. Over the years he'd established a relationship with a couple of photographers and could occasionally request a little indulgence. Some of them did actually have a streak of decency that could be appealed to. One of them had even been at the scene of his last drunken auto accident, but instead of taking pictures that would probably have been worth a fortune, he'd called B.T. instead. Bryan didn't know if that was for his benefit or

B.T.'s. The guy was probably on his manager's payroll, but nonetheless, he was grateful. Unfortunately, he didn't know either of these guys, so there'd be no goodwill forthcoming. Besides, they almost always expected some kind of payback in return, and he didn't like owing anyone, especially not those types of favors. He sighed, hoping against hope that they were there to harass some other poor slob.

After finishing his coffee and mangling a muffin, Bryan walked quickly back to the gate. When he saw the airline personnel opening the door, he knew Callie's flight had arrived. After a brief pause, passengers began to disembark. Kelly had booked Callie a first-class ticket, so she should be in the first group to exit the plane. Almost jumping out of his skin with nervousness, Bryan restlessly searched the face of each passenger, but didn't see Callie. Then just as he was about to give up, resigned to the fact that they were over, he saw her walk into the concourse. Looking pretty and feminine in a pale pink linen sleeveless vest and matching trousers, she literally took his breath away. For a moment he stood frozen in place, almost disbelieving that she had come to her senses at last. Then, startled out of his paralysis by announcements over the loudspeaker, he rushed towards her. She met him halfway and they just stood gazing at each other for a moment, absorbing the delight of being together again. Then as if someone suddenly flipped a hidden switch, they threw themselves into a fierce embrace and feverishly sought one another's mouth as if they'd been parted for decades instead of mere weeks. Those kisses promised that no matter what they had to weather to be together, it would be worth it. Nothing would ever part them again.

Certain sounds still penetrated the fog Callie's presence engendered in Bryan's fevered brain. He paused, positive that he'd heard the distinctive whir of a camera shutter. Damning all the gods who had apparently conspired to ensure his lifelong misery, he broke off the passionate kiss, grasped Callie's arms, and put her slightly away from him. Callie looked up, bewildered, still quite dazed from their intense embrace. He reached down and grabbed her hand, pulling her out of the traffic flow to somewhat limited privacy behind a column.

Watching her eyes closely to gauge her reaction, Bryan nodded his head in the direction of the shutter noise. "Paparazzi," he murmured. He didn't want to tell her, but knowing their relationship would not survive another shock like the one that had wrenched them apart before, he was compelled to reveal their presence.

Still not totally alert, her eyes widened in surprise. "Paparazzi? Where?" she asked, looking around wildly at the crowd of travelers.

Bryan wanted to scream as he watched her respond just as he'd feared. Seeing their relationship crash and burn before his very eyes, he pointed towards one of the two men he'd identified earlier. Knowing it was useless, he still tried diligently to pull their relationship out of the flames. "Baby, don't worry about it. They'll just take their pictures and…"

Callie shook her head and gave him an oblique smile as she placed two fingers over his mouth to silence him. Then, her succulent lips parting into a huge grin, she looked over her shoulder and waved energetically at the photographer Bryan had indicated to ensure that he was still watching. Turning back to Bryan, she threw her arms enthusiastically around his neck, clasping him to her body in a strong embrace and covered his lips with a long, lingering kiss, not letting go until she'd heard the camera's shutter whir several times.

After a long moment she broke the kiss, and then still smiling cheekily, waved at the reporter again as she said, "The hell with the paparazzi! I might even go on Oprah!"

Bryan, still disoriented from the effects of the kiss, stared at her bemusedly. Then he pulled her back into his arms, relieved that she was willing to accept one of the greatest liabilities of his career. He had to be sure; he couldn't take anymore uncertainty or confusion. Still holding her tenderly in his arms, he gazed into her velvety soft eyes, and raised a brow inquiringly. "My mate?"

If possible, Callie's grin widened, and she reached up to pull him down for another kiss. In her best imitation of a California surfer dude voice, she replied, "You bet your ass, dude, your mate for life."

## 2009 Reprint Mass Market Titles

### January

I'm Gonna Make You Love Me
Gwyneth Bolton
ISBN-13: 978-1-58571-291-5
ISBN-10: 1-58571-291-4
$6.99

Shades of Desire
Monica White
ISBN-13: 978-1-58571-292-2
ISBN-10: 1-58571-292-2
$6.99

### February

A Love of Her Own
Cheris Hodges
ISBN-13: 978-1-58571-293-9
ISBN-10: 1-58571-293-0
$6.99

Color of Trouble
Dyanne Davis
ISBN-13: 978-1-58571-294-6
ISBN-10: 1-58571-9
$6.99

### March

Twist of Fate
Beverly Clark
ISBN-13: 978-1-58571-295-3
ISBN-10: 1-58571-295-7
$6.99

Chances
Pamela Leigh Starr
ISBN-13: 978-1-58571-296-0
ISBN-10: 1-58571-296-5
$6.99

### April

Sinful Intentions
Crystal Rhodes
ISBN-13: 978-1-585712-297-7
ISBN-10: 1-58571-297-3
$6.99

Rock Star
Roslyn Hardy Holcomb
ISBN-13: 978-1-58571-298-4
$6.99

### May

Paths of Fire
T.T. Henderson
ISBN-13: 978-1-58571-343-1
ISBN-10: 1-58571-343-0
$6.99

Caught Up in the Rapture
Lisa Riley
ISBN-13: 978-1-58571-344-8
ISBN-10: 1-58571-344-9
$6.99

### June

Reckless Surrender
Rochelle Alers
ISBN-13: 978-1-58571-345-5
ISBN-10: 1-58571-345-7
$6.99

No Ordinary Love
Angela Weaver
ISBN-13: 978-1-58571-346-2
ISBN-10: 1-58571-346-5
$6.99

## 2009 Reprint Mass Market Titles (continued)

### July

Intentional Mistakes
Michele Sudler
ISBN-13: 978-1-58571-347-9
ISBN-10: 1-58571-347-3
$6.99

It's In His Kiss
Reon Carter
ISBN-13: 978-1-58571-348-6
ISBN-10: 1-58571-348-1
$6.99

### August

Unfinished Love Affair
Barbara Keaton
ISBN-13: 978-1-58571-349-3
ISBN-10: 1-58571-349-X
$6.99

A Perfect Place to Pray
I.L Goodwin
ISBN-13: 978-1-58571-299-1
ISBN-10: 1-58571-299-X
$6.99

### September

Love in High Gear
Charlotte Roy
ISBN-13: 978-1-58571-355-4
ISBN-10: 1-58571-355-4
$6.99

Ebony Eyes
Kei Swanson
ISBN-13: 978-1-58571-356-1
ISBN-10: 1-58571-356-2
$6.99

### October

Midnight Clear, Part I
Leslie Esdale/Carmen Green
ISBN-13: 978-1-58571-357-8
ISBN-10: 1-58571-357-0
$6.99

Midnight Clear, Part II
Gwynne Forster/Monica
    Jackson
ISBN-13: 978-1-58571-358-5
ISBN-10: 1-58571-358-9
$6.99

### November

Midnight Peril
Vicki Andrews
ISBN-13: 978-1-58571-359-2
ISBN-10: 1-58571-359-7
$6.99

One Day At A Time
Bella McFarland
ISBN-13: 978-1-58571-360-8
ISBN-10: 1-58571-360-0
$6.99

### December

Just An Affair
Eugenia O'Neal
ISBN-13: 978-1-58571-361-5
ISBN-10: 1-58571-361-9
$6.99

Shades of Brown
Denise Becker
ISBN-13: 978-1-58571-362-2
ISBN-10: 1-58571-362-7
$6.99

## 2009 New Mass Market Titles

### January

Singing A Song…
Crystal Rhodes
ISBN-13: 978-1-58571-283-0
$6.99

Look Both Ways
Joan Early
ISBN-13: 978-1-58571-284-7
$6.99

### February

Six O'Clock
Katrina Spencer
ISBN-13: 978-1-58571-285-4
$6.99

Red Sky
Renee Alexis
ISBN-13: 978-1-58571-286-1
$6.99

### March

Anything But Love
Celya Bowers
ISBN-13: 978-1-58571-287-8
$6.99

Tempting Faith
Crystal Hubbard
ISBN-13: 978-1-58571-288-5
$6.99

### April

If I Were Your Woman
La Connie Taylor-Jones
ISBN-13: 978-1-58571-289-2
$6.99

Best Of Luck Elsewhere
Trisha Haddad
ISBN-13: 978-1-58571-290-8
$6.99

### May

All I'll Ever Need
Mildred Riley
ISBN-13: 978-1-58571-335-6
$6.99

A Place Like Home
Alicia Wiggins
ISBN-13: 978-1-58571-336-3
$6.99

### June

Best Foot Forward
Michele Sudler
ISBN-13: 978-1-58571-337-0
$6.99

It's In the Rhythm
Sammie Ward
ISBN-13: 978-1-58571-338-7
$6.99

## 2009 New Mass Market Titles (continued)

### July

Checks and Balances
Elaine Sims
ISBN-13: 978-1-58571-339-4
$6.99

Save Me
Africa Fine
ISBN-13: 978-1-58571-340-0
$6.99

### August

When Lightening Strikes
Michele Cameron
ISBN-13: 978-1-58571-369-1
$6.99

Blindsided
Tammy Williams
ISBN-13: 978-1-58571-342-4
$6.99

### September

2 Good
Celya Bowers
ISBN-13: 978-1-58571-350-9
$6.99

Waiting for Mr. Darcy
Chamein Canton
ISBN-13: 978-1-58571-351-6
$6.99

### October

Fireflies
Joan Early
ISBN-13: 978-1-58571-352-3
$6.99

Frost On My Window
Angela Weaver
ISBN-13: 978-1-58571-353-0
$6.99

### November

Waiting in the Shadows
Michele Sudler
ISBN-13: 978-1-58571-364-6
$6.99

Fixin' Tyrone
Keith Walker
ISBN-13: 978-1-58571-365-3
$6.99

### December

Dream Keeper
Gail McFarland
ISBN-13: 978-1-58571-366-0
$6.99

Another Memory
Pamela Ridley
ISBN-13: 978-1-58571-367-7
$6.99

## Other Genesis Press, Inc. Titles

| | | |
|---|---|---|
| A Dangerous Deception | J.M. Jeffries | $8.95 |
| A Dangerous Love | J.M. Jeffries | $8.95 |
| A Dangerous Obsession | J.M. Jeffries | $8.95 |
| A Drummer's Beat to Mend | Kei Swanson | $9.95 |
| A Happy Life | Charlotte Harris | $9.95 |
| A Heart's Awakening | Veronica Parker | $9.95 |
| A Lark on the Wing | Phyliss Hamilton | $9.95 |
| A Love of Her Own | Cheris F. Hodges | $9.95 |
| A Love to Cherish | Beverly Clark | $8.95 |
| A Risk of Rain | Dar Tomlinson | $8.95 |
| A Taste of Temptation | Reneé Alexis | $9.95 |
| A Twist of Fate | Beverly Clark | $8.95 |
| A Voice Behind Thunder | Carrie Elizabeth Greene | $6.99 |
| A Will to Love | Angie Daniels | $9.95 |
| Acquisitions | Kimberley White | $8.95 |
| Across | Carol Payne | $12.95 |
| After the Vows | Leslie Esdaile | $10.95 |
| (Summer Anthology) | T.T. Henderson | |
| | Jacqueline Thomas | |
| Again My Love | Kayla Perrin | $10.95 |
| Against the Wind | Gwynne Forster | $8.95 |
| All I Ask | Barbara Keaton | $8.95 |
| Always You | Crystal Hubbard | $6.99 |
| Ambrosia | T.T. Henderson | $8.95 |
| An Unfinished Love Affair | Barbara Keaton | $8.95 |
| And Then Came You | Dorothy Elizabeth Love | $8.95 |
| Angel's Paradise | Janice Angelique | $9.95 |
| At Last | Lisa G. Riley | $8.95 |
| Best of Friends | Natalie Dunbar | $8.95 |
| Beyond the Rapture | Beverly Clark | $9.95 |
| Blame It On Paradise | Crystal Hubbard | $6.99 |
| Blaze | Barbara Keaton | $9.95 |
| Bliss, Inc. | Chamein Canton | $6.99 |
| Blood Lust | J. M. Jeffries | $9.95 |
| Blood Seduction | J.M. Jeffries | $9.95 |
| Bodyguard | Andrea Jackson | $9.95 |
| Boss of Me | Diana Nyad | $8.95 |
| Bound by Love | Beverly Clark | $8.95 |
| Breeze | Robin Hampton Allen | $10.95 |

## Other Genesis Press, Inc. Titles (continued)

## Other Genesis Press, Inc. Titles (continued)

## Other Genesis Press, Inc. Titles (continued)

| | | |
|---|---|---|
| Intimate Intentions | Angie Daniels | $8.95 |
| It's Not Over Yet | J.J. Michael | $9.95 |
| Jolie's Surrender | Edwina Martin-Arnold | $8.95 |
| Kiss or Keep | Debra Phillips | $8.95 |
| Lace | Giselle Carmichael | $9.95 |
| Lady Preacher | K.T. Richey | $6.99 |
| Last Train to Memphis | Elsa Cook | $12.95 |
| Lasting Valor | Ken Olsen | $24.95 |
| Let Us Prey | Hunter Lundy | $25.95 |
| Lies Too Long | Pamela Ridley | $13.95 |
| Life Is Never As It Seems | J.J. Michael | $12.95 |
| Lighter Shade of Brown | Vicki Andrews | $8.95 |
| Looking for Lily | Africa Fine | $6.99 |
| Love Always | Mildred E. Riley | $10.95 |
| Love Doesn't Come Easy | Charlyne Dickerson | $8.95 |
| Love Unveiled | Gloria Greene | $10.95 |
| Love's Deception | Charlene Berry | $10.95 |
| Love's Destiny | M. Loui Quezada | $8.95 |
| Love's Secrets | Yolanda McVey | $6.99 |
| Mae's Promise | Melody Walcott | $8.95 |
| Magnolia Sunset | Giselle Carmichael | $8.95 |
| Many Shades of Gray | Dyanne Davis | $6.99 |
| Matters of Life and Death | Lesego Malepe, Ph.D. | $15.95 |
| Meant to Be | Jeanne Sumerix | $8.95 |
| Midnight Clear (Anthology) | Leslie Esdaile | $10.95 |
| | Gwynne Forster | |
| | Carmen Green | |
| | Monica Jackson | |
| Midnight Magic | Gwynne Forster | $8.95 |
| Midnight Peril | Vicki Andrews | $10.95 |
| Misconceptions | Pamela Leigh Starr | $9.95 |
| Moments of Clarity | Michele Cameron | $6.99 |
| Montgomery's Children | Richard Perry | $14.95 |
| Mr Fix-It | Crystal Hubbard | $6.99 |
| My Buffalo Soldier | Barbara B. K. Reeves | $8.95 |
| Naked Soul | Gwynne Forster | $8.95 |
| Never Say Never | Michele Cameron | $6.99 |
| Next to Last Chance | Louisa Dixon | $24.95 |
| No Apologies | Seressia Glass | $8.95 |

## Other Genesis Press, Inc. Titles (continued)

| | | |
|---|---|---|
| No Commitment Required | Seressia Glass | $8.95 |
| No Regrets | Mildred E. Riley | $8.95 |
| Not His Type | Chamein Canton | $6.99 |
| Nowhere to Run | Gay G. Gunn | $10.95 |
| O Bed! O Breakfast! | Rob Kuehnle | $14.95 |
| Object of His Desire | A. C. Arthur | $8.95 |
| Office Policy | A. C. Arthur | $9.95 |
| Once in a Blue Moon | Dorianne Cole | $9.95 |
| One Day at a Time | Bella McFarland | $8.95 |
| One of These Days | Michele Sudler | $9.95 |
| Outside Chance | Louisa Dixon | $24.95 |
| Passion | T.T. Henderson | $10.95 |
| Passion's Blood | Cherif Fortin | $22.95 |
| Passion's Furies | AlTonya Washington | $6.99 |
| Passion's Journey | Wanda Y. Thomas | $8.95 |
| Past Promises | Jahmel West | $8.95 |
| Path of Fire | T.T. Henderson | $8.95 |
| Path of Thorns | Annetta P. Lee | $9.95 |
| Peace Be Still | Colette Haywood | $12.95 |
| Picture Perfect | Reon Carter | $8.95 |
| Playing for Keeps | Stephanie Salinas | $8.95 |
| Pride & Joi | Gay G. Gunn | $8.95 |
| Promises Made | Bernice Layton | $6.99 |
| Promises to Keep | Alicia Wiggins | $8.95 |
| Quiet Storm | Donna Hill | $10.95 |
| Reckless Surrender | Rochelle Alers | $6.95 |
| Red Polka Dot in a World of Plaid | Varian Johnson | $12.95 |
| Reluctant Captive | Joyce Jackson | $8.95 |
| Rendezvous with Fate | Jeanne Sumerix | $8.95 |
| Revelations | Cheris F. Hodges | $8.95 |
| Rivers of the Soul | Leslie Esdaile | $8.95 |
| Rocky Mountain Romance | Kathleen Suzanne | $8.95 |
| Rooms of the Heart | Donna Hill | $8.95 |
| Rough on Rats and Tough on Cats | Chris Parker | $12.95 |
| Secret Library Vol. 1 | Nina Sheridan | $18.95 |
| Secret Library Vol. 2 | Cassandra Colt | $8.95 |
| Secret Thunder | Annetta P. Lee | $9.95 |

## Other Genesis Press, Inc. Titles (continued)

| | | |
|---|---|---|
| Shades of Brown | Denise Becker | $8.95 |
| Shades of Desire | Monica White | $8.95 |
| Shadows in the Moonlight | Jeanne Sumerix | $8.95 |
| Sin | Crystal Rhodes | $8.95 |
| Small Whispers | Annetta P. Lee | $6.99 |
| So Amazing | Sinclair LeBeau | $8.95 |
| Somebody's Someone | Sinclair LeBeau | $8.95 |
| Someone to Love | Alicia Wiggins | $8.95 |
| Song in the Park | Martin Brant | $15.95 |
| Soul Eyes | Wayne L. Wilson | $12.95 |
| Soul to Soul | Donna Hill | $8.95 |
| Southern Comfort | J.M. Jeffries | $8.95 |
| Southern Fried Standards | S.R. Maddox | $6.99 |
| Still the Storm | Sharon Robinson | $8.95 |
| Still Waters Run Deep | Leslie Esdaile | $8.95 |
| Stolen Memories | Michele Sudler | $6.99 |
| Stories to Excite You | Anna Forrest/Divine | $14.95 |
| Storm | Pamela Leigh Starr | $6.99 |
| Subtle Secrets | Wanda Y. Thomas | $8.95 |
| Suddenly You | Crystal Hubbard | $9.95 |
| Sweet Repercussions | Kimberley White | $9.95 |
| Sweet Sensations | Gwyneth Bolton | $9.95 |
| Sweet Tomorrows | Kimberly White | $8.95 |
| Taken by You | Dorothy Elizabeth Love | $9.95 |
| Tattooed Tears | T. T. Henderson | $8.95 |
| The Color Line | Lizzette Grayson Carter | $9.95 |
| The Color of Trouble | Dyanne Davis | $8.95 |
| The Disappearance of Allison Jones | Kayla Perrin | $5.95 |
| The Fires Within | Beverly Clark | $9.95 |
| The Foursome | Celya Bowers | $6.99 |
| The Honey Dipper's Legacy | Pannell-Allen | $14.95 |
| The Joker's Love Tune | Sidney Rickman | $15.95 |
| The Little Pretender | Barbara Cartland | $10.95 |
| The Love We Had | Natalie Dunbar | $8.95 |
| The Man Who Could Fly | Bob & Milana Beamon | $18.95 |
| The Missing Link | Charlyne Dickerson | $8.95 |
| The Mission | Pamela Leigh Starr | $6.99 |
| The More Things Change | Chamein Canton | $6.99 |

## Other Genesis Press, Inc. Titles (continued)

| | | |
|---|---|---|
| The Perfect Frame | Beverly Clark | $9.95 |
| The Price of Love | Sinclair LeBeau | $8.95 |
| The Smoking Life | Ilene Barth | $29.95 |
| The Words of the Pitcher | Kei Swanson | $8.95 |
| Things Forbidden | Maryam Diaab | $6.99 |
| This Life Isn't Perfect Holla | Sandra Foy | $6.99 |
| Three Doors Down | Michele Sudler | $6.99 |
| Three Wishes | Seressia Glass | $8.95 |
| Ties That Bind | Kathleen Suzanne | $8.95 |
| Tiger Woods | Libby Hughes | $5.95 |
| Time is of the Essence | Angie Daniels | $9.95 |
| Timeless Devotion | Bella McFarland | $9.95 |
| Tomorrow's Promise | Leslie Esdaile | $8.95 |
| Truly Inseparable | Wanda Y. Thomas | $8.95 |
| Two Sides to Every Story | Dyanne Davis | $9.95 |
| Unbreak My Heart | Dar Tomlinson | $8.95 |
| Uncommon Prayer | Kenneth Swanson | $9.95 |
| Unconditional Love | Alicia Wiggins | $8.95 |
| Unconditional | A.C. Arthur | $9.95 |
| Undying Love | Renee Alexis | $6.99 |
| Until Death Do Us Part | Susan Paul | $8.95 |
| Vows of Passion | Bella McFarland | $9.95 |
| Wedding Gown | Dyanne Davis | $8.95 |
| What's Under Benjamin's Bed | Sandra Schaffer | $8.95 |
| When A Man Loves A Woman | La Connie Taylor-Jones | $6.99 |
| When Dreams Float | Dorothy Elizabeth Love | $8.95 |
| When I'm With You | LaConnie Taylor-Jones | $6.99 |
| Where I Want To Be | Maryam Diaab | $6.99 |
| Whispers in the Night | Dorothy Elizabeth Love | $8.95 |
| Whispers in the Sand | LaFlorya Gauthier | $10.95 |
| Who's That Lady? | Andrea Jackson | $9.95 |
| Wild Ravens | Altonya Washington | $9.95 |
| Yesterday Is Gone | Beverly Clark | $10.95 |
| Yesterday's Dreams, Tomorrow's Promises | Reon Laudat | $8.95 |
| Your Precious Love | Sinclair LeBeau | $8.95 |

# Order Form

**Mail to: Genesis Press, Inc.**
**P.O. Box 101**
**Columbus, MS 39703**

Name _____

Address _____

City/State _____ Zip _____

Telephone _____

*Ship to (if different from above)*

Name _____

Address _____

City/State _____ Zip _____

Telephone _____

*Credit Card Information*

Credit Card # _____ ☐ Visa  ☐ Mastercard

Expiration Date (mm/yy) _____ ☐ AmEx  ☐ Discover

| Qty. | Author | Title | Price | Total |
|------|--------|-------|-------|-------|
|      |        |       |       |       |
|      |        |       |       |       |
|      |        |       |       |       |
|      |        |       |       |       |
|      |        |       |       |       |
|      |        |       |       |       |
|      |        |       |       |       |
|      |        |       |       |       |
|      |        |       |       |       |
|      |        |       |       |       |
|      |        |       |       |       |

|  |  |
|---|---|
| Use this order form, or call **1-888-INDIGO-1** | **Total for books** _____ <br> **Shipping and handling:** <br> $5 first two books, <br> $1 each additional book _____ <br> **Total S & H** _____ <br> **Total amount enclosed** _____ |

*Mississippi residents add 7% sales tax*